THE BOOK OF THE WITCH'S SON

OCTOBER K SANTERELLI

Contents

To the people who feel like they don't fit into either world.
You fit into mine.
And to Dillion – you are my favorite sounding board.

Content Warnings

These stories feature:
Death
Grief
Abduction
Ignoring Consent
Sexual Assault (Kissing only, twice)
Implied Abusive Relationship (Off page)
The last four are portrayed as being the negatives they are. They are in the context of faerie lore.

GLIMMERS IN THE NIGHT

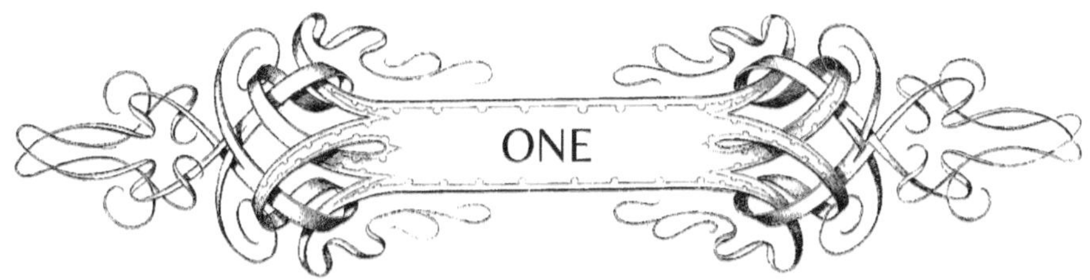

ONE

The wind howled and knocked the naked tree branches together, rattling them like bones in a basket. Jeth would know - he'd seen his mother at work. She was dead now, dead and burned in a pyre that melted the snow around it and left behind nothing but ash and steam and mud. The cottage was empty. It was dark. The fire had died in the hearth while Jeth was at the funeral, leaving it bitterly cold.

He had been the last to leave, standing in the snow as the sun set. The villagers left long before the last ember had died. Jeth did not.

Faint moonlight struggled through the window, casting layers of shadow and revealing nothing. He knew this house like the back of his hand, but it was different now. It wasn't his. Tomorrow, the villagers would walk the winding path up the hill to his door and tell him he had to leave. This was, after all, the Witch's Cottage.

And now there was no witch.

They'd find one, fully trained and ready for a posting. They always did. Jeth would have to make room for them. Those were the rules. He would have to leave, and he was not allowed to take any of his mother's jars and herbs and tools.

Jeth stood in the open doorway facing the darkness, the cold wind at his back urging him inside. He couldn't get his feet to move.

I don't want to go home without you, Mother.

"I'm here," she seemed to whisper behind him. When he turned, however, there was nothing but the woods.

She's gone.

There wasn't much time. The villagers would come to oust him at first light. Jeth had this one night to pack a satchel with a few essentials and some food, and then he would have to leave. Alone, and at just fourteen. No one in the village had the means to take on an extra mouth this late in the winter, even if Jeth wasn't so...strange.

Where will I go?

It was one of a litany of thoughts that kept circling in his mind like vultures over a carcass. None of them would change what was going to happen. None of them would bring his mother back. Yet there they went, over and over and over again.

Where will I go? What will I do? Can I do this? Set out on my own? What would Mother say? What would Mother want for me? What should I take? Where do I even start? Where will I go?

He stepped inside and let the door swing closed, sinking onto a worn wooden stool by the worktable that dominated the center of the small room. His breath curled away as he sat, mired in his racing thoughts. His heart was racing. His chest was tight. Watching the barely visible clouds of white that dissipated into nothing was the only thing keeping his breathing steady. It was almost impossible to truly hold the mounting panic at bay. There was a lump in his throat that he couldn't swallow, that threatened to choke him.

Breathe. In, he reminded himself. *Out. In again. Out.*

Jeth fought the urge to scream. He wanted to tear through the cottage and destroy it. He wanted to sweep the jars with all their spells and ingredients off their shelves and let them shatter on the cobbled floor. He wanted to shred the bundles of drying herbs hung in the eaves. He wanted to crush every crystal and stone his mother had collected with a hammer until there was nothing left but dust. He wanted to ruin everything that reminded him of his mother, to take it away from *them.*

He did nothing. He just breathed.

The villagers needed this cottage. They needed their next witch. The kingdom of Hallanor needed magic like it needed water, even if most of its people feared and despised it. Every town had at least a hedge witch. They were necessary to bespell the fields and the livestock. They were needed to bless the people and the buildings. They were important guardians, managing the deep rivers of magic that flowed, invisible, all around them. Most importantly, the witches were needed to protect their homes from the fickle, wonderful, terrible, and dangerous faeries.

Destroying the supplies would doom over a hundred people in this small, almost meaningless village to terrible fates. No witch would come without a place to stay and supplies to use. With no witch, the faerie's woods would creep closer and closer to the village until one day it would swallow them whole. It wouldn't survive a turn of the year.

Mother would hate that.

After all, she had spent fifteen years as the witch of this nameless little hamlet at the edge of this small kingdom, doing all she could to keep it safe. So Jeth did nothing. Not for the villagers, but for her.

Jeth was not a witch himself. Not yet. The plan had always been to be made his mother's apprentice once he came of age, at fifteen. Not that a barrier so flimsy as age had stopped his mother from teaching him everything she knew. She was always fond of breaking rules she thought were useless. He had grown up here. He had spent hours grinding herbs that were sharp in his nose for a sore throat potion at the workbench, days learning the meaning of the deck of oracle cards to tell love fortunes, weeks reading about all the plants in the kingdom and what they could be used for. He knew salves and spell sachets for fever and sleep, he foraged for roots and mushrooms at her side, and he learned some of the secrets of the faerie forest.

She taught Jeth how to use his magic, too. She guided him through tracing invisible fingers along the unseen leylines, on stirring just enough power to do something small. He could light a candle, stir a breeze into being, and sing a bird out of a tree. Anything more was beyond his reach for now, but she had promised him that as soon as he turned fifteen, she would teach him spellcraft in earnest.

Except now she was gone, snuffed out like a candle. One moment she had been walking in the village market, swinging her basket and greeting everyone who called out to her with a smile. The next, she crumpled to the ground. Jeth had been there at her side as she was wracked with spasms, as her ears had bled and her breath caught in her chest. Then she fell still, sightless eyes looking up at the falling snow, lips parted in the barest hint of surprise.

No one knew what happened to her. The villagers whispered of strange illnesses, dark curses, and bad luck. The only part that really seemed to matter to them was that *they* were at risk now, without her. They had lost their witch.

Jeth had lost everything.

The heat of his anger faltered, then died. The chill set in to his skin. He could hardly see through the tears he refused to shed. They made the shadowed gloom around him waver. His chest was tight, as if a barrel band had been fastened around it. His hands were curled into fists. Even if he couldn't feel his fingertips in the frigid winter cold, he could feel his nails biting into his palms. The lump in his throat grew larger.

I wonder if it will be like a dam. If I open the floodgates and let it out, what will happen? It felt dangerous, bottomless and wild—like he might cry for a hundred years, like a boy in a faerie's tale. What if it swept him away forever?

No, he couldn't risk it. Jeth forced himself to his feet, fighting the sting in his eyes. He hunted blindly across the table for the satchel he'd laid out before they had come for his mother's body. He had washed and dressed her himself, right on this very table, in preparation for her journey to the beyond. It was customary for the family. It was supposed to help.

It hadn't helped Jeth at all. He still had not let a single tear fall over the loss of his mother, afraid that if he started to, his grief would overwhelm him. He just felt as though he were walking through deep water. Everything was so much harder. It took all his strength just to keep moving.

His fingers brushed over the heavy cloth of the bag at last. Tonight, he decided, everything would be done in darkness. It suited his black mood. Forgoing the candle he had left out, Jeth turned instead to feel his way through the only home he had ever known in shadow. Silently, he tucked away the pieces of his life he hoped they would let him keep.

Three shirts. Two pairs of trews. Three pairs of thick socks his mother had knit. A book on edible plants, though he wasn't certain if the villagers would approve of him keeping the birthing day gift if they knew about it. He buried it beneath the clothes, and for good measure added a loaf of bread wrapped in cloth, a sack of apples, a small round of hard cheese, and two sachets of salt. Wire next, for snares and fishing. A paper packet of needles and fishhooks. A spool of thread. He didn't know what color it was. It didn't matter.

When the pack was finally full, he buckled it closed, leaving it on the table.

Jeth, himself, was next. He didn't change out of the black-dyed funeral clothes. They were well-made and warm. He merely changed his shoes for sturdy boots. Jeth pulled on his blue cape-sleeved jacket, running his fingers down the front of the soft, warm cloth.

"This will keep you warm enough. There. It looks quite handsome on you!" His mother had said as she wrapped him in the fanciful garment. The billowing cape sleeves ended just below his elbows. The sturdy rows of buttons on the front were hand-carved by his mother and him, polished until they gleamed.

"They'll think I'm putting on airs in the village," Jeth had said, turning this way and that.

"Let them. You and I know the world is wider than this place. Stranger things exist in this world than a boy in a handsome jacket."

The memory faded, sunlight and joy swallowed by darkness once more. He swallowed. Twice. Then, he started to move again. Belt, next. Into his belt went his knife and a small hand ax, his only weapons. He tucked a thick pair of fleece-lined leather gloves into his belt as well.

There. I'm... He had nearly thought the word 'ready', but he wasn't.

Instead, he turned to tidy up. It felt good to be moving, to be doing. The distraction was more than welcome. He felt his way across the table and counters, tucking things back where they belonged. He brushed over the jars and bottles on the shelves, making sure every neat label, written in his mother's hand, was turned out. He tucked his wooden stool beneath the table so it wouldn't be in the way. What else? What else could he do?

His fingers brushed against something soft and plush. A velvet cushion, black as ink, blacker still in the shadows of the night. Resting nestled in the safe embrace of that fabric was–

Mother's scrying crystal.

It was the clearest orb anyone had ever seen. The entire village admired it when they came for their spells and fortunes. His mother used it for divining, and to peer at the leylines around the village. She had told him how it worked a time or two, but never let him try it. Other than that, however, she was strangely silent.

"All you need to know is that it was a gift, just like you." She had said. *"No, no! No more questions. I'll tell you when you're older."*

Now she never would.

I should take it.

It was a gamble. On the one hand, his mother had brought it with her when they came to this place. It didn't technically belong to the village or the cottage, just to her. On the other, the villagers knew about the orb. They would notice it was gone immediately. It was a rare treasure, and a powerful magical artifact. If they wanted a way to lure in a new witch, nothing would be better than a pristine crystal ball. There was absolutely no way Jeth would get away with taking it.

He picked it up from its cushion, cradling it in both hands. The cool stone warmed quickly. For just a moment, Jeth thought he saw a glimmer of light in its depths, like the flicker of a fish's scales beneath the water. *I think it likes me.*

That settled it. Jeth turned, shoving the orb into a leather pouch and tucking it away in his pack. The villagers might notice in the morning –

But Jeth wouldn't be there. He refused to let them take this, too. If they wanted the orb, they'd have to take it from him by force—and in order to do that, they'd have to find him first. He wouldn't let them chase him out of his home. He wouldn't wait for them to force him to go.

He shouldered his bag and flung open the door, leaving it ajar as he crunched through the snow toward the twisted, skeletal trees of the forest. With a whisper to the night sky and a ringing in his ears, Jeth commanded the wind to hiss, to howl, to sweep away all signs of his passage.

It listened.

TWO

The storm Jeth had accidentally breathed to life raged through the night. The wind had listened too well. Jeth's will had been stronger than he had intended. Above him, the bare branches of the trees whipped back and forth, rattling together in a cackling frenzy. More than once, entire limbs ripped free and crashed to the ground around him. The wind picked up snow and turned it into daggers, flinging little pinpricks of ice that bit into Jeth's cheeks and ears. He fought his way through the woods with one arm holding fast to his pack and the other raised to protect his eyes. Tree trunks loomed out of the fog and snow with little warning, forcing him to thread his way back and forth.

It was a nightmare. The night stretched on and on, not that Jeth would have been able to tell when the sun rose again with how thick the clouds were overhead. The only good thing about it was that he couldn't think beyond lifting his feet one after the other.

Don't stop moving. Don't give up.

He couldn't tell if it was his own thoughts or his mother's voice that whispered the words in his mind.

Eventually, Jeth tried to wrangle the storm he had created, lifting his hands into the wind and reaching for a leyline. The stinging needles of swirling ice and snow broke his concentration every time he stretched his consciousness out, fumbling for the magic he knew was somewhere around him, somewhere nearby. He gave up, shouting his frustration into the wind. He couldn't hear himself.

Hours later, the wind suddenly just...stilled. As quickly as he had summoned the storm, it vanished. Jeth stopped in his tracks, dropping his arm and staring at the clear, bright forest around him. The sun had broken through the clouds, though it offered little in the way of warmth. The sky was clearing, spreading pale blue sky overhead. The snow glittered and sparkled like a thousand tiny diamonds, as if it hadn't been trying to kill him only moments ago. The only sound in the sudden calm was Jeth's breath coming in pants.

It's over? As the thought struck him, so did overwhelming exhaustion. His knees buckled. He sat down abruptly, staring at his snow-caked gloves and arms. For a while, that was all he could manage to do. Slowly, his breath calmed. The fog of fatigue lifted.

What now?

Jeth needed a plan. Wandering aimlessly away from his village was only a beginning. It wouldn't be enough.

If you run away, you will always be running away. If you run toward something, eventually you will get there. His mother's encouragement had been about learning to ride Farmer Hugo's horse, but it was no less true in this circumstance.

But what was there to run toward? He had no other family, no grandparents or cousins or aunts and uncles. He knew nothing about his father or his father's side of things except that he was gone. That was all his mother would say. He didn't know much about anything but witchery, about herbs and spells and magic. How many options did that really leave?

"I didn't think," he said aloud, "that I would have to know what I wanted to do with my life this soon."

A twig snapped. A hare took off through the snow, a gray shadow breaking up the pristine white until it vanished in a bush with a rattle of dry branches.

Jeth held his breath for a moment, then breathed out.

I thought it was one of the villagers.

His heart still raced in his chest as he pulled the small leather pouch from his bag. He had never done scrying magic before, but now might be the time to try. Jeth pulled his gloves off. The orb was warm when it rolled into his hand, as if he had left it lying in the sun.

Jeth cradled it in both hands. He took a deep breath. He closed his eyes.

When he reached for the leylines, he was surprised to feel one directly under his feet that was as broad as a river. He felt it like a roll of thunder in his chest and shoulders, heard it like a rushing waterfall, tasted it like copper on the tip of his tongue.

His mother had taught him how to touch a leyline safely, how to dip in one finger at a time until you held enough power to do what you wanted. He pulled the narrowest thread he could, her warnings ringing in his ears.

"Too much magic will kill a person. It hollows out their body to make room for itself and leaves nothing behind."

Pulling magic into himself made his whole body feel like it was full of lightning that would arc from his skin if he didn't hold it tight. Quickly, worried he might lose his grip, he directed the flow of power up to his head.

"Show me...Silas."

Silas the woodcutter was the unspoken leader of the tiny village Jeth had grown up in. If anyone were after him, it would be him.

Jeth opened his eyes and released the magic, staring down at the orb in his hands. Ghostly images flickered in its depths, outlined with the barest hint of gold. There was nothing distinct, no background or detail. Two broad-shouldered shadows mounted two horses. He couldn't tell if either of them were Silas as the horses began to trot. He didn't know where they were, what their expressions looked like. Nothing.

With a gasp, he lost his hold on the magic. The images vanished in the blink of an eye.

They *were* coming for him.

"It isn't fair. I had a plan."

Whatever else happened, he would not grow up in his remote village, learning magic at his mother's side and taking over her duties when she grew old. His theft and her death had dashed that plan to pieces, shattered beyond all saving. It was too soon. She was taken too soon.

The lump was back in Jeth's throat. He dusted the snow off of his coat and hands.

Don't cry. Just think. What will I do instead?

Any choice he made now would only drive him further into the unknown. He had never left his home. He never thought he would have to. Jeth shook his head, letting out a frustrated huff. He tucked the orb away.

Focus. Just think!

He had powerful magic for a child, and more control over his abilities than many his age. He could still be a witch's apprentice somewhere else, if he wanted. Maybe he could find a different village, or a town, or even a bustling city. He could lie and say he was fifteen already whenever he found a place that suited him. Well, if he found one in the next ten months. Otherwise, he wouldn't have to lie.

It was enough of a plan, at least, to get started.

The nearest town to his own was called Last Stop, and apart from his own village, it was. The rest of the kingdom of Hallanor lay beyond it, every clear inch of it won from the forest that covered the whole country. The same forest he was in right now. It was a few day's walk from Jeth's home, to the north and east. Jeth had never been that far from home, but he knew where it was. Twice a year, the farmers took three wagons full of crops and goods to Last Stop to sell and trade.

The world seemed very vast to Jeth, now. He had thought everything was closer, smaller. Hallanor might have been a small kingdom, but it would still take weeks on horseback to cross it from end to end.

The same trees marched across the entire thing, one great faerie forest that the humans had carved little holes into. Jeth couldn't tell if that made him feel connected to everything, or smaller still.

"Stop that," he said, an edge to his words. "You won't figure anything out just sitting here."

Jeth pushed himself to his feet, dusting the last of the snow off. Last Stop would be his next, and from there—who knew? Besides, he was not yet far enough away from his village — and the villagers — for his comfort.

Invisible deer trails wove through the woods, barely discernible in the way bushes curved, the way the trees leaned, the way the snow drifted. Jeth had followed them a hundred times in his life. Even if the snow was hiding the paths, he knew how to see. Jeth followed them, ducking under branches and threading through the underbrush.

When he lost the path, he would stop. If he closed his eyes, he could *feel* the forest around him. Not just the leylines—he could sense the trees, the bushes, the burrows with rabbits and foxes and badgers inside. The forest teemed with life, all of it sleeping, waiting.

Jeth could picture it in spring. Sunlight dappled through the leaves instead of pouring through bare branches. The paths were made of little runnels in the grass and creeping groundcover. Herbs and flowers and mushrooms grew everywhere, just opening their first buds. It was a riot of life. His mother would be just ahead, her head bent to scan the ground and her basket over her arm. He could see her. She felt so real, like he could just reach out and touch her—

Jeth opened his eyes, staring at his outstretched fingers. There was nothing there. It twisted his heart in his chest to see the empty space where he had pictured her. The warmth of a remembered spring faded. The chill crept back into Jeth's very bones. He dropped his hand.

"Why did you leave me?" he asked the air.

I didn't want to, his mother's voice whispered.

He turned, hoping to see her again—but of course she was gone.

"How long will you be with me?" he asked the last remnant of her in his heart.

This time, she didn't answer.

THREE

Four days had passed. Four days where every snapping twig and soft thud of snow falling from a branch above made Jeth's heart race. Four days of nightmares, where shadowy figures moved through the wood and surrounded him, then tore him apart. He was looking constantly over his shoulder, waiting for the villagers to appear behind him. At night, he dreamed of waking to a mob with torches and pitchforks, furious with him for robbing them. No one had ever stolen anything more than pastries there. Would they make an example of him if they caught him?

I don't want to find out.

The moments in between those heart-pounding seconds were worse, when silence and peace threatened to let his grief claw its way out of his chest. He almost preferred the fear. It filled his body and his mind and left little room for thoughts of his life before.

Maybe the villagers aren't following you at all.

Jeth didn't know them well enough to know if the thought was true. He knew their names, their faces, the broad strokes of their daily lives—but he didn't know any of them as individuals. None of them really bothered to speak much with him or his mother. Jeth was the son of the witch, and the villagers had always thought them strange.

It's because of the faeries. They can't understand faerie magic, and our magic pulls from the same sources. That's all they know. Even if they need it to protect them, they think every magical thing is strange and dangerous.

They weren't entirely wrong.

Jeth didn't know if they would be angry at all, let alone angry enough to come after him and the stolen orb.

Maybe they'll lop off my hand and call me a thief – like Silas said they do in the cities.

Silas the woodcutter was one of the only three people who ever left the village, riding in a wagon to Last Stop to trade. He would know what they did to thieves. Silas was leading the mob, small as it was, if the vision in the orb had worked.

But maybe they won't. Maybe they'll think I vanished like a faerie spell, and the orb is the price they paid. I just have to stay hidden.

Neither option made him feel much better. He would still be strange, still other, still alone.

Four days had passed in near silence, unless Jeth spoke to himself. They were uneventful. The weather held fair, even if it was cold enough to numb his ears and nose. He walked all night and well into each morning. He slept when the day was at its warmest, tucked into hollows made from the roots of trees or under thick evergreen bushes. Twice, he had tried to start a fire with his magic to keep himself warm while he rested. Twice, he had managed little else but smoke, and blamed the sticks being wet for his failure even though he wasn't sure that was true. Every day before he went to sleep, he tried to scry through the orb again and saw nothing but brief flickers of shadows.

Jeth woke when the cold seeped deep into his skin until it was painful enough that it was impossible to rest any longer. The sun was sinking, painting the sky with muted oranges and purples. After he had eaten, tucked into whatever safe little burrow he had found, Jeth rose and walked again.

He wasn't used to walking so much, or so far, or so often. His feet were sore. His legs ached. The heavy pack's straps dug into his shoulders.

Jeth reveled in the distraction of his pain. It was a relief to have his thoughts overwhelmed with mind-numbing discomfort, to have his only thoughts lean toward: *how much further?*

Last Stop *must* be nearby.

Once I get there, everything will sort itself out.

The thought was soothing. Last Stop might be the end of Hallanor, but it would be the beginning for Jeth. He didn't know where he was going to go or what he was going to do, but that would change when he arrived. He'd avoid Silas and Hugo easily, if Last Stop were as large as they had claimed. There would be trader caravans or solitary merchants, or maybe travelers. He would find some way to book passage or work, and then he would go east. Just east, to start. As they passed through towns and villages and cities, somewhere would call to him.

I'll know where I belong when I see it. I'll recognize my place.

He hoped.

Briefly, Jeth considered pulling out the orb again, asking it for guidance. He wasn't sure it worked that way. He never saw his mother use it to guide herself. *Some magics,* she said, *aren't meant for us.*

Was this one of them?

Jeth considered turning west instead, passing from Hallanor to Olmiven. After all, Silas and Hugo would never look for him there. Their neighbor-kingdom, however, had laws against magic. Olmiven had heard many tales of Hallanor and their encounters with the faeries. They feared the woods and did their best to ensure such tales never happened to them. If Jeth went west, he would have to hide his powers.

I would rather stay somewhere I can at least be myself.

His mother had told him stories about magicians who tried to smother their powers and instead were devoured by them. No, Jeth would find somewhere to go where he could be just as he was—magical, and a little bit strange.

The hardest part of these decisions, he decided as he struggled up a small hill made slick with snow and ice, *is that I can do anything.*

Anything he wanted. Anything at all. He could decide to take up in the woods like a hermit, or travel with a wagon and pass out blessings and spells in each place he came to. He could apprentice, as he planned, and set down roots of his own in a cottage on the edge of a different village. He could, he could, he could—

It made his stomach turn in knots and set his heart to racing. He felt small and vulnerable, like an insect scuttling about beneath the bare trees. The world was so very wide, and he was just one boy. How was he supposed to know what to do?

What would mother say?

Though the thought made his heart clench in his chest and his eyes grow hot and damp, it also summoned her voice in the back of his mind. She sounded so real, so close, that he slowed to a stop.

"Chin up, my lovely. Deep breath. We fall down, it's true—but then we get back up. Do you know what you do then?"

Jeth shook his head.

"No? I'll tell you. All you have to do is pick up your foot. Take one step, just one. Another will always follow. One little step. Ready?"

She faded from his mind. Jeth's eyes stung. He swallowed down his misery before it could swallow him whole, tipping his head back toward the sky. The midday sun was drifting in and out of sight as gray clouds built up.

One step, that's what she would have said.

Jeth hefted his pack, wading through the calf-deep snow. As he climbed, the scent of crisp, cold air was cut with the warm, welcoming spice of wood-smoke.

Wood-smoke!

Jeth lurched into a run, floundering up the last length of the hill as quick as he could. Wood-smoke could only mean –

He crested the rise, looking down on Last Stop. The town's two gates stood open, with mud-and-slush runnels leading in to roughly cobbled streets. The buildings were all packed close together, as though huddling for warmth against the winter cold. A single large town square was visible even from here, flanked by two towering inns.

I made it!

He felt his mother's presence behind him, leaning in with a smile. *One step. And the next would be...?*

Jeth's stomach rumbled. The thought of eating another chilled apple or gnawing at the heel of his loaf of bread was equally unappealing.

My next step is going to be a hot meal.

He could almost hear her laughing as she faded away again.

Down the hill he went, toward the western road that would lead him into Last Stop. He walked a weaving pattern back and forth so as not to slip and fall. He kept his gaze on his feet and his hands on the trees the whole way down.

When the ground beneath his feet abruptly gave way to frozen mud instead of snow, he stopped and turned toward the gate.

A single gatekeeper stood there, a wizened old man with a scraggly beard, leaning on a spear with a rusted tip like it was a walking staff. His eyes were wide, nearly bugging out of his head.

Jeth froze, staring back. What must he look like? His hair was wild and dark as a raven's wing, with waves that curled the tips up all on their own. No doubt there were at least a few twigs tangled in it. His skin was a perfect peach, neither ruddy nor weathered, free of any freckles or moles. His eyes were large and dark, with lashes so thick it looked like he had drawn around them with kohl like the women and girls of his village liked to do.

I must look like a faerie.

In fact, the only difference between Jeth and a faerie creature was that Jeth had plain human ears, round and smooth.

To the gatekeeper, Jeth had just appeared out of the forest, the *faerie* forest, in a handsome cape-sleeved coat with fey features. It was no wonder the man looked as though he wanted nothing more than to bolt – even if it might curse Last Stop forever. If Jeth *were* a faerie, a slight in hospitality might bring his ire.

Faeries had strict rules about such things. One must always be invited in, one must never lie, one must always be polite. If one strikes a deal with a faerie, both sides must always honor every word—so phrase your bargains carefully. To break these rules was to risk being turned into a beast or a toad or a tree, or taken away to the faerie lands forever.

Not wanting to startle the poor gatekeeper, Jeth moved slowly toward the gate. He tried to school his features into something cheery, but he could feel that it wasn't quite right. It was hard to smile, still, with his mother just buried. He gave up trying.

Jeth came to a stop a dozen paces away from the man.

"Hello," he said.

"Hello. Be you a faerie?"

"No, I'm just a boy."

The gatekeeper scoffed, brow furrowing. Jeth reached up to pull his ears forward, showing the roundness of them. Only then did the gatekeeper relax again. The reassurance did not stop the old man from shifting his hold on his weathered old spear, as if he hadn't quite decided Jeth was safe. As if he thought he might need to use it.

"Where are you coming from then, lad? We don't get many children passing through."

"From a village nearby. I'm not a child, I'm off to find an apprenticeship."

"Oh, aye? From that village two day's ride? Not the first to arrive in the past few days. Go on, then. Best chance for you finding an apprenticeship is somewhere else—so the folks at the inns or the market will be your best bet, eh?" The old man smiled and wagged the tip of his spear at the gate, entirely unaware of how his words had sent a chill down Jeth's spine.

They're already here?

Jeth felt as if the orb in his satchel were growing heavier and heavier, threatening to weigh him down like a millstone instead of a tiny crystal ball. He tried to force a smile, but his lips barely moved.

The gatekeep didn't notice. His business done, he tucked himself back into a little alcove in the crooked stone wall that surrounded Last Stop, warming his hands at a small brazier.

They've come for me.

Jeth's first instinct was to turn away, to circle the town through the woods and keep going. The villagers had never traveled far before. He could avoid them entirely. The promise of a warm meal swayed him.

It's a whole town. I can avoid them long enough to get something to eat, and then I'll leave. I'm only passing through.

Just take a step.

Through the gate he went. Jeth rounded the first corner he came to, weaving through crooked alleyways and crossing streets, working his way toward the town center. If he stayed off the main thoroughfares, they'd never find him.

The alleyways were like tributaries feeding into rivers feeding into that single central hub of a bustling marketplace in the broad, open square between the inns. The inns themselves loomed over the surrounding buildings, three and four floors tall to every other's two.

Jeth stopped in the shadows before stepping into the market, eyes wide. There were so many people! No doubt every room at both inns was full more often than not. Shoppers bustled back and forth with baskets over their arms. Merchants and tradesfolk mingled to swap stories and goods alike. Craftworkers sat beside the fruits of their labor at wooden stalls with colorful awnings that fluttered in the breeze. Errant flakes of snow drifted down from the sky, melting when they met braziers and torches that provided light and warmth.

This is more people than I've ever seen in my entire life!

The talking, the clatter of wagon wheels, the whinny of horses, the slap of boots on cobblestones, the screech of a crate being pried open—all of it set Jeth's ears to ringing and his heart to pounding.

If there are this many people here, *how many are there...everywhere else?*

Suddenly, his plan seemed more than daunting. Part of him wanted to turn back, to leave, to figure out something else, something smaller.

Then he thought of his mother. This time, she was not alive, not urging him on. No, this time she was wrapped in her burial shroud on a gray winter's morning, waiting for the torch to send her on her way. There was nothing for him behind.

One step at a time. One step, he urged himself.

I'll find an odd job to do for a shop or a stall. That might earn me enough for a hot meal. Then I'll go.

It would be safest to move on. Once he was on the road again, no doubt he could find a caravan of some sort. He was young, and his small stature could be used to feign that he was younger still. He wasn't above playing on the heartstrings of traveling merchants to get where he needed to go.

Somewhere in the back of his mind, he felt his mother's faint disapproval and pushed it aside. This was about survival until he was safely away with her orb. She would simply have to understand.

The taller of the two inns was across the square. It was more likely that the villagers were staying at the smaller inn. It was closer to the gate they had come through and looked a little cheaper. That meant that he might be able to circle around the back of the larger one and find work in the kitchens without drawing any notice. He would gladly wash a sink full of dishes in exchange for some stew and a fresh roll of bread. He'd wash two to fill his pack with traveling food before he left!

Jeth wrapped his hands tight around the straps of his pack and set off, weaving his way through the crowd. He hoped the hustle and bustle would hide him.

"--name is Jeth. He's got dark hair, a bit of a wan creature. Real small, belike."

Jeth ducked behind a market stall, heart pounding in his chest. He forced himself to relax his shoulders and straighten up. Skulking around would get him noticed. Being unremarkable would not. Slow as he could, he leaned against the wooden back of the booth and eased his head around the edge.

One row over stood a broad-backed man with sandy hair sticking out from under a knitted cap. It was Silas, the woodcutter. He was talking to a carpenter, gesturing.

"Never you mind that. We just need to find him."

Jeth quickly pulled back behind the booth again. His grip tightened on the straps of his pack until the fabric bit into his hands.

I won't let them take the orb. I won't!

It was the last piece of his mother he had left. He couldn't let them have it. Yet he didn't want to be arrested as a thief, either. He wondered if they would even let him explain. His stomach sank.

I never should have come in here.

Coming to Last Stop had put him right in the path of the people he was trying to avoid. He could have kicked himself. He *knew* he should have just gone around!

Enough of that, the voice of his mother chided softly, *what's done is done. All that matters is what's next.*

Jeth took off as quick as he could without attracting unwanted attention, hampered by the crowd around him. He had to weave around men and women with baskets and crates, around children running between legs, under a horse's head as it pulled a small cart sluggishly through a gap between two stalls. Everything became a blur around him, and yet somehow it was all sharpened into focus. He noticed little details in a flash, and forgot them just as quickly.

I just have to get across the square and to the eastern gate. Then I'm free and clear. It's just a little further.

"Jeth!" a deep voice called.

Before he could even turn, Jeth felt a tug on his pack. He twisted, eyes wide, to find himself face to face with Farmer Hugo and his bushy black beard, all shot through with gray. The farmer seemed just as surprised to see him, holding fast to the bag.

"Jeth. I can't believe we found you." The words were tinged...with relief?

I'm not a thief! It was only ever ours!

He couldn't get the words out. His mouth was too dry. Hugo's eyes searched his face, brow furrowing. Jeth didn't want to hear what he had to say.

You can't take it.

There was only one thing he could do. With a twist of his shoulders, Jeth slipped his arms free of the pack. His fist closed around one strap, pulling with all his might even as the other hand plunged inside the bag.

The orb was right there, right on top where he had left it.

"Stop it, boy! Stop!" Hugo was much stronger than Jeth. He easily wrested the pack back toward himself. "Stay still."

Jeth pulled the orb free and let his pack go. He backpedaled several steps, darting glances at the crowd that had pulled back around them. They wanted to see the show, to watch the little thief get arrested! Well, he didn't plan on going back.

Jeth turned and dove into the crowd, worming his way between one man's legs and taking off like a hare on the other side. He cradled the leather pouch that held the orb close to his chest.

"Jeth! Someone stop him, stop that boy!"

The residents of Last Stop began to search the crowd with interest, but by the time any of them saw Jeth, he passed right beneath their noses. Like a fox running ahead of the hounds, he wove his way through the last of the market and into an alleyway. Refuse bins and empty crates and barrels made an obstacle course of the already narrow path.

At least it will slow them down, too.

The men and women after him were all grown, and indeed, the junk hindered them enough that they quickly disappeared behind him.

Jeth didn't slow down. He couldn't stop until he was out of Last Stop entirely. They'd close the gates come dark, and he'd be trapped. They'd find him, and take the orb, and drag him back, and then...who knew?

His heart hammered in his chest, beating double time to his footsteps. He didn't dare look back. He could hear the distant shouts as people hunted for him.

Which way is the gate?

Jeth skidded to a stop at a narrow crossroads, gasping for breath and looking at the buildings on every side. He hadn't kept track of which way he had been turning, and he couldn't see the sun in the narrow strips of sky above.

I just need to find the gate. Then I can run right out of here and back to the woods.

It was a simple plan, an easy plan. He hoped he could carry it out. Picking one of the alleyways at random, Jeth ran once more.

Just get to the woods. They'll never find me out there. Not with what Mother taught me, and my magic, and –

Magic! As if struck by lightning, Jeth remembered his powers. He could use the wind to push himself up onto a rooftop, and then he'd be able to see everything. Even better, no one would be able to see *him*.

He gathered in his power, stretching his senses out to feel for the leylines. To him, they felt like a rumble in the earth, the stir of something sluggish and powerful at rest. Jeth only needed to borrow a bit of that might, just a trickle. He pulled a little here, and a little there, gathering the power into his chest, then guiding it down toward his feet and–

Jeth rounded a corner, running face first into a man's back. The breath was knocked out of him, and his concentration fell apart. The magic fizzled away into the air like static, shocking him as it went.

"Ow!" Jeth looked up at the man.

Not a man. He stared blankly, taking in the stranger's features. The planes of his face were angular and long. His eyes were a brilliant ruddy orange, verging on red. His hair was black as pitch and braided into a single tail that trailed halfway down his chest – which left his pointed ears plainly on display, even beneath his hood.

Jeth had run into a faerie.

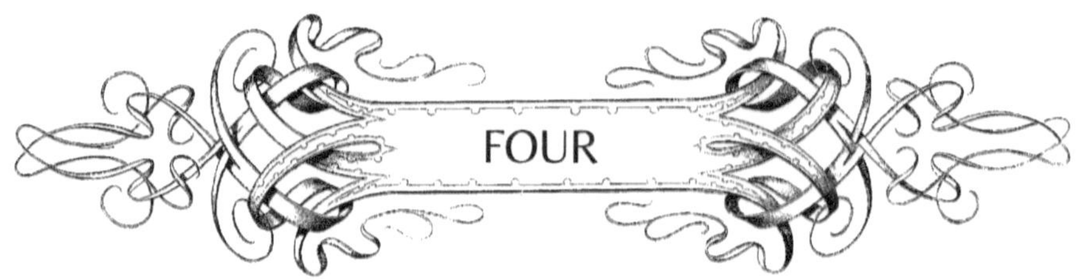

FOUR

What is a faerie doing in a town?

That was the first thought that crossed Jeth's mind. Swathed in dark clothes that seemed to be made more of a supple bark than of any fabric he had ever seen or heard of, the faerie studied him in turn. Jeth watched a flicker of something pass over the creature's face—too quickly for him to make out just what expression it was.

"Anyone see him?" came a woman's shout. She was no more than one or two streets away.

Jeth felt his stomach drop as he scrambled back to his feet. Whatever reason there was for a faerie to be in town, it wasn't *his* problem.

"Ah. You need to hide."

It wasn't a question. The words stopped Jeth from bolting away again. The faerie's voice was smooth and melodic, like a river running over stones. A hint of amusement played at the edges of his words.

"Allow me to assist."

No–!

With a sweep of his arm, the faerie's cloak enveloped him in a cascade of warm and heavy fabric. He pulled Jeth against his side, pinning him there with his arm and towing him along. Jeth writhed, trying to squirm his way free—until he heard voices all around him.

"Anyone seen him?"

"He can't have gone far."

"Don't worry, sir, we have the gates being watched."

"Thank you," Silas said, relief clear in every word.

Jeth stopped struggling, heart pounding so hard that he could hear the blood rushing in his ears. The cloak covered him entirely, woven so tight that he couldn't see anything. It was pitch black. The fabric just barely swept the ground, which meant that it would hide his feet. No one in their right minds would stop a faerie, if they even looked beneath the creature's hood at all.

This might be his only chance, even if it would no doubt come with strings. Faeries never did anything for free. He couldn't help but feel like a fly, choosing the spider to save him from the frog.

Jeth pressed the orb tight against his side, listening to the town around them. Footsteps, a squeak and clatter that must have been a cart. The bray of a mule in the distance. A door slamming closed. Every step they managed to go undetected was one step closer to his freedom.

If the faerie will let me go.

The thought rose in Jeth's chest until he felt like he couldn't breathe. He choked down the urge to fight his way free of the folds of the cloak and run back to Silas and Hugo.

Whatever else is happening, in this moment the faerie is protecting me.

Cobbles turned to mud beneath his boots, then to grass dusted with snow, and finally to snow a few inches deep. The faerie lifted his cloak.

Jeth lifted his arm to cover his eyes as they adjusted to the field of white. They were in a meadow in the forest, or what would become one come spring. Last Stop was still visible, barely, through the trees.

I'm safe. I'm free.

He stepped away from the faerie, still cradling the leather bag that held the orb. Reluctantly, he turned to face the creature.

His mother's voice whispered in his ear as his lips parted. *Never, ever, thank a faerie.*

"You helped me," he said instead.

The faerie nodded. "I did."

Silence fell. The creature watched Jeth with eyes that glittered in the way serpent's scales did when they moved.

If I do this right, I can still walk away.

All he had to do was dance the steps correctly. What exactly had his mother told him? He searched his mind for every word of advice she had ever said about faeries.

If only I were older. If he were older and wiser than fourteen, he'd know all these things on his own. He'd have a better chance. Then again, the faerie was an immortal creature who could be hundreds or thousands of years old. Maybe he'd never have had a chance, even if he were old and gray.

"What do I call you?" That was safe enough.

The corner of the faerie's lips turned up in faint amusement—though whether that was because of Jeth's careful phrasing and furrowed brow or his knowledge of faerie customs at all, Jeth couldn't tell. The silence stretched on between them as the faerie tipped his head to one side, weighing his options.

Maybe he won't answer at all.

Jeth had just decided that was the case when the creature spoke.

"Aneirin. May I have *your* name?"

"No," Jeth said firmly. It was the oldest trick in the book to steal someone's name away, making them and anyone who knew them forget it forever. He wasn't so wet behind the ears as to fall for it.

"Then perhaps you can tell me what to call you."

Jeth took a deep breath. He hadn't expected Aneirin to relent so quickly. There didn't appear to be any trick to the faerie's words this time. That only made the hairs on the back of Jeth's neck stand up.

Don't let your guard down.

"You may call me Jeth, for now."

"Jeth," Aneirin said, tasting the name. "Very well. You wish to leave this place, yes?"

Jeth didn't answer. Not for the first time, he wished his mother were there. She would know what to do. She'd met a faerie once, she said. He should have asked her more about them. The entire kingdom was carved out of a faerie forest! They co-existed with powerful magical beings that would tease and toy with someone before letting them starve to death or go mad or worse things still—and he didn't know enough to face one down!

Still, the rules of hospitality demanded an answer to a direct question before he could leave. He didn't know what would happen if he didn't. Jeth paced in the snow, carving out a packed trail. As he thought, he tied the orb's pouch securely to his belt.

I have no supplies. They took my pack. How long can I survive by myself with nothing to eat, in the winter, in the woods? How far is it to the next town?

His knowledge of Hallanor ended at Last Stop. He was no crafty woodsman, able to find squirrel caches or hunt rabbits without a snare. Was it worth trading food and directions for whatever a faerie might ask for? Aneirin could take his memories, or his ability to laugh. He could insist on Jeth serving as his page until he was old and hunch-backed.

He stopped pacing. Aneirin stood still as a stone, watching him. He hadn't moved at all.

"I will be leaving this place on my own. I don't wish for any help."

Aneirin's laugh was strange and brittle, like icicles falling to the ground. "Very well. I shall not offer aid."

Relief undid the knots between Jeth's shoulders. He hadn't even realized how tense he was. Jeth glanced up at the sky, taking a moment to find the sun and determine which way was east. No doubt he would come upon a village at some point. Or a road. Or anything. He'd be just fine.

"Well, goodbye then," he said, starting toward the trees.

"Jeth."

Don't stop. Don't turn.

He did both.

Aneirin gestured vaguely to a small rise to his left. "A trading caravan is just beyond that rise. I have been traveling with them for some time. Their business has concluded, and they are packing their wares to leave. Their path goes east from here. Perhaps they might need an extra pair of hands around their encampment?"

It was everything Jeth had wanted to find, offered on a silver platter.

This has to be a trap.

Why would a faerie offer so much, so freely? Aneirin hadn't even asked for payment or a favor for helping Jeth in his escape, and now he was offering—everything? Jeth's heart was racing.

Don't, his mother whispered.

"I hope they find the help they need. Goodbye."

Aneirin laughed again. Jeth's hands curled into fists as he turned and marched toward the trees. It was time to leave. This was too dangerous. He was no match for a faerie in a battle of wits and he knew it. As he stepped beneath the bare boughs of the trees, he breathed a sigh of relief.

That was when the trap snapped shut.

"About my favor…" Aneirin said, studying his fingernails. The words hung in the chill air.

Jeth froze. A wave of cold swept over him, followed by a flush of anger.

I'm a fool, falling for that. I knew it. I knew he wouldn't just let me go!

He had let his guard down, which was exactly what he told himself not to do. Slowly, he turned back around. He glared at the creature.

"What favor?"

"I rescued you, and one good turn begets another. You would agree, yes?" Aneirin smiled, but it was little more than a curl of the lips. His orange eyes never wavered in their stare, and the smile never reached them.

"What is it you want?"

Jeth's mind conjured all sorts of terrible answers. What if the faerie wanted his memories of his mother? What if he wiped Jeth's mind entirely? What if he took something more tangible—like the orb? Maybe he would want a limb. A leg!

"Do not worry so much. I don't want anything you own. Meager as your physical belongings are, now, you have nothing that particularly interests me. Not even that bauble on your hip. Where did you get such an artefact?"

Jeth didn't answer as the faerie walked over to him, footsteps making no sound and hardly an indentation in the snow.

"That wasn't an answer to my question," he said instead, trying not to sound cross and failing.

"I could ask for anything, and you would give it – for your freedom. For your very survival."

Aneirin circled Jeth, stride smooth and measured like a hunting cat. Jeth felt his eyes studying him from every angle. Jeth lifted his chin.

I am not afraid. Except, of course, that was a lie.

"You will travel with me, boy. That is what I want. The road is long and the humans I travel with are dull. Your presence amuses me, so you will come."

As simple as the request was, he knew it might come with hidden strings. He didn't dare agree too soon. What if he accidentally bound himself to the faerie for centuries? He didn't want that.

"How long? How far?" Jeth demanded.

"Clever," Aneirin said, still circling his prey. "Forever?"

"No."

"Fifty years."

"No!"

Aneirin stopped, heaving a great sigh. "Fine. Why don't you suggest your own terms?"

Careful! His mother's warning made him shiver.

Jeth whirled to face the faerie. "To the next town." His answer, he hoped, was vague enough that he could wriggle out of it if he had to.

Aneirin raised a brow. There was no sound beyond their breathing for several moments. A lone bird whistled a little tune in the trees nearby. A squirrel skittered across some branches, chittering as it went. Jeth's heart never slowed its racing.

"Agreed." Aneirin offered his hand at last.

Jeth didn't take it. He had never heard that it was necessary to seal a deal with a handshake. What if it was another trap? "Agreed," he echoed. "This way?"

Aneirin smiled again as he followed Jeth through the trees and up the rise, trailing after him silently. The space between Jeth's shoulder blades prickled. He fought the urge to fall back or look behind. They had a bargain. He would be safe.

I am not afraid.

He was.

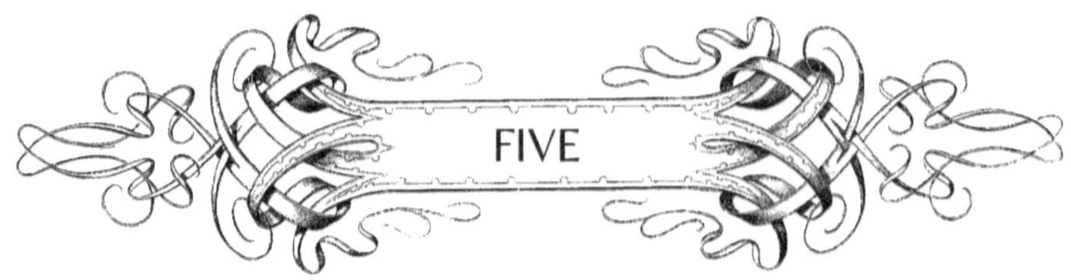

FIVE

The trader's camp was quiet. There were only six of them, three men and three women, all travel-stained and weathered no matter their age. Some few looked positively ancient, with gray hair and deeply lined faces. Three carts stacked high with crates and barrels and sacks, all fastened with ropes, were lined up between the traders and the thickest part of the forest. It was meager protection, but still better than nothing. There were plenty of horses, however, all picketed in a line. There were six for the wagons, broad-shouldered draft horses taller than any steed Jeth had ever seen, and three more besides. He assumed the smaller horses were for riding alongside.

Then there was the large black steed, standing alone on the other side of the camp. She wasn't tethered at all, and bore no bit, bridle, or saddle. Aneirin swept to the mare's side and put his hand fondly to her cheek.

Jeth had never seen a faerie horse before. He approached slowly, struggling to keep his eyes on her hooves and her face at the same time. The tales he had heard involved such horses appearing meek and docile before stealing someone away for a ride that would kill them, take them to the faerie lands, or never end at all.

"This is Shadowstep."

"Hello, Shadowstep." Jeth bowed slightly and made no move to touch the horse.

If she even is a horse. What if she's a Nightmare?

His wariness seemed to amuse Aneirin. His lips curled at the corners before his features went blank once more. He turned to the traders nearby.

Jeth had never seen a group of people more determined to ignore someone in his life. They spoke to one another in low voices, passing the last of the tents and bedrolls up and starting the process of harnessing the horses. Only one of them would even *look* at Aneirin.

A tall woman dressed in trousers and a thick jacket met the faerie's gaze. With a heavy sigh, she turned from the wagons to walk over. Her shoulders were broad, and her hair flaming red and bound at the nape of her neck. She lifted her hand in greeting.

"Ho, Aneirin. You're back. Who is this, then? Another stray?"

"An acquisition." Aneirin gestured at the wagons. "Are you satisfied, Burne?"

Burne folded her arms over her chest, studying their haul. The wagons groaned beneath the weight of so many goods. She shook her head. "You're keeping up your end of the bargain, and that's all I'll say on the matter. How much longer will you be with us?"

"Is three years not enough?"

"We're finished, then?"

"At the next town, I shall leave."

At the next town, when he's alone, Jeth thought. He couldn't wait to be free of his own bargain, and he wondered if Burne felt the same.

Burne nodded. "And the luck?"

"As you wished, your luck will hold for three generations."

"So this is it, then." Burne's gaze slid to Jeth.

"It is."

"Well, alright. I'll get this one settled in. You, boy. What's your name?"

"Jeth."

Burne leaned in a bit, brow furrowing. "Jeth?" She shot a glance at Aneirin, who had turned away to tend to his steed. "Jeth. I'm Burne Calder, and this is my team. Since you're with our...friend, here, you won't get much talk out of them. Not much point in trying. You can just talk to me, eh?"

Jeth liked how she grinned, and how she clasped his shoulder in a large, strong hand. He smiled back at her. "That sounds nice."

"You're going to ride with me in the lead wagon. Where's your things?"

Jeth spread his hands and shrugged helplessly. How could he tell her that he left them with the people hunting him for theft?

"Nothing but the clothes on your back? I've been there. Go on, get up in the seat there. We'll take care of the horses."

Aneirin cleared his throat delicately. "We leave within the bell."

Burne nodded at the faerie, then turned to help lift Jeth onto the wagon's tall seat and left him to settle in. Jeth couldn't help but lean around the side of the wagon to watch her and her crew. She moved among them, lending a hand where needed, doing jobs herself when everyone else was busy, and offering encouragement when she could.

Jeth liked Burne Calder. She had him smiling again, all because she was bright and cheery herself, even in the dismal gray weather.

In short order, the horses were fastened, the traders were mounted, and the wagons were rolling down to the road. Aneirin and Shadowstep rode in the lead, far enough away they disappeared if the road bent.

Burne watched the faerie's back with clear distaste, twitching the reins.

"You don't like him?" Jeth asked.

"No one likes or dislikes faeries, little Jeth. We make our deals and get on with our lives if we survive them. Aneirin is powerful. I don't know what deal you struck, but you'd do well to finish it quickly."

"You've been in a deal with him for years."

Burne laughed, low and bitter. "I have. I struck the deal when I first started out. He'd travel with my company and we'd go wherever he said, but in exchange? Riches. Luck. Safety. Not just for the duration of the bargain, but for the rest of my life. All because he wanted to find...something."

Jeth's brow furrowed. He had the strangest feeling that she nearly said something else.

What's so important that a faerie would travel the length and breadth of Hallanor to find it? Why won't she tell me? Is that part of their deal?

"Enough of that," Burne said, interrupting his thoughts. "What puts a boy like you out in the world alone? Why aren't you safe at home?"

He could tell she knew she had misspoken as soon as his expression fell. The guilt flashed across her face even as grief passed over his.

"You don't have to answer if–"

"My mother died. I haven't got anyone else."

"Damn. And damn me, too." Burne chewed on the inside of her cheek for a moment, gaze drifting to the faerie riding ahead of them.

"You didn't know," Jeth said softly.

"Doesn't mean it didn't hurt you. Look, are you hungry? There are cold meat pies in that chest behind you, fresh from one of the inns. Tuck in."

His mood lifted as he dug through the chest for his first proper breakfast in days.

"How did you meet him?" Burne asked.

Jeth paused, a meat pie wrapped in paper in his hand. He lowered the lid of the chest slowly, brow furrowing. *Does she suspect that I'm a thief?*

Aloud, all he said was: "I ran into him in an alleyway." None of it was a lie.

Burne cleared her throat. She scanned the trees on either side as if they were listening before crooking a finger. Jeth leaned in.

"Careful with Aneirin. I survive by doing exactly as he says, when he says it. He's in charge, and he knows it. You'd do well to do the same."

Jeth shivered. The paper in his hands crinkled as his grip tightened. "Why...why are you telling me this?"

Burne cupped his cheek in her calloused hand, gaze softening. "Because you're just a boy still, no matter that everyone else thinks you're a man. You're alone, and you're young, and I don't want to see that faerie chew you up and spit you out like he did me."

"But you got everything you wanted."

"The thing with faerie deals, Jeth, is that you get what you want but it's never how you wanted it. Now eat. No." She held up a hand, and Jeth closed his mouth again slowly. "Just eat."

They sat in silence as Jeth couldn't interpret as companionable or awkward as the sun sank, and the cold meat pie settled in the pit of his stomach like a stone. Jeth couldn't help but stare at Aneirin's back as the faerie came into view around a bend. As if he could sense the gaze boring into him, Aneirin turned in the saddle to glance back at Jeth.

Did he imagine the faerie smiled at him? Did he imagine that the smile was somehow taut as a bowstring, ready to fire an arrow into his heart? He couldn't tell. Dread built up like a weight on his back, heavier than his pack had ever been.

What have I done?

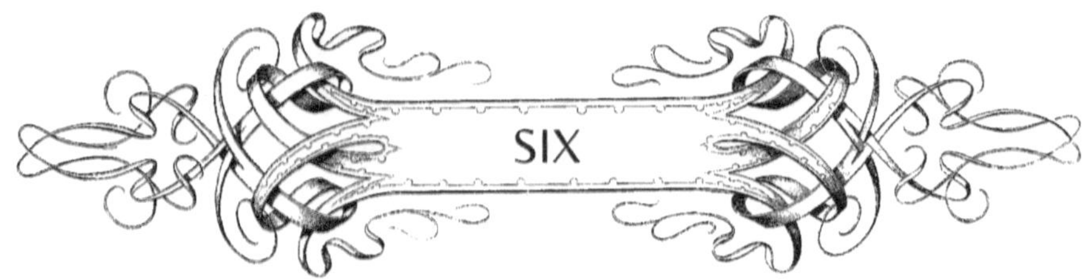

SIX

Jeth frowned at the length of rope in his hands, struggling to knot it the way Burne had showed him a dozen times. Three days had passed uneventfully. Aneirin had insisted that Jeth learn to ride, and Jeth had spent a few bells each day uneasily astride a horse. Burne taught him knots and ways to tell a good inn from a bad one before even seeing a room. True to her predictions, none of the other traders spoke to Jeth at all. The trader who loaned Jeth the horse simply handed the reins over without looking at him, and the rest pretended he wasn't there at all. Even when he spoke directly to them.

His only company was Burne Calder or Aneirin. Aneirin insisted on riding ahead of the wagons in silence, interrupted only by small observances of flora and fauna. Of the two, Jeth preferred Burne Calder. She was boisterous and warm, a balm to his lonely heart.

"Give it another go," she encouraged him. "Here, over. Now twist. Pull. Aha, you've got it!"

Jeth held the rope up, admiring the clumsy knot.

"Now do it again," Burne said, a playful grin on her face.

"Again?"

"Again."

The wagons rolled around a curve in the road as Jeth worked the knot free. Ahead, a dark shape caught his eye. He lowered the rope, watching the still form of Aneirin astride Shadowstep as the faerie waited for the wagons. Once they caught up, he fell in beside Burne Calder's wagon.

Burne's smile was gone. "What is it?"

"Trouble ahead. In keeping with our bargain, I shall handle it. No need to stop or change course," he said, as calmly as if he were discussing a walk to market.

Burne swept her arm toward the road ahead. "Well, after you, then."

Aneirin tucked his heels against Shadowstep's side and the mare practically flew, barreling down the road so quickly they were soon gone. Jeth shuddered at the quiet reminder that what appeared to be a horse...wasn't.

"Alright, Jeth, I don't know how much time we have." Burne pulled the rope from Jeth's hands.

"For what?" Jeth asked, feeling his heart beat harder at the urgency in her voice.

"You come from a small village outside of Last Stop, don't you?"

His heart was now hammering at his ribs, and a chill washed over him. *If I have to, I can run. I can make it into the trees and vanish.*

He didn't know what would happen if he broke a faerie bargain, but he wasn't about to find out. He braced himself against the wagon's seat.

"Why do you ask?"

"When we were in Last Stop, a man named Silas came to speak to us. He was looking for a boy named Jeth."

Jeth felt a flush of anger creeping over his cheeks and up to his ears. He considered defending himself, explaining everything—but what would be the point? He stood, prepared to throw himself off the wagon and flee.

Burne Calder was faster than he'd thought. She caught his arm, holding him fast. "They were worried about you, boy."

All of his anger vanished abruptly. The wagon rocked, tipping him back into his seat. "What?"

"Silas told us quite the tale. They went to your cottage to move you to some little house on the other side of the village, and you were gone."

Jeth remembered the empty shepherd's house, smaller than his and his mother's and long abandoned, with the crooked little fence falling to pieces at the side. "They wanted to move me?"

The villagers hadn't planned to abandon him at all.

"When they went to your cottage, though, someone else was there. A man was looking for you by name. When the villagers couldn't turn you over to him, he set three houses on fire before he decided they were telling the truth."

"I don't understand." Jeth felt as if someone had put a handful of snow down the back of his coat. He shivered. "I don't believe you!"

If Burne Calder was right, that meant Jeth was wrong. That meant that Hugo *was* relieved. That meant...that he didn't have to leave home in the first place.

"I don't know how to convince you. I swear, I spoke to Silas myself in Last Stop. There were others with him."

"Hugo," Jeth murmured.

Burne shrugged, glancing up the road. There was still no sign of Aneirin. "Now, I don't know what deal you struck with the faerie, but if it doesn't include protection from whatever's hunting you–"

The villagers aren't after me, but someone else is. And now I don't know why.

He shook his head. "No, you have to be wrong."

"We can argue all day and all night, Jeth. I can't turn around and show you proof. You have to take me at my word." She took a deep breath, closing her eyes as if her next words physically hurt. "You might need another deal with Aneirin."

"No, no more deals. One was bad enough!" Jeth's mother wouldn't want him indebted to a faerie forever. His hand fell to the pouch at his side, feeling the comforting shape of the orb through the leather.

The orb! Jeth had seen his mother use it a hundred times to scry for the villagers, to bring them news of washed out roads or when to expect the tax collector. He managed to use it himself once before, even if what he saw was brief and indistinct.

His fledgling powers were mostly used to stir the air or light candles. He had never perfected much more than that.

"I know how to see if it's true." Jeth said, fingers fumbling with the ties of the pouch. With a huff, he bit the fingertip of a glove and pulled his hand free, untying the orb at last. It rolled into his hands, catching the late afternoon sunlight and glowing soft and gold. It was warmer than he expected it to be.

Burne leaned over to study it. "Well, that's a mighty fine bauble. How exactly is it going to help us?"

"It's a crystal ball. My mother–"

"Was the village witch. Yes, Silas told me."

"Well, this was hers. Not the village's, but hers," he said, a challenge creeping into his voice.

Burne met his eyes and gave a solemn nod. "I understand."

"I can scry with it."

A breeze rose and stirred Jeth's hair, making him shiver. His fingers closed over the orb. *Spoken like a prophecy, but can I even do it?*

"Huh! With magic that powerful, it's no wonder Aneirin took an interest in you. He likes collecting things, that one."

"I'm not a thing, and I'm not collected." Every word was firm.

Burne shrugged, turning back to the road ahead. "Cast your spells, Jeth. Before Aneirin comes back."

Jeth held the orb in both of his hands, studying the depths intently. He summoned his will, feeling it build up like electricity in his chest. When he had enough that he felt like his teeth were rattling in his skull and his hair was standing on end, he pushed it down his arms and into the crystal.

The depths flashed a brighter gold, winking in and out of existence like a firefly.

It faded.

Jeth frowned, holding the crystal up higher. *What had mother said? What did she tell me to do?* He closed his eyes.

Her ghost didn't come. He frowned, straining to summon her, willing her to appear. *Don't be gone!*

I'm not, she seemed to whisper in his ear. *You can do this. For a scrying spell, you must let your mind drift. Draw in the power slowly. Through your chest and into your fingers. Do you remember how?*

"I remember," he murmured. He hadn't before.

"What was that?" Burne asked.

"Nothing." When Jeth opened his eyes, his mother's presence was gone again. She was growing fainter every day.

I don't have time to think about that. I have to figure out what's going on.

He held the orb aloft once more, staring into the depths. As branches passed overhead, the shadows flickered and rolled across the crystal. Jeth watched the play of light, of gold and darkness, relaxing until he felt everything else drift away piece by piece. The wagon stopped creaking. The horse's tack stopped jingling. The cold bite of winter began to fade.

It was then he pulled at the power again, reaching out to the leyline that ran parallel to the road. He imagined himself as a sluice gate, opening the link between the power of the forest and the orb just enough to let a trickle through.

It took a moment, but then he felt the magic *catch*, like a fish at the end of a line. He opened the conduit a little more, feeling the power build up, watching the golden gleam in the center as it began to glow. It was captivating—quite literally. Jeth found he couldn't tear his gaze away from the heart of the orb.

It must be ready.

My village, he willed.

He felt as if he were falling, as if the wagon rocked forward and threw him from his seat and he was plummeting to the ground. His breath caught and he tried to brace himself.

He couldn't move.

Instead, he seemed to be flying. So quickly it made his stomach roil, Jeth was flung into the sky and over the undulating ocean of the forest, speeding faster than a thought to his home. He closed his eyes, relieved to find he could.

Everything stilled. He could hear the clatter of a spinning wheel. The petulant bleat of a goat. He cracked one eye open – and gasped.

Jeth was standing in the center of his village, still holding the orb cradled in his hands. The image was so vivid, so *real.* The scent of burnt wood and snow filled the air, nearly overpowering the aroma of bread and stew from the nearest house.

The tiny one-room tavern was gone, replaced with a black pit of ash and charred wood. A few beams still stood in stark contrast against the snow behind. Hugo's house was gone as well, now just a ring of soot-covered stones with a pile of debris inside. Jeth recoiled, turning his gaze toward the cottage. He knew he wouldn't be able to see it from here, but he had to know if it was...

The house nearest the little path that wound to his home used to be bordered on one side by Silas's house, and on the other by the home of the baker and her sister. The baker's house was gone. Only the two massive stone ovens still stood, painted with fire residue until they looked like two holes in the very air itself.

Jeth swallowed. *Burne Calder wasn't lying. The village was attacked.*

He willed himself to the nearest lit window at Silas's house, peering through the bubbled glass. When he walked, he left no footprints and made no sound.

Inside Silas's house, the barkeep, his wife, and his two children were settling in on straw pallets that covered every inch of available floor. Hugo's wife, heavily pregnant, was settled into a rocking chair by the hearth, her pallet stacked double.

Silas's wife, Maeve, was pouring mugs of tea for everyone at the table, speaking soothingly to her stunned neighbors.

"When the men get back, they'll put it all to rights. You'll see."

Jeth didn't know how he had stepped through the wall, but now he was in the cramped cottage's living space, beside the door.

"And don't fret, they'll be back any day now. Them and young Jeth." Maeve gave a firm nod, pressing a mug into Hugo's wife's hands. *What was her name...?*

No one responded to Maeve. They took their mugs in near silence, even the children. A few tried to smile at her, but the attempts ended quickly.

"They'll be back," Maeve repeated. "Any minute. You'll see."

They lost everything, too. Not over a misunderstanding, but over me.

Jeth's heart sank, and the bottom of his stomach with it. A cold pit was left inside him. He knew how awful it was to lose your home.

I want to leave.

It felt as if a rope around his waist was given a sudden tug, yanking him back a step. He dropped his gaze to his boots, then back up to the window. For a moment, his eyes met Maeve's wistful gaze. Could she see him? He lifted his hand –

The rope tugged again, harder than before. He stumbled and fell backwards...onto the wagon seat beside Burne Calder. The light in the center of the orb flickered and died. Slack jawed, Jeth scanned the woods rolling by on either side of the wagon.

He'd gone there and back again in the space of a thought.

"Are you alright?" Burne asked, her hand clasping his shoulder. "It was like you went to sleep sitting up. You couldn't hear a thing."

"I'm fine. I'm alright," he assured her, even as a wave of exhaustion washed over him. His voice sounded far away. "You were right. Half the village is gone."

If Burne was right about the village, then she was right about something else, too. Someone was after Jeth. What could one boy do against an unknown man who was powerful enough to set three buildings aflame before anyone could stop him? Who could escape a half-dozen men and twice as many women unscathed?

What if I have to make another bargain to protect myself?

He shuddered. Any more bargains might come at a higher cost. Could he take such a risk? What would Aneirin ask for?

As if the thought summoned him, the wagon rolled around a corner and the faerie and his horse stood waiting in the center of the road. Parts of his cloak and doublet gleamed strangely in the fading light. A strong, coppery smell floated in the air, covering even the scent of snow.

Jeth quickly tucked the orb away. Aneirin's eyes seemed to follow the gesture.

"Just look straight ahead, boy, don't look around. You hear me?" Burne said, voice taut. She didn't slow or stop the wagon.

Jeth froze, keeping his eyes on the road ahead. "Why? What is it?"

"Just do as I say."

As they drew up alongside Aneirin, the creature mounted Shadowstep and fell in beside them. "In another league, there will be a nice clearing. We can make camp there."

"Good to know," Burne said, keeping her voice light. Jeth could hear the barest waver to the words, though.

His eyes slid slowly to one side.

An arm lay limp on the ground. At the top, where the rest of a body would be, there wasn't. A small pool of crimson stained the grass and snow beneath it.

Jeth looked ahead again. His stomach tied itself into a knot. He knew what that smell in the air was, now.

Blood.

They rode on in silence.

SEVEN

"It's been two weeks." Jeth was getting suspicious. Even if his time with the caravan had taught him how to start a fire, how to set up a tent, how to hitch and groom a horse, how to ride, how to tie knots—his intention was to strike out on his own.

They hadn't reached a town, a village, or even a little hamlet yet. They made camp in clearings Aneirin directed them to and found roots beside them. Three times they stayed at a waystation along the road, little more than a roof and walls with a massive hearth and a pantry full of flour, oats, and beans. One evening had been spent with their wagons parked in a field and the traders in the barn of a farmer in the middle of nowhere. Sometimes they ran into merchants on the road and bought or traded for fresh provisions. None of that took them to a town.

Every night, Jeth had nightmares about a man following him, a man made of shadows. Every day, shadows that flitted past beneath the trees on either side of the road made Jeth jump, made his heart race, made his spine go cold. How far behind him was the man who burned the village?

Jeth was keenly aware of his bargain with Aneirin. It chafed to know he might have to make another.

He's trying to keep me here with him. I can't trust him.

Jeth held the reins of his horse tight in his hands. It was quiet apart from the jingle of the bridle and the dull thud of the horses' hooves. Aneirin sat astride Shadowstep, leading the way as usual. The wagons rolled along a few lengths behind them.

"Two," Jeth repeated.

"Yes," the faerie affirmed, as though agreeing there might be snow later.

"We should have reached somewhere by now, and we haven't. Why?"

Aneirin's brows drew down. He didn't like questions. "The goods that Burne Calder has obtained will sell better at one specific market than they will anywhere else. I am keeping up my end of her bargain."

Jeth sighed. *Another half-truth. Why do faeries always do that?* He knew they couldn't tell lies, but it was frustrating how they were so obvious about omitting important information. Aneirin was avoiding the subject of his own bargain with Jeth on purpose.

If they never reached the next town, the deal would stand forever.

"You are displeased." It wasn't a question.

Jeth shrugged. "I'm just not sure what you want from me. When we ride, we hardly talk. When we talk, it's about plants or animals. Everything else has been...normal things."

"Normal things or human things?" Aneirin gave a small, brief smile. "Things such as learning to make camp, care for horses, and speak of likes and dislikes? Plain things, not magical faerie things. Yes?"

"Well, yes." Jeth heaved another sigh. Aneirin patrolled the edge of camp every evening, listening to Burne Calder and Jeth. They discussed what food he liked, what books he had read, what kind of music he liked, what weather he preferred. Over the weeks spent with the caravan, Jeth's answers had gone from curt, one-word answers to lengthy explanations and stories.

He tried to resist. It just felt so good to have someone to talk to like that again. Burne always listened, always laughed at his jests, always had something clever to say. Once his deal with Aneirin was complete, Jeth hoped Burne would let him go with her until he found an apprenticeship.

Part of him wondered if his mother felt betrayed to see him smiling again so soon. Did she hate him for being comfortable in his bedroll, tucked into one of the wagons? Surrounded by crates and burlap bags, Jeth was warm and safe. Did she hate him for that? He couldn't summon her at will anymore. She came less and less frequently, and said fewer words in his ear before she left.

Someday, she wouldn't come at all.

Jeth twitched the reins, guiding his horse toward the opposite side of the road from the faerie. "I just don't understand what you're playing at."

"Playing? I am not playing," Aneirin said, a firm finality to his words.

"Then what–"

"How did you sleep?" the faerie interrupted.

Horribly, Jeth thought. Every night, tucked in his bedroll away from everyone else, he wrapped around the aching hole in his chest and let the hurt swallow him until he fell asleep. He cried silently long into the night, trying to process his mother's passing, trying not to drown in his own grief.

Then, all night long, he had nightmares of fire, of reaching hands out of the darkness, of someone breathing behind him that he could never turn fast enough to see.

Yet every morning when the sun rose, he was back on his feet as if nothing had happened at all. Jeth didn't feel safe enough to let Aneirin know how he felt, but he suspected Burne Calder knew. She never said anything about it, just passed him a water skin every morning before sending him to do his chores.

It was an unexpected gift to find a friend in Burne – or perhaps an unintended side effect of his bargain with the faerie.

"I slept as well as I always do," Jeth answered at last.

Aneirin smiled. Could he tell that Jeth had given his own faerie lie? They rode in silence for several minutes.

"I expected something different," Jeth blurted.

"Oh?"

"I grew up hearing stories about faeries that dragged mortals below the hills for a hundred years to live in their courts, or about great revels where humans danced until their feet wore away entirely or they starved to death."

"Those stories are not entirely false," Aneirin said with an elegant shrug of one shoulder.

"What about the ones where you put mortals under spells that erase who they are, or disguise them from all their loved ones?"

"Also true."

Jeth leaned forward. "Can you cast a spell so that someone doesn't know where they are, and instead sees somewhere different?"

"I can."

"Have you cast that spell on me?"

Aneirin paused, brows lifting in faint surprise. "Very astute, Jeth, but no. I have cast no spells upon you."

Jeth turned to watch the trees pass on the side of the road. Faeries couldn't lie. No one knew why. He was safe. Well, as safe as one could be when traveling with a faerie.

Every story he had ever heard about faeries ended in tragedy. *I hope I can escape my own story unscathed.*

All he had to do was get to the next city or town, and then he would be free.

"You asked me why we did plain things." Aneirin's words cut through Jeth's musings.

Jeth nodded.

"I am training you. To be companionable, one must be able to keep up with me."

"I don't need to keep up with you. I'm leaving at the next town."

"You will change your mind."

"You don't know that," Jeth said heatedly.

"Would you like to learn a spell?"

The change of subject left Jeth floundering. "What? A...a spell? What makes you think..."

"You were gathering magic when you ran into me. I felt you fumble with it when I rode away to kill the bandits, as well. I know about the focus you have in that little bag on your hip. I can see it. I can feel it."

Jeth's breath caught. *I didn't know faeries could feel magic.* No one had ever mentioned that in any of the tales or written it in any of the grimoires his mother had let him read. *How...?*

"We faeries have an innate ability we call True Sight. It's easy enough to learn to use it, for some. It sees through glamours, and clings to those who use magic. When magic is pulled from the leylines, one can see it, like a little thread of starlight tying the caster to the deep pools of this world.

"Would you like to learn to do it?" Aneirin's sidelong look was smug. He knew Jeth's answer.

"I can learn it, too? I can see all that?" Jeth tried to imagine a life with that sort of power. He could go to the Royal Court of Hallanor and offer his services, spying out magic-users that might threaten the Queen. He could track new witches for villages that didn't have one. He could take to the hills and fight the faeries themselves! The possibilities were overwhelming.

He could go back to his village and help them rebuild, and they would welcome him. Even untrained, with an ability like True Sight, he could become a witch for the home he never wanted to leave.

"You can do quite a lot with that focus of yours. It amplifies one's natural abilities. I have seen its like before."

Jeth's hand fell to the orb at his hip. "What? You have? Where?"

"In a town called River's Tor."

"Do you know anything about it?" Jeth might not have another chance to learn about his crystal ball. They *had* to be close to a town, now. Who would he ask when he and the faerie parted ways?

For a moment, Aneirin tipped his head to one side. Jeth's heart picked up to a gallop in his chest. *Is he going to ask for a trade for the answer?*

"It is a conduit for power, something like a mirror and a cup in one. Power pools within it and reflects back to the user, allowing them to push their will further than they could on their own. Did you think it merely a pretty bauble to tell fortunes with?"

A flush crept over Jeth's cheeks. "No."

"You planned to use it to predict harvests? Find lost little pigs? Tell people who their one true love is?" Aneirin mocked. There was a disdain dripping from the words that Jeth didn't like.

"What's wrong with small magics?"

"Mortal magics are barely worthy of the word. Humans are like children playing with candle flames and calling it a bonfire."

He hates humans.

"Why did you ask me to accompany you, then?" Jeth asked.

Aneirin didn't answer. Silence fell over them again. After a few minutes, Jeth sighed and turned back to the trees.

Why did he make a deal with a trading caravan of mortals if he hates us? Why make a deal with me? Why come to Last Stop at all?

All Jeth had found on his journey so far were more and more questions. There was so much to learn!

"Pull out the focus," Aneirin said, gesturing to the pouch on Jeth's hip.

Brow furrowed, Jeth did as he was bid, pulling his gloves off and tucking them into his belt before pulling the orb free. He cradled it in one hand, though it barely fit.

"Reach out for the magic and pull it through your chest and into your fingertips."

For a single heartbeat, Jeth thought his mother had spoken. The advice was the same as her lessons, even if it came from the faerie's lips. He swallowed his surprise; he didn't want to give Aneirin anything to interrogate him about later.

Jeth stretched his consciousness out to the nearest leyline, which ran several lengths back in the woods. Once he had his 'fingers' in it, he opened the barrier in his chest and let it flow through him, down to his fingertips.

"Feed the power into the focus."

Jeth pushed the magic from his hands. Just as it had when Jeth used it to scry, the orb drank up the steady trickle of power until the center of it flickered to life with a golden glow. The glow grew brighter the more he fed it.

"Good. Now, close your eyes and will it to open them again. Will it to show you the leylines." Aneirin's instructions sounded far away.

Mother showed me the leylines, once. When he first began learning magic, his mother had sat him down and shown him the rivers of silver power that flowed through the world, using the crystal ball as a lens. Jeth remembered staring through it in awe, turning this way and that to see every inch of the magic he might use.

No, Jeth, you can't. Too much magic will burn right through you and leave you an empty shell. Drink sparingly from those rivers, or you'll drown. His mother's warning nearly shattered his concentration. He felt the power waver.

No, don't go! Show me the leylines, show me the magic.

The orb warmed in his hand. With a deep breath, Jeth opened his eyes.

The deep river of a leyline ran through the woods to his left, fed by tributaries of smaller magic. The smaller magics split off further or pooled into little knots of power before continuing on their way. The bright silver radiance of the lines themselves nearly overpowered the softer glow of the sleeping trees and shrubs along the road. When he looked back, the tradesfolk and Burne Calder on her wagon had the same barely perceptible sheen.

Aneirin and Shadowstep glowed nearly as bright as the leylines above. *Do all faeries glow that way?*

Jeth looked down at his own hands. His own light was stronger than the tradesfolk, but far softer than Aneirin's. The orb, however, shone gold, even to this other sight. Jeth twisted in the saddle, tracing the paths of magic. His jaw hung open in awe.

Could you see like this, Mother?

She didn't answer.

"Now, reach for the magic you put in the focus," Aneirin said after giving Jeth plenty of time to gawk.

We aren't finished yet? Jeth dipped his senses into the golden pool of power at the heart of the crystal ball. The hair on his arms stood up. Every inch of him tingled from the top of his scalp to his toes. His eyes widened. *This is much more than I gave it!*

"Good," Aneirin said. "Now pull the power free and stretch it into a mask. Place the mask over your eyes."

Jeth concentrated, teeth clenched as he wrestled the magic free of the focus and into the air. Holding that much magic was overwhelming, and letting his attention wander even for an instant could spark a backlash that would leave him senseless for the rest of his life, hollowing out his mind until nothing remained. It was like trying to hold a lightning bolt. It twined and writhed in his grasp, trying to escape.

That's enough! He forced it flat, pulling it into the shape of a mask he had worn one Hellsfire Night a few years ago. Strangely, giving it shape seemed to soothe the wild power. Magic, it seemed, liked to be molded.

Jeth imagined putting the mask on.

The golden light within the focus flickered out, but the silver shimmer of magic all around them did not. Jeth's skin was warm where the magical mask touched it. He tucked the orb into its pouch.

"There. You've done it. You now have True Sight," Aneirin said, a bloom of pride rising in the words.

"Will I see this way forever?" Jeth couldn't feel the strain of maintaining the spell any longer. How would he diffuse the power he wasn't really using? The silver overlay to the world would very quickly lose its charm if he had to see this way day in and day out.

"Simply take the mask off." Aneirin waved a hand.

Jeth imagined reaching up and pulling the mask from his face. It took a moment, but the glow of magic slowly faded away, like a sunset rather than a snuffed candle. He put the mask back on, just to make sure he could activate his new power again, then turned his True Sight off. It hardly took a moment of concentration.

"You will not need to cast the spell again."

"Why? How?"

Aneirin tipped his head to one side in thought. "You've not opened a door, which will swing closed behind you. You've removed a wall."

Jeth had never heard of spells one never had to cast again. His heart pounded. *Am I the most powerful witch in Hallanor?*

What would that mean for his plans, for his future?

"Why doesn't everyone learn to do this?" Jeth asked.

"Because not everyone is like you."

His brow furrowed. The vague answer left him uneasy. Aneirin answered the question without answering it at all. Jeth was getting tired of faerie games. He opened his mouth.

"There. Through the trees. Do you see it?" Aneirin pointed.

The interruption worked, which frustrated Jeth to no end. The road curved to the right, and behind a stand of birch trees, he could just see...a wall. A building? The sky was pale and blue and clear today, and twining columns of smoke rose from dozens of chimneys.

They had made it to town.

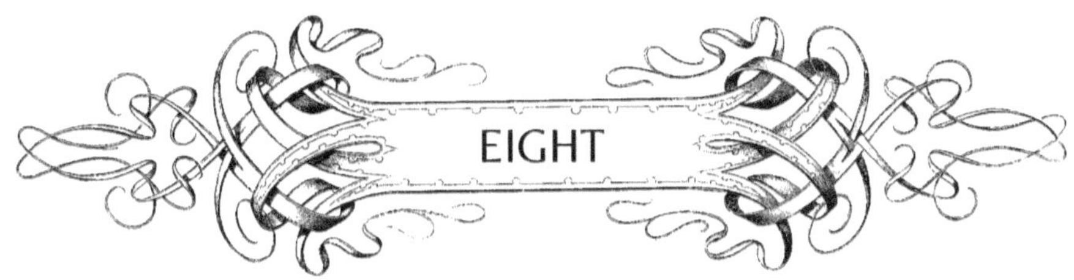

EIGHT

"We made it!" Jeth tapped his heels against his horse's sides, urging it into a canter toward his freedom.

Shadowstep easily fell in beside him as they rode around the bend. A simple wooden wall with a base of stones surrounded the small town. Rooftops huddled behind it. The gate stood open and unattended.

None of it mattered so much as being free of the faerie.

A hand snaked out of the corner of his eye, grabbing the horse's bridle and reigning the creature in. Jeth tore his gaze from the road, staring at Aneirin as the faerie pulled them both to a walk, then a stop.

What's going on?

"Let go," Jeth said.

"A moment." Aneirin calmly guided them to the wayside.

Jeth eased a foot back in the stirrup, ready to fling himself off the side and run to the safety of the village. Chances were they were simply waiting for the wagons, but there was always the possibility of worse with a faerie. His fears prickled down his back and spread over his entire body. What if his earlier suspicions were true? What if Aneirin was going to keep him? He wasn't going to go any further with the creature, not for all the gold, luck, and protection in the world.

The caravan trundled into view, with Burne in the seat of the lead wagon. Jeth lifted his hand to wave to her, but she was avoiding his gaze. Her jaw was set.

"Burne," Jeth called.

She didn't turn. She flinched. Her face twisted with guilt instead of a smile.

Confusion congealed into icy dread in the bottom of Jeth's stomach as the first wagon rolled past. He twisted in the saddle. "Aneirin, what are you doing?"

"Holding your horse."

"I want to go in. Let go."

"No."

"Why?" Jeth cried.

Aneirin fixed Jeth in a cold, distant stare that was strangely hypnotic. His orange eyes glinted like a dagger catching the light. "Because I will never let you set foot in a village, town, or city again. You are mine."

No. No, I knew it!

The time for questions was over. Nothing mattered now except getting away. Jeth swung off his horse, stumbling as he landed and catching himself on his bare hands. They stung, and he ignored it as he bolted for the town gate.

"Burne!" he shouted.

The wagons didn't stop. None of the traders jumped down to help. There would be no daring rescue. Jeth was on his own.

Hooves pounded on the road behind him.

That isn't fair! He could never outrun a faerie horse. Jeth flung himself sideways, landing hard on his shoulder as he tumbled off the road and into the trees with a crackle of branches. With a dozen new scrapes stinging all over his face and hands, Jeth scrambled between the tree trunks. The gate was so close. If he could just stay out of Aneirin's grasp for a minute longer–!

A normal horse might struggle to navigate its way between the trees, but Shadowstep was no normal horse. She plunged into the trees, threading between them like a needle through fabric. Bushes caught at Jeth's clothes and scratched at his face, but seemed to part around the faerie steed like water.

Aneirin was catching up.

Jeth burst out of the trees mere steps from the gate. Burne Calder stood by the gatepost, one hand on the wood.

"Burne, help me!" he cried.

Aneirin caught him by the arm and yanked him off the ground, wrenching Jeth's shoulder. Jeth lashed out with fists and feet alike as he was hauled onto Shadowstep's back. Aneirin's arm locked around his waist like a vice, tightening until it hurt.

Panting, Jeth stilled. *I can't get away.* They stood only a few feet short of the gate, and yet his freedom was further away than ever. He turned an accusing glower to Burne Calder.

"I'm sorry, Jeth," she said, tears welling in her eyes.

"Why? Why won't you help me?"

"My bargain was luck and good fortune, so long as he gets what he wants."

"And Aneirin wants me." Jeth said bitterly.

"Yes," the faerie said.

"You knew!" he shouted at Burne. In the town beyond, a few townsfolk gathered to watch the scene at the gate, their eyes wide. How many of them had actually seen a faerie in their lifetime?

Burne hung her head. "I knew. I knew as soon as Silas told me the story of your village."

But why would she know then?

Jeth's mouth went dry. "Aneirin, did you burn their houses to find me?" His voice wavered, betraying him.

"I did."

Jeth shouted, struggling anew. He writhed and punched and kicked and shouted, and none of it mattered. None of it helped. All he managed to do was pinch himself against Aneirin's arm.

"Are you not yet finished with this tantrum?" the faerie asked coldly. There was a bite to his words that suggested the creature would end this himself if Jeth didn't.

Jeth slumped, gasping for air. He glared at the faerie, willing every ounce of betrayal and hatred into his eyes in hopes that Aneirin would see it, would *feel* it. *You tricked me. You hunted me, and then you tricked me!*

Flinging a hand out toward the leylines nearby, Jeth pulled in power. With a crack of magic like a whip, the faerie shocked him, sending pain like static through his entire body. Jeth yelped.

"Stop that," Aneirin commanded. "You have no right to be angry with me. You'll understand. When we make camp, I will explain."

"I don't want to go with you! Let me go, please! Burne!"

Burne flinched again, covering her mouth with her hand.

"Our bargain is completed, Burne Calder. I am pleased. Your luck will pass to your children, and your children's children."

Burne's eyes were wide, a tear falling down her cheek. "I sold a child to a faerie and got a blessing for a child I haven't even got?" She gave a bitter laugh. "Some bargain."

"You will have children soon enough. After all, you have the good fortune of the faeries on your side." Aneirin smiled.

Burne Calder turned away from the gate, passing her hand over her eyes. "I hope that good fortune means I'll never see you again, Aneirin."

"Burne!" Jeth wailed, feebly trying to pry the faerie's arm off of his chest.

Aneirin turned Shadowstep away from the gate. A whistle summoned Jeth's horse from where it stood up the road. It trotted up to Shadowstep's side and matched her sedate pace as the faerie guided them into the woods.

Jeth craned his head to watch Burne walk away, rounding the corner and vanishing from view. The townsfolk pushed the gate shut. The booming echo of it closing followed Jeth like a death knell.

NINE

Jeth sat across from Aneirin, fingers curled against the bark of a fallen log doubling as a bench. He said nothing to the faerie, stewing in silence. Aneirin didn't seem to notice or mind. He added a log to the fire between them.

What am I going to do? What would Mother say? Where are we going to go? What is his plan? A welter of questions echoed in his mind, and he knew all of them would go unanswered. There was no way out of his contract with the faerie, unless...

Unless Jeth came up with a clever solution.

Maybe I will, in five years or ten or twenty.

His heart sank in his chest, vanishing into that yawning chasm within him and threatening to take all his will with it. What point was there in struggling? In trying again and again, year after year, to escape?

You must, his mother whispered, barely there and quickly gone. It was enough to pull Jeth from his misery. It was enough to let despair spark into something hot, and urgent, and *angry.* Jeth glared across the little fire between them.

Aneirin was patient. No doubt the faerie had lived for thousands of years, and would live a thousand more. Despite that, Jeth's stubborn refusal to engage grated on the unflappable creature's nerves. Aneirin's frown grew more and more pronounced with every passing minute.

If there is to be a war between us, I will win, Jeth vowed.

The fire crackled. A log popped and sank with a spray of embers. The horses shifted beyond the circle of firelight. One whickered. Jeth's glare never wavered.

Aneirin stood abruptly, abandoning the stone he used as a seat to pace, snow turning to slush beneath his boots. Another minute passed. Two.

Five.

Ten.

"I met your mother fifteen years ago," Aneirin said, coming to a stop and tipping his chin toward the night sky.

Of everything the faerie could have said, that was the last thing Jeth expected. His brows rose, lips parting in surprise. "You did? You...knew her?"

"Yes. Gleda was powerful, even then. She caught my attention. She caught my...fancy. I thought if I had her, the fervor I felt would wane. I offered her wish after wish, and she turned me down each time. As her disinterest continued, mine grew."

Jeth's nose wrinkled, and he looked away from Aneirin toward the trees. *I don't want to hear how this murderous, horrible thing pined after my mother.* His beautiful, magical mother, who had more kindness in a single fingernail than the faerie had in his entire body.

Aneirin laughed, a soft and melodic sound like a wind chime in a gentle breeze. "She became the first to discover who I was. Who I *am.* More than just a faerie, I told her, thinking it would impress her—or frighten her. It did not matter either way, so long as it made her mine."

Shifting where he sat, Jeth contemplated making a run for it. Anything would be better than this story. The silence settled over them like a blanket.

Why isn't he saying anything?

Jeth peered at the faerie. Aneirin's eyes trailed over the glittering stars above. The moon was full, glowing silver and blue low in the sky, not yet clear of the forest's branches.

He wants me to ask who he is, Jeth realized. He scoffed. *I'm not playing this game.*

Aneirin sank back onto his seat, staring at Jeth through the flames. "I am the King of the Blackthorn Court, tucked beneath what you mortals call the Heartwood Hill, near the village of River Tor."

Wait, I know that name. River Tor? Jeth's brow furrowed as he tried to remember.

"It lies near the heart of Hallanor, two day's ride from your Queen's great city." Aneirin laughed. "She and I are neighbors of a sort."

Jeth didn't think it was funny. He shuddered, realizing an entire court of faeries lay so close to people, to the palace, to the heart of his homeland. *Isn't that dangerous? Didn't anyone notice?* In all the stories, a faerie court was a bustling hub of magic, full of creatures of all sorts. Some were better to meet than others, but none of them could be called 'good.' "Didn't people disappear? Didn't they fall prey to faerie curses, or get dragged into the water by nymphs or caught in the traps laid by sprites?" he asked in spite of himself, biting his lip as soon as the words were out.

"Yes, all that and more—despite the best efforts of the witch at the time. Gleda was her apprentice, nearly ready to set out on her own."

"My mother wouldn't have been impressed by you," Jeth said firmly.

Aneirin smirked. "She wasn't. She told me that if I truly cared for her, I would go back to my court, never to emerge again. It was unfortunate that I hadn't the time to do as she wished. I had a plan, you see. I was going to expand the borders of my court. Your Queen was newly crowned, young and supple. I would give her an heir, and the power of faerie magic in her bloodline...but in return, I would get the kingdom. The entire kingdom. I would become the power behind the throne and run the mortals into the ground. Within a hundred years, the forest would have been ours again, only ours." Aneirin's words came faster and faster, his hand balled into a fist. "*If* I hadn't gotten...distracted."

Jeth shivered. The faerie's hatred of humanity was laid bare in the feral gleam of his eyes, in the bared teeth, in the way Aneirin's nails dug into his palm. "You didn't. You couldn't have."

"I didn't," Aneirin agreed. His gaze drifted to the sky. "My court was a thing of beauty, Jeth. It was a place between reality and dreams, more dangerous than you can fathom. All the old covenants would shatter once one of us sat on the throne, and I was going to be the hero to do it."

"Covenants?"

Aneirin waved a hand dismissively. "The magic built into your kingdom at the founding."

"I've never heard of them." Could these covenants help him escape?

"When the first king of this land lay the first stone of the castle, he bound a spell around it. All of his subjects would be safe, within reason, from our magics. We cannot stay in human dwellings. We cannot go where we are not invited. We may not make deals with the unwilling. We can only curse those who break the rules of hospitality. We may make our bargains—but are bound to honor them to the letter. If we break these covenants, our power vanishes forevermore."

Jeth's mind raced, but he couldn't see a way to twist that information to his benefit.

"With a child of mine on the throne, I could have bid them to undo the spell. I could have freed us all."

Unleashed, more like.

"Fate, perhaps, had me emerge from the Blackthorn Court right at the edge of that little village. I saw Gleda at a festival, dancing with a young man. She distracted me from all my goals. The way she moved like the breeze itself, the way she laughed like chiming bells, the way her eyes shone in the bonfire's light. They can wait, I told myself. I have thousands of years yet to live. When she walked home that night, I introduced myself.

"I came to her again and again, but she danced around my traps with word and act alike. She bested all my efforts until I went mad with need. She was the white hart in the woods, and I had to have her."

Jeth's hands balled into fists. He didn't like hearing his mother talked about like a prize to be won by this uncaring faerie.

"In the end, *she* tricked *me,* and I revealed my plan. That was when she offered a bargain of her own. Gleda saved your kingdom, for a time. A fascinating woman."

A chill crept down Jeth's spine. *I don't want to hear any more.* He fought the urge to cover his ears. "What did she bargain for?"

Aneirin smiled wistfully at the moon, as though it were Gleda herself. "Ah, our deal was so simple in the end. She offered to lie with me, to love me, to be beholden to me and only me for the rest of her days. In return, I would go back to Blackthorn Court for a decade...and give her a child."

What? Jeth's mouth went dry. His breath froze in his chest, ice spreading down to his fingertips. *My mother swore to never love another for the rest of her life, and in return she got...me.*

He sat facing his father. His *father!* His father was a faerie.

Jeth was a faerie.

"No," he breathed.

"Yes."

My magic is strong because I'm the son of a witch and a faerie. Even a drop of faerie blood in someone's lineage gave them power and changed them from human to something more, something powerful and old. Jeth didn't have years to survive with Aneirin. He had *centuries.* As the years passed, would he turn as vile and callous as his father?

"She promised to be mine, and to return the babe to me when I came to her again. Imagine my surprise when I went to River Tor and Gleda wasn't there."

She ran. Everyone in the village told me that she arrived already pregnant with me. She told them she was a widow, that her husband was gone—but he's a faerie!

"She thought to protect you by *hiding* from me," Aneirin snarled. "You were mine by rights. You are the son of a king, a prince of the faerie realm, and my heir. You were meant to be *mine*."

Jeth's ears rang. The world reeled around him. His mother had never told him about his father. He thought it was out of grief. Instead, it was out of...what? Shame? Fear?

How could she?

This was worse than anything he could have imagined.

"Our agreement lasted only until I left court. She told me before I left that she wanted to strike another deal when we met again, but she fled. The thing you will learn about faeries, Jeth, is that we can hold the flame of our anger for centuries if we must. It took me years to find her."

"You burned Hugo's house down, and the tavern, and—"

"That was after," Aneirin interrupted.

After? Jeth closed his mouth with a click of his teeth.

"When I first saw you, it was in the market. She was swinging a basket, and you were beside her, more handsome than I had imagined. I was filled with pride and fury. I regret striking her down. It seems to have...affected you more than I anticipated."

Jeth's eyes widened. He had thought his world couldn't be rocked again, not after the revelation of who—what–he was. He was wrong. Horror crept through every inch of his skin with tingling fingers and a rush of blood as his heart raced.

"I thought giving you the time to grieve would make your transition to my realm...easier. I planned to explain, after you laid her to rest. You fled before I could, and I couldn't track you in the storm. That was when I burned the houses in the village. You understand, of course."

He killed her.

Aneirin killed her.

Fury ignited in his chest in a sudden inferno. It took every ounce of his will not to leap across the fire and strangle the monster on the other side.

"You murdered my mother?" Every word was taut as a bowstring.

"I lashed out in anger. It was, perhaps, hasty of me."

Jeth laughed a high, shrill laugh. Once he started, he couldn't stop until his stomach ached and his eyes watered, until he wheezed. The laughter faded at last, but his ire did not. He scowled, hands balling into fists.

"We are united now. We may return to Blackthorn Court. It is not a city, a town, or a village. Your contract with me shall never end."

"That's cheating. I'm not your property, and I don't want to go."

Aneirin frowned. "You are my son, and–"

"I am not, and never will be, your son!" Jeth shouted.

The silence that fell was deafening. Even the fire stopped making a sound. It was as if the whole world had inhaled, bracing for the inevitable blow that would follow such reckless rebellion.

Aneirin rose from the stone, fluid grace replaced with the clipped movements of ice cold rage. The shadows gathered around him, huddling on his shoulders like a second cloak. Jeth could feel the build of magic in the air like the ozone before lightning struck, the sharp coppery scent of it filling his nose.

His anger was lost in the overwhelming *power* of it, building up like a mountain behind the faerie. His mouth went dry.

He felt his mother's hand on his shoulder. *Run.*

Jeth flung himself off the log and bolted for the trees.

The darkness behind Aneirin swelled, spreading through the air and sky and swallowing all light as it raced after him. Nothing stopped it, nothing slowed it. Trees and shrubs were consumed. The flickering fire vanished. The stars disappeared one by one. Faster and faster it surged behind him, until Jeth could see fingers of it flashing in his periphery.

"No!" Jeth shouted as the shadows closed in, threatening to swallow him like the jaws of a massive beast. The moonlight vanished. He threw himself forward–

–and was enveloped in darkness.

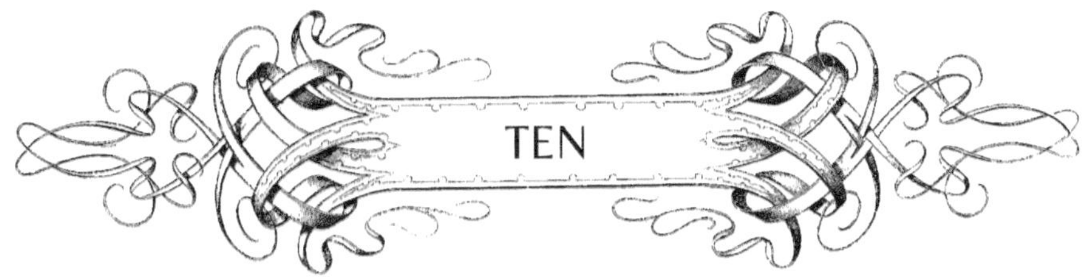

TEN

Jeth woke up to nothing.

Nothing stretched away from him in every direction. It was ink-black, but not dark. He could still see *himself,* his hands, his boots, his clothes. He felt a floor, cool and smooth as marble, leeching the heat from his body as he lay on it. There was nothing else, though. No walls, no corners, no lights. No windows, doors, or distinguishing features at all. All Jeth could see was...nothing.

Jeth pushed himself up. Every rustle of fabric and clunky step he took whispered off through the nothing until it faded away, soft echoes resonating like a chorus of ghosts. The thought sent a shiver down his spine.

Am I dead?

Had Aneirin killed him? Was this all there was in the beyond? He hunched his shoulders and wrapped his arms around himself, even though he wasn't cold. It wasn't warm, either. It was nothing.

Jeth felt vulnerable, alone in the vast and empty space.

"One step," he whispered.

The ground rippled beneath his feet like water, the barest glimmers of gold curling away from him as he walked.

Gold? Like magic from the orb. Jeth closed his eyes and pulled on the mask of his True Sight, only to be blinded when he opened them. He gasped, doubling over with his hands over his face as he turned the ability off.

A cell built entirely of magic, he realized. He was imprisoned in power itself.

All magic has a source. Jeth straightened, hands curled into fists. *I may not be able to see it, but it* must *still exist. I just need to find it.*

He walked. He ran. He walked again, panting. The nothing around him never changed. Who knew how large it truly was?

"Damn!" he spat.

The echoes repeated. "–amn,–mn,–mn,–n."

Jeth knew what Aneirin wanted. He grit his teeth and felt the bubble of anger rise in his stomach.

He tipped his head back, flinging his arms wide. "Hello?"

"Hello,–ello,–ello,–lo,–lo,–o?" His own voice called back.

"You're awake."

Jeth whirled as Aneirin's voice echoed off into the dark, recoiling instinctively. The faerie stood just behind him. His black clothes were gone, replaced with glittering silver finery. When Aneirin paced around him, the ripples at his feet were silver, too. Jeth endured his scrutiny, glaring.

"How do you feel?" Aneirin asked, coming to a stop at last.

"Where are we? What did you do?"

"I have detained you in a faerie prison. A jar, if you must know. Perhaps a century in here will improve your mood."

A century! The prospect of an eternity trapped in this place, speaking to his own echoes or walking endlessly through the dark pressed on Jeth's shoulders, threatening to crush him to the ground with the sheer weight of it. His heart fluttered in his throat. The hairs on the back of his neck stood up.

I'll go mad.

Or he would give up, which was exactly what Aneirin wanted.

Some father.

"Shall we make a bargain? We can shorten the length of your stay if you agree to behave." Aneirin idly studied his nails.

Jeth's mind raced. What would his mother do? What had she done in the past? Aneirin had said she danced around his tricks. How could Jeth sidestep this?

I can't.

...but he could eliminate a different problem.

"I agree to make a bargain only if our previous agreement is rendered moot," Jeth said. *A deal to strike a deal.*

Aneirin's brows lifted, and he studied Jeth with renewed interest. "A clever turn. Very well, I agree. If you make a new deal with me, your previous deal will be moot."

The faerie extended his hand. Jeth clasped it. His mouth had gone dry.

He'd done it. He'd evaded Aneirin's trap. This was a deal, newly made. His old bargain was broken, the power it had to bind him to the faerie now shattered.

Had Aneirin noticed?

"About the new deal," Jeth burst out. "What do you propose?"

He needed time to figure out the next step.

Aneirin paced, the silver ripples at his feet painting him in a cold, distant glow. "Gleda promised you to me. The bargain I have is for you to honor that promise and travel with me, live with me, and learn magic at my side. One day, you will take my throne. In return, I shall free you from this place."

"That's hardly any sort of deal!"

"Propose a countermeasure." Aneirin turned to face him, hands clasped behind his back.

Jeth didn't know what to say. He fumbled through option after option, brow furrowed. He only realized he was pacing when the golden glow around him grew brighter, painting him in its warm light.

I have my hunting knife, but that won't help me if Aneirin knows how to fight at all. If I were him, I would. I can't take that risk. It would be foolish to assume a faerie king couldn't fight. The only other thing Jeth had tucked into his belt was a pair of gloves.

And the orb.

The seed of a plan began to grow. He loosened the ties at the top of the pouch and thrust his hand in, feeling the crystal grow warm beneath his fingertips.

"When we leave here, you still plan to break the covenants."

"Yes," Aneirin affirmed. "I will bed the Queen of Hallanor, and in twenty or thirty years, faeries will be free. No time at all to us. A lifetime to the humans."

"The bargain you made with my mother, tell me about it. The exact words," Jeth said, hoping to buy more time.

Aneirin lifted a hand. "The deal shall be thus," he intoned, fingers glowing. The surrounding magic thrummed like the plucked string of a lyre. "You shall lie with me and love me. You shall be beholden to me, enamored of me, bound to me and only me until the end of your days. In return, I shall grant you a child. I will return to the Blackthorn Court for one mortal decade, and then I shall come for my heir and take it back to my dark realm. Do you agree?"

Is that where we are? His realm, or some small corner of it?

If the jar they were in was considered part of faerie lands, Jeth would have as much power as Aneirin did.

"And she replied to me thus." Power rippled through the air from Aneirin's outstretched hand.

Gleda's voice filled the air, the words slow and measured. Jeth felt a lump in his throat as he listened to her, for what he knew would be the last time.

"I shall lie with you, love you, be beholden to you, and enamored of you. I shall love no other until the end of my days. In return, I shall be given a babe. I will return to you a babe. You will spare Hallanor for ten years, then come to me and take the babe to be your heir. When you come, you will offer me the chance to make another deal."

Jeth bowed his head, clutching at his chest as the black pit of grief inside it swelled until he thought his ribs might split open, until he thought he would fall apart.

"Then I gave her a wedding gift, a focus that would grant her mortal self the power of a faerie, a beautiful crystal ball—and the deal was struck."

The orb beneath Jeth's fingers thrummed with power as he wrestled a trickle of Aneirin's tightly woven spell free, opening himself up to channel it. *Just a little longer, just a minute more!*

Jeth froze, a rush of elation rushing up his spine that warmed him from head to toe. He stopped his spell. "She broke the deal."

Aneirin sighed. "Don't mumble, boy. Speak clearly."

"She broke the deal, and you broke the covenants." Jeth's voice reverberated in the nothing. Though he wasn't moving, shimmers of gold pooled around his feet.

"What? How? Liar!" Aneirin glanced at the darkness around them, as though he feared invisible hands were reaching out even now to rip his power away.

"My mother said she would return to you a babe, but I'm not."

The faerie's brows drew down. "That's hardly–"

"I don't belong to you," Jeth said firmly. The gold at his feet glowed brighter. "You must follow your agreements to the letter. You had to take a *babe* from my mother. You killed the only chance you had."

"You had,–had,–had,–ad,–ad," the echoes chorused.

The whispers faded to silence. The gilt pool pushed back the darkness.

"A clever turn," Aneirin said at last, teeth grit. The silver glow of magic around him winked out of existence, never to return. "A mistake, as well."

"How?" Jeth demanded.

"I was the only one who could release us. Now we are both trapped for the rest of our days." He laughed, a bitter edge to the sound.

The power around them squeezed in, the vast space suddenly claustrophobic. Jeth fought a rise of panic. *Trapped?*

"You–" Jeth looked up, the words dying on his lips.

Aneirin was gone.

ELEVEN

"How long have I been here?" Jeth asked the nothing.

The whispers murmured around him, but gave no answer. He couldn't even summon up the ghost of his mother, not since he heard her strike her bargain with Aneirin all those years ago. That didn't stop him from trying.

"Mother?" He willed her to come, sending a hum through the nothing around him along with the echo.

Nothing. She was gone.

She's gone.

The bottomless well of pain bloomed in his chest, and this time there was no reason to stop it. He sank to his knees, burying his face in his hands as he sobbed. He let wave after wave of regret and shame and misery wash over him.

I should have told her I loved her more often.

She only died because Aneirin wanted me.

I'll never see her again. I'll never hear her again. Everything is different now.

The world had fallen out of step long before Aneirin trapped him in this place. Jeth had ignored it, choosing instead to pretend alongside everyone else that everything was fine. He remembered that the sky didn't seem as blue, the whinny of a horse seemed shrill and harsh, the cold seemed stronger—but who was to say that wasn't normal, now, in this strange new world where he was alone? Where she was gone?

Day by day, it grew more peculiar and fantastic. Jeth traveled with a faerie. He learned to cast powerful spells. He grew.

Maybe that's why I can't feel her anymore. Maybe I've changed so much she doesn't recognize me.

Maybe his faerie blood pushed her away.

There was nothing to be done about that. He couldn't imagine going back, even if he could. Not just because he now knew what he was, but because the world was wider than his nameless village on the edge of the kingdom. He wanted to *see* it. He wanted to be part of it.

The seemingly endless chasm of his grief had a bottom, after all. Though he didn't know how long he cried, eventually the tears stopped coming. Jeth felt like a rag wrung dry, but there was a lightness to it, too. It made his head spin.

"Aneirin?" he asked the nothing, the words coming out in a petulant croak that he hated. The faerie had vanished, and no matter how Jeth stretched his senses, he could not find him again. Aneirin knew how his prison worked, and apparently he could do as he pleased within it, magic or no. Their cell was vast enough to avoid one another for as long as the faerie wished.

The last echo of his question faded, leaving Jeth in silence and darkness.

I don't want to see him again, anyway.

The hole in his chest left by his mother's death filled with something hot, like he swallowed coals raked from a fire.

It was Aneirin's fault his mother was dead. He broke their bargain, and he stole her. Even after that, he tricked Jeth into an agreement that he never intended to honor.

He's sly and full of tricks. They all are. No faerie ever makes a good deal.

Even Burne Calder, who had gotten the best possible outcome in her deal, was left reeling. She looked like her heart was breaking when Aneirin took Jeth. Even with all the good fortune and wealth the faerie had given her, she was left with regrets.

No faerie ever makes a good deal.

And what about me?

The heat in his chest ebbed as Jeth studied his hands. The blood of faeries ran through his veins, making him one of them. How long before that blood swallowed him whole? How long before he made bargains and deals that would leave every life he touched ruined, if he ever got free? How long before madness made him like his father? What would his mother think of him in a hundred years, in a thousand?

Jeth closed his hands, nails digging into his palms. "I won't be like them," he said.

"Like them,–ike them,–them,–em,–em," his echo argued.

"I refuse. I can't!"

Gleda had not raised her son to be a monster. She taught Jeth the names of flowers and animals. She encouraged him to help her with the healings and blessings and tinctures and salves. She ran with him in sun-bright meadows, laughing while her dark hair streamed behind her like a banner in the wind. She teased him over dinners of stew and fresh bread. She read to him and with him, encouraging him to find new things to learn around every corner.

She taught him...to be human, he realized. All the best things of this world, of this kingdom, she instilled in his very being. Even now, alone and trapped in the dark, he rejected the barest *hint* of that behavior.

"But I'm still a faerie."

The whispers murmured.

Jeth frowned, pushing himself to his feet. "I was a witch's son first. I'm both. I'm...me. Just me."

Something stirred in the nothing.

"Even if I stay trapped in here for an age, when I come out, I will still be myself. I will only make good bargains if I have to make them at all, and I will never, ever trap someone. I am not a monster."

"Monster," the echo agreed. A glimmer of gold rippled away from Jeth's feet.

Jeth stared at it, watching it fade. Aneirin's light had vanished when his magic did. Were the glimmers in the endless night of this place...power?

He stamped a foot on the ground, watching the gold undulate off into the darkness. The light of it painted him in gilded ripples.

Jeth turned in place, studying the nothing. "Magic is never stagnant."

His mother had told him that. *"Look at the leylines. They flow like rivers, always moving. Even when they pool, there's a current beneath the surface, and the power flows out again. Magic is never stagnant."*

The proof of it was at his feet. He felt the nothing stir again, turning to trace the unseen shift of magic like a hound scenting the air. Wherever it went, it ran and pooled and arced in little rivulets of silver that glowed like starlight.

"The problem with this cell is that it is pure magic," he said, as if lecturing someone. He had seen it himself when he tried to use his True Sight upon his arrival. "If the power is flowing, that means my prison isn't as solid as it seems. I might be able to direct the flow, to change the shape."

To escape.

Jeth activated his True Sight. His eyes watered. The silver glow surrounding him was blinding, but he kept his eyes open.

They'll adjust. Just hold on, hold on!

The light abated, fading until Jeth could just make out the shifts in the walls around him. How far away they were, he couldn't tell—but he could see the ripples, the layers, the knots.

He could see the weaknesses.

Jeth's breath caught. *I can tear through.*

He let his True Sight fade, blinking away tears as the nothing closed in around him. He opened his senses.

Magic was in the very air. It threatened to overwhelm him, battering at his consciousness like a storm swallowing a ship. With a shout, Jeth closed his mind, clasping his head in his hands.

The pain faded. The only sounds were his breath coming in pants and the echo of it.

I need help.

No, not help. He needed a focus. Jeth pulled the orb from his hip, cradling it in both hands. Already a flicker of golden light danced in its depths. Cautiously, Jeth opened his mind again, slower than before.

The magic poured through the small channel he made for it, setting his teeth on edge and making his hair stand up as it ran through his arms, into his hands, and then into the orb. The glimmers of gold around his feet swelled into a puddle, growing with every moment he channeled. He felt it through every inch of his body. It was more power than he had ever touched in his life.

The orb glowed brighter and brighter, the golden core of it bulging, growing, swelling. Jeth's breath caught as he opened a second conduit to the power in the focus, only to find an ocean of magic raging inside.

That must *be enough!*

He gathered his will. "Let me out," he breathed.

"Out, out, out," the echo chanted.

Crack. The surface of the crystal fractured, a spray of golden light pouring out of it. Jeth's heart began to race. *Did I pull too much?* He tried to bring up the walls around his mind—and failed. His will was in control now.

"No, no, no!" he cried.

Crack! Another fissure formed. The orb shattered, shards flying in all directions. Jeth howled, staggering as several pieces struck his hands and face.

He lifted his arms over his head, waiting for the inevitable wash of power to consume him.

And it never came.

When Jeth lowered his arms, it was to find himself facing a golden gateway that hung in the air in the shape...of an orb. He walked around it in awe, a similar pool of gold at his feet. The edges of it flickered like it held barely contained lightning in its heart.

Jeth lifted a hand toward the power.

"Stop," Aneirin commanded.

Jeth froze, glancing over his shoulder.

The faerie stood tall behind him, hungry eyes fixed on the glittering gate. "You will take me with you."

"Why?"

"Because I am your father."

Jeth frowned. "You're a murderer, a monster. I don't have to take you anywhere."

"And what does that make you? My blood flows through your veins. You are as much a faerie as I am."

Jeth laughed. "What does it make me? I am the son of a faerie king."

Aneirin lifted his chin, a smug smile forming on his lips.

"And I am the son of a witch. I straddle the magic of two worlds, and I can pull from both." The gold around his feet swelled, and the nothing stirred, pressing in.

Sparks flew from the edges of the gateway like embers in the night, there and then gone.

"I don't need to take you with me. When I leave this place, it will be to prove that faerie magic can be used for good, and that none of you creatures choose to use it thus. I will change the world."

"You cannot be released!" Aneirin shouted, rushing forward.

Jeth slammed a wall of will into being between them, taking no small amount of satisfaction in watching Aneirin crumple against it. The faerie king howled, banging his fists against the barrier.

"I don't need your *permission* to be released, Aneirin. I can leave on my own."

"No! No, you cannot leave!"

"Watch me."

With a pull on the magic of the nothing, he made the wall around himself and the gateway stronger, thicker. With no magic of his own any longer, Aneirin wouldn't be able to break through. He'd be trapped. He wouldn't be able to use the gate.

Jeth stepped through the portal into the unknown.

It was too bright to see. With his eyes closed and his arms shielding his face, Jeth walked. Whatever he walked on still felt like the nothing, cool and smooth like marble. Then it crunched, giving way beneath his foot.

Jeth lowered his arms as the cold air of morning enveloped him. A single bird trilled somewhere nearby, the first promise of the impending spring. A rustle of bare branches dropped icicles to the ground in a tinkling symphony as two squirrels raced overhead. All that was left of the campfire were ashes covered with a thin layer of snow.

For several moments, Jeth didn't move. He breathed deeply, reveled in the light of the sun, and let his nose grow cold in the winter air. Breathlessly, he laughed.

"I did it. I did it!"

A whinny answered his words. Jeth turned to find his horse, still tethered where he had left it with a neatly cropped circle of grass around its feet. Shadowstep was gone without a trace. There was no sign of the portal he had stepped through, either. No mark on the ground, no shimmer in the air. Just a little clay jar in a leather holder, the top stoppered with a cork. Unassuming as it was, the vessel radiated magic in a hum that Jeth could *hear,* with no need for his True Sight at all.

Jeth bent to scoop up his father's prison, only to stop short.

He was...different. Where his skin had been peach-pale, now it held a golden warmth. The sleeves of his coat glittered with gold that he couldn't dust off. When he looked down, he realized that all of him was coated in a layer of gold. He brushed his fingers over the supple cloth of blue and gold.

It looks like the night sky, he marveled.

Jeth curled his hands into fists, hissing as he prodded one of the cuts left by the shards of the orb. He sat in the snow beside the jar, studying his wounds. *Those bits can't stay in there, they'll get infected.*

Only there weren't any. Each scrape was clean, if still fresh. Blood welled, but it would soon scab over. Another laugh bubbled up from Jeth's chest.

"What is happening to me?" he asked his gelding.

The horse tossed its head and stamped a foot, giving his tether an impatient tug.

"Alright, I hear you." Jeth picked up the jar and fixed it to his belt next to the empty leather pouch, then untied the reins. He paused when he caught sight of his reflection in the horse's dark eyes.

The face that looked back at him was different enough that, for a moment, he thought it was someone else. His dark hair was gone, replaced with blond hair down to the very roots. His eyes were still dark, but there was a faint gleam to them, a spark of power he knew he could summon at will.

"Good. I still have magic." He patted his horse gently on the cheek. "Let's go use it."

First, he would go to his village and help them rebuild their homes, and find them a new witch. Then, he would warn the Queen.

And after that? he asked the air as he swung into the saddle.

The breeze rose, tickling along the back of his neck.

Anything, it seemed to say.

UNDER THE HILL

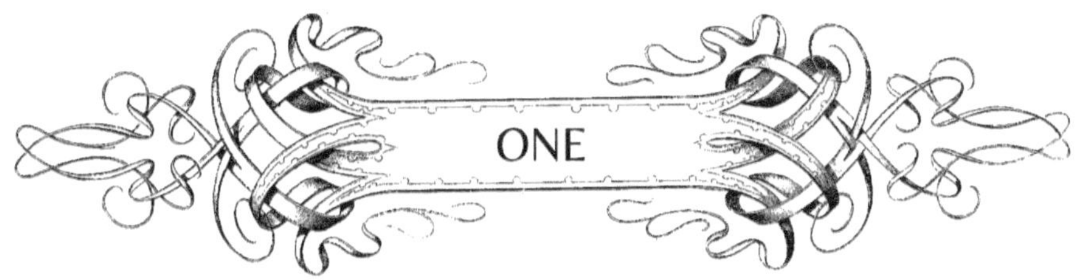

The heavy drone of pixies filled the late summer air. The longer Jeth walked beneath the gnarled, twisted branches of the forest, the more certain he was that it was them, not insects, humming endlessly. The closer he got to Heartwood Hill, the door to the faerie court, the louder they grew. Insects would have fled before the creatures, no doubt. Pixies were notoriously cruel to anything smaller than they were and anything they thought was weak.

Jeth was glad he'd grown so much in the past six years. A flock of tiny fae folk would no doubt think the twig of a fourteen-year-old he once had been would make an easy target. Now that he was a young man, he might be spared the worst of them.

If only I should be so lucky.

The trees grew close together. The underbrush was thick and wild, making it difficult for Jeth to thread his way through. He ducked beneath a low-hanging branch.

Clunk.

Jeth's head jerked back and he bit back a swear, lowering his head before ducking beneath the branch. His newly growing antlers, proof of his faerie blood, threatened to catch on everything. He was still adjusting to their length. They'd grown another inch in the past moon alone.

A growing buzz reached his ear and he stopped in his tracks, snapping his gaze to one side. With a flutter of beetle-like wings, the pixie hissed and darted back out of sight, diving headfirst into a clump of wildflowers.

With its green skin, stick-like arms, and its little hat of flower petals, it blended right in.

That one is brave, to mess with me now.

Jeth was ten times the creature's size. Broad in the shoulder, all lean muscle, and at near six feet tall—not counting his horns. A moment of weakness, however small, and the creature felt bold enough to test him.

At least Jeth was as prepared as he could be.

He pushed a branch out of the way, stepping over a circle of wild mushrooms hidden between the bushes. His past six years had all been leading to *this*, this harebrained scheme of his.

His hands were rough from scrubbing floors, weaving rope, chopping wood, and digging holes. He was all muscle from the work of pulling on ropes, hauling boxes, and lifting stone. Jeth had worked his way across the length and breadth of Hallanor, learning whatever he could, wherever he could. Earning his keep was easy, but convincing the people he met to show him something new, something he didn't know? That was harder.

Jeth stepped high over a root that arched above the path, perfectly poised to catch at the foot of an unwary traveler. As soon as he passed, the wooden tendril curled itself back into the loamy forest floor with a groan and a crackle. He paused.

A dryad? Or just magic?

It would be harder and harder to tell what was plant and what was fae as he neared the court. The forest was teeming with magic and life. Even his True Sight, which enabled him to see magical auras, was useless in determining which was which.

There was only one forest in Hallanor—*the* forest. Every town, village, and city had been painstakingly won from the woods. Rings of wards and constant spell work were all that prevented the faeries from taking them back, burying them beneath vines and roots.

There wasn't a person alive in Hallanor that didn't know the stories. Once upon a time, Jeth knew them only in passing. They were cautionary tales he'd learned at his mother's knee or in his bed, while she whispered them soft and low.

Gleda Penistone knew the ins and outs of the fae better than most, after all. She'd bedded one.

Her son was the result of that ill-fated match, and the downfall of his father. Everything turned out the way Gleda had planned, but for one thing. She didn't plan for Aneirin, the faerie king of the Blackthorn Court and her thwarted lover, to murder her.

Jeth stopped in the dappled shade beneath a spreading oak, pulling a waterskin from his belt and sipping at it. The heat was oppressive. A shimmer hung beneath the tree branches. Sweat ran down his back.

As he always did when he thought of her, he reached for the corner of his mind where she once was. It was empty and had been since he was a child. Her death began his adventures. He'd stolen her crystal ball and fled before his neighbors could give away the only home he'd ever known. Gleda had been the village witch, and the cottage needed to pass to another as quickly as possible.

Witches protected against faeries. They cast the wards and blessings to keep everyone safe. He'd understood the reasoning even then, though it hurt. He just didn't want to give up that one piece of Gleda Penistone. So he took the crystal and ran.

And he ran right into Aneirin's hands.

Caught like a fox in a trap, he was lured into making a bargain with the faerie. That was when he learned how faerie bargains worked—or rather, didn't. There wasn't a single one that didn't come with a catch.

He watched the tradeswoman, Burne Calder, cheery as a bird in spring and tough as nails, go through her bargain. Her deal had been luck for generations, in exchange for helping Aneirin find Jeth. She hadn't known she was looking for a person. She regretted everything when she watched Aneirin take Jeth away.

His mother, Gleda, died for her bargain. In running from her deal to save him, she'd lost everything.

Jeth himself narrowly escaped his own bargain by discovering Aneirin had broken one of his, and shattering his power.

He walked on again, scanning the sky above the trees. Heartwood Hill rose above them like the bald pate of a friar. He was close. Well, closer.

Damn the heat, *though!*

Jeth rolled his sleeves up as he walked, his fingers brushing over the small scars that speckled his forearms. They were part of his childhood, too. The crystal ball he'd taken with him wasn't a crystal ball at all. It was a faerie focus, a much more powerful artifact. In his fight against his father, Jeth had poured so much magic into the thing that it shattered. The pieces that flew into his skin were absorbed. At least, that was Jeth's best guess. Not a fragment could be found in a single wound. If the cuts hadn't existed, he'd have thought they'd missed him entirely.

He emerged from his battle entirely changed. Where once his hair had been black, it was now as gold as wheat. It curled over his ears and around his cheeks. Where once his skin had been a perfect peach, it was now dusted with gold that caught the light when he moved. Even though years of work tanned his skin, the gleam remained. His brown eyes lightened to a honey-colored amber flecked with brighter gold.

And two years ago he started to grow antlers.

The crackle and snap of branches nearby stopped Jeth in his tracks. He turned, craning to see what caused it. The forest was relatively still. Branches swayed gently in the breeze, but otherwise...

No, wait, there it was. A distant Hawthorne tree took another heaving step, wood groaning and roots crawling through the earth. It settled into a sunnier spot, swishing its branches at the encroaching stand of aspens that drove it to move in the first place. As far as Jeth could tell, the aspens were unapologetic. He suppressed a shudder. No matter how many times he saw it, he hadn't gotten used to the fact that the forest was alive, not just growing.

Jeth peered through the canopy at the growing mound of Heartwood Hill.

'Hill' is a bit of an understatement.

It rose well above the canopy of the forest, shouldering out of the trees like a monolith. The sides were too steep to climb. Someone—or something—carved steps out of the stone that wound around it to the very top. The hill was crowned with a perfect circlet of stones. Humans who stepped into it had a way of disappearing.

Less than half of them ever returned.

The hum of pixies grew louder as he passed beneath a flowering serviceberry tree. He kept his eyes fixed on his goal. He was so close he could taste it. It tasted like bile, or maybe that was just his churning stomach.

For six years, Jeth traveled every inch of Hallanor. He stopped in at every witch's collective, house, or cottage. He visited every magic shop, apothecary, and healing house. He'd even stopped to speak with the odd faerie on the road. Carefully, of course. Battered scrolls, ancient grimoires, and tomes made entirely of leaves the size of his palm had been memorized or copied over—usually both. He'd practiced his craft with a single-minded fervor until his power was under perfect control. Now, he had only one thing left to learn.

How to make a faerie bargain.

Jeth couldn't quite get the hang of it on his own. He'd experimented, but none of his deals had any binding magic behind them. The fae folk held their secrets close to their chests at the best of times. And with something this important? Their lips had been utterly sealed.

The first bit of magic he ever learned had been a spell called True Sight. Aneirin had taught him in an attempt to earn his trust. During his travels, he spoke of it often and learned something very interesting indeed.

There wasn't a single human who had heard of the spell.

And there wasn't a single faerie who hadn't.

The wards, spells, and blessings used by village witches were clearly visible in that other vision. It showed up differently to all, but to Jeth it looked like streams of sparkling gold. The lines and sigils of the protections were bright as sunshine. The fae knew exactly how close they could get to human settlements.

That made Jeth nervous. Humans were at the mercy of the fae, struggling to thrive in their constant shadow. Faeries toyed with their mortal neighbors, tormenting them and fawning over them in turns until they grew bored. After that, they discarded them like rags hardly worthy of the trash pile. Each magical creature presented its own unique dangers. Each had their own unique abilities.

Jeth alone knew that there were advantages and powers that faeries didn't share, that humans didn't know, that weren't in the stories. He knew how the creatures resented the people that lived beside them. They pushed at the edges of the covenants built into the kingdom itself, the rules that tried and failed to protect its mortal residents. Jeth alone knew how dangerous the tentative balance between the two species was.

That wasn't True Sight's only ability, however. Seeing spells was one thing, but Jeth could also see an aura around anyone with magical abilities. They glowed when viewed through the spell. The stronger their magic, the brighter their light. It helped him find witches to study under. Twice, it let him connect a witch with a new apprentice.

Most important of all? Through True Sight, leylines were visible. The powerful rivers of magic flowed through the very earth, air, and water. They ran all over the world, as far as Jeth could tell. Tapping into those streams gave a caster far more power, though anyone who used it ran the risk of taking *too* much. Too much magic burned a person alive from the inside out.

Jeth used the leyline overhead now—not to cast, but to follow. It ran straight overhead in a clear trail, leading straight to Heartwood Hill. He could feel it thrumming above him even without his True Sight activated. It was a tingle down his back and a shiver in his chest.

It was leading him toward a node, a tangle where multiple leylines came together to make a single powerful source. It made sense that Heartwood Hill, and the Blackthorn Court beneath it, were formed beneath that nexus.

Some stories said that Heartwood Hill wasn't formed so much as molded. Nearby towns and villages whispered that the sheer-sided slope was pulled from the earth by magic.

Not that it mattered if it was nature or spell work that made it. What mattered was the door.

Jeth stopped at the edge of the trees, tucked in the shadows beneath the boughs. The forest fell away at the base of the hill, leaving behind a strip of meadow. It ran, as far as he could see, the entire way around, uninterrupted. Long grass stirred and whispered in the breeze that tickled over his skin. Wildflowers bobbed their heavy crowns. A few scrubby bushes with waxy green leaves popped their heads up from the earth here and there.

It was idyllic. Jeth didn't trust it.

He circled the hill, using the shelter of the trees to keep himself from view. One ear was constantly listening to the woods behind him. The stairway to the top, carved from the slope itself and winding crookedly back and forth on its way up, was easily found.

Too easily.

Faerie circles were a way for humans to be trapped and taken to the kingdom below, but that couldn't be the door Jeth was looking for. It couldn't be how the magical creatures of Blackthorn Court went back and forth. He turned away from the steps.

No, what I need is something barely out of the ordinary.

Something subtle. The fae folk wouldn't paint a bright red circle on a wall or post a sign. The door would be hidden. It could be a large round stone, or a clear patch of earth ringed with stones or mushrooms. It could be a tunnel through the trunk of a large fallen tree, or the hole of a large den that wouldn't lead to a den at all.

It could be something like two trees growing against the sheer side of Heartwood Hill, when no other trees grew there.

Jeth stopped.

Two twisted alder trees all but leaned back against the near-cliff behind them. Their branches twined together in a tangle, making it hard to tell where one ended and the other began. Over centuries, they had formed against the hill's face, molding to every bump and ridge. They created an archway to nothing—or so it seemed.

The solid earth behind them was real enough, Jeth could tell. Glamours didn't work on other faeries. It would have looked like the mouth of a tunnel to his eyes, then. Closing his eyes briefly, Jeth imagined pulling a mask over his eyes. The tingle of magic raced down his arms as he activated his True Sight. He opened them.

And closed them again immediately.

The glow of the node was powerful, washing out any other traces of magic near the hill in a brilliant golden light that rivaled the sun itself. He turned his True Sight off quickly, cursing beneath his breath.

I won't be doing that again for a while, he thought sourly.

He could sense the veritable sea of magic that lay beneath the earth, fed by the leylines. It thrummed like a plucked string, trilling through his very bones. The node would drown out both sight and feel. Clever of the faeries to build where they wouldn't be able to see one another's auras, where they wouldn't be able to tell who was the more powerful being. Clever of them to build where no one could detect anyone else's spells.

Clever and dangerous.

But this was the way. It had to be. Jeth stepped into the sunlight, the gold in his skin a-gleam. He held his head high. It was time to start the act. From the moment he set foot in the forest, he knew this was coming. Every creature, great and small, would be watching him for any sign of weakness. He was a mouse stepping into a pit of snakes, and doing so willingly.

So he had to pretend to be a snake.

He imagined himself as the confident prince, returning to claim his throne. It was true, after all. His father, Aneirin, was the King of Blackthorn Court. So he drew himself up and adopted an expression of idle boredom.

Internally, however, he was sweating buckets.

Eyes bored into him from every shadow once he left the shelter of the trees. He could feel them. The faeries were watching, measuring, and judging him. They didn't know who he was. Curiosity and distrust filled the air until he could almost taste it.

Jeth fought the urge to swallow his nerves, the urge to fidget. He consciously kept his hands flat at his sides, though he wanted to ball them into fists. After a pause he hoped seemed dramatic and intentional, and not born of nerves, Jeth stepped forward and into the role of a future king.

I wish my palms weren't so sweaty, he thought, though he was fairly certain the faeries couldn't tell.

The alder trees stirred, the giants shaking off a doze as they realized someone was near. The pale silver-green undersides of the leaves shivered and rattled in the breeze, somewhere between a welcome and a warning.

The invisible gazes in the forest sharpened. The hum and buzz died down to a whisper behind him. Even the pixies wondered. Who is he? They wondered so loudly he could hear it without words.

Who dares?

Now came the hard part. Jeth's nature was quiet and reserved. He was clever, yes, but helpful and kind. In short, his humanity won out over his faerie side in every way. Now, to survive his own harebrained scheme, he had to act against it.

Jeth ran his hand over the iron seal of the small ceramic jar that hung from the belt at his waist. It made his skin sting as though he'd shoved his hand into a thicket of nettles. Iron was toxic to faeries, but Jeth's lingering humanity prevented it from doing more than that.

But it was better safe than sorry. Contained within that sealed little bottle was an unending faerie prison. He had once escaped it—and his father had not.

What would Aneirin's subjects think if they realized Jeth was carrying their ruler at his hip? Unpredictable beings at best, he could picture them tearing him apart in fury or welcoming him with open arms. Each was as likely as the other. Jeth wasn't going to take the risk.

Jeth, a voice whispered.

He froze for only a moment. Ice ran over his skin from the center of his back down to his fingertips and toes. Jeth quickly pulled his hand from the jar.

I did not just hear my father's voice, he told himself.

If he ignored it, maybe it would prove true. He did not hear his father, Aneirin, the being who murdered his mother, kidnapped him, and threatened to lock him away for a century to get him to behave. It was impossible. No, Aneirin, faerie king, was the last person he wanted to hear. He was also the one person who could help him the most.

After all, it was Aneirin's throne that Jeth was here to claim.

No. I don't need him.

With nothing more to rely on than his father's blood in his veins and his own abilities, Jeth strode forward confidently. He came to a stop before the archway.

New problem.

He didn't know what to do to get the portal between the human and faerie lands to open. He didn't know if there were special words, or a key, or if his bloodline alone would be enough to open it with a mere touch. There were a thousand tales of doorways to other realms, and not one of them opened the same way.

The faeries in the forest were watching. Word of what he did here would race ahead of him to Blackthorn Court through other doorways, messengers, and spells.

This was his first test. A powerful impression might be all that saved him from his own kind. After all, Jeth was not a very faerie-like faerie. Being raised human had its advantages, and now he learned it had its difficulties as well. What would a faerie do?

Standing still as a statue, despite the tickle of a breeze stirring his hair, Jeth studied the ancient trees that formed the curving gateway. He turned his head slowly, watching out of the corner of his eye. It was an old hedge witch secret, taught to him by a bent old woman. If he couldn't use his True Sight, perhaps this would –

–Aha!

There. Down near the base of the trunk, he saw faces in the tangles of the wood. The twisted alder trees weren't trees at all.

They were lovpu.

The tangled branches were the gate, and the gatekeepers dwelled within them. That would, he hoped, make opening the door easier.

Jeth turned back to the stone.

"I demand entry to the Blackthorn Court."

Everything around him fell utterly silent. The world around him held its breath. The buzzing pixies, the chatter of hobgoblins hidden in the shrubs, the lilting song that could have been birds or could have been sylphs—all of it came to a stop.

Jeth counted the heavy pulse of his heart as it beat. One. Two. Three. Four. Five.

Like his words were a stone thrown on the still surface of a pond, a murmur rippled away through the trees. His audience, unseen as they were, was listening closely now. After all, who *demanded* entry to a faerie court?

The alder trees shuddered. With a creak like a branch bending beneath a great weight, two creatures stepped out of their trunks. It was hard to tell if they had been part of the trees, fitting themselves into the bends and folds of the trunk—or if they opened a door of some sort and stepped through. But suddenly, there they were. Both of them looked to be made of the same wood they had come from, with skin crackled like bark and spindly, twig-like fingers.

And swords.

Each held a wooden sword, lacquered and polished, with a wickedly sharp edge.

Gate guards, then, not gatekeepers.

"And who are you to demand we let you in?" The taller of the two lovpu, hunched of back and with hair and beard of gray-white lichen, knelt down with a crackle and groan of their joints. They leaned in until they were face to face with Jeth. Their enormous eyes were entirely black. They glittered in the sun like polished obsidian stones.

"We don't like strangers here," the shorter said firmly. Their hair, if it could be called such, was made of thick, squat branches that ended in points made of the same bark-like brown as their skin. They looked like a flame made of wood, and their eyes were alight with a spark of suspicion that only made the resemblance that much clearer.

"We've been told not to let anyone in or out."

Jeth arched a brow. "I'm not 'anyone.'"

The shorter one scoffed, brandishing their sword as they stepped forward. "What if we just killed you, then? Problem solved. No one to go in or out."

Jeth didn't move even a fraction of an inch as the lovpu swung their sword, stopping less than an inch away from his throat. To show fear or uncertainty would ruin any reputation he had before he even built one. Though his heart was racing so quickly he could taste copper on his tongue, he didn't flinch.

Good, Aneirin's voice whispered in the back of his head. Jeth hated how pleased it sounded.

The weapons carved by lovpu from the wood of their trees was deadly as a poison to a magician. They were the only weapons that could kill a caster with a single blow. A scratch was as dangerous as being impaled. It was only supposed to work that way on humans, though Jeth wasn't entirely certain his faerie half would save him.

He didn't want to test it.

"Do it, or don't," he said, glad his voice didn't shake. "I don't think you will."

The two faeries exchanged looks. The shorter drew their sword away and stepped back. Their frustrated frown softened with uncertainty.

The taller leaned forward, their gaze brimming with curiosity. "What is your name, stranger of the woods?"

"I am Jeth, son of your King, Aneirin."

Both lovpu reeled back as though he'd struck them. They retreated a few steps, putting their heads together and murmuring. The shorter made sharp gestures, scowling darkly. The taller wore a frown and bared teeth of pale wood. After a minute or two, the taller seemed to win their quiet argument. They faced him.

"We are Lock," the taller said, gesturing to their companion. "And Key." They touched their own chest.

Lock crossed their arms, a stubborn frown still furrowing their brow. "We heard rumors that our king had a son. They said the child was born of a human woman. You don't look very human to me."

Jeth didn't bother to answer. It was common knowledge to human and fae alike that even a drop of faerie blood would turn someone into one.

"Have you seen him? King Aneirin?" Key asked hopefully.

"My father is lost," Jeth said, careful not to lie. "I've come to take my place on the throne in his stead."

"His Majesty wouldn't just die."

Key reached out, long fingers curling over Lock's shoulder. "But the fire *did* fade."

Jeth didn't know what that meant, but he didn't let it show on his face. Both lovpu fell silent.

It must be the way of trees, Jeth decided, *to think before they speak.*

He didn't mind that. It bought him time to think. Lock's gaze was brimming with distrust. They kept looking him up and down, drinking in his appearance.

Jeth didn't look like a prince. He long ago outgrew the blue cape-sleeved jacket his mother made him, but he kept a few scraps to have tailors match the dye. Now he was dressed in a rough-spun, travel-stained shirt that had once been white. It was tucked beneath a long blue tunic, belted at the waist. His pants were plain brown, as were his boots. Pouches, the jar, and his water skin hung from his belt, rattling faintly with each step. On his back was a worn canvas pack of the sort sailors used.

And he was armed only with a simple dagger.

Lock's expression said that Jeth didn't look like a prince, much less a king. He didn't even look like he could feed himself tonight.

And they'd be right. I can't. Jeth fought the rising uncertainty inside his chest, focusing on remaining still. The urge to turn and walk right back into the forest was growing with every passing moment.

Stop that. You know who you are, his father whispered.

Jeth tasted bile in the back of his throat. Where was that voice coming from? He wasn't imagining it, because he'd never imagined it before – but now? Now he heard it clear as day, and it wanted him to do this.

It would be so easy to just turn around and leave.

"If you really are the lost prince, the hill will know," Key said slowly.

Lock sneered. "Yes. Prove your bloodline, if you can."

Prove it? How could he prove he shared blood with someone who wasn't there? After all, he wasn't about to tell them he was carrying their ruler in a jar. He pictured popping it open and calling inside for Aneirin to tell them the truth of things, even though it was impossible to do that with the iron seal on the thing.

He bit back the anxious laugh that bubbled in his chest.

Think, damn it. Think.

The hill would know, Key said. Faeries liked their riddles and turns of phrase, and this one seemed very pointed. Prove his bloodline, Lock said. The hill will know. Prove his blood. The hill will know…

Jeth stepped forward, smoothly drawing his dagger from its sheath. He stepped into the shade beneath the boughs of the alder trees. Key and Lock drew back, watching him closely.

His blade wasn't made of iron, but copper. Its hilt was wrapped in black leather and copper wire. It was a fine blade, and he kept it sharp. It took only a single moment to draw it across his palm and leave a clean cut behind.

I really hope I'm right about this.

Jeth lay his hand against the rough, cool stone of Heartwood Hill.

The ground beneath his feet heaved. He stumbled, clutching at the hillside to stay upright. With a rumble like thunder, the very earth rippled away from him. The trees swayed madly as the land undulated in a wave.

A bit of drama wouldn't go amiss, suggested Aneirin in his ear.

With the node so close, it was stupidly simple to grab a tendril of the air and whip it into a fierce wind that swirled around him like a miniature storm. The leaves overhead rattled like dice in a cup. Several ripped free to swirl around him. His hair was whipped into a cloud of golden froth. The hem of his tunic flapped wildly, like pennants atop a castle tower.

The earth stilled. Jeth allowed the breeze to go on its way with a sigh. Everything settled around him, and only when all was quiet and calm did he drop his hand. He healed it with a twist of his wrist, leaving a thin pink line across his palm that would fade in a few days. The dark red smear of his blood on the stone glinted in the sunlight, but even that was fading as the porous earth drank every drop.

Jeth turned.

Both lovpu were on their knees, the tips of their blades sunk into the earth before them. Their heads were bowed reverently. The woods beyond burst with a sudden cacophony of buzzing, chirping, screeching, and howling—each one from faeries he couldn't even see. Their words were just garbled enough that he could hardly make any of them out. Only snippets reached his ears.

"The prince?"

"Who is he?"

"–his blood did you–"

"–was proof."

"Who is he?"

Who is he, who is he, who is he?

"Will that serve as proof enough for you, or do I need to do something more drastic?" Jeth asked idly, pulling a handkerchief from his belt to wipe off the last of the blood on his skin.

"Yes, your Highness. That will do quite well," Key said quickly. They slid their gaze to Lock.

Lock sucked in air through their teeth, brow furrowed as they mulled it over. It required both of them to agree, Jeth realized—and Lock earned their name by preventing entry more than they allowed it.

"We'll open the door," the shorter of the lovpu decided at last.

"Good," Jeth said, fighting a heavy sigh of relief.

That took care of step one.

The lovpu passed him on either side, both taller than he was by head and shoulders. Their trees were twice that. Their limbs creaked and groaned as they walked until they pressed against the bark of their trees. Lock and Key melted through the wood as though they were stepping into water. Once they were in place, there was hardly even a seam to denote where they had been.

Jeth still couldn't tell if that was because they passed through some sort of magical door into their trees, or if they simply *were* them.

Pebbles rattled down the side of the hill. Jeth stepped back to watch the gate open. It was much less impressive than his claim had been, magically speaking. The doorway grew from where the hill met the earth up toward the boughs of the trees, as if the earth itself were being shouldered aside by some invisible giant.

The sun couldn't penetrate the looming darkness of the tunnel beyond for more than a few feet. Shadows gathered thick among the pitted, pockmarked walls of stone. Ripples of pale blue and green and white ran over the rocks, remnants of water that vanished long ago. The walls undulated like waves, with holes that ran away in all directions. They turned into little black pits on the ceiling and walls and floor alike. Some were too small for a hand to fit inside. Others were large enough to fit two or three people side by side. The rest were every size in between.

There was one flat path, worn smooth by centuries of feet, that ran down the center of the tunnel. It was narrow and ran steeply downward, but the tunnel curved and the rest of its path was hidden from view.

Jeth would be king of whatever lay beyond this point. He was keenly aware of the need to act like it. *Weakness,* he reminded himself, *will tell them far too much.*

After all, he wasn't going down there to make friends.

He didn't hesitate to step through the opening. His footsteps made a scuff on the tunnel floor, but there was no echo.

The light behind him faded with the roll of stone against stone. The spot between his shoulder blades grew tight and his breath caught—but Jeth turned slowly so his audience wouldn't think he was alarmed.

Alarmed was one word for it, as he watched the earth itself crawl back down behind him. His pulse fluttered like a hummingbird's wings. The gateway was closing. He didn't know how to open it again. He wasn't sure he could.

The tunnel sealed behind him.

It was pitch black. Jeth couldn't so much as see his fingers right in front of his face. The quiet was loud, but it wasn't silent. The soft clack of stones somewhere ahead of him. The scuff of something tiny scurrying. Water dripped quietly down a wall nearby, the soft *pit-pit-pit* of it slow and steady. Something squeaked. He couldn't tell if it was a faerie or a bat. His own breathing seemed unreasonably loud.

Jeth lifted his hand. The faintest golden gleam formed in his palm and swelled until it was the same size and shape as the faerie focus he'd once stolen in the wake of his mother's death. He kept it dim, but it pushed back the darkness, painting a pool of light around him.

"Well, no turning back now," he murmured under his breath, softly enough that the walls didn't pass the words along ahead of him. It was time to do what he came here to do. It was time to claim a throne.

Jeth took his first steps down to the land under the hill.

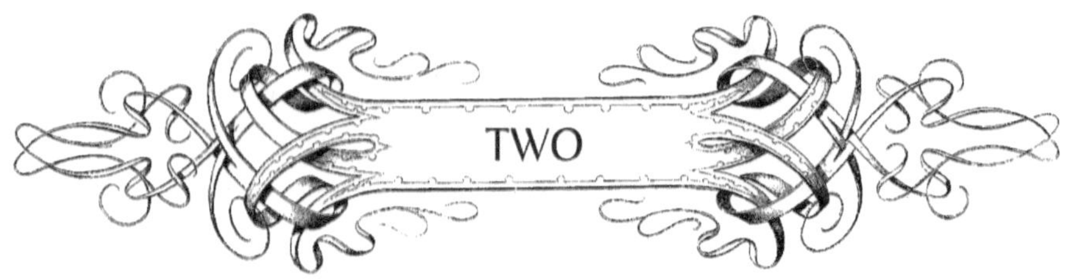

TWO

Every step Jeth took set the shadows ahead of him to lurching, stretching, twisting. The tunnel was cast in sharp edges as his dim mage-light passed over uneven rock walls. Beyond his light was an unending darkness that reminded him uncomfortably of the prison his father once trapped him in.

He didn't know how far beneath the earth he would have to go to reach the Blackthorn Court. Already, time distorted. A minute felt like an age, an hour like a lifetime. He'd been walking endlessly. The horrible thought that he might be wandering in circles tickled the back of his mind, sending a chill through him. It was a common enough faerie trick, to set someone wandering endlessly.

The earth sometimes opened wide around him, forming massive caverns dotted with stalagmites, stalactites, and pillars of stone. Sometimes, the ceiling and walls pressed in as the tunnel narrowed. One of his antlers scraped the ceiling and he ducked, swearing softly. His breath was shallow as he realized how much earth was above his head. What if this were a trap, a path to a dead end?

But the walls widened again to the pitted, undulating stone. Jeth had been walking at least an hour by now. There was no sign of the Blackthorn Court.

Something skittered in the dark. Jeth whirled, catching sight of something with hands and feet and a jagged face with teeth of sharp stones. It was short, barrel chested, clothed in tattered swaths of gray fabric. Milky white eyes were fixed on him. It wore a scowl that twisted its visage into a stone-like mask. When it growled, it sounded like stones being rolled in a basket.

Duergar, Jeth identified, his breath catching. The small troll-like beings were dangerous. Their only weakness was sunlight, which was currently in short supply. He swallowed.

The scowl eased into a cold, cruel smile.

Instinctively, Jeth took a step back.

The duergar gave a single barking laugh that cracked like a whip before it vanished through one of the many tunnels pitting the walls, crawling on all fours.

Jeth's pulse thrummed like a plucked lute string. He didn't let it show on his face, but he felt the fear coursing through him like lightning. Every piece of him screamed to turn, to run, to move.

He turned back to the path and his heart went from racing to stopping entirely—at least for a moment. A few pebbles skittered away and vanished into the gaping chasm at his feet.

"Fire and fury!" he swore, backing up a pace.

His breathing was ragged and uneven, loud in the otherwise silent cavern. He slowly leaned forward, peering into the darkness. He could tell how deep it was, only that his light certainly didn't reach the bottom from here. It wasn't wide, but it was wide enough that Jeth wouldn't risk jumping over it.

Duergar, he thought bitterly. They delighted in luring others to their deaths.

"I can't die before I even get there," Jeth muttered. He stepped back, pouring a trickle of magic into the light in his hand, letting it glow brighter.

The worn path curved here, and a few yards away it ran into the edge of a bridge. It was a beautiful piece of carved stone with arched railings and the illusion of leaves and vines growing on the edges and dripping into the chasm below. It was carved thin, the railings across the top were smooth and polished, and it was only a few steps long.

It also looked like it wouldn't hold the weight of a cat, let alone a grown man.

You can always turn back, Aneirin's voice murmured.

"Never."

Jeth stepped onto the bridge. It didn't crumble; it didn't drop him to his untimely death. He let out a breath he didn't realize he'd been holding. He might have been ageless, now, but he was certain a few years had been shaved off his life anyway by this particular surprise.

On the other side, the path continued into the darkness. Back into the tunnels and caverns he went. One passage was lined with ghostly white stone that held the light after he passed, fading slowly back into the dark in his wake.

Another scuff, a gentle knock on the wall. Jeth paused, listening. Knocking was a kobold habit, a gentle warning from a gentle faerie. Danger lay ahead, though the creature didn't explain what kind.

Other faeries caught his attention as he passed. He heard the steady *tink-tink-tink* of a dwarf in the distance. A shuffle of feet passed in front of him, and when he reached the spot he'd heard them, he found the flat, round-footed prints of a trow. The bell-like hum of nixies raced overhead. The scent of sulfur met his nose, already fading from the air.

The caves were *alive* with things moving just beyond his sight. Shadows darted away, never resolving into something he could recognize. More than once, he nearly jumped out of his skin.

I am a prince. I am their *prince. Keep up the act, damn it. You have to.*

For the first time in his life, Jeth regretted his childhood. The days spent with his mother as a simple country boy in a small town could never have prepared him for this. Gleda knew, she *knew* who and what her son was. She knew who he might one day have to become.

Why didn't she prepare him?

I would have raised you properly. You would have known how to walk these paths without fear. I would have been better for you.

Jeth grit his teeth, putting a hand over the iron seal of the jar on his hip. That voice in his head couldn't be real. Aneirin had no power. He was sealed away.

And he was wrong. Gleda may not have prepared him for a faerie court, but she did prepare him for the day when the fae would find him. She prepared him for an endless life with the gift of humanity.

The darkness ahead of him ended abruptly in a wall of moss that perfectly filled the rounded hall. It smelled strongly of brackish water and rot, like a swamp. Jeth stared at it, brow furrowed. This couldn't possibly be the wrong way. There had only been one path this entire way.

The moss wall moved slowly out, then back in with the sound of a bellow.

It was a faerie. A large one, probably some kind of troll, Jeth realized. A very large one.

What now? Jeth wondered, mulling over his options.

Easy, Aneirin whispered. *Lash out at it with magic, boil the moss from its hide. How dare it stand in your way?*

Jeth swore and pulled the jar from his belt, studying the seal. It was intact. That was exactly what Aneirin would do, though, exactly what he would say.

The question wasn't what Aneirin would do, however. The question was, what was the least he would do?

His expression smoothed as he tied the jar back onto his hip, lifting a foot and prodding at the mossy mass with a toe. It squelched and gave way with the consistency of watery mud. The troll grunted in confusion.

"Move," Jeth commanded, putting a hint of his magic into the word.

The troll groaned, then shifted. It rose, and massive round, flat-bottomed feet appeared beneath it. It stood at least twelve feet tall, looming far overhead. The ground where it rested was dark with damp. With another grunt, the creature pulled away from the path.

Beyond it lay another massive cavern, but this one was different.

This one wasn't entirely dark.

Jeth dimmed his mage light, just to make sure. On the far side of the cavern, a faint yellow-white light shone. The tiny floating sparks of devas drifted in and out of sight like fireflies.

Water trickled over the stone somewhere, and moss and mushrooms grew on the walls. Some of them glowed faintly. He extinguished the light in his hand, stepping into the open cavern. The troll sat on an outcrop of rock nearby, studying him. Jeth ignored the creature as he passed.

Chin up. Look straight ahead. Calm and confident, that's what you need to be. You belong here.

Part of him wanted to turn back, and that part grew stronger with every step. There was still time. No doubt the echo of the bloodline magic that shook the hill and forest had reached the court, but he hadn't claimed the throne. He could leave.

But he had yet to learn to make good faerie bargains, or break them. He hadn't even started looking.

There were tiny giggles and the flutter of wings around his head, there and then gone. A will-o'-the-wisp glimmered to one side, dancing enticingly, but faerie magic didn't work on Jeth. The pull was barely there and quickly gone.

The glow grew stronger as he reached the far end. The tunnel was high and wide here. The air grew warmer. In fact, the soft, buttery yellow light reminded him of strong morning sunlight. It *felt* like sunlight. He rounded the corner, fully expected to see a golden globe of fire suspended in the ceiling. It wouldn't surprise him to find the faeries had made a second star just to light their kingdom.

Instead, he saw nothing. The golden glow streamed from everywhere and nowhere. Some of it came from golden mushrooms that crept over the walls in little cascades. Some of it seemed to radiate from the very rocks itself.

And that nebulous light from nowhere lit the entire massive cavern and took Jeth's breath away.

A mist almost like clouds coiled among the stalactites that dripped from the ceiling. A river rushed, filling the entire space with the dull roar of water, which was an oddly soothing sound. The path turned into a flight of stairs at his feet, leading down to the river's edge and another delicate bridge. It wove back and forth across the cavern floor, but led inevitably to the absolutely massive pillar in the center of the room.

Which was also a castle. A tower crowned the structure, with turrets and walls cascading down to the ground itself. A courtyard sat high above most of it. Jeth could just make out the tops of trees. A massive bonfire glowed in its center like a beacon, which was exactly what it was.

Come, it whispered. *Come closer, come see who we are.*

Jeth felt the magic tickle the edge of his mind, tug at his heart, then fade. It was a potent spell, no doubt meant to lure any humans foolish or unlucky enough to make it this far. He felt a spark of anger at the thought. He wanted to turn back, and he *was* a faerie. He could only imagine the horror a human would feel as they struggled to break free while the magic reeled them in.

Suddenly exhausted, Jeth crouched down, drinking in the distant sight of his new home—at least for a while. A light went on. Another went out. A shadow leapt over the castle wall as someone passed between it and the bonfire.

Jeth had made it to the Blackthorn Court.

THREE

Get up. You can do this, Jeth urged himself. It took an incredible amount of effort to push himself back up to his feet. The walk through the tunnels had been hellish, but now he had to face an entire court of fae.

Worse, he had to rule them.

His experience with the fae was varied, with some faeries being helpful if treated correctly and most being malicious. Humans stole their land, as far as most fae were concerned, though the humans had been there when they claimed it. Deemed unintelligent and primitive, the humans had been ignored until they stood up for themselves.

The kingdom of Hallanor was a faerie bargain. In exchange for marrying a faerie, a young ruler made a treaty that limited their power. It was all that stood between the humans and utter destruction, now.

Jeth encountered dozens of people who suffered at the hands of faeries. He, too, knew how cruel and thoughtless they could be. What lay ahead was a den of vipers dressed as butterflies.

He steeled himself with a deep breath and started down the steps.

Careful, boy. Any weakness and they'll pounce. Aneirin's insidious words were tinged with glee.

It had been years since Jeth had seen his father, but as he walked down the steps, he pulled the persona of the faerie king on like a cloak. Cold, haughty, and distant. That was what would protect him here.

As he descended, threads of music caught his ear. The delicate strains of a flute were muffled by the rush of the underground river as he neared it, but he could just glimpse the nyads on the rocky shoreline. When they caught sight of him, they froze, studying him intently.

He turned back to the path. The river roared before him, the edges frothing white. Spray made the stone slick beneath his feet. A glint of blue-white skin made Jeth pause at the foot of the bridge. Even as he watched, a hoof melted into a hand. A man pulled himself up to rest on the bridge's edge, his features impossibly perfect, and his eyes fixed on Jeth. His eyes were too large and too far apart, but there was a light in them that was undeniably magnetic. His hair was blue and green in turns, coiled in hanks like...seaweed. It was seaweed.

Jeth didn't move. His knowledge of water faeries was slim. They were difficult to find on the surface. From what he could remember, however, only one had hooves and hair of seaweed. Kelpies, cannibal faeries.

"And who might you be?" the handsome man asked in a rich, deep voice. He leaned to the side, muscles in his chest rippling.

"Someone not to be trifled with," Jeth said coldly. Aneirin wouldn't allow someone so brazen to get away with it. This was a test. Whether it was the one kelpie testing him, or whether the kelpie had been sent by others, he couldn't tell.

"Don't be like that. Come, sit with me."

The telltale pull of faerie magic slid off of Jeth like oil on water, and he lifted his chin. He stepped onto the bridge, advancing like a soldier, each foot solidly planted. The kelpie's eyes sparkled, and he grinned. His teeth were sharp and gleamed yellow in his mouth.

Jeth knelt down beside the creature, and it lifted its hand.

"Touch me, and you will live to regret it," Jeth said firmly, each icy word laced with a hint of power.

The kelpie froze. It's hand lowered.

Jeth rose and walked past him, fighting the urge to look over his shoulder as he turned his back. The space between his shoulders prickled.

He stepped off the bridge. A splash behind him was all that told him that the kelpie had taken to the water once more. He let out the smallest sigh of relief, careful not to let it show on his face.

How had his father ever survived this? Already, the weight of his adopted persona was heavy on his shoulders and his heart, which was thundering in his chest like the water behind him.

The castle was close, now. Before him, the stone pathway was now polished, gleaming darkly beneath his feet. It was impossibly smooth. Jeth couldn't help but long for the cracked and uneven cobblestone roads from above, or even the pounded dirt paths through the trees. A path like this couldn't have been made by hand.

He hadn't encountered something built entirely by magic before. He believed he was about to.

The massive gate before him was made of silver and gold, studded with gems and precious stones arrayed to make beautiful images. Dozens of colors were aligned to make a forest scene, and to depict a faerie revel with dozens of different creatures. Elves, dwarves, dryads, pixies, brownies, hobgoblins, trow, and more besides.

Jeth stopped before them, facing a tiny carved pixie with her hands thrown up in a rapturous dance. His gaze slid up the seam of the door, and he frowned.

Will they even let you in, boy?

"Open the gate," Jeth commanded, fighting a trill of fear. Aneirin's voice seemed stronger somehow. Louder.

A door in the wall cracked open, and a tiny creature dressed in homespun clothes stepped out. She curtseyed to him, her head bowed.

"Beg pardon, sir, but they bid me ask you why," the brownie said apologetically. Brownies were house fae. They liked to clean and tidy and hide things if you put them in the wrong place. They didn't do things like confront strangers—unless they were ordered to.

A shadow flickered over the wall inside the little guardhouse.

Jeth stepped back, turning slowly to face her. "Because I am here to claim my throne. I am Jeth, son of Aneirin." He raised his voice slightly at the end, directing it toward the creatures he couldn't see.

She stepped back, as if waiting for instructions on what to say next. Jeth lifted a hand. "Whoever they are, they can face me themselves. Or did they not feel the shift when I touched the earth of Heartwood Hill?"

The door swung open with a ponderous groan. Rather than face him, the unseen faerie simply let him in.

Good, they're already afraid of you, Aneirin whispered.

With a bitter twist of his lips, Jeth turned toward the corridor...

...and stepped into a forest. His eyes widened in spite of himself. The plants on the walls were real. Flowering vines and rich dark ivy curled up over the carved branches of stone tree trunks, giving the illusion that they were really trees. Ferns with their delicate fronds bobbed in the breeze of the passing door. The floor itself was still clear, the hall lined with planters on either side, he realized. That was made of plain polished marble, but he couldn't see a seam.

The air was alive with the tingle of magic. It crept over his skin like ants as he walked. Doors large and small and every size in between lined the walls at irregular intervals, and they were all carved with different sigils, frescoes, and faces. No two were alike. Neither, Jeth guessed, were their occupants.

A multitude of scents filled the air as he passed them, from the crisp salt brine of the ocean to the loamy earth scent of the forest. He heard the call of birds and the chirrup of little frogs.

And the eyes. He felt the eyes on him, heard the sound of doors opening and closing behind him. Jeth couldn't turn his head to see without ruining his act. Like a rustle of leaves, he heard the swish of fabric and the faint whispers as his future subjects followed him along the hall.

The walls fell away abruptly, leaving him standing in a large, oval-shaped room with a lake in the middle. An actual lake, with sand and stone at the edge of the water. Waves lapped at the shore. Tiny houses of seaweed and wood bobbed on rafts. A few small huts dotted stone islands near the very center of the water. Below the surface, as Jeth walked around it, he saw swaying seaweed. It grew dark quickly, too deep to see any further.

Selkies, naturally curious creatures as they were, climbed out of the water swathed in their seal-skin cloaks. Kelpies snorted, their heads just above the surface of the water, watching him with narrowed eyes. Undine and merfolk appeared, their tails flashing in the water as they followed his progress around their home.

It was a salt-water lake for faeries of the sea. Jeth wouldn't have guessed that land-locked Hallanor would *have* sea faeries.

He left the chamber behind and climbed another set of steps lined with doors. That one, too, came to an end—in a small stone tunnel with beautiful carvings, which opened into the courtyard.

The bonfire Jeth saw from above crackled and roared. Up close, it was as large as a ship. The wood it licked at never seemed to burn. Fueled by magic, the bonfire once again cast out the net of its spell—or perhaps it had never really stopped.

Come, come closer. Come and see.

Jeth stepped into the warm, open air and circled the fire slowly, admiring it. It was a powerful bit of spell work, powerful and dangerous. At last, he tore his gaze from it and turned to face the waiting faeries before the gilded doors.

A cluster of them stood there, each garbed in elegant finery. Sweeping sleeves, delicate coronets, actual flowers and leaves woven into cloth. The colors were as bright and varied as a field of flowers.

Keenly aware of his travel-stained clothes and dusty boots, Jeth slowed to a stop before them. He smoothed the front of his tunic. "Is this how you greet your prince and future king?"

He spoke loud enough for the impromptu parade behind him to hear. A murmur coursed through the crowd. Jeth felt the first prickle of sweat at his hairline as the cluster of faeries before the doors leaned close to confer in whispers.

His chest was tight with nerves. He hadn't taken a full breath, it felt, since he stepped foot under the hill. Now he was left the sole figure of scrutiny, and that was his entire future. The king, the one set apart.

This was a terrible idea.

And it was too late now to change his mind.

A faerie stepped forward, looking down his strong nose. He was stunning, even amongst the fae folk, tall and broad and with eyes the color of sapphires. He carried a small clay pipe in one hand, which he put between his teeth as he circled Jeth.

Jeth didn't move, though his skin crawled. This faerie was a Gean-Cánach. A dangerous faerie—if one weren't careful. A faerie that, like Aneirin, sought love with humans. Jeth hoped his faerie blood would continue to protect him.

"And who are you to claim you are our king?" The Gean-Cánach's voice was smooth as supple leather and just as thick. It echoed in a way that sent a tingle up Jeth's spine.

He wasn't entirely immune, then.

"I am the one who shook the earth. I am Jeth, son of Aneirin."

"That would be most interesting, if it were true."

Fear arced through Jeth like lightning, a tingle that ran out from his chest and all the way down to his fingers and toes. He hid it with a scowl. "And what is that supposed to mean?"

"*We* didn't see you touch the hill."

"Eoghan," one of the other faeries said, an edge to the word.

Jeth's eyes flicked to the side, just catching sight of the slim faerie, fair of feature and skin, and yet the most human looking creature there apart from their pointed ears. He spun back to the Gean-Cánach—Eoghan, he now knew.

Eoghan slowed to a stop, his head turning. His dark hair gleamed with red highlights where the firelight caught it. For a moment, Eoghan and the other faerie were locked in a silent battle of wills.

"Oh, very well," he sighed at last, turning away. "If you are the heir to our throne, then you may enter."

The cluster of faeries before the doors stepped aside, clearing a path—but not one of them made a move to actually open them.

I am getting tired of the tests, Jeth thought, feeling a weight settle on his shoulders.

He lifted a hand, pausing. Dramatics were once again in order. With a tug on the power of the node surrounding him, he summoned a wind that sent fabric billowing and blew dust away in a cloud. The bonfire behind him danced in agitation, dimming.

"Open," Jeth said, lending just a hint of power to the word so it would echo throughout the courtyard.

With a bang, the doors flew back, swinging wide. As quickly as he'd stirred the air to life, it stilled.

Jeth steeled himself and stepped inside his castle.

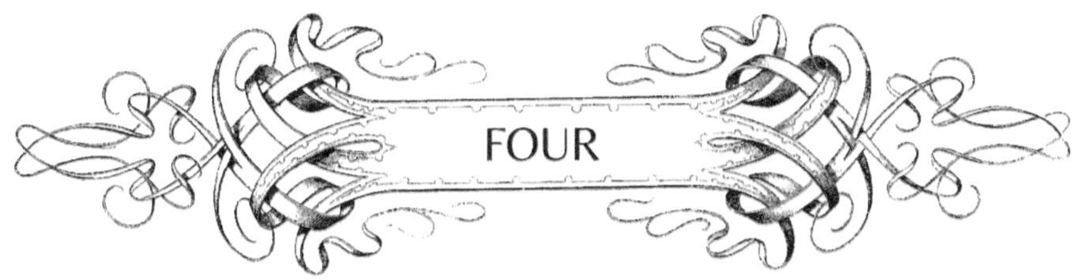

FOUR

The interior of the castle was bright and warm compared to the courtyard behind him. The balmy stir of a summer breeze swept through the air and toyed with Jeth's hair. Where the corridors had been covered in plants to look like a forest, the throne room was entirely transformed.

Pillars stood at irregular intervals, and Jeth couldn't tell if they were carved to look like tree trunks, or actually were. Roots crept over the ground, vanishing into a thick carpet of verdant green moss. The ceiling was festooned with leaves that stirred in the air, wrapped around and supported by branches. Long trailing vines, flowered and plain, dripped down to the floor in places.

It was impossible to tell where the walls began, though the room echoed softly like it was an enclosed space. Powerful illusion magic had painted the walls to look like the sky, and the light was roughly the same color as the sky above-ground would be—and changing.

At Jeth's feet, a pathway of pristine white stone ran arrow-straight across the floor to the bottom of a dais. The white stone of the platform was decorated with silver and gold, and it glowed in the magical light around it.

Ah, what once was...

Aneirin's words sparked the connection in Jeth's mind. This was a replica of the Blackthorn Court as it had been, before the humans and Hallanor had driven them underground. No magical expense had been spared, though who knew how many hundreds or thousands of years ago the spells were cast.

Atop the platform lay Jeth's goal: the Blackthorn Throne. True to its name, it was a monstrous nest of brambles, artfully arranged into a beautiful seat. Jeth couldn't tell if it was grown and shaped, or carved of a rich black wood, polished to a gleam. The tips of the thorns were dipped in silver and gold that dripped down them like blood. Somehow, the very tips of them were made of a clouded crystal.

With every step Jeth took, it seemed to grow. Its back was high, and the base wide. He felt heat creep up his neck toward his ears.

I can't sit on that. I'll look miniscule!

It isn't about your size, it's about commanding the room, Aneirin sneered.

Jeth's self-consciousness disappeared in a split second, replaced with a new rush of heat as he dropped his gaze, briefly, to the bottle on his hip.

Stop that.

Aneirin didn't answer.

The dais' steps appeared before his feet, and Jeth lifted his gaze to his throne. A gleaming green cushion covered the seat, and a darker green velvet drape. At head height, there was a spiral of thorns that held a green jewel in place. It was dull, almost black, and the size of Jeth's head.

And dangling over the arm of the throne, as though Aneirin had planned to come back in moments instead of years, was Jeth's crown.

Jeth stopped, reaching down to run his fingers over the wood and crystal. It was designed to match the throne, but this one was all in gold, with black tipped thorns fading into that same crystal at the very tips. It was lighter than he thought it would be. He lifted it with two fingers and let it dangle.

An outraged gasp sounded behind him, and he paused.

You mock us, treating that crown so casually. Aneirin's voice was still just a whisper in his mind, but it came with a force this time, a rising tide of anger.

Jeth spun the crown on his fingers once, then caught it. Several gasps came from behind him. He smiled slowly, then turned.

Silent as the down of dandelions, the faeries of Blackthorn Court had filed into the throne room after him. The doors were closed with a rumble that rolled through the room, cutting the silence like a knife. Fabric rustled. Bells jingled softly.

Jeth swept his gaze over the room. Every eye was fixed on him, weighing him, judging him. After all, they looked upon their king.

Jeth looked upon his people.

His people. His to care for, even as they plotted against him as they no doubt would. His to look after, even as they fought to make him leave. His, each and every one—from the cannibalistic to the peaceful, from the dangerous to the helpful.

A murmur rippled through the room as Jeth lifted the crown, studying the play of light over the gleaming gold. He lifted it over his head, over his antlers. He lowered it carefully—he couldn't imagine what reaction the faeries would have if he caught it on a tine or two as he tried to put it on his head. Wouldn't that make an exciting first five minutes of his reign?

It settled atop his hair. The entire room sucked in a breath at once, and a pulse of magic raced through the room. It left Jeth's skin tingling. His heart lurched uncomfortably in his chest.

A trap?

No, nothing else happened. The crown was on his head. The faeries stared in stunned silence. A pale green light played over Jeth's hands as he lowered them.

Wait–

Jeth turned slightly, looking up at the gemstone in the throne. It flickered and danced with a fire deep inside that turned it from a green so dark it was nearly black to a bright, brilliant emerald.

What had Key said above? *The fire went out.* Not the bonfire, but this one.

"Shae–" Eoghan hissed behind him.

The faerie from before, the one that looked almost human, turned toward the crowded room. "To King Jeth," they called.

One by one, faeries knelt. Faster and faster, until they all seemed to be dropping at once, creatures great and small dropped to a knee if they had them, or lowered themselves if they didn't. A sudden rising feeling of unease crept up his spine like a spider.

Jeth claimed his throne. He sat, hands running over the polished wood of the arms. His hands settled neatly into dips worn into the seat over centuries. His father's hands had rested in this same spot.

He nearly pulled them away. Nearly.

You can't control me. You are powerless, he thought toward the bottle.

Am I?

Eogan rose from where he knelt, a smile on his face that was all too warm and pleasant. "What are your commands, my king?"

Commands?

Jeth hadn't thought of any commands. He hadn't come to make grand proclamations or sweeping change. All he wanted was to survive his reign long enough to leave it.

Show them you're in charge. Show them you aren't to be trifled with. Show them your power! Aneirin urged.

He had to do something. His mind raced until he remembered the bridge. The bridge, and his first test.

"There was a kelpie who attempted to stop me on my way here," Jeth mused, keeping his voice light and airy.

The crowd stirred. Several faeries exchanged knowing looks.

"See it put in a tank here in the throne room." The command left a bitter taste on his tongue. It was just what his father would do. He'd want to see it trapped and suffering. When he was tired of that, Aneirin would have the creature murdered. Jeth's stomach turned at the thought.

I will never be a killer like my father, he vowed.

When enough time had passed, he would see the kelpie released again. He'd find a way to play it off as boredom. He had to.

The doors at the far end of the hall opened. Several faeries slipped out to do his bidding. Jeth exhaled slowly. A few days and he could say he was tired of it staring at him. A few days.

The longer he sat here, the easier it was to see his persona falling into place. Aneirin ruled like a sword, ready to cut down anything in his path. Better to be mercurial and fickle, better to be unpredictable. All he had to do was something unexpected.

He had no doubt he could do *that.* Such traits were expected of a faerie. He could turn them into an art.

"Anything else, your Majesty?" Eoghan sidled closer to the foot of the dais. His head was bowed deferentially, but the look he gave Jeth through his lashes was anything but. His gaze burned, promising whatever Jeth wanted.

Jeth looked away. The Gean-Cánach was getting on his nerves. "See to it that those who serve the Blackthorn Court present themselves to me over the next three days. I would see the state of the kingdom my father has left for me."

"About that, sire..."

Irritation flickered over Jeth's face. He turned to face Eoghan. "About what?" he asked, the words clipped and crisp.

Eoghan held up his hands placatingly, bending in a shallow bow. "I meant no offense, sire, it's simply a question. We here at court don't rightly know what happened to your father. The light went dim, it's true, but how do we know King Aneirin won't return for his throne?"

Another murmur. The faeries stood, craning around one another to peer at Jeth, their curiosity quickly growing almost predatory. They pressed forward, crowding the foot of the dais. Jeth was keenly aware of how far away the door was, and how many bodies lay between him and it.

The jar on his hip felt heavy. He didn't touch it, didn't even so much as glance at it. He merely lounged back in his seat, idly picking a bit of mud off his tunic. "I was with him in his last moments in the open air," Jeth said carefully, walking that fine line between truth and lies. "He is lost to you, and he will not return to this place."

The art of a faerie's fib lay in crafting a truth that wasn't the truth at all. His words set the crowd aflame, whispers rising into a chattering throng as everyone tried to guess at what had befallen the previous king.

The only still point in the sea of turning heads and wagging tongues was that of Eoghan. The red-headed faerie stared at him intently, expression hard and cold.

Jeth tore his gaze from the Gean-Cánach and pointed at Shae, the human-like faerie. "You. Come here."

The talk did not subside. Shae mounted the steps, pausing beside the throne. They said nothing.

"Was there no sign of his power fading?" Jeth asked.

"Oh, there was," Shae said in a lazy drawl. They folded their arms over their chest and shrugged a shoulder. Their green eyes were the color of new spring leaves, and hard as agates.

Even this one, who appears to be on my side, doesn't like me.

"Explain," he said aloud, waving his fingers through the air.

"The throne went dark." Shae gestured at the glowing emerald above Jeth's head. "They're testing you. But you already know that, don't you?"

A small smile curled the corner of Jeth's lips up before he could hide it. He shrugged, going back to idly picking at his tunic.

Shae scoffed, rolling their eyes.

It was refreshing, having a faerie dislike him to his face. No subterfuge or fawning, no secret. Shae didn't like him.

Jeth pushed to his feet, and the room went abruptly silent. All eyes turned to him. Shae slowly backed down the dais steps.

"I am weary. Take me to my chambers. I will see to no other business until morning. Go." He pointed at the doors at the end of the hall, sending a thread of magic across the way to pull the doors wide. The dismissal couldn't have been clearer.

The babble rose again at once. Faeries broke off in clusters, gathering in corners of the courtyard and around the bonfire to speak. Clusters of pixies darted overhead, spying on their fellows as much as gossiping with them. Ponderously large trolls perched on the walls like they were seats and bent to speak to anyone who came to them. Their voices rolled like low thunder. Elves drifted like swans on the water, speaking behind fine fans and dainty fingers.

Eoghan and Shae remained at the foot of the dais.

The Gean-Cánach bowed, his eyes fixed on Jeth, glittering. "I serve as a keeper of this place, your Majesty. A second in command and...a confidant, should you need one."

Jeth arched a brow, turning his gaze to Shae.

"That one is just a changeling," Eoghan said hastily.

"And what is wrong with that?"

"They aren't a *real* faerie."

Jeth looked Shae over. For their part, they merely rolled their eyes. Clearly Shae was used to Eoghan. "And are you a real faerie?"

"I'm Shae," they said sourly.

"Is that all?" Jeth stood, descending the steps of the dais.

"It's good enough for me. Anything more you wish to know, you can ask about later. You said you were tired."

Shae tipped their head toward a curtain of vines hanging from a branch. When they walked over to it and pushed it aside, a corridor was revealed. Jeth followed slowly, taking in the elegantly carved stone. Eoghan's footsteps were light behind him, merely a scuff now and then. It made the hair on the back of his neck stick up, but he pointedly avoided looking over his shoulder.

Shae led the way to a staircase and up, and up, and up. Jeth's chamber, it seemed, was in the tower that overlooked the entire keep and cavern. It made sense, and at the same time...

This is so many stairs.

Up they went on a curving staircase. The center of the tower was hollow, with nothing between the steps and a long drop but a spindly metal bannister. Windows were few and far between, but glittering jars of magic lights in dozens of hues lined the walls. Everything was painted with splotches of color, like stained glass.

Jeth had to admit, even if he hated faeries on principle, they built the most beautiful things.

At the top of the steps, Shae stopped before two double doors. A pair of trees in massive planters stood on either side, and Jeth could sense the lovpu guards within them, unobtrusive and sentinels to protect him. He hoped. Shae pushed the door open.

The walls were carved and painted to look like a field of flowers stretched away as far as the eye could see. The light came from everywhere at once, as though he stepped outside, and as below in the throne room, illusions made the walls change with the time of day above. A tiny stream babbled as it flowed around his bed, with a small pool at the foot of it. Water lilies floated on its surface. On either side of the bed, short, elegant bridges crossed the water. A canopy of flowers and trailing vines hung over his bed, forming natural curtains that didn't quite hide the rich silk sheets and heap of cushions piled high.

It was hard to tell where any of his furniture ended and the room itself began. It looked as though it had been grown naturally from trees and placed around the room. Bark textured the outsides, knobs looked like knots of wood, and there wasn't a perfectly straight edge among them. Wardrobe, desk, dresser, and chair. He had windows on all four walls, the only thing that looked strange as they hung in the glamoured sky. Cushioned benches sat beneath all of them, looking so much like logs with pillows on top that Jeth was wondering if they were fashioned or merely placed.

"Will it suit?" Shae asked, as if they didn't really care what the answer was. Their gaze was sharp, though. They were listening.

"It will," Jeth said, stepping inside. The floor was moss, plush beneath his boots.

"Anything else, your Majesty?" Eoghan asked, leaning against the doorway. He looked through his lashes, a suggestive smile on his lips.

"No, thank you." Jeth spoke firmly, the dismissal clear.

Eoghan rolled his eyes, turning and sweeping back down the stairs. Shae pulled the double doors closed, pausing when they were open but a crack.

Sharp green eyes met Jeth's gold.

"Be careful."

The doors closed with a clunk. Jeth stared at them, a chill running down his back. The soft sound of water and the twitter of birdsong, illusory as it may have been, were the only sounds in the room.

There were no eyes on him here, but Jeth couldn't relax. He paced, looking out the windows as he passed them, drinking in his kingdom. His! He'd done it, he claimed the crown.

Still, something told him this was going to be more difficult than just putting on a crown and demanding what he wanted. How would he learn about faerie bargains without raising suspicion? His mind went through a dozen plans and discarded them all.

At last, fully clothed, he dropped onto his bed. The crown rattled against his antlers. He tugged it off with a soft scowl, tossing it against the pillows. He turned his back on it. Curled up at the foot of his bed, surrounded by the scents of flowers and water and earth, Jeth closed his eyes.

Eventually, he slept.

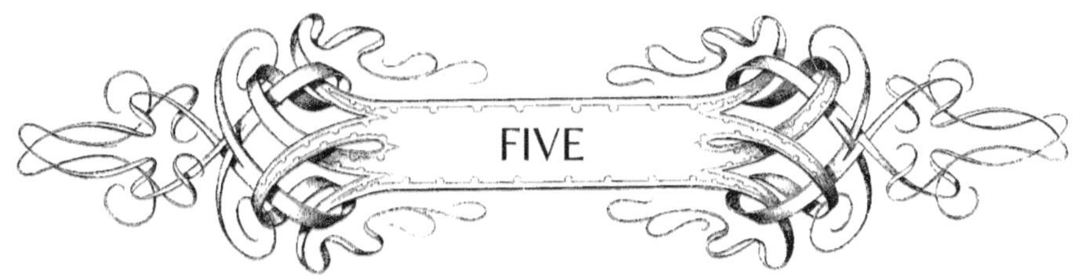

FIVE

Trust is a fickle thing. Amongst the denizens of the Blackthorn Court, it was downright mercurial. From moment to moment, Jeth couldn't tell who wanted to help him and who was trying to maneuver him into a trap that might cost him his crown at best, or his life at worst.

It had been three weeks since he set foot under the hill. Three harrowing weeks.

Pixies tried his food before he ate his meals—apparently standard practice. Two died of poison, and no culprits had been caught. Still, the pixies tried his food. His tower room was his own, but the study he used to run his kingdom was a prime target. Thorns and pins were found on his chair. Once, his inks were replaced with a toxic tincture he only recognized because he grew up as the son of a witch.

The throne room was no better. Faeries were subtle, at least, so no one dived at him with a knife. But the sly offers of help and advice were many. Jeth always turned them down. Help here had strings. Petitions were their own kind of trap, where faeries demanded he weigh in their favor in order to gain one in return. He was taxed to his mental limit finding ways to disappoint both parties—but only slightly, so no one felt offended.

Eoghan hovered at the edge of everything, eager to offer his advice, standing too close, and admiring Jeth with every glance.

Shae was the opposite. They were around, it was true, but the reluctant faerie rarely spoke. What words they did offer were irritable and short. They watched Jeth, always at the edge of things. Of every faerie in the Court, Shae was the one that made him most nervous. He felt as though the changeling could see right through his masks.

Masks which he felt he was mastering, thanks to a new wardrobe. Flowing robes in rich silks, tooled belts, and boots in every color he could wish for became part of the persona he was cultivating. The aloof, careless king. All that mattered to his persona was his own comfort. Today, he wore a robe with draped sleeves at the shoulders in his favorite rich blue, accented with gold. His undershirt was plain white, but the lantern sleeves were made of delicately pleated silk. A tooled belt around his waist held a sheath and a knife, and the clay bottle he never left alone. His trousers were two shades darker a blue, and he wore knee-high boots in a rich, dark brown.

He paced the paneled floor of his study, scanning the shelves that ran all the way from floor to ceiling. The throne room sat just beyond the door, which was painted to blend seamlessly in with the walls. It stood open. Reading books was no crime, after all, and Jeth couldn't imagine what ammunition it could give his subjects to use against him.

Every spare moment had been spent here, scanning the shelves for books on faerie magic and pouring over them. He didn't dare ask for help, but he needed the answer. He needed to know if there was a way another faerie could break a terrible bargain, if there was a way to make a good one. As soon as he had that information, he could leave.

He had perhaps an hour before his next meeting. The chief of a Goblin tribe wanted to discuss a lichen shortage. Apparently, they needed it desperately. Apparently, it only grew in certain caves. Apparently, all those caves were in troll territory at the edge of the cavern, and the Goblins wanted permission to go harvest it. The trolls kept mostly to themselves, and they didn't want a farming operation in their quiet homes.

Jeth couldn't blame them, honestly.

He'd decided what to do, but until the representative showed up, he had time. Light streamed in from the ensorcelled window, painting the shelves. He paused, glancing outside. He could see part of the keep and the paths across the cavern clear as day, but around those things was a field of grass and rolling green hills instead of stone walls, stalagmites, and stalactites. It was easy enough to peer through it with his true sight if he really wanted to see those things, but this was...nice.

He sorely missed sunlight, actual, genuine, beautiful sunlight. The throne room and his bedchamber each had skies, and those skies echoed the weather and light of the world above—from cloudy to brilliant and blue, from stars to sunrises, from moonrise and sunset.

It wasn't the same as fresh air, though. No true breezes, no feel of the shadows playing across his skin. So he took the little glimpse from the window as a gift, pretending for just a moment that he wasn't under the very crust of the earth itself, as far away from humanity as he could get.

Jeth rubbed his brow as he turned back to the shelves, sweeping the floor before them. As light as it was, after a few hours, the crown gave him a headache. Still, he never took it off. It was part of his mask.

A knock on the door dragged his attention from his search.

Eoghan stood in the doorway holding an armful of scrolls. A sharp-toothed smile curled his lips. He smelled of cedar and leather, today, and the scent filled the modestly sized room in moments.

"Majesty."

"Eoghan," Jeth said, affecting as bored a tone as he could. He went back to scanning the shelves, this time with a distracted disinterest. "What is it?"

"I brought you the maps of the Blackthorn Court and its surrounding caverns and tunnels." The faerie unfurled one across the desk. "It ought to help you with your decision."

"I didn't ask for maps."

"I am anticipating your...needs, sire." Eoghan cast a look over his shoulder as he set the maps down. "I can handle many needs."

"I didn't ask for that either."

Shae suddenly bustled in with a pitcher of water and a crystalline goblet in hand. "Here's what you asked for, your Majesty." They set both down right on top of Eoghan's map.

Eoghan bristled, but Jeth waved a hand to forestall the argument that was brewing.

"That will be all, Eoghan."

The flash of rage directed at Jeth was there only for a moment, gone so quick he thought he imagined it. Instead, the faerie turned his ire where he could. Glaring daggers at the changeling, Eoghan left. Jeth waved a hand, a trickle of magic pushing the door most of the way closed. He frowned at it, troubled by the ever-bolder attempts of Eoghan to control him or lure him to bed.

"These maps aren't bad, though." Shae said idly after a moment. They perched on the edge of one of the cushioned chairs in front of the study's massive desk. A finger idly traced over the flowers and leaves set beneath the desk's polished quartz surface.

"What do you mean?" Jeth asked cautiously, moving to weigh the map's corners down with little paperweights shaped like pixies.

"He brought the ones where the territories are marked. Look, here and here. Goblin and troll." Shae pointed.

Jeth sat, pouring over the map. "Not just those, but every territory. This *is* a good map."

He's keeping his enemy close, trying to earn my trust.

A headache was starting behind his brow. It wasn't the crown, either, but the constant wariness. It wore on him until he was exhausted every night when he fell into bed. He had hours yet today to get through.

Jeth felt eyes on him. He looked up. Shae studied Jeth with an inscrutable expression on their face, head tipped slightly to one side. Their fingers toyed with the hem of their sleeve.

"What do you want?" they asked suddenly, the words clipped.

"You saved me from Eoghan. That's the fourth time in three weeks."

Shae scowled, standing abruptly. "I'm not saving anyone. Don't be conceited."

"Sit, please," Jeth said, gesturing at the chair.

Please. That one word made Shae's scowl ease. They sank back into their seat. After a long, awkward moment in silence, they cleared their throat. "You didn't answer my question. What do you want?"

"I want to know why you hold yourself back. You've been here long enough to change, and to gain status, but you never engage with the other faeries if you can avoid it. Why?"

The question was blunt, but subtle overtures had been part of every conversation he'd had for three weeks. Dancing around what he really wanted to say grew old after a single day, let alone most of a moon.

Besides, part of him instinctively trusted Shae, and he wanted to give in to that feeling very, very badly. The other part whispered that there were no good faeries, that he couldn't trust them, that this was a bad idea. That other part, however, sounded like Aneirin's voice in his head. Jeth idly traced his fingers over the lines of the map, waiting for an answer.

He had a guess, after all. He guessed Shae was more than they seemed. He guessed they could help him learn how to make a faerie bargain—in exchange for their own freedom from the Court.

"Because I don't like it here?" Shae said with a shrug. "I would have thought that was obvious."

"Why not?"

The scowl returned in earnest. "Why does it matter to you?"

"Because I'm trying to trust you." Jeth leaned back in his seat, the fingers of one hand tapping idly on the desk.

Shae ran a hand through their fair, curly hair, a messy, wavy thatch that grew fluffier every time they touched it. "Why would you trust anyone down here?"

"Because you say things like that, and be careful. So why?" Jeth pressed.

"Because I'm a changeling, of course." Shae lifted a hand, gingerly feeling over their pointed ear tips. "I was stolen as a child and raised here. You try enjoying a life among your kidnappers like nothing ever happened."

Jeth knew quite a lot about changelings, having met the faerie halves of them on the surface on more than one occasion. The faerie food and the very magic in the air changed the human children over centuries until they were impossible to tell from their captors. At the same time, that taste of faerie food bound them to their court and sovereign as a servant.

Shae wasn't raised to their position. They were bound to it.

"Did Aneirin bring you here? Did he change you?"

Sullenly, Shae shrugged and stared out the window. "So what if he did? He didn't leave his own kin behind, if that's what you're worried about. Your throne is secure. It was over a century ago, anyway. Anyone I knew before is gone. It's too late to be upset about it all."

But they were still upset. It was clear as day on their face.

Jeth smiled. *I was right.*

Don't, you can't trust them. You can't trust anyone, Aneirin whispered.

Insidious as the thought was, Jeth pushed it aside. He needed an ally to get through this place with his own mind and soul intact.

"I've finally put my finger on why you're so different from the rest."

The changeling tensed, green eyes sliding slowly to fix on Jeth.

"You still have some humanity in you."

Shae surged to their feet. "Don't you say that, don't you dare! You'll set them on me, and I won't take it anymore. Do you hear me? I swear, I'll –"

"You misunderstand," Jeth interrupted calmly. "I recognize it because I have some, too."

The words died on Shae's lip. Indeed, the changeling looked as though they'd been bopped on the head. "What?"

"Aneirin may be my father, but that's nothing more than an unfortunate coincidence. My mother was human. I was raised up there, with them, as one of them."

A hungry look stole over Shae's face. They leaned forward, lips parting as they hung on every word. Thousands of questions rose in their eyes, and Jeth waited—but they never reached the air. Their hope faded as quickly as it came.

"So? Why should I care?"

"So, if I can trust you, if you can help me, I'll not only tell you about the surface world you left behind, I can give you permission to go back to it. Can't I? Now that I'm the king?"

Shae ran their tongue over their lips, eyes darting to the window, roving over the rolling green hills. "I don't know."

"You do."

"What does it matter? I'll tell you right now, you can't trust anyone. Do you understand me? You can't trust anyone down here." Shae turned a glare on Jeth. "If you turn your back on anyone down here, there will be a knife in your spine before you can blink."

"I know."

"You have no choice now but to play their damn games. For as long as you live."

"I know."

"You might die any day, all because everyone has their own agenda and doesn't care about another living soul."

"I know."

"Then why did you come down here?" Shae asked, voice cracking. They were on their feet again without realizing it. "If you truly had any humanity left in you, why on earth would you take a single step into this court? Why would you claim the crown?"

"I want to tell you, but I can only do that if you let me trust you, Shae."

"No!" Shae spun on their heel and marched toward the door. A moment later, they whirled back. "You're an idiot. You're being a stupid, reckless, idiotic fool.

Don't trust me. Don't trust anyone who won't tell it to you straight. And down here? That's everyone. Got it?"

They flung the door open and vanished into the throne room beyond. The moss cushioned all sounds of their passage, but Jeth could tell they had left. He wasn't sure how he knew. He just did.

A flash of dark red hair in the depths of the throne room, far enough away that he was certain he and Shae hadn't been overheard, drew his attention. Eoghan arched a brow and tilted his head, a silent question.

Do you want me there?

Jeth turned his chair away, ignoring him entirely. He lifted a hand to his temple. The headache was back, and this time it throbbed in time with his heartbeat.

In his past, someone else told him who he could and couldn't trust. A woman named Burne Calder had taken him under her wing while they traveled with Aneirin. Shae's impassioned speech summoned her to Jeth's mind. He could see her weathered face and solemn expression, the tendrils of bright red hair escaping the tail tied at the nape of her neck. He could almost hear her voice, repeating the advice she'd given him when he was but a boy. His mother, Gleda, raised him human, but Burne Calder was probably why he held on to that humanity even now, after his faerie magic was triggered.

Strange how Shae's words summoned that face to mind. Strange how the changeling said not to trust anyone who didn't tell it straight—and told him straight that they couldn't be trusted.

A small, soft smile formed on his lips. He covered it with a curled finger to hide it from view, turning back to the window and the elegant meadow beyond.

He could trust Shae.

He knew it.

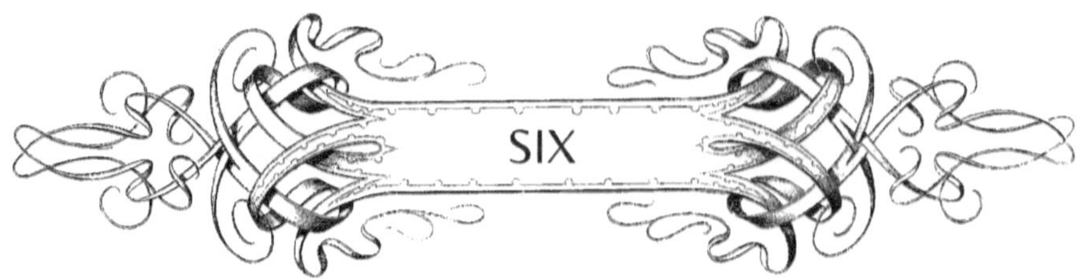

SIX

Jeth sat in the cushioned wooden scoop of a window seat in his bedchamber. The crown sat on a pillow beside his bed, far across the room, and he was glad for that. It was rare that he got to lower the mask, to be himself. It was rare enough that in the two moons since he'd come to this place; he had only ever felt safe enough to do so in the confines of this room.

He raked his fingers through his hair, scritching gently at his scalp. It felt so good to be able to, without that damn circlet in the way. The more he wore it, the more he felt as though the poison of Aneirin seeped into his very being. The whispers were almost constant now. It got bad enough that Jeth crammed the clay bottle into the back of a drawer and left it there, just to find peace.

The golden light in the cavern faded in time with the enchantment on his walls, growing dark as stars winked into life across his ceiling. Both were complicated magics that weeks of research hadn't puzzled out. He studied the glittering constellations with a frown.

No, stop. That's a problem for tomorrow.

For now, he had just changed out of a stiff tunic with piles of beading and embroidery weighing it down and a pair of trews that fit like a second skin. He traded them for soft, simple clothes he could sleep in, loose and comfortable—and blessedly plain. Loose silk pants in a sage green that flowed around his legs. A supple knit shirt with shortened sleeves, made of gray thread, its sleeves ending just below his elbow.

And nothing else. Thank the heavens. No sashes, no robes, no trains—and no crown.

A knock came at the door. Two raps, short and sharp.

"Come in, Shae."

Jeth turned away from the window as the door swung open. The changeling, dressed as casually as they always were, slipped inside. Their scowl was there as always, their lips pursed. The door swung shut behind them.

Arms folded over their chest, they glowered at Jeth.

"Hello," Jeth said at last, when it became clear that Shae wasn't going to talk first.

"What do you want, then? I told you to leave me alone."

"No, you told me I shouldn't trust you. Repeatedly." Jeth smiled faintly. "What were your exact words since you started avoiding me? Don't trust anyone who won't tell it to me straight?"

Shae snorted, looking anywhere but at Jeth.

"Tell me, Shae. Can you lie?" Jeth could, though it was more difficult every year as his faerie magic grew stronger.

A faint, triumphant smirk flickered across their face, smothered as quickly as it flared to life. "...faeries can't lie."

"And you're not entirely a faerie. Just like me." Jeth gestured at the cushion beside him. "Come sit."

"Why? Why me?" Shae asked as they crossed the room. They studied the massive window seat, set beneath the equally massive window. After a moment of thought, they settled into the scoop on the window's other side. The two of them were seated far enough apart that their hands couldn't touch if they stretched them out.

So why, then, did Jeth's heart pick up its pace? He studied Shae's face. Their cheeks were softly rounded, a uniquely human trait among the angled features of the faeries. Their lips were full, their nose just barely brushed with freckles.

"I told you, didn't I? I was born to a human mother," Jeth said.

"I was thinking about that. How many people down here know that?"

Jeth shrugged. "I don't know. I don't think any."

Shae nodded. "I thought so. You came out of nowhere, but you have the Blood. I think you should leave that little detail out, just...say you were raised elsewhere."

"Why?" Jeth asked, brow arched.

"Because if they think you're a full-blooded faerie, they won't try so hard. They'll still try, mind you, but they'll give up faster."

"Try what?"

"To kill you, of course. Or depose you. Take the crown. Drive you out. Maim you, perhaps." Shae mused over the options a little too calmly.

Jeth grimaced. "Of course it would be something like that."

"Just don't bring up a human parent. Humans aren't treated very well down here. I barely escaped that sort of thing, being a proper changeling."

"I haven't seen any humans down here."

Shae snorted, waving a hand to take in all of Jeth, from head to toe. "Because the most exalted and highest ranking faerie would see the lowly human slaves and pets."

Jeth frowned. *I knew humans wandered down here, but I thought they were lured to revels and then...*

Or maybe they never were released. He shifted uncomfortably where he sat.

"Just...say it, alright? You're from elsewhere. Aneirin left you in your mother's care on the other side of Hallanor. It's all true, right?"

"It is." Jeth sighed. "And it's true that I can still lie, but it's getting harder. The more I use faerie magic, the harder it gets. So the truth, however twisted? That's good."

"I thought so," Shae said smugly.

"Thank you. For your help."

"It's not help." The scowl was back on their face in a heartbeat.

"What is it, then?"

"It's...Well, it's..." A flush crept over their cheeks, their brow furrowing all the more.

Jeth laughed softly. "Thanks for your help," he repeated.

The flush on Shae's cheeks deepened. They looked out the window, glaring into the utter darkness of the cavern. A faint silvery moon glow filled Jeth's room, but it didn't reach the ink black darkness below. The soft sound of water filled the air. This time, the silence wasn't strained or awkward. It was contemplative, quiet, comfortable.

"What did you ask me here for?" Shae asked at last, voice hushed.

"I've decided I can trust you," Jeth said slowly, drawing a knee up and draping an arm over it, looking up at the stars on his ceiling again. "I need help. I need *your* help."

"Help with what?" Shae hedged, eyes narrowing.

"I'm here only to learn the magics I don't know. The most important thing I want to learn is how to make a faerie bargain. How to make the magic catch, the bargain stick."

Shae scoffed, turning back to the window. "Faerie bargains are traps. You must know that. Why would you want to learn something like that?"

"So I can make better bargains. So I can do better for the humans I bargain with. And so I can help break bargains, I hope, after I study the spell."

The changeling said nothing. They didn't take their gaze off the darkness below. Their scowl eased, a faintly wistful look flickering to life in their green eyes.

As green as the emerald above the throne.

"When I was young, my mother died," Jeth said slowly, studying Shae's face. "Aneirin came after me. I didn't know he was my father. He trapped me into a bargain with him, and introduced me to a woman. He had a bargain with her, too. Her name was Burne Calder, a merchant. You remind me of her."

Shae turned toward him, a brow raised. "I do? How so?"

Jeth laughed. "You both have tongues sharp as daggers and a deep sense of honor."

Shae blushed, tearing their gaze away with another scoff, this time to take in the flower-dotted meadow of the bedchamber. Jeth saw their lips, however, turned up ever so slightly at the corners in the faintest of smiles.

Jeth smiled, too. He turned back to the sky, missing true night as much as he missed the sun itself. No breeze tickled over his cheeks. The air didn't cool. It was just what it was—an illusion.

"Burne Calder told me to be careful with my bargains. She wasn't so lucky with her own. She didn't know she was bargaining for me, for my capture. I was just a boy. In the end, she couldn't do anything to stop Aneirin when he took me. It was her end of the bargain—to help him find what he wanted, what was stolen from him."

"You," Shae echoed.

"Yes. Me. His son, stolen away by the human woman who so charmed him with her defiance." Jeth sighed, looking down at his hands. "I barely escaped him, and only because of her."

The jar loomed in the forefront of his mind, and his gaze was drawn to the drawer he had stuffed it in. Aneirin wasn't speaking, but his presence loomed, his fury becoming a rising tension that filled the room like smoke.

No one noticed whether he wore it or not. He was glad for that, glad that no one came to find it or investigate.

"So you want to learn a faerie bargain to be like him? Your father?"

"No. I want to learn to make them for Burne Calder and my mother. I want humans to have a chance. I want to use my humanity for something more. I want to use it to help the people I choose, not the people I was forced to become." He pointed up at the ceiling. Beyond, above the cavern, in the open air, was the kingdom of Hallanor. He'd grown up in a nameless village at the border, and crossed back and forth across it a dozen times. In just six years, he came to love it as deeply as he'd loved his mother.

Shae laughed bitterly, startling Jeth out of his thoughts. "You want to learn to make good faerie bargains? You'll get humans in trouble that way, you realize. No? Well, picture this. Humans start spreading the story of good faerie bargains. Suddenly, all a faerie has to do to trick a human into one...is pretend to be you. You might as well set the traps yourself. It will save time."

Heat bloomed across Jeth's cheeks. "I hadn't thought of that."

"Obviously." Shae folded their arms over their chest, one foot swinging as they studied him. "Tch. You're an altruistic fool. I'm sure I've said that to you before."

"*I'm* sure you'll say it again."

Shae fought a smile. "Probably."

Jeth sighed. "Well, I still want to learn. If I know the spell, perhaps I can still learn how to break them."

"You can't do that, and it won't stop faeries from making bargains. How many people can you reach in their lifetime, before the deals go sour?"

Jeth frowned. "I have to try."

"You might as well ask the sky to trade places with the sea." Shae snorted out a laugh. "You can't stop them, not without the Moot Crown."

Jeth's gaze fixed on Shae, sharp and curious. "The Moot Crown?" He kept his voice light, idly curious.

Shae's laughter stopped abruptly. Their shoulders hunched up toward their ears. They stared at him, eyes wide. "No. No way. You have no idea what that thing means. I'm not saying another word."

"Tell me. Please. What is the Moot Crown?"

Shae squirmed in their seat. "Well, it's the...it's the crown of the highest of faerie rulers. The crown of the Ruler of faerie rulers."

"And?" Jeth pressed, sensing there was more to it.

Shae hesitated, then sighed. "It has the power to give commands to all faerie-kind. If you're wearing it and you speak a command in the court of a faerie, in the hearing of a faerie, all creatures must obey."

"Must?"

"It's deep magic, old as the earth itself, almost. It was meant to keep the courts from warring with one another."

"How did you even learn all this?" Jeth asked, leaning forward curiously.

Shae stood, pacing quietly back and forth. Plain gold rings encircled their fingers, and they twisted them anxiously as they walked.

"Shae?"

"I know, I know. I learned about it. I've been reading every book I can get my hands on, including the ones in your study. I know I wasn't supposed to, but Aneirin was gone, and no one was going in there, and information is power, and I...I just didn't want to be powerless anymore."

Jeth's expression softened. He knew that feeling inside and out. It summoned up a black stretch of nothing and a deep sense of grief even thinking about it. He stood, reaching out to grasp Shae's arm, stopping them as they passed.

"I understand."

"You don't," Shae said bitterly. "When I read about it, I thought I could get ahold of it. I thought, if I could win, I could..."

"Could?" Jeth urged.

"Could leave this place." They sighed. "I want to go back to the world above. I know it won't be the same, but it would be better than here. It has to be better than here."

Jeth lifted his gaze to the ceiling. If he ached for the sun after just a few moons, he couldn't imagine how desperate he would be after hundreds of years. He missed the sun, the moon, the breeze. He missed the barely controlled chaos of towns and villages, the open kindness most humans offered one another, the twitter of birdsong and the chirrup of crickets.

I can do something about this.

"I can free you, if you want." He lowered his gaze. "No catch. Right now."

Shae was as stunned as if Jeth had slapped them, their lips parted and eyes wide. Shock was replaced with an intent, hungry gaze, as if Shae were a person starved. "I do."

Jeth turned toward the crown on its cushion, only for slim fingers to close around his wrist, stopping him short.

"I do, but not until I earn it. A trade. A bargain."

"I can't even cast that spell."

"Not a formal one. One we build on...trust."

The word on its own meant little. Down here, however? Down here where they were two people in hiding in a sea of monsters? Down here, it meant everything.

Jeth smiled. "Alright. A bargain of trust, pure and simple."

"You have magic. Strong magic?"

Jeth cleared his throat and shrugged. He used his magic often to prove he had it. In his persona, he used it as part of his aloof and lazy facade. "Yes."

No one down here knew exactly how strong, how the tingle and surge of golden power lingered always at the edge of his senses. How every inch of magic he drew in was doubled and tripled by the focus he'd absorbed. How his power, born of two worlds, was twice as strong even before that.

"You can win the Moot Crown," Shae said urgently, grasping both of Jeth's shoulders—and then quickly drawing back as if their hands had been burned. "It requires a magical duel, a battle of wits and power. You have to challenge the current ruler, the High Queen." They ran their tongue over their lips. "Once you command the faeries to leave the humans alone, then...*then* I can leave."

"We," Jeth corrected. "We can leave."

"What?" Shae's brow furrowed. "But you're..."

"I didn't come down here for the throne or the crown. I didn't even know about the High Throne and its power. I came down here to learn how to protect the people I care about. I'll leave, too, once that's done. I can go with you, Shae, help you navigate the world above until you're ready to go on your own."

I hope that takes a while.

Jeth smothered that thought quickly, watching Shae's face flicker through a dozen emotions in a matter of seconds. In the end, they settled on a slow, soft smile. Color crept over their cheeks and up toward their pointed ear-tips.

"Okay," they said at last. "I can agree to that."

"So my end of the bargain is to free you, and teach you. And yours is –"

"To summon the Moot."

Jeth took a deep breath. "How many are there?"

"You mean courts? There are eight courts besides the High Court. Blackthorn Court is one of the oldest."

"Eight others and ourselves?" Jeth grimaced. "Nine. How do I summon them, then? Do I just declare I want to fight for the Moot Crown?"

"No, that's too obvious. But don't worry, it won't be hard." Shae turned, sweeping their arm toward the crown on its cushion, the gold, black, and crystal gleaming softly in the silver light. "After all, you haven't had a coronation party. Yet."

SEVEN

The fabric of Jeth's elaborate tunic weighed on his shoulders like a yoke, threatening to topple him if he stepped wrong. Blue cloth picked out with black and gold thread hung over his shoulders. It was something between a cloak and a robe, belted at his waist over the fine white shirt, embroidered with white thread in a subtle pattern of thorn-laden vines. The crown sat atop his golden hair. His fingers were adorned with gold rings with black stones that glittered every time his hands moved. He paced the dais before his throne, staring up at the flickering emerald overhead.

The soft scuff of a foot behind him made him pause. He closed his eyes, listening.

There, there it is again.

He knew that step.

"Hello, Shae."

"You always know it's me, and damned if I know how." Shae stood at the bottom of the dais, an apple in each hand. They tossed one.

Jeth caught it, running a thumb over the smooth red skin. "Just a guess. Now it's time to plan." He took a bite.

Another week had passed. Jeth was losing track of how much time he spent beneath the ground. He'd sorted out the goblins and the trolls, a clash between the undine and the selkies, handled the kelpies and their brief and unsupported rebellion, and more. He told himself it would all be worth it—*if* this worked.

At least there are no more threats against my crown.

No more today, came the whisper-faint sneer of Aneirin's voice.

Jeth closed his eyes and took a deep breath. What mattered was that he had things under control. He felt certain he could make it to his coronation date in one piece.

That meant it was time to plan the party.

"I can't believe we're actually doing this," Shae muttered, scanning the throne room.

Jeth watched them for a moment, studying the slope of their jaw, the bridge of their nose, the way a single curl coiled over one of their pointed ears. He wanted to reach out and tuck it back into place with the rest of his hair. He took a deep breath.

"I'll release you from the court before the coronation, so if things get out of hand afterward, if I..."

Shae wrinkled their nose and shrugged one shoulder. "At least there's only a slight chance you'll die?" they offered.

"Very reassuring," Jeth said dryly.

A flash of red hair showed between the trees. A moment later, a resplendent brown robe embroidered with gold caught the light. Eoghan came up the center aisle as if he were the king, not Jeth. His gaze swept over crowds that weren't even there.

Jeth lapsed into silence, shoulders square and chin lifted, every inch the perfectly regal prince. Shae glanced back, and at the sight of Eoghan, their shoulders tensed, creeping up toward their ears. It was a posture Jeth should have recognized sooner.

They have a history.

A pang of jealousy and a wave of concern and sympathy ran through Jeth in moments. Had the newly arrived Shae kissed Eoghan when they first came to court and found themselves enchanted until their change was far enough along to protect them? Had Eoghan toyed with Shae, never quite giving them what they wanted and delighting in the power struggle? There were dozens of possibilities.

And I never asked...

Eoghan stopped at the foot of the dais and bowed, barely tipping at the waist. Jeth bit into his apple, the crisp crackle of the soft yellow flesh splitting apart the only sound. He chewed as he observed the Gean-Cánach without a word. Only after he swallowed did he speak.

"Eoghan," he said simply.

"Sire. May I ask what you and your little...pet," he said, eyes sweeping over Shae dismissively, "are doing here at this time of day?" He turned back to Jeth, a brow arched.

Jeth studied the half eaten apple in his hands. "I want to throw a party."

At that, Eoghan's face lit up in earnest. He smiled, his teeth just a hair too sharp and white. His eyes glittered with the possibilities.

"A party, is it? I love parties."

"Yes. A coronation gala, to be precise. I want to open the doors to our neighbor courts as well. No expense is to be spared. No detail overlooked. Knowing this, who do I assign to the preparations?" Jeth knew what the answer would be.

Eoghan set one foot on the lowest step of the dais, leaning forward like a hound straining at their tether. "Me, your Majesty. I throw the best ones. Everyone knows it," he said pointedly, turning to look at Shae.

Shae grimaced. Reluctantly, with a sigh and a roll of their eyes, they nodded. "It's true, he does."

Jeth took a deep breath. "Very well. I want this to be on everyone's mind for the next thousand years. Am I clear, Eoghan?"

"Crystalline, sire. I can manage that easily, though it will take a few weeks. I'll need to–"

"I don't care. Summon my tailor and send him to my chambers. I want something new to wear for the affair."

"Of course, of course," Eoghan said, rubbing his hands together with a faint rasping sound, like smooth wood grinding against itself. "And do I have free rein to do as I wish?"

Jeth paused, holding up a finger. "You can do as you wish *for the party*, and within reason. I'll not have you taking the ceiling off the throne room or some such."

Eoghan's eyes gleamed as his subterfuge was caught, bowing deeper this time. "As you say. And who shall I run everything by? I can come to you personally, if you wish..."

"I can help there, my king. I'm told I'm far too reasonable," Shae said, glowering faintly at Eoghan.

"Of course you can," Eoghan hissed, acid in every word. "You're such a stick in the mud that you never let anyone have any fun. Trust me, sire. Let me take things right for you. Let us work together." His voice smoothed as he turned to Jeth, looking up at him through his lashes.

"You'll work together," Jeth said firmly, feeling his skin crawl beneath Eoghan's intent gaze. He felt like a rabbit in the eye of a hawk. The man was determined to get at him.

Did the faerie know what Jeth and Shae were planning? He must have suspected something. Even as he bowed again, his smile turned sinister. His eyes never left Jeth's face.

"As you command." He turned, clapping his hands. "The servants, get the servants in here! We need lanterns, ribbon—who can go speak to the nixies?"

A sudden flurry of activity had people coming out of various hidden corridors and doorways in the walls. Jeth watched idly as a troll was summoned to hang the lanterns in the ceiling above. A pixie messenger was dispatched to ask the nixies—who glowed, unlike their smaller droning cousins—to flitter in the branches overhead. A handful of elves discussed the floor and what they could get the green faeries to grow there.

...and then his gaze swept over a cluster of humans approaching Eoghan with their heads bowed and shoulders hunched. They were dressed in rags, or dressed like dolls, with no in between. Several had bruises on their faces. All of them had expressions that swung between fear and a dazed lassitude, between wariness and enchantment. Many bore heavy collars. One had a collar with a cowbell on it that clanked with every startled jerk. A few others were hobbled, wearing manacles around their ankles and chains long enough for only a shuffling step.

Eoghan looked them over with clear disgust. "Get to work on polishing, and some of you go down and get the thrones for the other courts. Bring them up. You –"

As the humans turned, Eoghan shifted a foot to step on the hobble-chain of a young man, and he fell to his hands and knees. He looked back, swallowing. "Sir?"

Eoghan bent down and cupped the man's cheek, kissing him softly.

Jeth tensed, nails biting into the apple he held forgotten in one hand.

The young man's face smoothed. He leaned eagerly into the kiss. When Eoghan stepped back, the human gave him a fawning, wide-eyed look.

"Keep me company while I work, yes? You're a pretty thing."

The human blushed and beamed, standing beside Eoghan. Nothing else in the room seemed to exist. The other humans, small as their numbers were, all but fled.

Jeth was struggling to breathe.

Shae cleared their throat pointedly. "Perhaps we might get a head start on the menu, your Majesty?" They swept their arm toward a corridor.

"Yes. Yes, that will do until the tailor arrives," Jeth said hollowly. He swept down the stairs, tearing his gaze from the doting human and Eoghan's smug smirk.

Changeling and king walked in silence until they were well and truly alone in a sweeping curve of the corridor.

"He just…"

"I know."

"And the rest–"

"They're treated like pets, or serfs. They're dispensable toys either way."

Jeth's jaw worked.

"I thought he was going to catch on to us," Shae said, letting out a relieved sigh.

"But those people–"

"Your Majesty, the best way you can help them is to get that crown. The plan doesn't change." Shae stopped him with an outstretched hand. "You have to hold on."

Jeth rubbed a brow. His crown felt heavy again. "You're right. Let's hope the party planning distracts everyone enough to spare the humans their attentions." He stared back up the hallway, worried about the young man Eoghan had enchanted. A few weeks might be enough for the faerie to lose interest, and when a Gean-Cánach lost interest? Their human lovers wasted away.

But Shae is right. There's no way to do this any faster.

For a moment, they stood in silence. Shae ran their hand gently down his arm, raising goosebumps in its wake. When their hands met, their fingers intertwined with his.

"I can tell you one thing," Shae said slowly, looking the same direction as their king. "Whatever else this party does, it's going to turn the entire court on its head. Either you win or you lose…and then…"

Jeth's gaze hardened. "That's the plan."

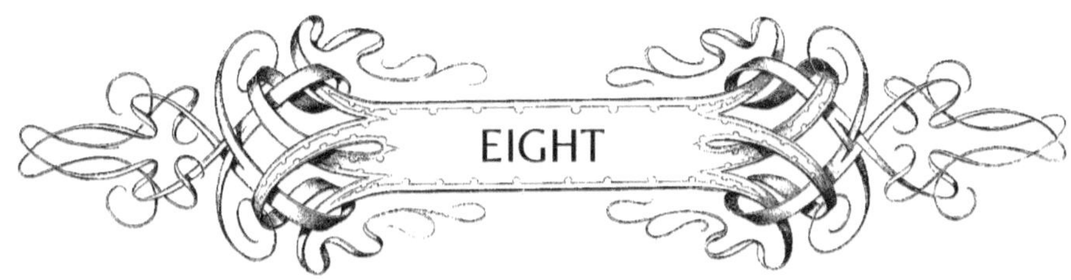

EIGHT

Jeth's hands curled around the railing of a low balcony until his knuckles were white, though the rest of his posture was carefully relaxed. He could see most of the keep from here, including three of the pleasure gardens—each one bespelled to grow and flourish, tended to by green faeries who lived among the plants.

Someone was throwing a small gathering, an elegant tea affair of some sort, in the flower garden. The bright, gauzy clothes of the faeries came in as many colors as the blooms around them, each trying to out-do the next.

The thin, dazed, and dirty forms of humans made their way through the crowd with food and drink. Jeth watched as a faerie stopped a young woman, whispering softly in her ear. She smiled. Her eyes grew glassy, but she simply stepped away to return to her task.

Bespelled just to serve tea cakes, he thought, disgusted.

She wasn't the only one being targeted. It seemed the humans lay mostly beneath their captors' notice, but when they *were* seen, they were toyed with.

There was a buildup of tension in the air. Jeth ground his teeth, gripping the railing to keep himself from storming out of his castle and down to the gardens. He could demand every human servant be given to him. He could free them one by one.

But that was rash, and they would all be free in three days. The coronation was so close.

A chime of dainty laughter carried up to him. A human crumpled like a dropped towel at the feet of a handsome elf. The young man was on his knees, prostrating himself, hands clasped together as he pleaded. He begged, his face twisted in misery—for what, Jeth couldn't hear.

The elf looked at the dryad beside him, a beautiful woman with long green hair and clothes like gossamer. He asked her something. With a shrug, she gestured toward a doorway into the keep. Her lips moved.

The elf knelt, whispering something to the young man groveling before him, and then swept toward that door.

The young man followed, face brimming with joy, his smile wide and his entire bearing eager.

Too eager. Jeth's frown deepened. Whatever was about to happen, it wasn't genuine. The young man was bewitched. A pang of guilt twanged in his chest, followed by a rising fury. He had to wait. Wait! It was the worst feeling in the world to stand there and do nothing, knowing he could, if he wanted to. Knowing he would, if time would just move faster.

The urge to march down to the garden and save that young man rose like the bile in the back of his throat, acidic and urgent. If he couldn't stop this now, why was he here? His entire purpose had been to help humanity.

And yet here you are, watching them fall, Aneirin whispered.

Jeth scowled. He didn't even have the damn bottle on him, and his father's voice was growing stronger.

I am just one man against an army of monsters. All of them were as far from human as they could get. Did faeries even have morals, or did they only possess the perverse need to trail from one pleasure to another? They flitted from joy to joy like demented butterflies.

Jeth's nerves frayed strand by strand, the last little threads barely hanging together. Three. More. Days. He could last three more days, couldn't he?

In three days, he would either have the Moot Crown upon his head, or he'd be exiled. Either way, it would be the end of this.

"Your Majesty?" Eoghan said gently, his voice as syrup sweet as ever.

Jeth forced his grip to relax before he turned to look at the Gean-Cánach. He leaned back against the rail, folding his arms over his chest, the perfect picture of boredom. "What is it?"

"Guests will begin to arrive on the morrow. I know you wanted them hosted here. Perhaps you'd like to inspect the preparations? I've been trying to find Shae to finalize everything, as you commanded, but..."

Jeth pushed off the railing, waving a hand idly. "You handle it, Eoghan. You're much better at all this than Shae is, anyway. I can trust *you* to do a good job."

In reality, Shae was preparing for after. Jeth didn't want Eoghan to find them. After the party, no matter what else happened, Jeth and Shae were leaving. Somewhere in the keep, Shae was packing bags with essentials, checking routes out of the cavern and tunnels, and bribing or blackmailing the faeries that would stand between the two of them and their freedom to clear the way—all without anyone the wiser to their plan.

To say it was a delicate dance was an understatement.

Jeth swept toward the open double doors and the corridor beyond. Eoghan moved, appearing suddenly before him. The faerie looked down at him, lips faintly parted. A hand came up to Jeth's waist as he instinctively recoiled, and he found himself pressed against the glass door.

Eoghan's lips curled up in a smile as he gave Jeth a heated look, his long red hair falling over his shoulder as he leaned down, separating them from the outside world like a curtain. "You've finally come to trust me, haven't you?"

Jeth's heart skipped a beat, but not out of the desire the faerie was attempting to kindle. Out of unease. His mask threatened to slip, his stomach twisting. He put a hand on Eoghan's chest. The cloying smell of wood and flowers filled the air between them.

Calm, stay calm.

"You prove yourself to me more with every day," he said carefully, coldly.

Eoghan cupped Jeth's cheek, a thumb running gently over his skin. He leaned in.

Their lips met, and Jeth felt the surge of magic, stronger than the other spells the faeries had tried to cast, envelop him. It searched his protections, hunting for a weak spot, a place to dig in despite his faerie blood. Jeth returned the kiss, his own power thrumming beneath his skin, ready to fight back if the spell caught.

But it didn't. It slipped away, and Jeth's relief was enough to make his knees weak. The kiss ended when they were both breathless.

Eoghan leaned in, murmuring softly in Jeth's ear. "Perhaps we could discuss that trust more...in depth? In private."

Jeth's mouth went dry. Slowly, he lifted his hand to cover Eoghan's, studying the Gean-Cánach idly. His mind was screaming to run, to push him away, to *do* something. He kept his expression idle, tongue running over his lips thoughtfully as he ignored his instincts.

"Why don't you come to my rooms after the fete? We'll have all the time in the world then to...speak."

Two could play at this game. Eoghan wouldn't find him in those rooms that night, or any night thereafter. It was the best he could do to protect himself. He knew Eoghan wanted power, wanted control. The coy, triumphant smile that bloomed on his handsome face was proof enough of that. He thought he'd won. He thought he had Jeth at his mercy, wrapped around his finger.

As if party planning were enough to win Jeth over.

Jeth felt disgusting. He wanted a bath, and he wanted it yesterday. "I'll see the rooms in the morning. I have a fitting this afternoon. Besides, knowing you as well as I do now, I can tell you've done a good job. You'll impress me, won't you, Eoghan?"

"Of course, your Majesty," Eoghan said gently, brushing his fingers over Jeth's jaw and down his neck.

"After breakfast, then?" Jeth ducked under the faerie's arm, smoothing his silk tunic and straightening his shoulders.

"I'll be there." Eoghan's head tipped to one side, his smile warm as honey in the summer sun.

Bile coated Jeth's tongue. He swept into the hall and made his way to the one place where people would leave him alone.

Every day, it was harder to breathe beneath the mask he donned. Every day, he felt the faerie king chip away another piece of the witch's son. He knew who he wanted to be, and he was fighting that person, poisoning him. He couldn't do this much longer. Three days would be the outermost edge of his limit.

It had to be.

He raced to his bedroom, closing the door behind him with a thud. He pressed his back against it with his eyes closed, listening to the babble of the water, inhaling the scent of earth and flowers and clean air.

"Are you alright?"

Jeth's eyes flew open, fixing on Shae. The changeling stood before the wardrobe, a small stack of fine clothes in their hands, neatly folded. A bag sat at their feet, half full at best. They bent, slowly tucking the clothes inside without taking their gaze off his face.

"I'm...I'm fine," he said harshly, striding across the room to sit on the edge of his bed.

"You know, just because you can lie doesn't mean you should, especially when you aren't any good at it," Shae muttered. A drawer slid closed with a firm clunk.

"I heard that."

"You were meant to."

Jeth couldn't help the small smile that crossed his face, chasing away some of the oily feel on his skin, the taint that Eoghan left behind. It faded as fast as it came.

"Shae, I'm not sure how much longer I can play this part."

"These bags will be waiting for us on the surface. I'll move them out tonight, or first thing in the morning."

Their light footsteps on the floor were all the warning Jeth had that they were coming. The scent of cloves mingled with that of flowers, earth, and water as the changeling sat beside him, the sinking mattress pushing them both closer together.

"Your Majesty," the changeling began.

"Jeth, please."

"...Jeth," Shae said softly, looking away and clearing their throat. They lay their hand over his. "Things like this get harder when there's an end in sight."

His fingers laced with Shae's, his gaze studying the way they twined together. It felt comfortable. It felt natural. It felt *good.*

"Why is that?" Jeth asked suddenly. "Why does it get harder?"

"Because you can see the other side of things. Because you know all the horrible things will end, and you are *so close* to after. Later. Whenever." Shae waved their free hand idly.

"Eoghan kissed me," Jeth confessed.

Shae's grip tightened. Their voice shook faintly, though when they spoke it was with mild curiosity. "Did you like it?"

"*No,*" he said firmly, harshly. "Not even for a moment."

The changeling's grip relaxed.

"It was so hard not to push him away. I was afraid that if he kissed me..."

"He'd ensnare you. He did that to me, when I first arrived."

I knew it. Jeth frowned, a fresh surge of dislike sparking to life. *That damn bastard.*

"But when I stopped...being human...the enchantment just faded away. I got lucky. Others haven't. And even with all that happened, all that he did, I'd go through it again to be who I was."

Jeth turned, studying Shae. The changeling dressed plainly, though their clothes were still made of silks. They weren't prone to gauzy, delicate things or flashy, bright robes. The only jewelry they wore was the rings on their fingers, which they twisted whenever they were anxious. Apart from the pointed ears poking out of their hair, they could almost pass for a human.

Slowly, he lifted a hand to his own head, brushing over the antlers growing there. They had gotten longer, and a new tine was starting. Jeth dropped his hand with a sigh.

"Neither of us will ever be human again."

Shae cupped his cheek, a gesture that echoed what Eoghan had done earlier. But where Eoghan's touch inspired unease and disgust, Shae's sent a small electric shock through him, warming him from head to toe in a single second. The smell of cloves grew stronger as Shae leaned in.

"That doesn't mean we've lost our humanity."

Jeth closed the distance between them, pressing his lips to the changeling's. That one perfect, heated kiss turned into two, and then he lost count. Shae leaned back, a hand on Jeth's neck guiding him over them.

For a while, there was nothing else to think about. The brush of skin against skin, the taste of nectar-sweet lips, the soft sound of them murmuring one another's names. The sounds Shae made sent thrills through Jeth, spurring him to move faster. Their bodies fit together as though they were made to.

And when they finished and Jeth rolled onto his back, panting, Shae shifted to lie against his chest, and his arm fit perfectly around their shoulders.

Content silence filled the air. Shae drowsed against him, and Jeth studied the flowers and vines overhead. One by one, his thoughts came creeping back in. A flicker of uncertainty crossed his features, a crack in his composure.

"Shae?"

"Mm?"

"I have a bad feeling about this," he confessed.

"Good. You should." Shae propped themself up on an elbow, frowning. "This is a crazy idea. You say you have powerful magic, but you haven't had a chance to let it loose. You can't even practice, not with so many eyes on you."

For a moment, they were both silent. Shae's hand rested on Jeth's chest, fingers playing slowly over his skin. Jeth frowned. It was true, he hadn't channeled the full brunt of his power in a very long time. Not since...

Not since me, Aneirin murmured, sly and cold.

He hadn't tested his power after that, either, not to the extent of what the faerie focus he'd absorbed could hold. He hadn't had to. Until now.

"Jeth," Shae said softly, drawing his attention with two fingers on his jaw. "Someone has to say this. Someone has to give you the choice. You don't have to do this. You can leave. We can just *leave*. To be completely honest, that's exactly what we should do."

Jeth caught Shae's hand in his own, bringing their palm to his lips, kissing it gently. He met the changeling's eyes. They both knew he wasn't going anywhere. He couldn't abandon the others. Instead, he looked at the only person in the whole damn Court that he could trust, and spoke the truth.

"I'm scared, too."

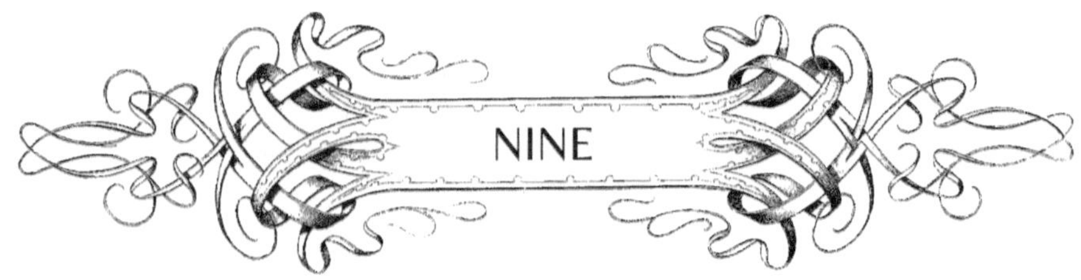

NINE

If there was anything the faeries did well, it was parties. The coronation itself had been grand, but the fete afterward was where Eoghan truly shone. The festivities were in full swing. Musicians played on either end of the room, swapping back and forth between slower songs and dancing reels, and far enough apart that the sound didn't overlap. Jeth suspected there was magic involved in that.

Nixies glowed like rainbow fireflies as they floated through the false branches and leaves above, each a different color. Lanterns glowed. The doors to the courtyard were thrown open, and herbs had been thrown into the bonfire's flames that made it flare in blue and green and red in turns.

In the gardens, Jeth knew, there were single musicians playing soft, soothing music and faeries indulging in more physical pursuits. But here, in the throne room, everyone spoke, laughed, and cavorted until there was a musical cacophony filling the air.

Jeth sat on a newly erected raised platform on his dais, his throne and one other elevated above the rest. The other massive throne was for the Moot Queen, Orla. She was more beautiful than she'd been described. The elven woman was tall and slim, with long silver hair that gleamed like moonlight when she moved. Her eyes were pitch black, but the way they caught and reflected the light made them look like they were studded with stars, as if the very heavens themselves were in her gaze. They were framed by long pale lashes that brushed her cheeks whenever she lowered her gaze. Her gown was made of spider silk, gossamer thin and with a faint iridescence to it that captured the eye. The neckline plunged to her navel, and the back had a high collar that stood against her neck. Her jewelry was all silver and diamonds, glittering like frost.

Atop her hair sat Jeth's goal. The Moot Crown. It was a single piece of crystal, curved into an oval. Points and clusters alternated, uneven but beautiful in their flaws. A ring of gold had been poured around the bottom of it to create the perfect fit, with the texture of stone pressed into the metal. Even from a distance away, he felt it hum with power.

It reminded him of the faerie focus his mother once held, the one he absorbed. Every trickle of power put into it doubled or tripled.

Queen Orla drummed her fingers on the arm of her large throne, fashioned from crystals polished until they looked like ice. Otherwise, she showed no sign of approval on her sharp features—or disapproval.

On either side, their shared dais was flanked by more thrones. Each held one of the kings or queens of faerie upon it, the glittering spread of crowns catching the lamplight as they turned and spoke to one another.

Jeth's heart hammered in his chest. He lounged indulgently on his seat, half bored by all appearances, but inside he was ready to scream. He knew he was a spy amongst the enemy, the rabbit amongst the hawks. Outwardly, however, he looked just like them.

He was *resplendent.* His robes, tailored just for this occasion, ended just above the knee. It was a rich blue, his favorite, and a color that matched a coat his mother made him once when he was a boy. Gold trim and delicate beads of mother-of-pearl were woven together to look like moonflowers on their vines. Beneath that was a gold silk shirt. The trousers tucked into his black boots were also black, tying everything together with his thorn-wrapped crown.

To add to his brooding and idle persona, he'd lined his eyes with kohl. A lotion rubbed into his skin made the gold dusting all the more radiant. The gleam of his clothes and his flesh caught the light whenever he moved. He was the only faerie with skin like that, so far as he could see.

Yes, Jeth was every inch the equal of his fellow sovereigns, as far as appearances went. If only they had *anything* else in common.

Creatures great and small gamboled and danced among the tree trunk pillars, engaged in a spirited reel that sent fabric swirling everywhere he looked. He'd never been to a faerie revel, but this one more than matched the stories of them he'd heard growing up.

I have to admit it, Jeth thought grudgingly. *Eoghan has talent.*

The dance at this end of the hall ended, and another began on the far side. The crowd before them surged toward the new song, fanatically eager to celebrate until they dropped.

"Is it time, High Queen Orla?"

Jeth's attention drifted to King Kiniveth, a frost faerie from a remote mountain near the edge of Hallanor. He built an entire city for faeries on the icy, unforgiving slopes, and had a reputation for collecting humans in a menagerie if they were foolish enough to wander too close. He fought his distaste for the man.

"I believe it may be, yes." Queen Orla lifted a hand festooned with silver rings, gesturing at her companions. "King Jeth of Blackthorn. Now that you are officially one of us, we find ourselves back at full strength for the first time in some years."

Jeth lifted a brow, leaning on the arm of his chair, a finger curved over his lips. He said nothing. His heart stuttered beneath his ribs.

I have a bad feeling about this.

You should, whispered the distant, gleeful voice of Aneirin.

"Before your sire left this place, he was part of a grand plan. We were all working together, which is quite a feat." Orla laughed, a dainty sound like bells.

Jeth snorted. "I can imagine."

Faeries didn't like or trust one another at the best of times.

"This plan will benefit all of us," Queen Periphea said, studying her nails. They glittered with real gold dust that accented her beautiful bark-brown skin and elegant cloud of curled green hair. She was a dryad from the south. Her lands were partly in Hallanor, and partly across the border.

"Long ago," Queen Orla continued smoothly, "when this kingdom was founded, the High King of all faerie fell in love with the first daughter of the first king." She rubbed idly at the curved arm of her throne. "They lay together, and a child was born."

Jeth felt a chill creep up his spine and out toward his fingertips. "Oh?"

"Yes. And now the most recent of the human queens has passed her throne on to another. A daughter."

"A shadow of our beauty, our power, and our grace," sneered Queen Cirsa, who lived on an island men thought was a mirage, protected by vibrant reefs from most intrusions.

"And a sham of a ruler." This came from King Lorcan, whose own underground kingdom in the west lay in another kingdom entirely.

"Once, your realm was part of ours in every aspect," King Kiniveth drawled over the rim of his wineglass. "Now the border has shrunk and left you stranded."

"If we went by mere human borders, perhaps, but we do not," Lorcan snapped.

The air noticeably chilled around King Kiniveth, frost creeping over the arms of his chair.

Jeth cleared his throat, staring at both kings with a single raised brow. The dancers whirled in the distance, the music played, and both men settled back in their seats with faint frowns.

Silence reigned over the dais—but the air warmed.

"My apologies, King Jeth," King Lorcan said at last. The man was not handsome, being half troll, but he was built broad and tall. He was the largest of those on the dais by a full head.

Jeth waved a hand idly, dismissing the incident. "What does a previous lineage with faerie have to do with the new queen?"

"Simple," High Queen Orla said, leaning back in her seat to bask in the light of the lanterns and nixies overhead. "There is a chance that I can command her, if I can get close enough. If she has but one drop of faerie blood, she will answer to the Moot Crown the same as all others."

Jeth muffled the shock that ran through him in a jolt, ensuring all that showed on his features was a lift of both brows. He turned to look at his most esteemed guest. "If that is true, you wield a mighty and terrible power, indeed. Why have you not yet moved?"

"Because when we take the kingdom over, there shall be a bit of turmoil. As faeries reclaim their lands, the humans shall be displaced. We wish to be ready to move all at once, so they may not mount a resistance," Queen Periphea said, words sharp with savage glee.

His stomach twisted in a knot. "My father mentioned he, too, wanted to move against the human queen. On his own." He kept his voice light, feigning boredom.

"This is true. And how did it work out for him?" Kiniveth laughed. "He went above to marry a royal and fell for a common woman instead. At least he sired you before he went. A right proper faerie child."

Jeth nodded his head in acknowledgement. His antler tines, capped in gold, gleamed. He turned his attention back to the party. "Still, he didn't have to leave me with the woman. The bastard."

Forgive me, Mother, he thought, the words bitter in his mouth. He had a part to play, damn it!

"You are returned to us. The mistake is corrected." Queen Cirsa waved a hand fluidly through the air. The sea glass bangles around her wrists rattled with the motion. Her pale, blue-tinged skin was the only way to tell she was a nymph.

"As we are all gathered here, I should like to call a meeting of the Moot Court on the morrow." The High Queen's voice was calm, careless. The heartless faerie could have been talking about a trip to the market rather than a plan to displace an entire kingdom and ruin countless lives.

Finally, Jeth's eyes caught what he was looking for. A single dark-clothed speck in among the rainbow of hues, eyes fixed on his. A single point of stillness in the sea of movement. A single nod of the head. Shae had done everything they could.

It was time.

"A meeting to discuss this coup of the human lands?"

"Yes, and reclaim what was ours, what was always ours!" Kiniveth said eagerly, leaning forward. There was a manic gleam in his pale gray eyes.

"Then, no."

Shae vanished into the crowd as every head on the dais turned toward Jeth. They retreated quickly to a safe spot beside a pillar. They knew what came next.

"No?" High Queen Orla repeated, sitting up in her seat, her voice as frigid as the air around Kiniveth. She fixed Jeth with a glare. "I showed kindness in making it a request, King Jeth. Do not make me command you."

"Your command holds no power over one who challenges you for your crown," Jeth said, outwardly as calm and bored as ever. Inwardly, his heart banged against his ribs like a drum. "Which I do."

He may as well have projected the words with magic. The music ended abruptly, a ripple of silence racing away from them. The dancers stilled like so many birds alighting on the ground. All eyes turned toward the dais at the head of the throne room.

Jeth pushed to his feet. A touch of his power was all it took to set his voice reverberating through the entire cavern of the Blackthorn Court.

"I challenge you, High Queen Orla."

Thank heavens my voice didn't shake. His legs certainly did.

"What?" The word was clipped and sharp. Slow as a hunting cat, she rose beside him. "What did you say?"

"I challenge you for the Moot Crown."

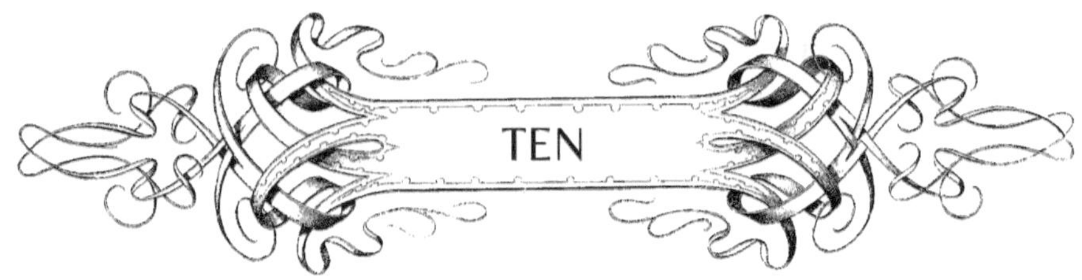

TEN

The silence was deafening after the din of the music and revelers.

I've done it. I've said it.

Jeth was enveloped in a wave of calm. The mask could come down. No longer did he have to wonder what his father would do. He could shed the stifling persona of the careless faerie prince for what he really was.

Everything around him sharpened to a razor's focus. Though his heart was racing, he felt confident. This was what he was here for, now. This was his purpose.

The people of Hallanor would be safe if he had anything to do with it.

High Queen Orla flicked her hand toward the crowd. Faeries scattered, retreating toward the walls. Some were pushed away by her magic, sliding across the floor with startled shouts. Pixies went flying. Once they cleared away, she swept down the steps of the dais, her long train spreading behind her. She stopped in the dead center of the throne room, then turned to face him. Slowly, she lifted a hand to brush over the crown on her head. The crystals glittered in the light.

"You want my crown? Come and take it," she said, the words laced with venom.

Jeth stalked down the steps, every pace smooth and measured. "You think I can't?"

"Aneirin had power, but it was paltry compared to mine. A candle flame in the face of the sun!" She stamped her foot. An arc of brilliant light raced out across the floor, splintering into sparks before they vanished.

"A spell circle, hurry!" Shae called from the depths of the crowd.

Just like we planned it.

Aneirin's voice in his head was cold with fury. *What are you doing? We were so close!*

Close to what? Jeth clenched his jaw. Close to settling into this role, into this throne? Settling into being a faerie king? Close to giving up his humanity, perhaps?

Put away these foolish notions. Rescind. You cannot win.

Jeth swept his arms wide as a dozen faeries formed a ring around him and High Queen Orla, as if he summoned them himself. The ring was as wide as they could make it, each caster pressed back against the crowd. Jeth felt the tingle in the air as they channelled. They moved with haste, as though they doubted the pair would wait for the rest to be protected.

In most cases, they might be right.

With a flick of his eyes, Jeth watched the thin gold sheen of magic. The edges of the spell faltered when they met, the casters fumbling. Cooperative magic was not a strong suit down here. Finally, they knit their power together into an arching dome. He dropped his gaze to the High Queen.

"This is your last chance," she hissed, pacing forward, beautiful and terrible in her livid fury. "Prostrate yourself before me, or face the consequences."

"I will not."

Jeth knew, he *knew* he had the power of two worlds within him—but that wouldn't be enough to face Orla on its own. Not with the Moot crown on her head. But he also had something else. Slowly, he unbuttoned the cuffs of his sleeves and rolled them up. The faint white lines of scars on his forearms were clearly on display for the first time. No one here knew what they meant.

No one knew he absorbed a faerie focus, becoming one himself. He had a Moot Crown of his own, at least so far as power reserves went. He had a chance.

The spell crackled around them, solidifying into a faceted dome, iridescent like a dragonfly's wing. According to Shae, the duel began with a build of power. Then, it would turn to blows. As though the hardening of the spell circle were a sign, Orla drew.

Jeth closed his eyes, his mind stretching toward the golden magic he knew was all around him. Blackthorn Court was built within the absolutely torrential power of a node, where three ley lines came together in a tangle of energies. To touch it was like a drug. To dive into it, as it urged him silently, was a death sentence. Magic would burn a body from the inside out if one tried to take more than they could handle.

Delicately, Jeth dipped his mental fingers into the vast golden sea. Just a touch was like sticking his hand in a pit of lightning. Every inch of him tingled. His golden hair stirred in a breeze that wasn't there. He felt it pool inside him, could almost watch it race through his veins. It gathered in a knot in his chest, a place where the power of the focus still lived.

Just as he had done once before when he was fourteen, he poured power into that spot until he felt his teeth vibrate in his skull. He spread his feet slightly, feeling the power grow denser and heavier in his chest as it grew, and grew, and grew. Bracing himself, he filled the last of his reserves—and his body — with a trickle more.

Anything else and he'd be crisped in a heartbeat. As it was, his skin was warm, and it felt tight over his muscles and bones, as though it were the only thing containing the vibrating energies he held inside.

Across the way, High Queen Orla transformed. She grew more beautiful and terrible by the moment. Her face was twisted in silent fury, her eyes glowing brilliantly white. Her hair lashed around her. Her gown billowed. She looked like a maiden on a cliff over a stormy sea, and the sparks of energy that arced through the air around her like lightning only reinforced that image.

She was a vengeful maiden, however. Arched into claws, her hands lifted into the air.

She thrust them forward with a screech.

Jeth reacted instinctively, pushing his power out just enough to form a shell around his body. It took a mere moment, a split second—but it was still nearly too late. He held his hands up, protecting his eyes from the sudden burst of radiance. It crackled over his shield, searching eagerly for any weakness, any place too thin to protect him. Every hair on his body stood on edge. The smell of ozone was thick in the air.

Between one breath and the next, the High Queen's white lightning disappeared.

Jeth lowered his arms slowly. He pulled his shield back until it was the thinnest layer above his skin. He stood with his head held high. Murmurs raced through the crowd watching them. To their eyes, the High Queen stood in sudden stillness, her clothes and hair settling around her, her hands still lifted.

Jeth, haloed in a soft golden glow, stood entirely unharmed.

Her eyes widened, then narrowed. Jeth felt the tug in the surrounding power. She was drawing again. He took a deep breath, trying to settle his racing heart. She had tried to crush him, in earnest, with her very first blow. She wasn't playing simply to defeat him. She wanted him dead.

Another deep breath. To do this right, he had to make it a show. No one could question his power, and no one must know that he was fighting for his life.

Every inch of Queen Orla crackled with light. She glowed with it, radiant as a star. The more she drew, the more a weight seemed to fill the room. It pressed on Jeth's shoulders. It took all his will to stand tall against it.

"What do you think to gain from my crown, little faerie? You are a babe still in a cradle compared to one such as I. I am older than Hallanor, older than humanity itself." Her voice rippled out across the room, echoing with a vast depth. The cosmos themselves did not hold as much power. "When the world was formed, I was first to set foot upon it. You are nothing, a speck, a gnat, a mere annoyance. I will *crush* you."

Jeth's teeth rattled with every word as they washed over him like a riptide, threatening to drown him. He took a single step backward.

The faeries gasped eagerly, pressing against the shield surrounding them. They wanted to see him crushed.

I will not be so easily beaten.

"I have something I want to protect," he said firmly. A trickle of golden power flowed into his words. He knew it was not the same strength as the High Queen's. He didn't want it to be. The more she underestimated him, the better.

Still, his voice moved through the room, audible to all. They were smooth, warm, and sweet. He laced them with every feeling he'd been smothering for moons. His heart ached for the nameless village, the little cottage, the beautiful forests. The call of people at the market, the low of a cow and the murmur of the milkmaid, the laughter of children. He pushed the feeling of life, fleeting and imperfect, into his spell.

That was its own kind of power.

Though soft, the words made the crowd lean forward, hanging on every one.

"And what is it you wish to protect? Your little kingdom, small as it is? Perhaps a little faerie *pet*." Her eyes swept the crowd.

Jeth's instinctively flicked to Shae, then back. Eoghan stood behind the High Queen, outside the shell, and followed Jeth's gaze. His expression turned stoney, though fire flickered in his eyes.

He ignored it, ignored him. The red-headed faerie couldn't control him, couldn't bespell him. Eoghan didn't even *know* him. None of them did.

It was time to set the mask down.

Jeth stepped forward, advancing with every proclamation. "I am Jeth, son of Gleda," he said, louder than before, more power seeping into the words. "I am born of the faerie king Aneirin, yes, but I am more than that. I am the son of a human witch." He lifted his arms, and the golden power arced between his fingertips. "I am of two worlds, and I refuse to watch one devour and destroy the other."

Orla's laugh was high and sharp, like shards of glass tumbling from a height to shatter around him. He felt the sparks of power burst against his shield as she tested him, as the wind built up around her once more, as a breeze turned into a gale.

"You think you can protect the humans? Pitiful, temporary, weak little creatures as they are? There will always be a challenger for your crown, for your throne. I have faced a hundred of them. I have squashed a hundred of them like bugs. How many have you eliminated?" she sneered.

"I will only need to crush one."

The words drew a murmur from the crowd.

The High Queen laughed again. "Oh, it will be so much fun to watch you writhe. When I have finished with you here, I shall take you to my kingdom and tear you apart piece by little piece."

Jeth said nothing. He closed his eyes, mind wandering. He pictured Burne Calder with her weathered face and flaming orange hair, her hands on her hips before her wagons and her boisterous laugh in the air. He pictured his mother, reaching out to cup his cheek and scold him lightly for getting muddy before dinner. He could smell her, like leather and herbs. He could feel her. He thought of the people he had seen on his travels, the numerous innkeepers and musicians, hedge witches and merchants, traders on the roads, simple farmers. He thought of the nearest town, the one his mother called home, the little hamlet of River Tor. He thought of the sleepy little village nestled in the curve of the river, with people strolling languidly down its streets. He saw it only from a distance, but he knew it still felt like home.

Decades from now, every person he would save today would be a distant memory. The humans would never know what he did. His descendents wouldn't know, either. There would be no mention of this in any histories, not even a whisper of when Jeth, the faerie king, saved all of Hallanor from his own.

No word of Jeth, the witch's son, protecting everything his mother taught him to love.

Then why do it? Why bother? The small voice whispered, the tiny, cruel voice of his father. It echoed in his mind. *Why save them?*

Because the alternative, he told him fiercely, *is the end of a kingdom, the end of a people.*

Is that so bad?

He clenched his hands into fists. "You will *not* win," he said aloud. He was speaking to his father's insidious voice in his ear as much as to Orla.

The High Queen drew herself upright with a scoff, her shoulders squared, her chin held high. Her mask of outrage wavered, the first flicker of doubt crossing her brow.

After all, faeries could only speak what they believed to be the truth.

With another scream, she threw her head back and released a tidal wave of pure power. An arcing wave of brilliant white light swept through the space between them and crashed against the spell circle, pouring back over him. It rose like water until the shielded area was full, until the very air threatened to crush him.

Jeth held on to every image of what he was protecting, adding to it with every measured breath. The young man Eoghan charmed, now wandering the crowd despondently, fighting the broken heart that threatened his life. The people the faeries dressed like dolls and treated like animals. Shae.

Shae.

He exhaled, relaxing at last. His eyes closed.

He released the power he held at bay, the power that vibrated beneath his skin.

Hers came like a wave.

His rose like a sun.

It swelled, little more than a glimmer at first. Then it spread out from him, radiating, the warmth of it fragmenting her cold white light, driving knives through it, shredding it to bits.

Jeth, with the focus in his very blood, let every ounce of power double as he released it, feeding more through himself with every passing moment until his ears rang. He could hold more than the High Queen. He could do this endlessly.

A scream rent the air.

Jeth let the power drain away into the node that surrounded him, panting. In the sudden silence, the crackle of the spell circle was loud. It melted away like ice in the summer sun, oozing back into the faeries that stood around them.

The High Queen Orla—no, just Queen Orla, now—lay sprawled on the floor, her resplendent skirts a pool around her. Her crown had fallen from her head. It lay on its side, softly rocking back and forth. Breathing raggedly, she stretched a hand toward it.

A shock jolted her arm, and she drew her hand back with a cry of pain. Queen Orla, indeed, for the Moot Crown was hers no longer.

Jeth stepped forward slowly. He bent to pick it up. It was light in his hands, as light as a feather. How was that possible? He pulled the Blackthorn Crown from his antlers, replacing it. It fit his head as though it were made for him.

"Humanity is protected. Faeries cannot take them to torture them, harm them, or enchant them in any way," Jeth said firmly, coloring the words with a brush of power.

The focus inside him and the power of the Moot Crown doubled it, then doubled it again. He felt the power lace through the crystals, thrumming. His voice echoed with strength, as Queen Orla's had before. The faeries gathered around him shuddered, a motion that ran through them like a ripple in a pond. All the way out to the edge, then on. Everyone in the cavern heard his words, he knew.

His gaze swept the crowd, meeting every incredulous look. "All human pets, slaves, captives, hostages, whatever you call them—*all* humans shall be released to the surface with no further harm."

He *saw* as faeries turned, summoning their humans, almost entirely against their will. Eoghan was white with fury as he lifted his fingers to the brow of the young man he'd been tormenting, as the enchantment snapped. The human looked as if he'd woken from a nightmare, clutching at his chest.

Other spells were broken, too, the crack of them like whips in the air.

"Faeries are not welcome to set foot in any human settlement, or on any human land," he said, louder. He turned to face the dais. "Every faerie court shall prepare for a visit from their High King. Every faerie, no matter how great or small, shall assemble in the throne rooms to hear my words."

None would be spared these edicts. None.

The royals shuddered violently, almost convulsing. Disgust painted Periphea's face. Dismay and despair sat on Kiniveth's and Cirsa's. The rest kept their faces like stone. It didn't matter, Jeth's words had become law. They would do as they were bid.

"You filthy mongrel, with your tainted blood. You should not even *touch* one of our crowns!" Queen Orla spat.

"You said it yourselves, your Majesty," Jeth said, barely sparing her a glance. "Even a drop of faerie blood makes someone a faerie."

The crowd stirred restlessly, as if none of the creatures gathered knew what to do, where to go. Shae pushed their way to the forefront.

Jeth stepped over to them quickly, catching both their hands in his. "I freed you," he said, voice low. "I told you that you should leave while I was fighting, just in case."

"And I told you not to do this, to run away with me. Looks like we both were wrong." They smiled.

"Then let's go. Let's get out of here. Come with me, Shae. I know once we reach the surface, we can go anywhere, but come with me."

Shae stilled, their eyes on his face, their grip tight in his hands. "Is that an order?"

"No." It was true. He put no power behind the words, just feelings. So many feelings.

Eoghan's eyes burned into Jeth's back, the malice from the Gean-Cánach palpable as he realized the lies he had been fed. He never had a grip on the faerie king at all.

The changeling did.

"Let's go," Shae said at last, a smile breaking out on their face. "Hurry up, before someone tries to stop us and you have to command them into oblivion."

"I wouldn't command them into *oblivion*," Jeth protested.

Shae huffed, towing Jeth into the crowd. Heads swiveled to follow them, the path before them opening with rustles of fine cloth as faeries stepped out of their way. Jeth kept his gaze on Shae's back, not wanting to see what his subjects felt about his commands.

A hand caught at his arm, stopping him in his tracks. His eyes met those of a human servant. She was dressed in worn, patched clothes, her hair tangled, her cheeks hollow with hunger. "Take us with you," she pleaded.

"Of course," Jeth said at once. "Spread the word. Everyone will meet us at the North tunnel. Go quickly. We leave in an hour."

The humans who heard him scattered in every direction like startled starlings. They would be there, he knew. The faeries drew away from their former pets and servants as though touching them might burn.

Jeth and Shae ducked into the corridor while the attention was elsewhere, breaking into a run in the empty hallway, their footsteps echoing back to them along with breathless laughter. *His* breathless laughter, he realized.

He upset the world order with a party, and he'd do it again, and again, and again after that. The faeries would hate him. His father's voice was silent, but he knew the man would be furious. His jar was hidden in a secret drawer in the back of the wardrobe, in the bedchamber only the king could give permission to enter. It was safe. It would no longer be able to reach him once he was on the surface.

They raced through the kitchens, where several humans were quickly gathering what meager belongings they had, packing them in baskets or blankets with the corners tied. The kitchen door let out onto a beautiful, fruitful vegetable and herb garden, the air heavy with scents of sage and pea flowers. A narrow path wound around the outside of the keep, clogged with crates and barrels. It was the only part of Blackthorn Court that wasn't beautiful, he realized, which made sense because it was to be used by mere humans, and humans alone.

Shae stopped, panting. They crouched and shoved their hand between a stack of crates, only to pull out two packs. They were bespelled to hold twice as much as normal, and be twice as light. It was easy to swing one onto his back and fasten it in place. Jeth hefted it on his shoulders with a small smile.

It's been a while since I had a bag on my back. He found he'd missed the comforting weight pulling at his shoulders. How strange and simple a thing to miss.

A few humans caught up to them, then, and Jeth smiled at them encouragingly. They all seemed stunned, as if they couldn't believe their luck. As if they couldn't believe the faerie king was really, truly, on their side.

It was a small, silent group that set off toward the North Tunnel, crossing the bridge and climbing the same stone path that brought Jeth here. As they walked, more and more humans caught up to them. Some came alone. Some in pairs, or small groups. They glanced constantly over their shoulders, but no one could be seen following them.

Jeth couldn't help but remember when he came here. There were eyes on his back then, too, eyes that judged and measured and guessed at what kind of person he was. The eyes here were full of broken hope, quickly mending. Every step brought them closer and closer to freedom, to futures—actual futures.

He liked these stares better.

The maw of the tunnel opened before them, and still they were unaccosted. Jeth slowed, then stopped. As they waited, lights in the keep's windows came on one by one. The faeries were returning to their rooms and suites. The party was over, the coronation of their king come to an end with a new High King instead.

With no humans to serve them, Jeth wondered, *who is turning on the lights?*

"It's time," Shae said softly by his elbow.

No one new had joined them in the past few minutes, and no one was visible on the path below.

Shae was right. It was time to go. Jeth straightened from where he leaned against the stone, lifting a hand and forming a golden light to guide them all. He let it drive back every shadow, this time, enveloping himself and his freed captives in its warm radiance.

The walk down the tunnels had been never-ending when he arrived, a twisting warren of shadows and skittering monsters. The way out passed in moments, a flash of time that ended so abruptly he felt sure they must be lost. He lifted a hand, touching the blank stone wall.

"Lock, Key, let us out," he commanded.

The stone ground away, wrapping in on itself until the gateway was completely open, encircled by trunk and branches of the trees. The lovpu didn't appear. Jeth couldn't blame them.

Sunlight, honest to goodness sunlight, streamed in. Jeth let his mage light go out, lifting his arm to shield his eyes. Others did, too, murmurs rising behind him. The air was fresh, scented with damp earth and that savory-sweet scent of green things.

How I ever thought the light in the cavern could compare to this, I'll never know.

The people surged forward, splitting around him like he was a stone in a stream. They raced for their freedom. Some fell to the ground and wept. Others laughed and danced. A few just kept moving, as though they were afraid the faeries might follow them, as though they wouldn't feel safe until they reached civilization once again.

Jeth waited until every single one of them—and Shae—was free of the tunnel before he stepped out from under the hill. Shae stood by a tree at the edge of the meadow that encircled Heartwood Hill, watching him with their head tilted and a smile on their lips.

"Well, where do we go from here?"

Jeth smiled, holding his hand out to the changeling as he passed by. He'd once asked himself a similar question. *What now?*

"Where do we go? Anywhere. Anywhere we want."

DOORS OF GLASS

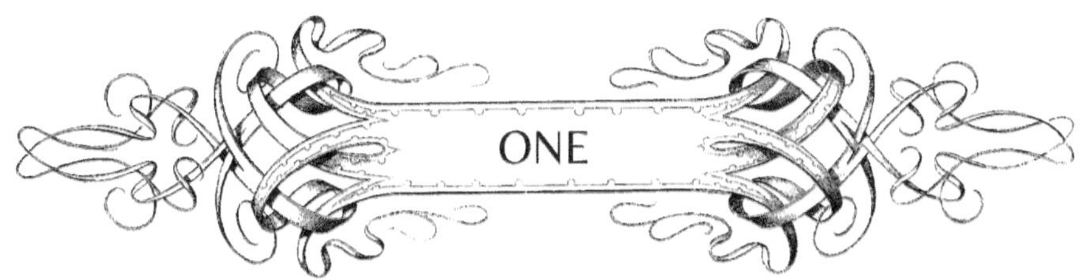

Jeth, High King of all Faerie and most powerful mage in two worlds, felt the earth give way beneath his boot a split second before he fell. He squawked like a startled chicken as his rump hit the ground hard enough to knock his teeth together, clutching at roots and shrubs as he slid several lengths down the muddy hillside.

How graceful.

He caught against a tree trunk, groaning. Peals of laughter followed him. Despite the damp soaking through his clothes, the mud on his hands and cheek, and the temporary throb in his backside, Jeth couldn't help but smile as he pulled himself back to his feet.

"You," wheezed Shae, clutching their side. "You looked so surprised. Are you alright?"

Jeth shook the mud off his hands, arms held out from his sides as he looked himself over. At the rueful twist of his mouth and the awkward stance, Shae doubled over laughing again.

"Your entire backside–" was all they managed to say.

Jeth rolled his eyes, but his smile grew until his cheeks ached. "Laugh all you want. I was just clearing the way."

He shook off what grime he could from his already travel-worn clothes, now *muddy* and travel-worn. He dressed like he always did when they wandered, in fine colorful leathers and durable clothes that would hold up to the abuse of the road.

Not that my own clumsiness really counts.

Shae picked their way down the hill far more carefully, their clothes just as worn, made of leather and cloth just as durable, though they preferred a vest and trousers over Jeth's long tunics and high boots. A large-brimmed hat made of woven straw sat on their thatch of thick blond curls. The pack on their back rattled softly with every step, full of trinkets and baubles they found on their journey, with very few practical things in between.

Jeth carried a satchel on his hip, slung over one shoulder.

Neither bag was large. They didn't need to be when they were enchanted to hold three times their visible capacity. They carried bedrolls, provisions, books, and treasures—and they weighed hardly anything at all.

Jeth patted his bag, feeling the lumpy crystals and points of the Moot Crown beneath the thick oiled canvas.

That damn crown.

"How much further?" Shae asked as they caught up.

Jeth held out a hand to guide them down the last bit of hill to his side. His skin warmed when Shae touched it. Something in his stomach fluttered.

"Oh, not far now, I'd wager. Down the hill and along the road a bit and we should see it."

They'd have to pick their way down the hill from tree to tree to avoid another rapid descent. The start of spring came with nothing but rain, rain, and more rain. Every night, and every other day, to boot.

"And you've been here before?"

"Once," Jeth admitted, gazing to their left. The trunks of the trees grew closer together there. The underbrush was thick. Moss and mushrooms grew in what little earth was visible between them, and up the trunks of trees.

That invisible line of rampant greenery denoted the faerie woods of Hallanor. Somewhere just beyond that border lay the town of Last Stop. It was aptly named, being the first and last trading stop at the farthest reaches of the least populated area in the little land-locked kingdom.

Jeth scanned the trees to his left as they picked their way along. They were only a few days' walk from the nameless little hamlet Jeth grew up in. He'd lived in the witch's cottage at the edge of the woods with his mother, Gleda Penistone. She was the witch, of course, but she taught him everything she knew.

After her death—*her murder,* he corrected himself—Jeth walked to Last Stop with her crystal ball in his bag and a heavy heart in his chest.

After that...well.

"There's the road," Shae said, interrupting his musing.

The track of dark earth wove along the base of a series of hills. Puddles of standing water gleamed in the thin spring sunlight. It'd warm up soon. Then it would dry out. At least it was rain now instead of snow. The past few months had been full of difficult weather.

The damp of the mud seeping through his pants and the cold, slick feeling of mud down one of his boots spurred Jeth down the hill. He longed for a hot bath and a change of clothes.

Last Stop was famed for two things: the constantly changing market of merchants and tradesfolk selling their wares, and the inns. There were half a dozen now, a sharp change from Jeth's last visit.

How long has it been?

More than sixty years, by his best guess. In all that time, he and Shae hadn't aged a day. After a while, seasons bled together. Years stretched and shrank in turns. Jeth had lost count.

Shae held their hands out. Jeth took them and helped the changeling hop down the last length of the hill onto the road itself. They stumbled, and Jeth caught them easily in his arms.

The changeling's slim body was familiar to him. They'd been together most nights of those sixty years, but it was...informal, at best. Shae was skittish, Jeth told himself. That was why neither of them broached that invisible line.

The line from lovers to love.

Shae flushed and elbowed him, driving the Moot Crown into his hip. "You don't need to coddle me."

"Alright, alright," Jeth said, holding up one hand placatingly. The other rubbed his hip where a crystalline tine had stabbed him. That damn crown.

That crown was the entire reason they'd traveled as much as they did. They sought out every faerie court. Once there, Jeth put on the crown and commanded all the faeries to leave the humans alone. Not to harm them, or cause mischief, or enter their settlements.

Inevitably, one to five faeries challenged Jeth to a battle of magical prowess, which was the only way to win the Moot Crown and take control again. The only way to undo his edicts. Jeth always won, but it didn't stop them from trying. At the courts, on the roads, once in the dead of night. The Moot Crown summoned trouble from all corners of the continent.

Jeth and Shae were faeries themselves, but neither of them started that way. Both had been born to humans.

Shae was a changeling, a pure-blooded human child, stolen for their beauty and replaced with a faerie turned mortal. A steady diet of forbidden fae food and a surplus of magic in the Blackthorn Court had changed them over nearly two centuries until they were a faerie themselves. Not a powerful one, but Shae was as immortal as all the rest.

In his quiet moments, Jeth was jealous of Shae. The only outward sign of their status was a pair of pointed ear-tips, easily hidden beneath hair and hat.

Jeth was born to a human mother, the witch Gleda. His father, however, was the faerie king Aneirin. Even a drop of faerie blood made someone a faerie to some extent. Casting magic seemed to activate that blood. Jeth, inundated with power from both sides of his lineage, used his as easily as breathing. The more he cast, the more he changed, his faerie blood winning out. He'd sprouted antlers, and his features grew more angular. He stopped aging in his early twenties. There were little nubs at the top of his ears that might one day turn into points.

And of course, his once black hair had turned yellow as gold. His dark eyes were now liquid amber, bright and warm as honey in the summer sun. Those two changes, however, were due to the shattering of his mother's crystal ball—which was actually a faerie focus. He'd absorbed the shards of it somehow, doubling his power and changing him irreversibly.

The only reasons the changes are this strong in me are because I cast. Shae doesn't.

That was what he told himself, when his antlers caught on a tree branch, or itched as they spawned a new tine, or got him stuck in his shirt in the morning. He wouldn't trade his magic for anything. Not even a life without branches of bone on his head.

"The last time I was here, the gatekeeper asked me if I was a faerie," Jeth recalled, smiling faintly at the memory.

Shae snorted. "What, he couldn't see the antlers?"

"I didn't have them yet."

They walked so close their hands brushed every few steps. The earth churned beneath their feet with every step, and they wove back and forth along the slim track to avoid the puddles.

Seven or eight years ago, Shae lost a boot to the sucking mud at the bottom of a puddle. They hadn't been able to wrestle it free again. They were more careful now.

"Shae, I –"

"How much further?" Shae interrupted hastily.

Every time, he thought with a frown. Every time he spoke soft and warm, Shae changed the subject.

The wooden palisade that surrounded Last Stop came into view as the path curved right. Jeth slowed, brows rising toward his thick gold hair.

What in the...

A new wall was under construction, several lengths out from the current barricade. Masons were laying stones one atop the other. It was already a good few feet taller than its wooden counterpart. Beyond those walls, buildings crowded every inch of available space. Inns three stories tall, the spire of the headwoman's house, the wood shingled and thatched rooftops of homes over shops.

"I guess Last Stop has grown since I've been away."

"Everything changes the longer you're away, Jeth." Shae paused. "Glamours?"

"Right."

Jeth slowed to cast the spells over himself. Shae didn't need them, though it would be as easy as thought to spell their pointed ear tips away for a bit. His own glamours were more complicated. It was impossible to make his antlers disappear completely. He could spell them most of the way invisible, but they still left a waver in the air over his head. It was easier to cast a spell of no importance on them. People might look at them, but they'd dismiss them right away and forget they were there.

It wasn't foolproof, but it worked well enough.

The spell itched as it settled over his antlers, a prickle across his tines and scalp that made him shiver.

"Done."

"Alright." Shae reached out for Jeth's hand, but stopped and dropped it by their side.

Jeth wished they'd held his hand.

The pair walked on, passing easily into Last Stop. The gatekeeper didn't even give them a second glance.

"Isn't this where you met your father?" Shae asked as they walked through the disorganized tangle of streets. The city grew one building at a time over the years, and the streets around them.

"I did. Aneirin found me running down an alleyway."

"And snuck you out of the city, right?"

"Under his cloak," Jeth said with a laugh. "I was fourteen, and a lot smaller then."

Shae grinned. Jeth told the story of his father a dozen times over the years, but it was different to see the place it happened in person. "Will you show me where you met?"

"If it's still there. Let's go get cleaned up and changed, at least, and then we'll go see."

The pair of them found an inn easily enough, paying for a room for the night and taking advantage of a fine washroom to get cleaned up. Both of them changed clothes, and it felt divine to be in something truly clean. After a warm meal, the pair of them picked up their things and went to explore.

Last Stop had grown, but not so much that they couldn't weave their way through it in less than an hour. They found the alleyway, and the gate Aneirin spirited Jeth through. The new wall had been completed on this side, and the palisade was being taken down. The second time Jeth passed through that gate would be the last. It would be gone within a moon.

On the far side of the stone wall lay the road and the forest. Hallanor had only one forest, one massive forest that humanity carved their towns and villages out of, every inch hard won. Jeth picked his way through the trees to a small meadow, gently sloped. The clearing was utterly unassuming.

"Here we are. Satisfied?" Jeth asked, spreading his hands wide.

"This is where you made the bargain?" Shae asked, turning slowly where they stood.

"It is."

"It doesn't look anything like I imagined."

"That's what happens when you take my story and spin it into some fanciful tale. The road was muddy, the trees were bare, the clearing was full of dead grass, and it was cloudy and gray." Jeth stood in the center of the meadow.

Despite his words to the contrary, the meadow felt powerful to him. Momentous. The stone wall was visible through the trees, the fresh-cleared land around it a bright stripe in the afternoon sun. Some day, this spot might not exist any longer. Someone would build a house or a shop on it, and it would never be the same again.

For now, it was the place he struck his first faerie bargain.

Later, who knew?

Is this why faeries lose their grasp on humanity? Because in the blink of an eye, everything is different, everything is gone?

Shae's hand slipped into his, drawing his attention.

"You alright?"

Jeth smiled softly, turning to rest his forehead against the changeling's, ducking beneath the brim of their ridiculous hat. "I will be."

Of course Shae knows. They always know.

The feeling of eyes ran over Jeth's skin like spiders. His grip tightened minutely.

"Jeth, look, I want to go home. I mean, I want to go to the town I grew up in. I want to see if I have any family left."

Jeth's brows rose. Distracted from his wariness, he lifted his head. "Of course. We can do that. And it isn't far from Valley Mill to River Tor. We can see if any of my family still lives, too."

They'd finished their duties. They went to every faerie kingdom and compelled every faerie to leave humans alone. They deserved a break.

A shrub rustled nearby. Jeth's head swiveled toward the sound.

"Show yourself," he demanded.

"It's probably a rabbit, Jeth," Shae said, walking toward it. A sense of foreboding washed over Jeth as their hands left his. "Maybe a bird."

Instead, a head of silk soft auburn hair glinted as the faerie stepped out from behind a tree. His face was in shadow, hidden, but Jeth knew instantly who it was.

So did Shae.

It was Eoghan, the Gean-Cánach.

Cold fury radiated off the creature as he stepped into the light, his sapphire eyes as cold as ice and fixed upon...Shae. Every step he took, the changeling retreated. Shae's hands trembled.

"I knew you'd come back, your *Majesty,*" Eoghan said, turning the title into an insult. "And now I find you in the arms of this little bug, this little thrall, this little mongrel."

Shae paled. Jeth's expression turned stormy. The air hummed with magic as he stepped forward and took the changeling's hand.

"I don't need to enthrall anyone to get their attention, Eoghan. What a shame you can't say the same."

The kiss of a Gean-Cánach was a powerful bit of faerie magic. Whatever human they kissed fell hopelessly in love with them, vying for their attention every waking moment. When the faerie tired of them, they pined away until they starved to death, dying of their broken heart.

When Shae was first taken, before the faerie magic finished changing them, Eoghan had claimed them as a pet. Jeth didn't know all that happened during that time. He knew it had been years. He knew Shae didn't want Eoghan to touch them. He knew Shae still had nightmares about it, two hundred years later.

Jeth didn't need to know what happened—Shae's reactions told him enough.

Eoghan's face twisted. He spat at Jeth's feet, tossing his hair. "Why you think having *that* is a measure of pride, I'll never know." His expression smoothed, turning coy as he sidled closer. "You could have so much more. You could have so much *better.*"

Shae trembled beside him, but they lifted their chin. "No, he couldn't," they said, voice wavering. "Especially because you're not better than me."

Fierce pride surged in Jeth's chest.

"He lo–"

"Don't talk when the real faeries are speaking," Eoghan interrupted Shae sharply.

Jeth's power crackled around him like golden lightning, his eyes narrowing. His grip on Shae's hand tightened. "I'm tired of this. Why are you here, Eoghan? Make it quick, or I'll fry you where you stand."

Just give me a reason.

"I want the throne. The Blackthorn Court. You're going to give it to me."

Jeth scoffed. "You show up here, bully Shae, and think I'll just hand over the crown? You're an idiot. Your magic is no match for mine. You can't beat me in a duel."

Eoghan's magic was based on touch. Jeth's was all around them, in the leylines, the nodes, the very air.

"Oh no," Eoghan said with a click of the tongue, putting a hand to his cheek and slumping dejectedly. "You're right. Now why didn't I think of that?" Their melodramatic misery faded to a small, wintry smile. "Oh, wait. I did."

The faerie dipped a hand into his elaborate traveling robes, his blue eyes never leaving Jeth's gold.

"This is your last chance, your Majesty. Make the better choice."

"I already have," Jeth said firmly. They may not have said it in so many words, but he loved Shae, and they loved him.

Eoghan drew out an old clay jar, its lid sealed in iron. He was careful not to touch the iron itself, as it would burn him. He held it instead by a leather strap wrapped around its neck—a strap Jeth once put in place to fasten the thing to his belt while he traveled.

Jeth stiffened. "Where did you get that?"

Shae stared, giving his hand a squeeze. They'd never heard Jeth sound this nervous.

"I thought so," Eoghan said idly, holding the vessel up to study it. "I thought it must mean something, since you took such pains to hide it away. And to seal it in iron! Bold, for a faerie."

"There's no way you can have that. You'd have to search my rooms to find it, and there are spells–" Jeth started.

His room at the castle of Blackthorn Court should have been impenetrable.

"Yes, yes, I know. I can only go in if I were invited. Well, I was. You invited me yourself, your Majesty. The day before your coronation, you said you would meet me in your rooms after the party." Eoghan smiled, a stiff smile with too many teeth. "So I went there whenever I wanted, waiting for you to arrive. Waiting for you to meet me. Imagine my surprise when I found that hidden compartment, when I found this little jar. It hums with magic. A powerful spell. What could possibly be in it, I wondered? But we both know that answer, don't we, Majesty?

"Leverage."

Shae gasped as Jeth's grip tightened. They twisted their hand in his grasp. "Ow, you're hurting me," they whispered.

Jeth hastily let go before he crushed Shae's hand, fingers curling into fists. From the corner of his eye, he could see Shae's growing concern. They wrapped their arms around themselves. They were uncomfortable.

I have to end this.

"What leverage?" he asked idly, glad his voice was steady. "All I see is one of my personal possessions in your hands. I want it back, Eoghan. I'm giving you a chance to hand it over."

His heart was racing, though it was easy enough to bury the swelling bubble of a scream beneath his anger. That jar held his greatest secret—and his greatest enemy. All it would take is one mistake, one slip of the hand and...

Eoghan swung it back and forth, watching it idly. "You know what I want. Give me the throne."

"Give it back."

"No. Not until I get what I want, either you or the throne! Make your choice."

"Give it back!" Jeth demanded, hand diving into his satchel. He yanked out the Moot Crown, lifting it toward his head.

"No!" Eoghan screamed, seeing the crystalline circlet, edged with textured gold. Even as Jeth lowered it, the Gean-Cánach raised his arm.

"Freeze," Jeth shouted, flinging his hand up as soon as the crown touched his hair. All it took was a trickle of power behind the word. The faerie focus he'd absorbed doubled that power. As it fed through the Moot Crown, it doubled again. The word came out fierce and strong–

–and too late.

Eogan froze as ordered, his face twisted in a mask of fury. He froze a moment *after* his arm went down. A hair's breadth *after* the jar left his hand.

It hurtled toward the ground.

Jeth dove forward, hands outstretched.

The sound of shattering ceramic broke through the cool spring air.

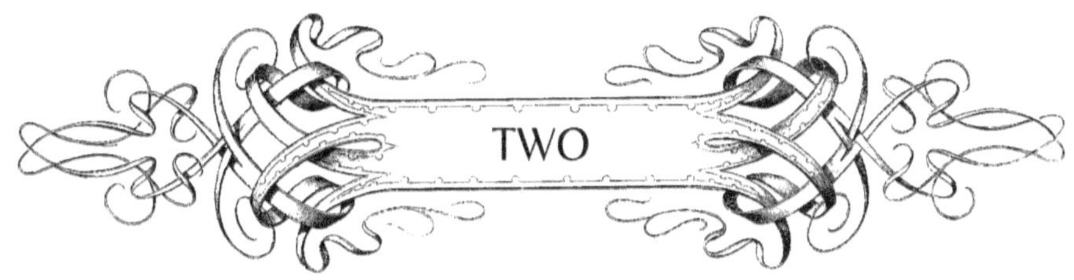

TWO

Jeth hit the ground as a cloud of darkness burst around him. He shielded his face with his arms, crying out. It didn't hurt, but it felt cold and stale.

It thinned, bleeding away quickly beneath the light of day, but it left behind something far worse than shadows. Where once three faeries stood in the meadow, now there were four.

Aneirin, the former faerie king, stood before them. His ruddy orange-red eyes were wide. His jaw, slack. He was still beautiful, dressed in the elegant and complex traveling clothes he'd worn when he went in to his own trap to taunt his captured son. His hair was longer, but it still hung in a silky black plait over his shoulder.

Jeth pushed himself to his feet, stumbling.

His father's shock turned quickly to cold fury when his eyes met Jeth's, sparking orange and calm gold locked in a silent, violent exchange.

Murderer, Jeth thought vehemently. This man killed his mother in cold blood.

"You," Aneirin spat.

"Your Majesty?" Eoghan said, as stunned as the former king was.

"Your father," Shae breathed, turning to Jeth. Shae knew the man. He was the one who stole them all those years ago.

Shae heard every bit of the story, from the murder of his mother, to the bargain Aneirin broke, and all the way to Jeth's escape from the dark nothing they were trapped within.

"I thought you said you buried the jar."

Alright, not the entire tale, then.

Aneirin lurched into motion, hands outstretched. His fingers closed around Jeth's throat, nails digging into skin, sharp as daggers. They threatened to break through the skin, to rip his flesh, to end him.

Jeth swept his hand between them, a surge of power flinging his father away. He lifted a hand to his throat, wheezing, eyes wide. With a flick of his fingers, he conjured a barrier around himself and Shae.

Aneirin rolled across the ground, landing in a heap. Slowly, the faerie pushed himself to his feet, his fine clothes and face spattered with mud. His face was twisted in disgust. His eyes raked over Jeth from head to toe.

I'm glad I took a bath, he thought, irrationally.

"You kept me imprisoned in that jar for who knows how long, and now you have the gall to glare at me, boy? To push me around with the power I created? You pathetic whelp, I have thousands of years on you."

Jeth's glare deepened. His gaze didn't waver. "But not the magic."

"And whose fault is that?" Aneirin snapped.

"I think you'll find that *you* broke the bargain. You set the trap. You did this to yourself. I just didn't save you when I found my way out."

"You broke a bargain?" Eoghan asked numbly. If he got any more shocks, his brows would disappear into his hair, never to be seen again, he was raising them so high. "But your Majesty, that means –"

"He has no power," Jeth said firmly.

He couldn't reclaim his throne.

Aneirin's hands balled into fists at his sides. He scowled and paced beyond Jeth's barrier like a caged animal. It was a flimsy spell, something any faerie with magic could break.

It remained intact.

Aneirin slowed, his fury trickling away like water being absorbed by a stone. His gaze cold, his face impassive, he weighed his options. His eyes slid to Shae, then to Eoghan. He weighed them, measured them. His eyes swept over the forest.

"Don't even think about it. You leave them alone," Jeth demanded. He channeled power into the word—but it was then he realized the Moot Crown wasn't resting on his head. It was caught on a tine of his antlers, dangling awkwardly. Uselessly. He let go of Shae's hand to reach for it.

Eoghan edged closer to Jeth and Shae, eyes fixed on Aneirin. Jeth lifted part of the barricade. No matter what else he was, the Gean-Cánach was still his subject. He ought to be rewarded for showing his solidarity.

...but he wasn't.

Jeth was watching Aneirin, ready to snap his barricade shut behind Eoghan, to fend off any physical attack. He was reaching for the Moot Crown. His fingers closed around it.

He wasn't watching Eoghan.

He should have been.

Eoghan lunged, grabbing his arm. With a rattle against his antlers and a shout, Jeth lost his hold on the Moot Crown. It fell to the earth at his feet. The rest happened fast after that. Eoghan reached out and put two fingers on the barricade, and it popped like a soap bubble, there and then gone.

Jeth turned, only for Eoghan to grapple him from behind, pinning his arms by his sides.

Shae was prying at the Gean-Cánach's hands, eyes wide, hands shaking. They weren't much of a fighter.

Aneirin was reaching for them from behind.

"Shae!" Jeth cried. Eoghan's grip was vice-tight. Try as he might, he couldn't wrest himself free. "Shae, look out!"

He toppled to the ground, Eoghan on top of him. His breath, like milk and honey and rot, rolled over Jeth's face as he leaned closer and closer, a hungry glint in his eyes. Jeth struggled, turning his face away. Memories of a kiss pinned against a door ran through his mind.

How much worse did Shae suffer?

Shae, who cried out somewhere beyond Jeth's current predicament, a cry tinged with pain.

With a roar, Jeth kicked at Eoghan, writhing madly. He just needed to get one arm loose, one—Something clanked against his antlers as he jerked his head away from Eoghan, whose eyes were on his lips.

Jeth twisted enough to look.

The crown!

That *damn* crown.

He yanked an arm free, grabbing it and shoving it quickly onto his head. He held it in place as he shouted.

"Stop and release me!"

He poured more power into the words than was needed. They slammed into Eoghan like a wall.

Eoghan stopped.

His arms pulled away, but he didn't get up. He didn't move away from Jeth at all.

"Get off," Jeth spat.

Eoghan stood, glaring down at his king.

Jeth stumbled to his feet, breathing heavily, his gaze sweeping across the meadow.

The empty meadow.

Shae was gone.

No.

So was Aneirin.

No!

"Shae? Shae, answer me! Shae, where are you?" Jeth shouted, staring at the tangle of footprints in the mud. Which sets belonged to who? Where was Shae? He whirled on Eoghan. "Where did they go?"

Eoghan said nothing, eyes narrowed.

"Answer me," Jeth commanded.

"I didn't see," the faerie said through grit teeth.

"Why would you do that?" His voice broke.

Eoghan lifted his chin, drawing himself up. "I did it for the Blackthorn Court. We deserve a real faerie king, not some bleeding heart wearing a crown. Do you know what your little edict did to us? Do you even care? The backstabbing and torture is still there, your Majesty, but it's faerie against faerie now. You've turned us into monsters."

"You were already monsters."

"It doesn't matter what you think. Aneirin will get his power back and return to us, and you'll lose everything. *Everything*, including that stupid little changeling." His smile was eager, sharp as a knife's edge.

"You bastard," Jeth hissed, hands balled into fists.

A spell wouldn't cut it, not this time. He swung, the satisfying smack of flesh on flesh sounding through the clearing. He shook out his aching hand, but the blow knocked Eoghan to the ground.

The faerie's eyes narrowed as he lifted a hand to the red mark beneath his eye. A tiny gash had been torn into the skin over his cheekbone. A single drop of silver-blue blood ran down his jaw.

Eoghan didn't wipe it away as he climbed to his feet. "You betrayed your own kind, over and over again. You are no king of faerie. You trapped us all and left us to rot! We'll have our own back. You'll see. Someday, someone will take that pretty crown from your head and set things right."

A chill slid down Jeth's spine. He'd never thought of that, of what would happen later. Of what would happen to the faeries and the humans of Hallanor when someone else wore the Moot Crown on their head.

Focus. There's more important things right now.

Jeth ground his teeth together, but he didn't say a word to Eoghan. He didn't punch the faerie again, either, even though he wanted to. Desperately. He didn't spell him into oblivion or command him to his death. A thousand other thoughts of how he could take his anger out on Eoghan flitted through his head. But Eoghan wasn't the problem here, not really. Eoghan was a buzzing fly, annoying and persistent.

Aneirin was the dagger in the dark.

Aneirin had Shae.

Jeth crouched over the mud, his gaze sweeping the damp earth until he spotted the uneven boot prints of two people heading into the trees. Leaving Eoghan behind him, Jeth followed. He was on the trail like a hound on the hunt. Beneath the shadowy boughs of the trees, all just beginning to bud with new leaves, the same thought circled through his head again and again, fuelled by helpless fury.

This time, I won't leave him alive.

THREE

Weeks.

It had been three weeks since the meadow. Jeth was at a disadvantage. For three days in a row, he tracked them from camp to camp, arriving always when the embers were still warm—but Aneirin and Shae were gone.

On the fourth day, he didn't find a camp. He found it late on the fifth day, the embers cold. Somehow, Aneirin was moving faster. On the sixth day, Jeth found a churned up road and couldn't tell which way they'd gone.

Damn it all.

Jeth paced, frustrated, hands clenched. He worried about Shae. Aneirin was wood-wise and centuries old. Shae and Jeth were children in his eyes. He was taller, physically stronger, and knew the ways of the woods far better than he did.

I don't stand a chance.

That didn't mean he wouldn't try. He sat on a rock, rooting through his satchel. He and Shae traveled together for decades. They slept next to one another, they walked, they rode, they sailed. Jeth hated sailing. But in all that time, Shae *must* have left something –

–Aha!

A smile passed over Jeth's face as he pulled out a handful of rings. They were plain things, smooth silver bands. They clinked softly in his palm. Shae had two sets. The other was gold, and no doubt in their own bags.

Jeth sorted through them until he found one that fit on his pinkie. A dowsing spell would do it, though it would need to be cast constantly. He'd have to drop it from time to time, but it would follow Shae's path.

I have to hope they'll stop.

Eventually they *had* to stop, right? He closed his eyes.

Find your owner. Find your home. Take me to them.

The ring tugged at his pinkie, gentle but insistent. It pulled to the left. Jeth followed it down the road, alternating between a walk and a trot, eating as much ground as he could. Maybe they were closer than he thought. Maybe he'd catch up.

Shae, hold on.

But at the next village, when he paused long enough to buy food and ask around, he was told that two faeries had ridden through town astride a great black charger. It was the talk of the town. They'd passed through early the day before. Jeth was miles behind.

And Aneirin has Shadowstep.

Jeth hadn't given the huge black faerie steed much thought over the years. When he broke free of his father's prison, he found only his own horse. Shadowstep had run away. It made sense, he supposed, that a magical horse might still be alive and loyal. Even all this time later. Being a creature of faerie, Shadowstep was probably as immortal as the rest of them.

It meant he would never catch up, unless...

Jeth purchased a sturdy horse with long legs and cast the dowsing spell again. They were on the road quickly. Jeth rode until sunset, then dismounted and walked his horse until he was exhausted, long after the moon came up.

The next morning, he poured healing magic into the gelding, ensuring he was in his best shape. They rode hard, stopping for Jeth to cast spells as needed. The only spell he cast while riding was the searching spell, dowsing for Shae.

I'm coming.

Could you be quick about it? Shae's voice whispered in his mind, strained. He was imagining it, he knew, but he picked up the pace anyway.

He was still too slow. He hoped he was catching up, but he couldn't know for certain.

The trail twisted off the road and into the woods in the fifth week. Jeth and his gelding were forced to pick their way through the trees, the thick underbrush slowing them down.

"Damn it," Jeth said, five days later. They were still following the insistent tug of the ring on his finger, but he was no closer to Shae or Aneirin.

And the worst part of it is that this isn't even magic. Aneirin isn't using magic to evade me, just a horse!

A magical horse, it was true. A horse that didn't tire, that didn't need to eat as often, that could run without breaking a sweat.

What did Shae think? Did they worry Jeth wasn't coming at all?

I should have said more when I had the chance.

They both danced around the word 'love' like it was a snake that might bite them. Jeth didn't want to scare Shae away. Shae always changed the subject. He should have said it anyway.

I will always come find you. You matter to me more than anything. I can't imagine another moon without you.

His horse picked up his pace, though he hardly noticed. Jeth's gaze was lowered, his thumbnail pressed between his teeth as he ran through every spell he knew, and every spell he didn't know but might be able to invent.

I'll be there soon, Shae, so don't worry. I love –

The half-shade of the trees vanished. Jeth and his horse burst from the trees onto a broad, well-traveled road.

With a startled snort and a creak of wood, two massive draft horses tried to turn and run. It didn't matter much to them that they were attached to a laden wagon. The man in the seat cried out in alarm, wrestling with the reins.

The gelding came to an abrupt stop, his ears alert and his entire body rigid as he tried to decide if he would stay or bolt.

"A faerie!" the driver shouted, voice cracking, eyes wide.

Jeth, momentarily stunned by the sudden chaos, jerked in his saddle. A hand flew to his horse's neck to soothe him. The last thing he expected was to pop out of the woods into the middle of a line of merchant wagons.

And they were shouting. About a faerie.

Damn.

That was him.

He looked down at his clothes with their intricate stitching and finely tooled leather. On the ground at his feet, the shadow of his antlers was clear, thin and long in the mid-morning sun. He hadn't cast a glamour. He hadn't even thought about it.

"Back off, faerie, and don't say a damn word," a woman shouted, rushing toward him from the wagon in the lead, brandishing a club in one hand and a dagger in the other. "Open your mouth and it'll be the last thing you do!"

She was solidly built, tall and broad of shoulder. A shock of red hair atop her head kept escaping the bun she'd twisted it into, coils of it framing her face in waves. She swung the club up over her head, face twisted into a scowl.

"Burne? Burne Calder?" Jeth asked, stunned. He must be seeing things. This was all so surreal.

She froze, her scowl melting into surprise. She stopped short a few feet away. "What?"

"But you can't be Burne Calder. By now, she'd be..."

"Ninety four," the woman said slowly. "But she hasn't traveled in a long time. How do you know her?" She drew back the club, eyes narrowing suspiciously.

A granddaughter! Burne Calder had a family, and that family had family. A thousand questions sat at the tip of his tongue, but the armed woman waiting for her answer kept them there. He held up his hands slowly.

"Once, when I was just a boy, I made a bargain with a faerie to travel with her caravan. We spent weeks together. She tried to warn me about my father, the faerie, and...well, in the end..."

If he closed his eyes, he could still see it. Him, running for the gate surrounding the town. His hand outstretched, Burne Calder's heart breaking in her eyes as she watched. Her turning away, the gate closing, and everything growing smaller as Aneirin rode away with him. Snow lay thick over everything. It was so cold. The sound of the gate closing had been strangely muted and twice as sharp at the same time.

"–Jeth?" the woman asked, the club lowering. She stared at him, looking him and down. "But you're just a tale," she accused. "And now you're a–"

"Yes, I know. A faerie." Jeth swung quickly down off his horse, keeping his hands up. "And yes, that's me! Jeth. I owe Burne Calder so very much. An explanation, at the least. I looked for her for a few years, but I never managed to catch up."

The redhead laughed, offering her hand. "Well, flame and fire! That sounds like her, never in one place for long if she can help it. It's nice to meet you, Jeth. I'm Anabette Calder."

He grasped her hand, beaming.

"You're like a bedtime story come to life. Grandma told me time and again about that trip, about the bandits and the evil faerie. And you're a faerie! I wonder if Grandma knew that."

Jeth laughed. "I've always been a faerie. The more I use my magic, the more it comes out."

"That makes sense. She told us you were magic. Well!" Anabette slapped her hands together. "There's an awful lot to catch up on. Stop for the night with us. There's a clearing just ahead."

Jeth hesitated, heart torn in two. Shae needed him, but it *was* getting late. He'd have to stop soon, anyway. And it was only for a few hours.

"Which way are you going?"

The tug of the ring on his finger had changed its pull. It wanted him to go up the road in the opposite direction of the caravan. Reluctantly, he pointed to where it led. "That way, I'm afraid," he sighed.

"There's a pretty large town that way, half a day's ride. And a keep. One of the baronies, I think," Anabette said, sheathing her dagger on her belt. "But I'm not going that way. I'm headed home." Her grin widened, eyes twinkling. "I can't *believe* I get to tell Grandma all about you. Sparks, why don't you write her a letter, tell her everything that's happened to you?"

Jeth looked down the path. Every moment he stopped was another moment he fell behind Shae and Aneirin.

But this was important. Burne Calder carried a guilt she didn't need to.

He nodded, turning back to Anabette. "I'd like to. I have paper and ink, I can write something up. But come morning, I have to be on my way. I can't stop long."

"In a rush, eh? Then let's get to it." She turned to her caravan, the bevy of drivers and guards quickly pulling their heads back as though they *hadn't* all been eavesdropping on this strange interaction.

Anabette narrowed her eyes, planting a hand on her hip.

"Oi, you lot, pull off the road! We're making camp."

"I have to be on the road again by dawn," Jeth warned as the wagons creaked to life and moved off the path.

"Don't worry, we'll break camp on our own in the morning. Load you up with a traveler's breakfast, too. Quick and easy, and something you can finish in the saddle. It's the least I can do. You look like you haven't seen a decent meal in weeks."

Jeth's lips parted to protest again, but she had a point. He hadn't eaten much in the past few weeks. His stomach gurgled. He shook his head with a soft smile.

"Alright, you win. And I can give you a faerie bargain for your hospitality. For Burne, too. No strings, no loopholes. Just a simple thank you."

It was magic he'd finally learned a decade ago, magic he rarely used. In an island court of faerie, actually. But for Burne Calder? For Anabette?

"Oh, pft," Anabette waved a hand. "I have more than enough for me. I mean, I'm just glad I got to meet you. We all thought you were dead, actually, but...but it's a family tale. Who else would know that story except—"

"Except someone who was in it." Jeth grinned.

"Exactly!" She laughed. "So now I get to bring good news and a letter, and that's enough for me."

"Then, in exchange for the food, let me expand upon a bargain already made. Let me extend your family's luck."

That was what Burne Calder bargained for all those years ago. Three generations of impossible luck in their travels and trades. Her, her children, her grandchildren. That luck was going to end—and soon. Anabette had the last of it.

But it was within Jeth's power to cast a bargain that would extend that luck for as long as he wanted.

For forever.

"That's it? Just give you dinner and a place to rest your head, and we get more luck?" Anabette's words held a careless lilt, her head shaking. She didn't believe him.

Jeth smiled and shrugged a shoulder. "I'm not like other faeries."

She'd find that out quick enough.

"Just write your letter. We can talk nonsense later." Anabette left him there.

Her companions started a nice fire on the side of the road, well clear of the trees. They took apples and cheese and bread from their stores. They cut pockets in the bread and pushed slices of the crisp fruit and yellow cheese inside, then warmed them over the fire until the crust was crisp and the cheese was melted.

Every one of them avoided Jeth's gaze, flicking worried glances at Anabette. He was certain they believed she'd lost her mind, welcoming him into their ranks for even a moment. Everyone knew what faeries were—dangerous.

Jeth couldn't change who he was, though, and Anabette wanted news. They might not have trusted the faerie, but they trusted her. Tents went up. The smell of savory cheese and crisp, tart apple filled the air.

Meanwhile, Jeth dug through his satchel to find parchment, pen, and ink.

He settled on a rock, staring at the page. What did he want to say to the woman who filled a gaping hole in his chest after his mother had died? What could he say?

Dear Burne, he started.

It's me, Jeth. I survived. Aneirin didn't win, just so you know. I don't know if you knew this, but he's my father, and just as terrible as you warned. But that means I'm a faerie, too. I'll live a long time, and thanks to you and my mother, I'll be a different kind of faerie. I'm not the only one, either. And I've done so much to protect people like you and Anabette. I'm changing the world, Burne, and part of that is you. There's so much I want to write here, but if I told you all of my adventures, you would get a book instead of a letter. I'll try to visit when my work is done. Anabette can tell me where to go. Then we can spend a week catching up.

I met Anabette! She looks so much like you and has the same deep voice. I thought I was seeing a ghost. She thought she was under attack! Luckily, we cleared both things up. I heard you're 94 now. 94! Has that much time really passed?

I'm glad that I get the chance to write to you before you leave this world. I looked, but I couldn't find you. You moved too quick with that caravan of yours. I've wanted to tell you I'm alright for years. You don't need to feel guilt for that day, not anymore.

I'm alright, Burne. I'm just fine, and you and your family will be, too.
Jeth.

It wasn't enough. There would never be enough words to describe how her kindness meant the world to him, how she helped him heal, how she became one of the pieces of humanity he wanted to protect. And the paper was too small. It would never hold them all, even if he did have the words.

He folded the letter and packed away his supplies. He shoved the Moot Crown out of the way to get around it. It winked in the light.

"What's that?" Anabette asked as she stopped in front of him, a warm roll of cheese and apple in either hand. She held one out to Jeth.

"Oh," he said. He cleared his throat. "Well, it's a crown. I sort of became a king of faerie." The High King, though he didn't mention that.

"That sounds like a bit of a story. Congratulations?"

"Thanks." Jeth took the roll, trading it for the letter. After a moment, he pulled the crown out and put it over his antlers, settling it on his brow. He could use its ability to multiply magic for this next part.

"Sit down," he gestured.

Anabette plopped down, taking a bite of her dinner, a brow raised.

"My gratitude is unending, and so too shall be your family's luck. In exchange for hospitality and the delivery of my letter to Burne Calder, this deal is struck."

The magic for a faerie bargain had to come from the faerie themselves. Jeth couldn't pull on leylines or nodes to flood himself with power. He could only use the power of the focus and the Moot Crown to strengthen it. So he did.

Jeth pulled a thread of power from his own chest, pulling it through the focus to double its strength before winding it through the crown. His magical reserve, the font inside him, tingled. He guided the thread to Anabette.

With his True Sight, the glowing golden rope was visible to him—but invisible to everyone else.

Usually, it was complicated to weave a new bargain. This wasn't the same. A silver thread was spun around her, the last bits of Aneirin's magic. It was a simple matter to tie his thread to that one, to set his intention to extend that gift indefinitely.

He tied it off like a bow, then pulled the magical thread taut, and...*crack.*

The feeling of a deal being made was like a twig breaking in two and a puzzle piece falling into place at the same time. It sent a rush of pleasure through Jeth from head to toe until his skin felt alive with magic.

Some faeries found that feeling addicting. Jeth was certain Aneirin was one of them.

Thanks to Jeth, they couldn't cast bargains anymore. Not with humans. Faeries had a bad habit of making poor deals, or twisting the words of a deal to suit their own ends.

Anabette shivered and gave him a sour look. "That felt like walking through cobwebs. Don't spell me anymore, alright?"

"Alright," Jeth agreed, biting into the roll. The sweet tang and crisp crunch of the apples paired beautifully with the gooey, salty cheese. It was delicious. He pulled the Moot Crown off his head with one hand, shoving it back into the satchel.

Jeth could almost hear Shae's exasperated sigh.

That is the most powerful artifact in all Faerie, and you're treating it like an old hat!

It is an old hat, he'd say.

You know what I mean.

Shae knew Jeth hated the damn thing, though. Maybe they wouldn't say anything at all. He wanted to ask them. His hand rested over his satchel, worry gnawing at him.

Aneirin doesn't torture people. If he thinks he can use them, he keeps them from harm. Like he had with Jeth when he was a boy. *Shae is just fine. They're fine.*

If the dowsing spell on the ring was still working—which it was, tugging at his pinkie even now—then Shae was alive, at least.

And unharmed, he thought firmly. He hoped.

Anabette waved her hand. "Hey, Hank, Pearl, come on over here. Meet Jeth, an old friend of the family."

"An old friend?" Pearl, a young woman with braids wrapped into a crown on her head, came over with her arms folded across her chest, a brow raised. "You do realize he's a faerie, right?"

Hank was a giant of a man, and he sat very near to Anabette. Their knees brushed, and the merchant woman leaned into him a bit.

"It's quite the story, actually," Jeth started.

He began the tale of meeting Burne Calder as night set in around them. Before long, he was ushered to the fire's edge so the rest could hear. Ale was passed around, though only one mug apiece. Jeth's tales went from his childhood to the kingdom of faerie, to all the different faerie courts. He talked until he was hoarse, at which point the traders filled his mug with water, let him drink, and then bombarded him with questions.

The moon was starting to sink by the time Jeth was shown to a bedroll. He fell asleep as soon as he closed his eyes. Exhaustion kept him from dreaming, both a blessing and a curse. He wanted to see Shae.

Come dawn, he woke without opening his eyes, a hand stretching across the bedroll. Nothing. No one. Empty. Shae was still missing. Jeth sat up and rubbed the grit from the corners of his eyes and prepared to resume his hunt.

The chill morning air was cold enough that his breath curled away in little puffs of steam. The rising sun in a clear sky promised much warmer temperatures later, thank goodness.

Anabette and her wagons were lining up again, the horses hauling them onto the road. Traders bustled around camp, taking down tents, dousing the fire, and packing things away with an efficiency born of years of travel. Hank passed by, pressing a cold breakfast roll into his hand. It had been baked with dried fruit and honey inside. Jeth ate his food and stood, gaze fixed down the road as though he could see just how far away his father was.

"Anabette?"

"Mm?" Anabette turned to him from where she was harnessing a horse.

"You said there's a town ahead?"

"Yeah, nice place. Ulma Dale. Old town, been there for ages. It's so strange, though..."

Jeth tore his gaze from the road, a brow raised.

Anabette shrugged. "Well, it's just that there was all this gossip about people saying their names were taken. But nobody believed them."

A chill ran through Jeth, freezing the blood in his veins in a slow crawl. His mouth went dry.

Stealing names was a faerie story.

Aneirin had to be in Ulma Dale, or at least stopped there. Jeth was catching up. And where Aneirin was, there would be Shae.

Jeth was on his horse before he realized it, spurring him on with a click of his tongue and a nudge with his heels. When he glanced back, Anabette was waving. The wagons were rolling away. He wondered if he'd ever see her again.

And then he turned back to the road, to the town where names were being stolen, and to the newest question looming in his mind.

How is he taking their names with no magic?

FOUR

The town of Ulma Dale was as large as Anabette promised. It was a cobbled together sort of place, where the roads meandered and dead ended into one another, and then wandered away again. Housing was built over shops, and what couldn't be bought in those shops appeared to be on sale in stalls scattered throughout the streets.

There were portions of walls left here and there, crumbling away, signs of the town's growth. A new wall encircled the whole thing—or at least a wall only a few years old.

From what Jeth could see, perched on a branch in a giant oak tree at the edge of the woods, the whole thing sprung up at the foot of the keep. A massive thing, too. Absolutely huge, squat, square, and stone. How old it was, he couldn't guess, but it was certainly one of the oldest structures in Hallanor. Once, it must have housed Ulma Dale's entire population. Now it sat as the town's sullen guardian.

The buildings below it were built of dozens of different things. Stone, plaster, and wood walls. Tile, thatched, or wood shingled rooftops. Chimneys made of metal or stone. The streets were half cobbled, in the process of being built throughout the whole of the town. Whether stone or packed earth, said streets bustled with pinpricks of brown, gray, green, and blue. It was a lively town full of people moving about on their errands.

Jeth climbed down, ducking beneath a branch carefully to avoid catching his antlers.

He had to go in. He had to ask about the missing names. That meant preparation was needed. He set his satchel down, sticking his arm in far deeper than it could possibly hold, feeling about for a set of plain traveler's clothes. They were drab and brown, with a thick vest and a wide belt to wrap around his waist. He didn't want to seem well off. That would draw too much attention.

Jeth frowned as he tugged his tunic off and the shirt on, always a process with his tines threatening to poke holes in everything.

Aneirin was stealing names.

I've traveled all over, learning every bit of magic I can find, and I never learned how to steal a name.

It didn't make sense that there was magic he didn't know, magic that could be cast by someone without any to speak of. Unless Aneirin was forcing Shae to use their meager reserves? What if they were being forced to—no. No, Shae insisted that changelings never had more than a trickle, at best. And Shae didn't like using their magic if they could help it, so it *stayed* small.

They had Jeth cast their glamours, for goodness' sake!

Dressed, he stood and cast one over himself. He took extra care, painting his antlers invisible—well, as invisible as he could. The air over his head wavered, and he looked to have two strange cowlicks in his hair. With another spell to have people dismiss what little was left to see as unimportant, he was ready.

He picked up his satchel and started down the road, his gelding trailing behind him. No one cast them a second glance.

Up close, the streets were wider than he'd guessed. The buildings were still chaotic, but signs of organization showed in the runnels along each side of the street that served as sewers, keeping mess and stink to a minimum. Little bridges crossed at every doorway. Just enough water swept through them to keep them clean.

Jeth slowed to study one, brows furrowed. There was magic in that water, in the design. Silver magic. He blinked.

Someone, at some point, must have made a faerie deal for the prosperity of Ulma Dale, and they made that deal with Aneirin.

Was that why Aneirin came here? Could he siphon some of it off? Could that be how he was able to steal a name?

Jeth turned, holding out a hand to slow three women passing by. "Excuse me, I'm a bit lost," he started. His mind raced, coming up with a plausible story. "I'm a scholar with the royal archives. Well, an apprentice. I was sent to talk to those people claiming they've lost their names. Do you know where I can find them?"

There, that ought to be safe enough. And technically all true—just not from the court they assumed.

Two of the women shook their heads. The third, with her hair braided into a loop atop her head, held up a hand.

"I think I remember Tibauld gossiping it about it. Wasn't he, Margaret? He's the one who told us about it. Tibauld is the ribbon merchant at the Hoof Street Market." She pointed.

"Thank you."

Thus began a long afternoon. Tibauld, the ribbon merchant, said he heard it from the clothier. The clothier heard it from a cobbler. The cobbler heard it from his serving woman at the tavern where he ate breakfast every morning. The serving woman heard it from their cook, who heard it from the delivery driver—who was due any minute, now. Did he want to wait?

Jeth sat on a stool with one short leg, nursing a mug of water outside the tavern's back door, waiting. It felt like an age before the delivery cart rolled up the alleyway to the kitchen.

Jeth was on his feet in a flash, mug abandoned. "Excuse me," he said, standing next to the man's seat.

The tavern's staff shuffled around them, unloading the cart.

"Hello, sirrah. What can I do for you?" The delivery driver, a grizzled old man with one missing tooth and a broad, open smile, asked.

"I'm a scholar," he repeated for what felt like the hundredth time. "I'm looking for the people who believe they've lost their names."

"Oh, right mess all that is. You're looking for Baker, the fellow I get the bread from. Thinks he lost his name, but I ain't recall ever calling him by anything else, aye? Baker's always been Baker, long as he's lived."

"Always?" Jeth asked, brows raising. "How strange. When did he claim his name had been taken?"

"A few days ago. Three? Four? Quite the stir, too. Once he started up, so did a few others besides. Right mess, like I said."

"Can you tell me where to find him?"

The driver leaned down, pointing this way and that as he directed Jeth. First a left, and two rights to the main thoroughfare, and then a right, and then the bakery halfway toward the keep, couldn't miss it, right on the corner.

Jeth clasped the man's shoulder for a moment. "Thank you. Thank you very much."

He took off at a quick walk.

This spell took not just a name, but even the memory of that name in other people's minds. While it was a common faerie story, it wasn't common faerie magic. Jeth hadn't learned how to do it. Something that powerful had to be Aneirin. He'd eat his fancy hat, crystals and all, if it were anyone else.

Especially since the orders he'd given with the Moot Crown meant faeries couldn't come into human settlements with any intention of harm or mischief.

The walk didn't take long. The bakery was unassuming, a plain storefront with 'BREAD' spelled out over one window. Still, it had a small line out the door and a crowd at the counter. Jeth joined the queue, waiting his turn to get inside the stuffy, over-warm building. It smelled of flour and yeast and something sweet. Shelves of bread were all but cleared out this late in the afternoon.

Jeth finally wrestled his way through the crowd to the counter, facing a young woman with her brows raised.

"And what can I get for you, sir?"

"I'm here to talk to Baker, please."

"You and everyone else," she said, rolling her eyes. "Buy a loaf of something or get out."

"I'm a scholar, sent by the court." The faerie court, at least. He could send himself places, couldn't he?

"Are you?" Her eyes widened. "Well, alright. I'll go see if he's interested in talking to you, at least."

She ducked through a curtain into the kitchen, a clatter of noise and a wave of heat rolling through. A moment later, she came out again, hurrying to Jeth's side.

"Go around the back. He'll meet you outside."

Jeth put a few coins on the counter with a nod of thanks, then wove his way through the throng and back to the open air. A quick circle of the building led him to an open kitchen door. A few barrels and crates were pushed up against the wall on either side. The baking ovens put off an enormous amount of heat. The air shimmered where it poured outside.

He perched on a crate, anxiously twisting the ring on his pinkie. He'd turned the spell off. Shae would have to wait. They'd understand, wouldn't they? They wanted to protect humans as much as he did.

A portly man with a thatch of dark hair came out, mopping at his red, sweaty face with a corner of his apron. He looked Jeth up and down.

"You're the scholar? Sent from the court, eh? I didn't think the Queen would have heard about all this yet. We only just sent the letter along."

"You'd be surprised, sir. What matters is that I'm here to talk about your situation. What can you tell me about the day your name was stolen?"

Baker's brows shot up toward his hair. "You believe me, then?"

"I'll be able to tell. Can I look at you? I have a special glass." He had a magnifying glass, but it would make a good enough excuse to hide his True Sight from the man. He pulled it from his bag.

Baker held his arms up a bit, standing stiffly.

Jeth activated his True Sight. It was the first spell Aneirin had ever taught him. All these years later, he still cast it the same way. It was as easy as breathing to picture the mask of pure power, golden and glowing, and pull it on over his eyes.

The world around him lit up with magic. Everyone's looked different, behaved differently. His was always gold and fluid, with sparks that drifted away from it like embers. Shae's meager as it was, always looked like the foggy breath exhaled on a cold morning.

And there, on Baker's brow, was a glimmer of magic that looked like molten silver.

It was Aneirin's.

He lowered the magnifying glass, letting his True Sight fade with the gesture. The knot of magic at the man's brow told him nothing about how the spell worked.

Damn it.

"I do believe you," he said with a sigh. "It's subtle, but you show the signs of magical tampering."

Baker, however, looked elated by the news. He grasped Jeth's shoulders with a wild laugh, shaking him. "You believe me! Hellfires, I was beginning to think I'd gone mad. Everyone else acts like I've always gone by Baker."

"Everyone?" Jeth repeated sharply.

"Absolutely everyone. Even my wife. My children! They call me Papa, still, but when asked what my name is, everyone I know says the same thing. Baker, Baker, Baker." His hands fell from Jeth's arms and he sighed. "Even I don't remember it."

Even the memory of his name, in other minds and his own, is gone.

"That sounds awful."

"Well, seems that way to me. But it would, eh?" Baker sighed, wiping his hands on his apron as he claimed the crate Jeth vacated.

Jeth crouched beside the man. "Tell me what you remember."

Baker was silent for a few moments, arms folded over his broad chest. "Well," he said at last with a sigh. "I remember it starting like any other day. I'm always the first one here, the first one awake, first to work. I start the ovens up and check that all the loaves rose. It was early. First light of dawn. I propped the door open—" he nodded at the kitchen door beside him, "—so my workers could come right in."

Jeth nodded slowly. "And then?" he asked softly when Baker didn't continue.

Baker shook his head, brow furrowed. "I heard something. I remember that. I turned around, and I saw a man. At least I thought it was a man. I heard the horse's hooves in the alley and didn't think anything of it. And there was someone shouting, but muffled, like their mouth was covered up."

Shae, Jeth realized with a pang. His jaw clenched. Shae was alive three or four days ago. "And after that?"

"And then my apprentice was here, helping me off the cobbles and saying I must have got sick from the heat inside, came out, and fainted dead away. Pah! Never gotten sick from the heat of an oven in my entire life. And then one of them called me Baker, and I *knew* it was wrong." He shook his head, brows drawn together. "I knew it was wrong, but for the life of me, I couldn't tell you what my name used to be. No matter how hard I try to remember, lad, it's just...gone."

"Even in your memories?"

"Just a blank space there, an echo you can't hear. Like when you stick your head in the horse trough and somebody tries to talk to you through the water."

Jeth nodded and stood. "I'm sorry, Baker. I don't know how to get your name back."

"I'll survive, lad. Worse things I could be called, I suppose. Just you do me a favor and pass our stories along to the court and the Queen. Tell her about us, yes?"

"Us?"

"Well, you didn't think I was the only one, did you? No, no. My friend Cook has had a go of it, I'll tell you that. She's up at the keep, and a more salt of the earth woman there never was. She's not the sort to pull fancies or make up tales. If she says her name was stolen, too, I believe her."

"You mean you don't remember if she had a different name before? Even though you know they can be taken?"

Baker sighed again, groaning as he pushed to his feet. "All I remember calling her, my whole life, is Cook. Same as everybody else only remembers me as Baker. Go on up to the keep, to the side gate. Tell them Baker sent you for Cook. They'll let you through. Get her story, and then tell the Queen. Please."

"I will. Especially if other names are disappearing," Jeth said grimly.

Baker disappeared back into his kitchen, barking orders before he was even through the door. Jeth wrapped a hand tight around the strap of his satchel, picked up his horse's reins, and started toward the keep.

More than one name is taken, which must mean something. What does taking a name even do? How does he do it when he hasn't got any power?

No matter how his mind raced, no answers came to him. By the time he reached the side gate, all he'd managed to do was give himself a headache. All he had were guesses, supposes, and what ifs.

He told the guard that Baker sent him, and he was waved through and directed toward the kitchen—which was right across the yard. Much like the bakery, the door was propped open and heat rolled out into the cool spring air of evening. Here, though, the scents were much different. Savory sauces, meat, and something spicy that tickled the inside of his nose and made him want to sneeze. They mingled in the air in a mouth watering perfume. His stomach growled. The gelding was content to crop the thin grass at the side of the kitchen yard, so he left him there.

Jeth paused in the door, wondering if he ought to knock.

"Here, now, and what are you after, lad?" A woman asked. She was tall and slim. Her brown hair was liberally streaked with gray, at least what wasn't hidden beneath her cap.

"I'm here to speak to Cook. Baker sent me."

"Baker!" She turned, passing the ladle in her hand to a young man before crossing the kitchen in three great strides. "I love that man. One of my oldest friends, you know. What did he send you here for, eh? Work?"

"I'm looking into the lost names, actually," he said slowly. His story about being a scholar might not be as helpful here as it was in town. What if they wanted him to be a guest? "I know someone who lost their name. Someone close to me."

Cook was standing right in front of him, after all.

"And you're out here trying to help them? Oh, what a good lad." She smiled, gesturing him to a chair at a small table against the wall—and well out of the way of the cooks still working. She dropped into the seat across from him with a sigh of relief. "Alright, what do you want to know?"

"What do you remember?"

"Oh, not much, lad. I was up here, just after dawn. Starting on breakfast and all that. Maid came in through the door with two of his Lordship's guests on her heels. Can you imagine? Guests through the back door instead of the front!"

"Maid?" Jeth asked, forcing his tone to remain light and inquisitive. Because her name sounded like...

"Hm? Oh yes, another one of us that seems to have lost their name. Not that any of us can remember any different. Poor girl. She lives with her mother in town, helps care for her little siblings come evenings. And she walks up the hill every morning. She said she lost it on the walk, as if you can drop a name out of a basket and not notice!"

She probably *had* lost her name on the walk, when Aneirin spotted another unlucky victim. He pulled on his True Sight as he listened. The same silver shimmer was tangled in a knot at Cook's brow. He lowered it with a frown.

"And she works here, too? Can I meet her?"

"I don't see why not. Wonderful girl. Worked here about five years now."

"Who?" asked a young woman in a neat kirtle and crisp white apron as she swept into the kitchen. She set down a tray laden with a long-since-devoured tea service on the nearest surface.

"Why, you! We were just talking about you and all this name mess. Maid, this is..."

"Jeth," he supplied, standing and bobbing his head politely.

"Jeth," Cook repeated. "Someone he knows lost their name, too. Someone close."

"Oh no," Maid said, putting her hand over her heart. "I'm so sorry. It's been difficult around here lately. Everyone's afraid theirs will be next. One or two more go missing every day. Lord says that it's nothing to worry about, that we shouldn't write any reports on the matter. He says it makes no sense to have your name taken, and –"

"Sorry, Lord?" Jeth interrupted. "The man who rules this place is just called...Lord?" He raised a brow pointedly.

"Well, yes. Always has been." Maid paused, her eyes widening. "Wait, you don't think...but why wouldn't he say so?"

"Maid," Jeth asked, "Are those two guests still here?"

"Yes. Why?"

"Oh, enough of this. You've got enough work to do without putting boogey men under the beds," Cook scolded, sweeping across the kitchen and turning Maid around. "You brought the tea tray back, now get on with the rest of it. Go, go, go!"

She shooed her out of the kitchen.

Jeth sank back into his seat, fingers trembling, heart soaring and falling in turns.

Lord, who had his name stolen, had two guests. Lord was telling his people everything was fine. He was either in on it, or under Aneirin's control. Because his father was here, and so was Shae.

Jeth had caught up.

And Aneirin had taken over Ulma Dale.

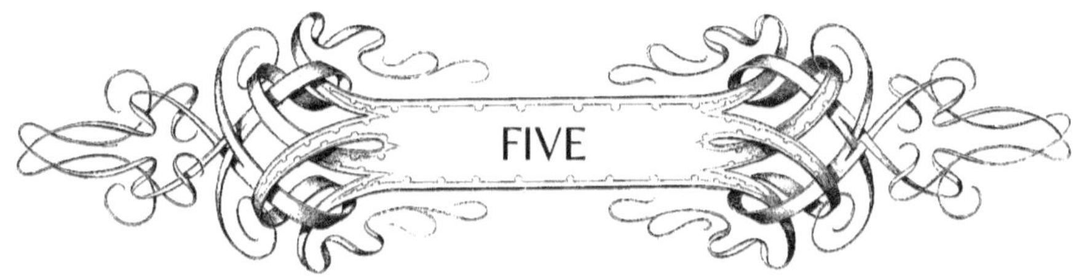

FIVE

Jeth slipped out of the kitchen and into the cool night air. The last light of the sun was fading from the sky, and the breeze promised another chilly spring evening. Soon it would get warmer. Soon, life would run rampant.

For now, he and the world needed sleep. Jeth made his way around the side of the keep. He kept close to the wall, head craned back as he studied the windows overhead. He tried to guess which ones belonged to Lord, which had been commandeered by Aneirin, and which might be holding Shae.

He was so close. He wanted to march right in and tear the place apart until he found the changeling.

Patience, he thought, closing his eyes. Rushing in would only result in someone getting hurt. Despite his anger and rising hatred for his father, he didn't want to kill anyone. He didn't want to stoop to Aneirin's level.

He absolutely did not want to get Shae killed.

The best way to get the lay of the land was to blend in, make friends, and ask questions. He rounded the corner of the keep. Cook was right—the stable was right there. He couldn't miss it.

Aneirin, once a king of faerie, was used to luxury or darkness, and little in between. He wouldn't suspect Jeth to hide himself among the servants, humbly hiding behind his glamours. Cook told him there was an opening for a stable hand.

The long, low building was twice as large as most stables Jeth had seen before. A modest paddock stood between it and the wall. No doubt it would hold dozens of horses at once—including Jeth's gelding. It was beside the fence, nose thrust between the rails to drink from the trough.

He gathered its reins and went inside. It was brightly lit by lanterns above the walkway, every one glass sided and fastened securely. There'd be no fires here if they could help it.

A soft snort came from the stall beside him. His horse danced away a few steps, tossing his head. Jeth tore his gaze from the ceiling–

–and looked right into the huge dark eye of Shadowstep. The faerie steed leaned over the railing of her stall, studying Jeth intently. She was a magnificent creature, black from head to toe, with eyes like an abyss. Intelligent, too. To this day, Jeth couldn't tell if she was just a faerie steed or a Nightmare.

Could she tell Aneirin that I'm here?

Jeth held his breath.

Shadowstep snorted, tossing her head in disdain. She nudged a bucket that hung on a hook near the stall door. Jeth eased closer to peer inside. A few oats littered the bottom.

"You want me to give you treats?" Jeth asked with a snort. "Good luck with that. You're on *his* side, aren't you?"

Shadowstep's head lifted in surprise, ears pinning back. She huffed an annoyed snort of her own, scraping a hoof over the ground.

"Well, look at that. Not afraid of that beastie, are you?" The stable master was a slim woman, her long hair plaited down her back. Despite her size, Jeth had no doubt of her muscle. She was carting a full bale of hay around, alone, like it weighed nothing at all.

"No, I'm not. I'm familiar with her kind," Jeth said dryly.

Shadowstep shook her head at the half-lie, very pointedly turning around in her stall. Her tail lashed to either side.

"What I'd give for a dozen of you, then." The woman laughed, and it was earthy and loud. It conjured a smile on his face, too.

"Well, will one of me do? Cook said you were looking for a new stable hand, and I'd like to stay on." For now.

A few days, a week at most. No more.

Her brows rose. "Angling to make my day, eh? How's your bale slinging arm?"

"Don't you need to use both?"

She grinned, dropping her bale with a puff of straw dust. She held out her hand. "I'm Halen."

"Jeth."

She clasped his forearm. "Pleasure's mine, if you can get that mare to let you in her stall. Drop that bag of yours upstairs in the loft and let's get to work. New stable hand gets to muck."

Halen watched his face intently at that announcement. Jeth shrugged and smiled. Her shoulders relaxed. She gave a firm nod, and bent to pick up her bale again.

"Thanks, Halen," Jeth called as she walked away.

He put his gelding in a stall and rubbed him down. The ladder to the loft was easy enough to find, as were the four cots. Only one was stripped bare, so that was where he put his things, tucking the satchel against the wall beneath it.

When he presented himself for work, he was briefly introduced to the other two stable hands, a broad-shouldered girl and a gangly young man, and then Halen set him to work. The length of the stables left plenty of space between all of them.

Which meant, Jeth quickly discovered, that he could wheel the barrow into a stall and use his magic to muck out any dirty hay. It took three heartbeats, maybe less, and allowed him to linger. He alternated between familiarizing himself with the horses and peering out the nearest openings to observe the keep, the guards, the comings and goings.

The day was nearly done when he'd arrived, so he didn't work long before Halen arrived.

"Well, I'll be. You did a fine job, Jeth. Mucked a stall or two before, eh?"

"Once or twice."

She handed him a wrapped paper packet. "That's your supper. Go wash up and then do as you like. Just remember you're up at dawn."

Jeth took it, nodding his thanks. He washed up in a trough. He walked around the keep as he ate his meat pie. It was too dark to see much, though, so he quickly gave up. He wasn't tired, though. The thought of Shae so close and yet so far electrified him. He climbed to the top of the stable roof with an apple for dessert.

There was something *right* about being beneath the open sky. He tipped his head back and took a deep breath, studying the stars.

Think. Just think.

All you have to do is find out where Aneirin is keeping Shae.

You can wait here. Aneirin will come down to see his horse. Shae will be alone. Maid will know where they are. Lie low, make friends, and wait.

And when Aneirin returned to his rooms to find Jeth waiting...

Yes, that was the plan.

Never in his life had a plan been such an abject failure. Four days were *gone*, and not only had Aneirin not come out to see Shadowstep, he hadn't left the keep at all.

Jeth volunteered to get breakfast for everyone, every day, so he could talk to Cook and Maid. He asked casually about all the things going on in the keep—Lord, the deliveries, oh...and what about those two guests?

The answer was always the same: they never left their suite.

What they *did* do was request a different person be brought to them each day.

Four more names were taken, and Jeth just watched. Each loss stabbed like a thorn in his foot. He couldn't let it keep happening, especially when he didn't know what taking their names gave Aneirin. Not when he didn't know if he could get the names back. But he needed one more thing.

He had to ensure Aneirin wouldn't get away.

Shae would know. Shae loved knowledge the way bees loved flowers. They would know what taking the names did, how to get them back, and what Aneirin's plans were. Jeth wished fervently that he could sneak in and speak to them *before* everything was set in motion.

I have to get them.

His other option was to slow Aneirin's escape. He could only do that if he could convince Shadowstep to run off—and this time not to come back. Considering Aneirin seemed to summon the horse from anywhere, he doubted he could do that, either.

He sighed heavily, rubbing a hand down his face. The other was wrapped around a pitchfork as he stood in Shadowstep's stall, staring at the mare miserably.

It was early evening. The faintest stir of a warm breeze toyed with his hair. The fresh smell of hay, dusty and earthy, tickled his nose.

Shadowstep, for her part, kept her hindquarters pointed in Jeth's direction, ignoring him and ensuring he *knew* he was being ignored. Still, it was a vast improvement over how she terrorized the rest of the stable. The mare would tug at Halen's braid, or grab the back of someone's tunic as they passed and yank them down, or startle them by kicking the stall, and so much more.

She tried none of that with Jeth, though he wasn't entirely sure why. Perhaps she recognized him, remembering him from when he was a boy. Perhaps she knew he was the High King of Faerie. Perhaps she just preferred the company of her own kind over humans. He'd never know.

"What is it about you?" Jeth asked the horse sourly, turning back to spreading fresh hay in the bottom of the stall. Shadowstep never left a mess inside. She had a stall open to the paddock, and she took herself out and back.

That didn't mean she shouldn't have fresh straw.

Shadowstep snorted, turning her head toward the sky. The sun was sinking, the sky quickly fading from orange to ink blue.

"What? Something catch your fancy?"

Her head swung around, her eye fixing on Jeth.

"Don't tell me you're mad I'm talking to you? At least I'm here. My father hasn't come down to see you once," he said, voice low. The last thing he wanted was for the others to find out he knew their guests.

Shadowstep's ears pinned, then lifted. She turned, putting her nose near Jeth's hair, lipping at it and his ear.

"Stop that!" Jeth jerked back. "Gross."

Shadowstep turned again, placidly marching across the stall to nudge the saddle hung over the wall. She gave Jeth a pointed look.

Jeth looked between the saddle, the horse, and the saddle again. "You want to go for a ride? With who?"

She kept her gaze on Jeth, a rising intensity in the air.

"With me?" He asked faintly.

The horse tossed her head, bobbing it in something alarmingly like a nod.

"I don't know if I want to. Your loyalty lies with my father, doesn't it?" Jeth set the pitchfork aside before he realized it.

Shadowstep nudged the saddle so hard it nearly fell, then turned and presented her back to Jeth. Her gaze was mesmerizing.

The lowering sun sent a slant of light through the stable, a brief moment of golden brilliance gone in moments. In that glow, Shadowstep's sable coat seemed burnished with copper, her mane glittering like obsidian. She arched her neck.

She looked satisfied.

He wanted to go with her.

Jeth reached out to stroke the horse's neck, unable to stop himself. Almost mechanically, he saddled her, double checking the straps. He was detached from himself, his mind floundering like a man drowning even as his hands moved steadily through the motions.

He was trapped. It was a spell, and he was trapped.

Strange how this brand of magic didn't dull because of his father's blood. Shadowstep was a faerie steed, and she had what she wanted. She entrapped princes, lords, heirs...and kings.

Jeth grit his teeth as he slid the bridle over Shadowstep's head. It had no bit. His mind raced, recalling as many of the stories as he could.

The horse returned at dawn, and the prince was mad. The horse returned at dawn, and the king was dead. The horse returned at dawn...

At dawn?

Everything plunged into gray shadow as the sun set. Jeth fit his foot into the stirrup.

This isn't faerie magic, he realized, his entire body chilled as he swung up into the saddle.

It was a curse.

Jeth took a deep breath. In a perverse show of concern, Shadowstep turned and touched her nose to his knee.

"Oi, Jeth, what do you think you're doing? Get off that thing right now!" Halen shouted.

Shadowstep reared. Jeth clutched both pommel and reins to keep his seat, giving Halen a wild-eyed look as she ran toward him.

"Faerie steed," he managed to shout—and the mare lurched into motion.

The black horse wheeled, charging out into the paddock. Muscles bunched beneath Jeth's knees, his only warning that she planned to jump.

They cleared the fence and tore across the yard, around the keep, and out the gate before he could so much as catch his breath. Cobblestones clattered beneath Shadowstep's hooves as she galloped like mad through Ulma Dale. What few people were left on the streets scattered before her with shouts of alarm.

The *clack-clack* of her hooves turned to the dull *thump-thump* of packed earth beneath them as they left the town behind.

They didn't stay on the road for long. Shadowstep veered into the trees. Jeth shouted in alarm, ducking low over her neck as a branch whizzed over his head.

Her flying mane stung his cheeks where it cracked against his skin like a thousand tiny whips. His grip on the reins was so tight he felt the edges of the leather digging into his skin. His knuckles were white.

Terrifying as it was, it was also exhilarating. He knew it wouldn't stay this way, that he'd grow tired, that she'd test him to his limit and then some. He wanted to shout, to whoop and holler, but he held it in.

This was another test of him, of his abilities. So far, he passed every test he'd been thrown. All he had to do was come up with a plan.

A plan.

Come on, damn it, a plan!

A low, lurching leap sent them over a fallen log. Jeth's heart skipped a beat as he raised out of the saddle, only to jolt back into motion as he landed again with a grunt. That moment of suspension, of floating weightless in the air, brief as it was, showed the first danger.

Falling off.

I can fix that.

Wildly, he cast his senses out, only to recoil a moment later. They were running *directly beneath a leyline*. The golden glow of it blinded his magical senses. Not much power would be needed for this spell, but Jeth needed a constant supply of it. He didn't give in to the temptation. It might be another trap.

Instead, he found smaller sources among the trees and earth and dipped his fingers into them, pulling a trickle of power, casting ahead for the next source even as he doubled what he had and used it to tether himself to the saddle and stirrups. He imagined sewing the seat of his pants in place.

Now hold it.

Already his muscles ached, but now he wasn't fighting to keep his seat. The next battle was to stay balanced, to stay low. More than once, branches whizzed over his head, so close he felt the tines of his antlers tingle.

Jeth avoided all thoughts of those antlers catching on tree branches and what could happen. It helped that Shadowstep was constantly wheeling, turning, weaving. He had his hands full.

The surrounding night turned from blue to black, the shadows beneath the boughs deepening. Those abyssal bits of darkness twisted and writhed as they flew past, turning the ride from an ordeal to a nightmare.

How long had it been? How far was the dawn?

A trickle of warm, sticky liquid on his wrist distracted him. He chanced a glance down, eyes widening. The leather of the reins had cut into his palms as Shadowstep's head sawed back and forth, as he wrestled for control he'd never get. He didn't let go, even as they grew slick.

How long had it been? How long was left?

Those questions verged dangerously close to madness, as if continuing to wonder would make it all the harder to hold on. Still, it echoed like a constant refrain. How long, how long, how long?

Jeth closed his eyes, pouring a constant stream of magic into the spell that kept him seated. Shadowstep's muscles worked beneath him, her sides heaving like bellows, the thud of her hooves all in a row. *Thudthudthud, thudthudthud.*

They lurched left and right. Branches flew overhead. Tree trunks flashed by on either side. Undergrowth slapped against his legs, leaving welts like they were lashes instead of branches.

Jeth held on.

He forced himself to breathe. Inhale. Exhale. The air hissed through clenched teeth. His heart raced beneath his ribs, faster than the horse herself.

The scent of freshly disturbed loam, rich and damp like the earth after rain, filled his lungs. It was accompanied by the crisp, clean scent of cold air. Air that flew past, whistling in his ears, turning his nose and cheeks red. The wind of their passage chilled his hands and ears until they were numb.

Branches snapped and crackled around them, but apart from that, their mingled breathing, and the wind, there was nothing. If he closed his eyes, it almost sounded like they were running through walls of fire.

Jeth's world narrowed to the horse surging beneath him, to the power he was drawing, to his own breathing. Inhale. Exhale.

Hold on.

Inhale.

Hold on!

Exhale.

Jeth's body went blessedly numb—after how long, he didn't know. He felt the sticky crust of dried blood on his arms and hands and ignored it. He felt the prickle of sweat on his brow and down his back. He ignored it.

The sound of Shadowstep's hooves changed. They raced along pounded earth, and no more trees or branches battered him. He clung with his knees despite his spell. His arms shook from exhaustion. All he wanted to do was let the reins drop. He could hardly feel his hands. He could hardly feel *anything.*

But I will tomorrow.

If tomorrow ever came.

Shadowstep slowed from her headlong gallop to a canter, and then down to a trot. A walk. She stopped.

His ears rang in the sudden silence, chest heaving with every breath. He didn't know when he'd closed his eyes, but it seemed almost impossible to open them now. He did. The open gate set in the wall surrounding Ulma Dale stood before them. The town itself stretched quietly up the hillside, almost every window dark.

The first light of dawn painted the horizon pale in pink and blue.

Shadowstep stepped through the gate, walking as sedately as an old pony as she made her way back up the hill to the keep. Jeth pried his fingers one by one from the reins in his hands, peeling the leather out of the cuts in his skin with a hiss. He let the spell holding him in place fizzle out.

They were back in the stable before he'd finished.

As though they were returning from a lovely picnic instead of a deadly race, Shadowstep stopped politely beside her loose box in the stable. Jeth snorted softly, slithering out of the saddle.

His legs buckled. Instinctively, he caught himself on Shadowstep. The mare turned to nose at him gently.

Jeth could *sense* her fondness and concern.

"Don't even give me that. I'm only like this because of *you,*" he muttered.

Shadowstep nosed him again.

It was necessary.

Despite his exhaustion and mounting pain, Jeth tended to the horse. *His* horse. He pulled off the saddle and bridle and draped them over the wall of her stall. He opened the gate, checked that there was water and feed, and gave her a brisk rub down—not that she showed any sign at all of their wild ride.

His arms felt like lead. His legs were like over-boiled cabbage, barely able to hold him up. His hands throbbed in time with his pulse.

As soon as Shadowstep was seen to, his knees gave out. The dusty, earthy scent of fresh hay enveloped him. It was clean. He'd replaced it himself.

Jeth crumpled sideways into it, the stalks prickling against his skin.

That was the last thing he remembered before he sank into darkness.

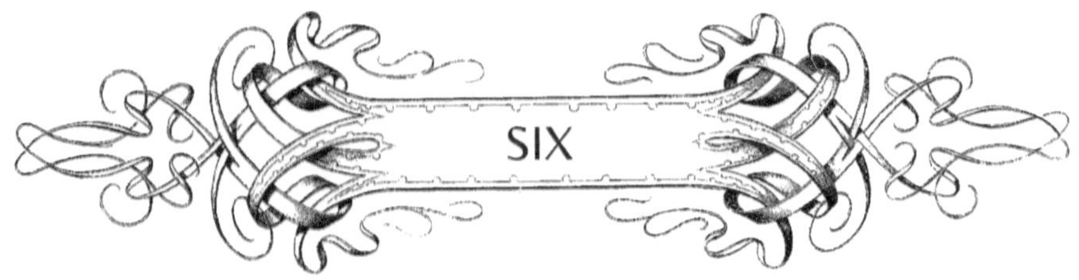

SIX

Halen clicked her tongue, dabbing at his hands with a damp cloth. She paused now and then to eye her work critically.

Jeth sat on an overturned bucket, his hands on his knees. "Ow," he said blandly as she poured water into the cuts.

Halen snorted, dabbing them dry before winding clean bandages around them. "What on earth were you thinking, mounting a faerie horse?" she scolded.

"I didn't really have a choice, Halen."

From her stall across the way, Shadowstep whickered in smug agreement.

"Well, you survived. That's all that really matters. Haven't heard of too many folk doing that. Earned the loyalty of the thing, too, didn't you?"

"I think so," Jeth said slowly. Her thoughts were certainly in his head, now. He could sense where she was, and he felt he could call to her from anywhere and she would come.

How many of the survivors in the stories were faeries? Jeth wondered. Aneirin must have done the same thing to gain the mare's services, sometime long in the past. Was he one of the tales?

Now he'd done it too, and he gained her loyalty. The loyalty of a terrible, needy, high-strung...

Shadowstep lifted her head, ears pinned back, and gave an indignant snort.

I'm not taking it back.

He'd never seen a horse give someone a withering look before.

Jeth was tired, too tired to deal with this revelation. He ached all over. His hands throbbed, and it hurt whenever he opened them fully—which Halen insisted he do, of course. Muscles he didn't even realize he had protested every movement.

At least Halen has given me the day off.

She saw him up the ladder and into his cot, where he sank into the mattress with a groan. In the quiet, with the soft sounds of horses beneath him, he dozed.

The wild ride through the night awoke something in him. A spark of frustration blazed into a bonfire of fury. It was time. He didn't care anymore. If he could survive Shadowstep, he could survive anything his powerless father threw at him.

No more names will be stolen if I have any say in it.

Just as soon as he...slept.

Jeth woke with a jolt, heart racing. The sun hung low over the horizon, and his muscles were stiff. Every movement ached. But his dream, convoluted as it was, had given him the answer. It was so simple.

Jeth had the Moot Crown.

Aneirin was still a faerie. The crystalline circlet commanded all the faeries of the courts. All Jeth had to do was walk inside and command his father to obey, to listen to him, to take no names and harm no humans.

To give him Shae.

He could end this right here and now.

Jeth flexed his hands, letting the sting wake him fully. Shae was good with herbs and poultices. They'd be able to help with his injuries after they were reunited. He could hear them now.

What the hells did you do to these? I swear, I leave you alone for a few days and...

I rode a cursed horse all night. It's fine, though. I didn't come back mad or dead.

No, you just came back near cut to pieces!

They'd pull faces and speak hard, but their hands would be gentle and sure. They'd fuss in their own way while they healed, constantly checking on him.

He closed his eyes. His heart ached.

I can't go another day without them.

It was time.

Jeth slipped out of bed, fishing his satchel from the shadows beneath it. He peeled himself out of his filthy worker's clothes, pulling on his fine traveling clothes instead. A soft shirt so light and rich a brown it was nearly gold. His blue leather tunic. A gold sash for a belt.

He dropped the glamour on his antlers, settling the Moot Crown on his brow. The time for hiding was past.

Heedless of the people who might see him, Jeth climbed down out of the loft, satchel banging against his side. By the time he stood on the ground, he was no longer the stable hand. He was every inch the faerie king.

Halen gasped, her pitchfork clattering as it fell to the floor. Her eyes were wide as saucers, a hand pressed over her heart.

Jeth's expression softened. He paused beside her. "I owe you a great debt, Halen. You'll collect on it before I leave."

She nodded numbly.

He turned away. As soon as he did, all warmth vanished from his expression. He forged his face into cold, unforgiving steel.

He swept through the kitchen door, startling a shout out of Cook. With gasps and clatters, the servants scattered through every available door. Jeth stepped into the broad stone corridors of the keep.

The stone floors and walls were softened by rugs and tapestries, rich and colorful. He passed them without pausing to admire the fine artistry. Up the sweeping staircase. Down the hall. He slowed, brow furrowed.

The corridors were lined with doors. Where would Aneirin be hiding?

"Oh!"

He turned at the soft gasp, eyes locking with Maid's. She stood in the center of the hall, her arms wrapped tight around a stack of linens. Her jaw hung slack.

"Jeth?" she breathed. "Are you..."

"Maid," he said gently. "Where is he? The faerie guest."

"But you have..." She lifted a hand to the air over her own head.

"Yes. Maid, please."

"But where did they come from?"

"Maid."

She swallowed once. Twice. "This way. He's this way."

She turned on her heel and led them down the hall to a tall, beautiful door. It was carved with scenes in the panels, images of humans at the hunt.

"These were Lord's rooms, before. He pushed him out."

"Don't worry, Maid. I'll do what I can." Jeth put a hand on her shoulder. "Go. Warn Lord. Warn everyone. Keep them away from here."

There would be no more collateral damage if he could help it.

Maid ran, her arms still full of bedsheets that wouldn't make it onto their bed.

Jeth didn't knock. He flung the door open and swept into the room.

Rooms. There were two, a sitting room and, through open double doors to his left, a massive bedchamber. Aneirin stood perfectly framed by the open entryway. Before him was a beautiful gilded looking glass with whirling golden edges. Aneirin studied himself critically in its polished surface. His gaze never shifted from his own face or the rich silks he held in his hands.

"Aneirin," Jeth said, the word edged with ice. "Where are they? Where is Shae?"

"Hm?" Aneirin glanced back at last, taking Jeth in from the tips of his antlers to the scuffed toes of his travel-worn boots. He paused at the bandages wrapped around Jeth's hands, a brow ticking upward slightly.

"Ah, Jeth. It's about time you showed yourself. I felt you lurking somewhere out there. Watching. Waiting. What did you see?"

"You're stealing names."

Aneirin's lips curved into a cold, careless smile. He sauntered to the wardrobe, tucking the fine tunic he held back among a sea of its fellows. He sorted through the rainbow of hues, pulling out two more.

"What do you think? Black and gold, or black and silver?"

"What?"

"I'm asking which suits me," Aneirin said slowly, as if it might make Jeth understand.

Jeth's brow furrowed. "How are you taking their names?"

"Are you sure that's the right question?" His father turned back to the mirror, lifting one tunic, then the other, studying himself critically.

Jeth's brow furrowed. His palms stung as his hands balled into fists. The pain grounded him, kept him from following where Aneirin led. He *wanted* him to get worked up and frustrated.

I won't give him the pleasure.

"You ought to be asking *why*," Aneirin said into the silence stretching between them. "It matters far more than the how. And don't you want them back? You haven't asked me about that at all."

"You have no power," Jeth said slowly.

"I have some, now. This holding swore its loyalty to me many, many years ago in exchange for prosperity. I've taken a bit of that power back, is all." His head tipped to one side. "I've never been a fan of gold. Too flashy for my taste."

Aneirin tucked the black and gold tunic back into the wardrobe. He changed into a silver silk shirt and the black and silver doublet as though Jeth weren't even there.

"Why, then? Why are you stealing names?"

"I'm so glad you asked." Aneirin smirked at his own reflection as he ran his hands through his hair. He pulled out black trews and matching boots with silver buttons up the side, next. Once more he changed as though Jeth mattered about as much as an ant.

Jeth's jaw clenched, but he didn't react. Aneirin was playing games, but he didn't know Jeth had the upper hand. He wore the Moot Crown. Whenever he wanted to, he could end this. He could demand answers. He was in control.

Aneirin loved the sound of his own voice, loved his own cleverness. If he were patient, his father would talk. He wouldn't have to show his hand. Not yet.

Aneirin sat on a massive clothes chest, tightening the laces on the sides of his boots. His head bent, his long black hair hanging like a curtain over his shoulder.

Jeth's patience was wearing thin. His lips parted.

Not yet, Shae's voice seemed to whisper. *Don't rush. You have a plan, don't you?*

Always cautioning him to think things through, that one. He did have a plan. *So stick to it a little longer.*

Where are you, Shae? Are you alright?

There was no answer.

"There's power in a name, you know, but there's more in an identity," Aneirin said suddenly. "A complex thing, that. Everything we like, everything we hate, everything we do, all tied up and topped with the bow of the name we attach to ourselves. Take it away and a person becomes one thing. One note. All they are, or were, or will be is suddenly all tied up in a single word. Lord, Maid, Baker, Cook, Smith, Drover."

Aneirin stood, studying himself in the mirror.

"An identity is made of so much more, and *that* is what I take. The certainty of who someone is. When all they have left is what they do, what are they? What happens if they stop doing that one thing? Will they cease to exist?"

He tucked his hair behind a pointed ear tip.

"They'll forge new identities," Jeth said, hoping it was true.

"Oh, of course. But it will take them years, as it took them years the first time. And while they do that, I have taken the power of who they were and distilled it, turning it into something new. Knowledge is *power*. A person knows themselves better than anyone else ever will. Their knowledge of self is a potent magic."

Jeth's brows drew down sharply. It took only a flicker of his True Sight to see it.

Aneirin's power was still much depleted, but it was *there,* which should have been impossible. He had magic. It was just a trickle, a thimbleful at most. Aneirin was filling a dry well from scratch. The names he'd taken weren't enough to allow him to cast. A single spell would take everything he had and more.

His father would have to steal more names, more identities, throw more lives into chaos, more people into crisis.

"You'll have to excuse yourself, now. Lord Perival—Oh, my apologies. *Lord* is having a luncheon, and I have so many powerful names to take. I need to finish getting ready."

Not again.

"Freeze," Jeth said. The Moot Crown swirled with power and sent it into the air.

Aneirin stilled, brows raised.

"Tell me what you're planning," he commanded.

Silence.

One heartbeat.

Three.

Five.

Aneirin laughed. He *laughed,* turning back to the mirror and fussing with his appearance. "Did you truly believe that would work on me?"

Jeth's heart hammered beneath his ribs, even though he swore he felt it stop. "What? No, it must."

"It works, oh High King of Faerie, on the creatures of the Courts. There are so, so few of us who have been ousted, thrown away, left to fend for themselves. I can count them on one hand, and that includes myself." His eyes narrowed.

Jeth's hands clenched tight, cuts throbbing in time with his pulse.

"I have not belonged to the Courts since my son stole my throne, my place, and my power." Aneirin's gaze was cold as ice and burned with fury. He stared at Jeth in the reflection of the mirror. His voice was a knife, sharp and cutting.

A thrill of fear and a rush of anger threatened to sweep Jeth beyond reason. Never in his life had he wanted to throttle someone so much.

"Imagine my surprise when I finally got that little changeling of yours to tell me what you've been up to."

"Shae—I swear, if you've hurt them–" Jeth said, surging forward a step.

Aneirin held up a hand, stopping him in his tracks. He turned away from the mirror at last. "You used all that power that I gave you, all that magic, to protect humans? Filthy, crawling, grasping mortals. A blink and they're gone. A touch and they crumble. Imagine my surprise when you followed in *her* footsteps instead of mine. That cheating *witch*."

"Don't you dare speak of my mother that way," Jeth snapped.

Gleda Penistone was worth so much more than Aneirin would ever be. Even after all these years, Jeth remembered her. Her hands, her voice, the lessons she taught him.

"You can't command me not to, Jeth. You can't control me at all. So tell me..."

Aneirin turned, his eyes cold, promising a frost that would cover the world.

"Are you willing to kill me to protect your precious, pathetic humans?"

Jeth's mouth went dry, his pulse rushing in his ears. He forgot to breathe. Kill? He'd never had to kill before. Every instinct in his body screamed.

No. This isn't me. That won't be me.

That's what Aneirin would do.

He remembered a wintery forest, riding on the seat of a wagon beside Burne Calder. Smears of red stained the snow. The lone arm of a bandit had lain tangled in a shrub, propped up by the snarl of barren branches. Aneirin killed. He killed without mercy, as though humans were dolls made of straw.

Aneirin killed his mother.

Her life mattered. Burne Calder, her children, her granddaughter Anabette, they mattered. Shae, and all the people Shae lost when they were changed, they *mattered.* A line of Queens he had never met. Lord, Maid, Cook, and Baker. Halen and the stable hands.

They didn't matter to Aneirin.

His father would tear their identities apart, and who knew if he would stop there or if he'd do something worse? Aneirin would see them all suffer horribly, but even then...

...even then, Jeth couldn't kill.

Aneirin smirked as Jeth's shoulders dipped ever so slightly. He crossed the room, a hand curling around the back of his neck, pulling him closer. Aneirin whispered in his ear.

"I knew you couldn't do it. You don't have what it takes. So you will leave. This world is mine."

Jeth's heart twisted in his chest. He was no coward. And death wasn't the only option, no matter what Aneirin thought.

"No, Father. No, it's not."

He started to channel a spell.

SEVEN

For decades, Jeth traveled across the known lands to learn as much magic as he could. Most spells he picked up to take apart, to learn how to break them. Faerie magic in particular was cruel and twisted, a flavor of magic he did his best to destroy.

Now he cast one of those spells.

The golden power surged in his chest and raced up through his ear tips, through the Moot Crown. Jeth's entire body hummed with magic, every inch of his skin tingling.

Aneirin stilled, eyes widening a fraction. His otherwise impassive face was set in a faint, disapproving frown. He didn't have the means to fight back. What little power he'd gleaned from stealing names wouldn't be enough to save him if Jeth attacked.

A flicker of fear kindled deep in his red-orange eyes. Aneirin thought he meant to kill him.

Jeth let his power crackle between his fingertips, reveling in it. He felt a thousand feet tall. And his father? His father was just an ant. He *could* crush him. He could rend him to pieces with a single thought.

Instead, he pulled magic out in thin wires from the molten pool of gold within him. They snaked through the air, spreading like the branches of a tree. Jeth arranged them just so, pouring his will into them.

He'd learned three variations on the imprisonment spell after Aneirin used one on him.

It was complicated work. He lifted a hand, weaving the strands into the edge of the mirror, lining every inch with magic as thick as a new layer of paint. The prison itself was decided by the caster. When Aneirin trapped him, he thought of nothing, and nothing was what they found within.

Jeth was kinder than that. He built a comfortable prison, bleeding magic into the mirror, *beyond* the mirror, to create a room for his father to spend the rest of his days. Windows that weren't real showed landscapes that never existed. Books he vaguely remembered, knowing the spell would fill them in. A fireplace that would never need wood and would never go out. Walls of stone. A bed, a chair, a desk. He could conjure whatever he wished, and he gave his father comfort. Peace.

All it took was the barest outlines of the objects. Magic flowed like water, filling each vessel until something solid was left behind.

The polished glass surface of the mirror turned liquid and silver, smooth and still.

It took only seconds to cast it all.

"You wouldn't dare touch me again," Aneirin snarled, his calm disintegrating. He watched the threads weave around him, fingers arched like claws, his teeth bared. The faerie didn't realize the power was not meant to trap him. He didn't see it pouring into the mirror.

Sparks danced across Jeth's hands and forearms. "Wouldn't I? After all you've done?"

"Disgusting little whelp. You can do *nothing* to me. You're too softhearted to stop me, too kind to kill."

"You're right. I am too kind," Jeth agreed, releasing the last of the power like a sigh. It faded from the air.

Aneirin looked smug.

"I could have trapped you in darkness again, but I choose this instead."

He swung his hands up. A rush of air swept through the room, slamming the wardrobe doors shut.

Aneirin shouted, lifting his arms to cover his face. The wind slid him backward across the floor.

Jeth did it again, advancing with each burst, until finally he charged Aneirin.

Their bodies met like crashing waves, slamming into one another with every bit of strength they had.

Jeth was younger, but he wasn't stronger. His arms trembled beneath the pressure his father exerted. But Jeth had magic. It surged through his arms and legs. He pressed forward, teeth grit, as his power matched Aneirin's.

Outstripped Aneirin's.

Step by agonizing step, Jeth pressed him backward. Three steps left.

Two.

Aneirin glanced back, realization spurring him to struggle anew. He clawed at Jeth, eyes wild, teeth bared in a snarl. He tore at clothes and hair. He couldn't touch the Moot Crown, but that didn't mean he didn't try.

One step.

"No!" Aneirin screamed.

Jeth heaved.

The silver surface of the mirror rippled, giving way without a sound. It was surreal to see Aneirin sink into it, to see the silver run over his face and hands like molten metal. The faerie's furious screech cut off abruptly. His hand caught at the edge, but the magic dragged him slowly, inexorably, in.

The distortions of the glass smoothed, leaving a fog behind. A fog, and the shadow of a man, his hands pressed against the glass from the inside. The door was locked.

Jeth panted, lifting a hand to his cheek. His fingers came away red with blood from scratches Aneirin had left behind. It stung. The longer he stood there, the more everything started to sting, to ache, to throb. His knees trembled with fatigue.

The fog slowly gave way to show Aneirin frothing at the mouth as he battered his hands against the glass. His lips moved, but no sound, no sound at all, came through the glass.

"There. Rob a name from *that*," Jeth muttered.

Aneirin threw himself at the glass, shoulder first, the faintest *clunk* coming through. And again. *Clunk.* And –

CLUNK.

Jeth whirled, instinctively reaching for power. That hadn't come from the mirror.

The lid of the clothes chest Aneirin had used as a bench rattled fiercely. Wariness gave way to relief. In two steps, Jeth stood in front of it. He threw open the lid.

Shae glared up at him. They were bound hand and foot with silk scarves, and gagged with a third. If looks could summon thunderstorms, Shae would conjure a hurricane.

Jeth yanked the scarf free. "Shae! Thank the heavens."

"About damn time!" Shae burst out, holding their hands up.

Grinning, Jeth picked at the knot holding the silk shackles closed.

"Do you realize it has been weeks? Weeks, Jeth. And for days, he kept putting me in this box when he was tired of me. Like I was a child's toy. Do you know how uncomfortable it is to sleep in a wooden box?"

The scarf fell away and Jeth bent to get Shae's ankles free, too.

"And he did the most terrible things. He stole the names of nearly a dozen people, all told, and he was going to steal an entire feast's worth tonight. You cut it really close, you know. I'm so mad at you."

Jeth helped Shae out of the box, then scooped them into his arms, kissing them deeply. It cut off any further tirade. Shae clung to Jeth, slowly relaxing. They were safe now.

"I missed you, too," Jeth said with a grin, his forehead resting against the changeling's.

Shae smiled—only for it to fade. They looked around warily, the tension returning to their shoulders. "Where is he?"

"In the mirror."

"What?" Shae pulled away, approaching the mirror like a deer in the woods, ready to startle and run at any moment. "Hells, this is the one from overseas, isn't it? It worked?"

"As far as I can tell."

"But it's a doorway spell!"

"He hasn't got the power to open the door," Jeth said firmly.

"Yet. Who knows what he can do, given a few centuries?" Shae stared at Aneirin in the glass.

His father only had eyes for Jeth, eyes full of murder.

"Shae, are you alright? He didn't hurt you, did—Shae, wait!"

Shae did not wait. They grabbed the edges of the mirror and heaved with all the strength in their small, slim body. The mirror tipped forward. Shae darted out of the way.

Jeth met Aneirin's stunned gaze only a moment before the whole thing hit the floor with a crash that could have woken the dead.

Glass went skittering across the floor in every direction, little pieces and great shards alike. For good measure, Shae stomped furiously on the delicate wooden frame until it cracked and splintered.

"What in skies' name is going on?" shouted a voice in the distance.

Jeth pulled Shae away from the mirror, even as the furious changeling kicked at the fragments. Panting heavily, Shae stood with their hands balled into fists and a challenge in their eyes.

A man came swinging around the corner. He was dressed in a fine doublet that stretched across his portly belly. The bald pate at the top of his head gleamed. Fine rings adorned his fingers.

"You must be Lord," Jeth said mildly. "Lord Perival?"

Lord paused, eyes widening, a thoughtful look crossing his face. "Perival. Lord Perival. Why, that feels like it fits. Like a nice hat. Why, that's *my* name, isn't it?" It clicked into place, and Jeth felt it, felt the tiny thread snap between Aneirin—wherever he was—and the lord before them.

Lord Perival's gaze dropped to the mirror. His face turned red. He puffed his chest out and turned on them. "Now, see here. I don't know who in the blazing hells you think you are, but I ought to have you—you…"

Perival faltered as his gaze lifted just a few inches from Jeth's face to his antlers.

To his crown.

Perival paled.

"Forgive me, your Majesty, king of the fae," he stammered, taking a large step back before he bowed.

"No, no, just call me Jeth," he said quickly. He pulled the crown off his head, shoving it into the satchel at his side. "I'm sorry if I upset your household. I needed to handle your…guest."

Lord Perival's lip curled. His nose wrinkled like he smelled something bad. "Ah, yes. My guest. And where has he gone?"

"There," Shae said smugly, pointing at the utterly destroyed mirror at their feet.

The lord stared at the shards scattered across the stone, realization dawning in his eyes. Then, Pervial sighed, shoulders slumping, something like pain crossing his features. "You have no idea how dreadfully expensive it was to get a looking glass like that. And now it's gone!"

Jeth picked his way across the room, glass grinding beneath his boot heels. "I can give you some gold to make up for your loss. It's a shame to lose a one-of-a-kind piece of art."

"I don't lament the loss itself, lad. Aneirin is—was—a bastard. I know he took my name, and others besides. But my greatest grandfather promised Ulma Dale to him as a playground centuries ago. Back then, it was little more than a stone lump on a hill."

Lord Perival sighed, shaking his head as he nudged a piece of the frame with a toe.

"And I'd certainly mourn this mirror less if it *were* one of a kind. I can always get someone to make a one-of-a-kind mirror. *This* one was part of a set."

The hair on the back of Jeth's neck lifted, his entire body tingling like lightning was about to strike. "What? What did you say?"

"A set?" Shae whirled on Jeth, flinging their arms wide. "You didn't check to see if the mirror was part of a set?"

"I didn't have much time, considering I was in the middle of a fight!"

"What's wrong with it being part of a set?" Perival arched a brow.

"Each identical piece becomes another door," Jeth admitted slowly. Shae was right. This was a problem.

"Can he open them?"

Jeth shook his head. "No, not yet at least."

Shae grabbed Lord's arm. "How many are there?"

"What?"

"How many mirrors are in the set?"

"Five. Well, four now, since you broke mine."

Jeth paced, chewing on his lower lip. "You don't happen to know where they are?"

"Yes. Yes, I know. One was given to the king of Olmiven, to the west. And one to the ambassador to Pelusir, to speak to the king about an arranged marriage. One of their princesses to our crown prince. Two more belong to the royal family. One in the summer palace, and one in the castle itself."

"The castle," Shae echoed flatly.

"Yes. In Sol Krona."

Of all the places he'd been in Hallanor, Jeth had always avoided the capital city and the soaring palace there. He cleared his throat. "I see."

Lord Perival planted his hands on his hips as he paced back and forth. Glass crunched beneath his feet. "The artisan probably still has the mold, too. Craftworker Olyver."

Shae rolled their eyes, casting an exasperated look in Jeth's direction. "The artisan still has the mold. Four mirrors, and the artisan *still has the mold.*"

"Then we'll just go get it," Jeth snapped. "Come on, let's go."

Shae sighed, fishing their pack out of the wardrobe and slinging it over their shoulders. They pulled on their hat. "For one solution, a dozen more problems."

"Only five," Jeth said. He smiled. It was good to have Shae with him again.

"You really couldn't have asked before you confronted him?"

"I didn't know I was going to put him in the mirror when I started."

The pair stepped into the hall, leaving the newly re-named Lord Perival and his household to pick up the pieces—literally and figuratively—of their lives. They had a new task. Ensure that Aneirin couldn't tear any more lives apart.

Break the mirrors.

"How far is it to Sol Krona?" Shae asked.

"Walking? Nearly two weeks. Maybe more."

"Weeks? *Weeks?*"

Jeth slipped his hand into Shae's. The ring on his pinkie brushed against the changeling's skin. He'd never have to use it to find them again, he vowed. Every argument, every sour expression, every roll of their eyes was sweet as honey on Jeth's tongue. He could kiss Shae to within an inch of both their lives and then some, if they'd let him.

"We can't take weeks to get there," Shae muttered.

Jeth brought the back of their hand to his lips, smiling as he kissed it.

"Don't worry, I've arranged a ride."

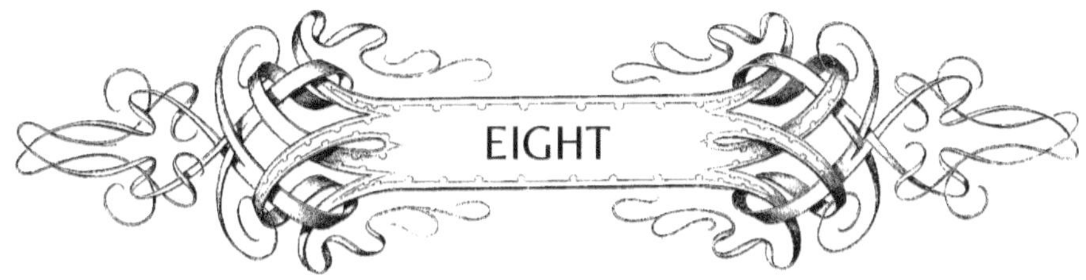

EIGHT

Sol Krona was beautiful.

I shouldn't be surprised. But he was.

On his travels, he'd seen towns and villages and tiny hamlets, cities, ports, and more. Sol Krona was the golden crown over it all, as its name implied. When Hallanor was founded, a faerie married a human, and they built the kingdom together. It was why the faeries had covenants they had to follow, why the humans could carve a living out of the faerie forest. The first king and queen built the city together, planning for it to be Hallanor's crowning achievement.

It showed.

The streets fanned out from the castle walls like the overlapping curved-to-a-point scales of a dragon. Major thoroughfares arched to meet one another in diamond shaped markets, and smaller roads wove between the buildings built within each layered scale.

Nestled across a huge round valley as it was, it was impossible not to notice the artistry of it. Every road into Sol Krona rose to the top of a hill before it wound down to the massive stone gates at every entrance. Stone! Stone and metal and not a bit of wood among them. How much did they weigh?

In the center of the petal-like spread of the city was the jewel in the crown – the castle itself. The pristine stone was so pale a gray that it looked white when the sun shone upon it, with peaked rooftops in blue and gold.

I don't even want to know how much that cost.

Turrets and towers stacked higher and higher beside one another until it was hard to tell where the original castle began. The whole thing was built up, not out, and it soared. It left ample room for its grounds and the surrounding city. It was magnificent, and it radiated *history*.

Shadowstep danced beneath him impatiently.

Shae tightened their arms around Jeth's waist. "Stop that," they snapped.

The mare stopped with a snort, head swinging around, ears pinned. She scuffed a hoof across the ground.

"Both of you, knock it off. You've been going at it all morning." Jeth rubbed his brow. They'd actually been going at it for three days, which was how long it had taken them to get here from Ulma Dale.

"Well, to be fair, my last ride with them wasn't very comfortable," Shae said with false sweetness.

Shadowstep snorted again, tossing her head. Her thoughts grew clearer in Jeth's head every day.

You weren't supposed to be.

Jeth didn't pass on the message.

He nudged Shadowstep into a walk, gaze on the castle. The entire way here, he was plagued with nightmares. He'd stop in front of mirrors, only for his father's face to stare back at him instead of his own. Hands would stretch out of the glass, clawing for his throat.

He hadn't slept well.

Shae didn't sleep well either. They spoke little of what happened while they were apart, but Aneirin hadn't treated them kindly. A moon, no, more than a moon separated the pair of them from one another, and it felt like a chasm.

"Can't we go any faster?" Shae asked, gaze fixed on the castle.

And I thought I was anxious to get this over with.

Jeth wrestled his own nerves with the need to blend in. They both wanted this over with. Shae had been stolen from their family ages ago—by Aneirin. Jeth's mother had been killed—by Aneirin.

And those were merely the worst things to happen to them both at his hands.

Jeth's grip tightened on the reins, the mostly healed cuts on his palms protesting the movement. The scratches on his cheek were nearly gone, too. Shae worked wonders with just a touch of power and a good salve.

Shadowstep flicked her ears as she walked, lifting her head to look at the quickly approaching gate.

Jeth cast his glamours over his antlers. Behind him, Shae pulled on their hat to hide their pointed ears.

They passed beneath the gate as the last of Jeth's spells settled into place. Even before Jeth had altered the balance between two species, it was common for the people of towns and cities to chase the faeries from their streets. If not that, then the humans avoided them. Faeries wore disguises—just like Jeth.

The streets were full of people, but it didn't feel crowded. The broad streets were full of cheery faces. The air brimmed with promise. Spring had well and truly arrived. New flowers grew in window boxes above the street or planters outside doorways and shops. Riding along the curved streets toward the castle took them through half a dozen markets, each strung with colorful pennants and full of stalls. It had the air of a festival, as if Hallanor finally stirred awake, and it all started here in its heart.

Jeth smiled at the sight of children running with hoops and sticks, shouting as they raced them down the road. The buildings were all three or four stories high, especially near the outer wall. Shared spaces, if the sheer volume of people were any indication. As they rode through the city, the houses grew no shorter—but for a time they grew slimmer. They became the abodes of single families. They swelled back in size as they neared the castle walls, becoming mansions and estates to house the wealthy and noble.

All of it paled to the eight story magnificence of the castle itself. Jeth dismounted Shadowstep at a park in the massive building's shadow. Shae slid down beside him.

"Why don't you stay here with Shadowstep?" Jeth asked.

"Absolutely not."

"Well, there's no stable here. We'll have to go back, and–"

Shadowstep tossed her head, turning and walking off into the park. *I'll keep hidden.*

Jeth stared after her. "You can do that?" he called.

She snorted, glancing back. If she had brows, one would have been raised.

Of course she could. Jeth shrugged, stifling a smile.

Shae gasped. "You like her."

"I do, a little," Jeth admitted, turning to brush his knuckles across Shae's cheek. "I seem to have a thing for grumpy and unapproachable, though, don't I?"

They smiled, rolling their eyes. "I did everything I could to warn you away."

"I'm glad it didn't work." He laced their fingers together.

Side by side, they approached the castle gates, which stood wide open. Guards stood on either side, stopping people coming in and monitoring who went out, but it was a simple enough task to distract them with a bit of magic. The same spell to avoid notice that Jeth cast on his antlers worked on entire people as well.

They were through the gate and walking up the broad path to the circular courtyard and the castle's front doors in moments.

"We need a plan," Jeth said, scanning the windows.

"You and your plans."

"Our first order of business should be the artisan, Olyver."

"Jeth."

"We need to see if he still has the mold. Or maybe he has the plans."

"Jeth," Shae said more urgently.

"And then we'll ask where –"

"*Jeth.*" Shae stopped in their tracks.

Jeth stared at them. "What?"

"Look, there's something above the door." Shae nodded toward it, eyes narrowed. "Worked into those carvings. Can you see it?"

Jeth studied the intricate geometric designs, lips parted to say no, no he didn't—but out of instinct he glanced at it with his True Sight.

Shae was right. Words hid within the carvings, worked into the design so cleverly they were almost impossible to see unless they were highlighted with the magic they'd been carved with.

Whosoever wishes to step within, be they human or not, must an invitation have: through spoken word or thought.

He dropped his true sight, frowning. "It's a faerie covenant."

Normally, this would be wonderful news.

The Queens and Kings of Faerie, including his father, all had designs on the royal family of Hallanor at some point or another. They wanted to control the Queen, whose lineage had a drop of faerie blood.

That blood would bind her to the Moot Crown's command. Jeth ran his fingers over his satchel and the pointed lumps beneath, unease growing between his shoulder blades. That damn crown.

At least it would never be easy for a faerie to set foot inside the castle to get to the royal family.

I wonder if they knew, or if they thought they could just sweep right in and command their way to power?

Had he gotten further than any of the faeries had?

Well, any of the other faeries, he corrected himself with a frown. No matter how he felt, he was one of them.

"What do we do?" Shae asked. "Stand in front of the door and look lost?"

"By spoken word or thought," Jeth mused. "Let's try the kitchens instead. We're grimy enough to pass for mid-level servants, I think."

Shae sighed and looked down at their clothes. "I want a bath."

"Tonight, I promise." Jeth towed them toward the side of the castle. "Let me hide your ears."

Shae pulled off their hat, nose wrinkled. It took barely a breath of power to settle the glamour over the changeling's ear tips. As the spell settled, Shae sulked.

"Glamours itch."

Jeth laughed softly. "I know. Would you believe me if I said I was sorry?"

"Not even for a minute."

Jeth knew they did.

It took half a bell of careful wandering, avoiding as much notice as possible, for the pair to happen upon a quiet corner tucked into the join of three walls that weren't quite square with one another. It had been fenced off. Chickens clucked and chattered as they wandered about their little yard. A maid sat on a stool outside the fence, basking in the spring sun even as she plucked a hen, shoving the loose feathers into a bag at her feet.

Jeth cleared his throat softly as they approached.

"Heavens be," she gasped, looking up. "You near turned my hair white." She was far too young to go gray yet, a fair thing with dark hair and dark eyes over a delicate nose and a full mouth. She was pretty, and there was a cleverness in her eyes that Jeth liked. She studied them intently.

"Our apologies. We're a bit turned around," He said gently.

"What are you looking for?"

"Work?"

"Ha!" She smiled, waving a hand idly through the air. "Not turned around, then, just not far enough. You keep on going around this wall. The kitchen's a little way on."

"Would you mind showing us?"

"Oh, sure. I can always finish this inside." She gathered up her chicken by its feet, and the bag of feathers in her other hand. "Come on."

Jeth glanced at Shae as they fell into step behind her, a brow lifting.

Shae stared back, then sighed, gesturing at the girl. *Go ahead.*

"We owe you for this. What do you want, more than anything?" Jeth asked idly.

The kitchen maid laughed. "You mean besides a lot less plucking and pot scrubbing? Thanks for the offer, but not even you can send along a handsome stranger to whisk me away to a better life," she teased.

Jeth grinned. Shae snorted. That was exactly the sort of thing he *could* do. Jeth sank into the magic, letting Shae lead him by the hand.

A faerie bargain was a complicated piece of magic. With Anabette Calder, it was much easier. Extending a bargain already made was as simple as stretching.

Weaving an entirely new deal was a completely different matter. Jeth let his mind run along the threads that connected everything, moving faster than thought as he followed each trail.

It would be all too easy to pick the nearest noble to turn her into a mistress—that was how most faerie deals turned sour. They were hasty, with faeries only doing enough to meet the terms of the agreement.

Jeth wanted better for her, which took doing.

He skipped along the threads between the maid and everyone she knew. He found nothing. So he expanded his hunt to others in the kitchens, searching, hoping...

Aha.

There, a thread from the castle's top pastry chef led to his cousin, a kind and wealthy merchant—who was looking for a wife.

From there, Jeth raced along the man's suppliers until he found a tradesperson with a rare pink sugar to sell. He tied the first thread between that sugar and the merchant, planting the thought that the pastry chef would pay handsomely for such a rare thing. The next thread was tied between the maid and the chef, to ensure they'd develop a friendship that would ensure she was around when the merchant arrived. And the last, between her and the merchant...

Dark and dainty was the man's type, and she'd feel compelled to help him unload his cart of all the fine goods. She was clever, very much so, and curious besides. She'd make a good merchant's wife, running numbers and helping to plan routes. She wouldn't sit idle and spend his coin, like he feared. And he wouldn't be old or unkind, like *she* feared.

He tied off the threads. With a *snap,* the bargain settled into place. Immediately, his head throbbed, and he lifted a hand to his temple.

Faerie bargains required magic from inside the caster. They were draining, at best. Still, he didn't regret it.

"Got it, then?" Shae whispered.

"Yes. It's a good match. They'll be happy."

Shae smiled softly.

All the kitchen maid had to do was invite them inside to set it into motion. Within six moons, she'd be the lady of a manor, managing accounting books for her doting new husband.

"Alright, you two, come this way," she said, stepping through a door.

Jeth grinned as the magic around her stirred to life, as he and Shae stepped beneath the stone lintel and into the castle itself. The deal was met. He cast one last spell.

"We just need to talk to—oh!" The maid turned, but there was no one behind her.

Invisible, Jeth and Shae raced down the corridors, closing in on their goal.

NINE

Expending magic made one tired, though not from channeling it. Jeth could channel for a week straight if he tapped into a leyline and be none the worse for the wear. No, it was the *control* of it, like lifting a heavy boulder and maneuvering it through a series of hoops. Finesse was exhausting.

And faerie bargains, I suppose.

As Jeth and Shae prowled down the fine halls of Sol Krona's castle, he worked on yet another finely tuned spell. It made his headache throb in his temples with every beat of his heart, but their clothes had to change.

Or at least improve.

Jeth wove his magic through his and Shae's clothes, changing the fabric slightly. His tan travel shirt became gold silk. His blue tunic, a thick, soft suede. Shae's clothes melted into fine silks and a tunic that fell just below their knees, belted at the waist. Their hat, however, was tucked away in Jeth's bespelled satchel, beneath the Moot Crown.

The satchel was changed, too, the worn leather bespelled to fine, embossed, polished leather, beautifully tooled.

"That should be enough to get us by," Jeth murmured, releasing the spell and letting it settle.

Shae squirmed from head to toe. "Guh! That one almost stung. What did you—oh." They studied their clothes for a moment, then smirked. "Did you just faerie godmother us?"

Jeth laughed softly. "I gave you trousers. I figured you'd like that more if we had to run."

"I do. The tunic is nice too, thanks. How long will it last?"

"A few hours."

"Let's get to work, then." Shae shook out their hands to chase the last tingles of spell casting from their skin.

They hurried along the halls, pausing to eavesdrop when they could and poke about when they couldn't. The castle had stairs that went up and down and halls that dead ended and more that seemed to lead in circles.

In short, they had no luck.

The rattle of mail and the fall of heavy footsteps echoed up the hall ahead of them. Jeth yanked Shae into a small curtained alcove with beautiful windows, holding them against the wall, where the curtains would hide them from sight.

The small group of guards marched past, murmuring among themselves. Once they vanished from view, Jeth exhaled, turning to look at Shae.

Shae stared at him, eyes wide, cheeks flushed.

"Sorry," Jeth said quickly, stepping back.

"No, it's alright. We've just…it's been one emergency after another for a bit, hasn't it?" Shae rested a palm against Jeth's cheek, thumb running over the skin beneath his eye. "You look tired."

"We can rest when we're through all this."

"Can we? Can we settle somewhere, Jeth?"

Jeth paused. "I thought you wanted to go find whatever family you have left."

"I don't have family left. I have distant descendents at best. I have *you*."

The words hung between them, invisible, heavy as thunderclouds. All Jeth had to do was open his mouth and say them. All he had to do…

He cupped the back of Shae's neck, pulling them in for a deep, lingering kiss.

I'll say it, he promised quietly. *I'll say it when I'm not afraid you'll disappear.*

"We have to go," Shae murmured.

"Alright," Jeth said. Neither moved. He rested his forehead against the changeling's, eyes sinking closed.

"We really have to go," Shae said again after a time. "The spell…"

"Right." Jeth sighed, lacing his fingers with Shae's and stepping out of the alcove.

They nearly ran into a small army of servants laden with brooms, buckets and cloths, and mops.

"Oh, begging your pardon, noble guests," one said, bobbing his head apologetically.

"No pardon needed. Great timing, in fact," Jeth said with a broad smile.

"Is it?" Shae asked dryly.

"Yes," Jeth said, trying to reassure Shae that he had a plan with that single word. A plan he'd just thought up this second, but a plan none the less. "Yes, we're completely lost. Came into town to commission that brilliant craftworker of the Queen's, Olyver? And..."

"And you can't find his suite, my lord?" the servant asked, shifting his broom to his other hand.

"Precisely. Can you direct us?"

"I can do you one better, if you like. I'll take you there myself."

He turned to the other servants, murmuring low. A few nodded. He passed his broom off and the others continued on their way.

"Ready, my lord?"

"Yes, thank you," Jeth said, inclining his head.

They set off down the halls at a sedate pace.

"Do you have a name?" Shae asked carefully. In the wake of Aneirin's name-stealing adventures, they were both careful of their phrasing. Just in case.

"I'm Leofric." The servant grinned back over his shoulder. He was scarcely out of his teens, strong and tall. He had a restless energy that showed in the flick of his hands, in the way his head turned to look at everything they passed.

"Leofric. A pleasure," Jeth said.

"What's the matter?" Shae asked suddenly.

Leofric stumbled over his own feet, turning to look back at them in surprise. "What? The matter? No, nothing. Why would..."

"I can tell," Shae said, stopping stubbornly in the middle of the hall. They folded their arms over their chest.

Jeth studied Leofric, noticing at last what Shae saw. The cheer was false, forced. "Tell us. We won't hold it against you."

"I'm just doing what my brother told me to do. He's older. He thinks I can follow in his footsteps. He got out of the servants' wing and into the guard." Leofric shrugged helplessly.

"And you don't want to be a guard?"

"No, sir. I'll get sent somewhere, like he did. He got stationed outside the city. But our parents are here, and our baby sister, and if I get stationed somewhere else, they'll be on their own."

Jeth nodded, taking him in. "And if you could get any job you like that would keep you here in town?"

Leofric grinned, sheepishly rubbing the back of his neck. "In the kennels, sir, and with the huntsman. I like the dogs. But I haven't any training."

"Things work out from time to time." Jeth slid his hand into Shae's and gestured for Leofric to lead on.

The changeling cast him a worried glance as they led him down the hall.

Jeth sank into the magic of a faerie bargain once again. Knives stabbed into his skull at both temples as he drew, gritting his teeth. In exchange for being their guide, Jeth would set Leofric's future in motion. The prince's prize hound was whelping a litter. One of the puppies would get away, would be lost. Lost, but safe, he added. Leofric would find them and bring them back. The Mistress of the Hounds already knew him. She'd offer him a position for his help.

Leofric would get twice the pay, and the opportunity to impress the Master of the Hunt later. He'd get to stay in town near his parents, too.

Snap.

Jeth stumbled, and Shae caught his arm, steadying him.

"Don't cast anymore, not today," they whispered.

A blinding headache rolled behind his eyes. His ears rang. "You're probably right," he murmured. "Wouldn't be a good idea."

"You'll be dry if you do."

"What if I need to?"

Shae frowned. "You didn't need to cast this time, or the last," they hissed. "Your bleeding heart is showing again. You could have just handed over some gold."

"If I can match them one good turn to another, shouldn't I?"

Shae swore softly under their breath, but Jeth won that argument and they both knew it. After all, there was a time Jeth risked both life and freedom to rescue two dozen human strangers from the fae.

My bleeding heart saved us both.

To his relief, Shae didn't argue any further. They just held his arm while his ears rang and his eyes refocused. Leofric, oblivious, led them on down the halls.

"Here you are." He stopped in front of a plain, unassuming door.

"Thank you," Shae said, granting him the rare ghost of a smile.

Leofric bowed slightly, then left.

Jeth leaned against the wall, gesturing at Shae. "Would you do the honors?"

Shae sighed. They reached up and rapped firmly on the polished wooden portal.

After a moment, the door creaked open. A woman peered out at them.

"What do you want, then?"

"We're looking for the Queen's craftworker, Olyver," Jeth said, straightening.

"My husband isn't here," she said flatly, pushing the door closed again.

Which is how Jeth saw her hand, or more accurately, her fingernails. Two of them had paint beneath them. Dust covered the hem of her sleeve, sawdust if he had to guess.

He stuck his boot out, wincing as it was pinned between the door and the jamb.

"What are you–?"

"I said we were looking for the craftworker. We were told it was your husband, but it's not, is it?" He met her gaze.

The woman's eyes widened, her grip on the door tightening. She yanked the door open, peering down the corridors. Her hand flew out. She grabbed Jeth by the front of his tunic and yanked him inside. Shae followed quickly of their own will, not wanting to be next.

Jeth stumbled, catching himself on the edge of a worktable laden with half-finished wood carving projects.

The door closed firmly behind them.

"How in the blazes did you come to that conclusion, exactly?" The woman asked, acid in her voice.

"The hands of a craftsperson never lie." Jeth straightened, smoothing his tunic rather than looking at her. His gaze swept the room appraisingly.

There was a small bedchamber off to one side, the door standing open to show a modest bed with a handmade quilt, the colors long faded. The only other doors were those that led to a small balcony. They stood open to the spring air, stirring wood shavings on the floor in the barest whisper of a breeze.

But the bulk of the space was a workroom. Drawings littered the walls and tables alike. Tables, saw horses, easels, and platforms bore a thousand different projects of all scopes. Tools of every sort, many of which Jeth had never seen before, were all neatly arranged in wooden trays.

No sign of the mirror or its mold, though.

Damn. Of course, it can't be that easy.

"Well, you can't tell anyone. Only Queen Cailea knows, and she's sworn to secrecy."

"Why?" Shae asked, folding their arms over their chest, lips twisted sullenly. "That seems stupid. Is it because you're a woman? Why can't a woman be an artisan?"

"Because I don't want to be," she said with a shrug. "I want to work on my things. That's all I want. But the craftsperson is expected to go to dinners, and court events, to present things as gifts and be fawned over, to go on trips to measure something or other. Besides, Olyver gets better prices for being a man. We both benefit from him pretending."

Jeth's brows rose. "So you do it to protect your peace?"

"And give Olyver something to do. That dear, dear man *likes* to attend parties. He knows what I do well enough to pass a cursory inspection of his knowledge, and I love that he's interested."

"But?" Jeth said quickly, catching the pause.

She shook her head, waving a hand. "It's nothing."

"Please, I'd like to understand."

She turned away, moving things around on a worktable. "I'm busy."

"I'm Jeth. And this is Shae."

"Lily," she said reluctantly. "What do you want, then?"

He glanced at Shae, who shrugged.

"Lily, we have a proposition for you. A trade, if you will."

She scoffed softly, picking up a rough piece of paper with sand glued to it. She set to work on a carving of a rosebush, her brow furrowed.

"What kind of trade?" she asked at last.

"Anything you want, in exchange for anything you have relating to the mirror you made five copies of."

Lily's hand slowed. She looked back at him, eyes narrowed. She was slim in the shoulder, built with the dainty grace of a dancer, and yet Jeth knew she was ten times stronger than anyone thought.

"And who in the blazes do you think you are, promising me anything I want? What if I want the moon? Fetch it for me. No, wait, I want a unicorn to ride about, with ribbons in its mane. No, no, I want to be the queen of my own kingdom!" Lily snorted loudly, throwing up her hands. "*Anything,* ha!"

"This is very important, Lily, and I can get you anything you want. Well, nearly."

Jeth glanced at Shae, a hand playing over the front of the satchel.

Shae grimaced, then shrugged. "That might be a bad idea," they whispered.

"How else can we convince her?"

Shae shrugged again.

"And how can you promise me that?" Lily asked, turning toward them.

Jeth dropped his glamour, pulling the crown out and settling it over his antlers. He gave her an apologetic smile, looking her right in the eyes.

No more hiding.

"I'm a king of faerie."

She stared, eyes widening slowly until they were the size of saucers.

The next thing Jeth knew, he was ducking as a mallet swung through the air where his head had been a moment before.

This damn crown!

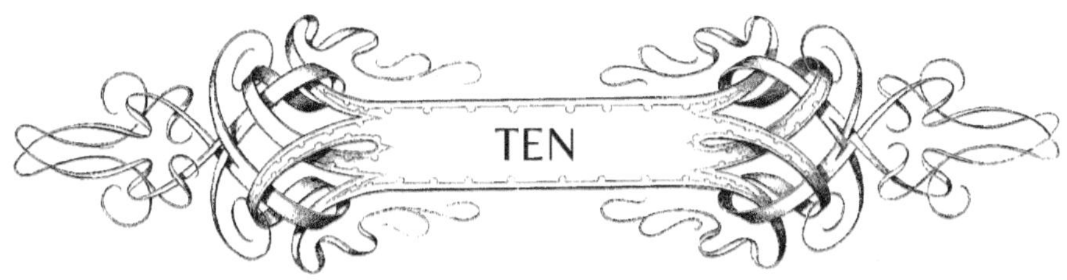

"Wait!"

Lily did not wait.

Jeth jerked back. The mallet swung down right in front of his nose, so close the wind of its passage stirred his hair. "Wait, wait, I'm not–"

"Shut your silver-tongued mouth, you monster!" Lily shouted, charging him. Jeth dove sideways.

"He's right, though," Shae called from behind a worktable across the room, keeping it between themself and the angry craftswoman with a hammer. "He's the one who stopped all the other faeries, you know."

"What?" Lily's head whipped around.

With a strangled shout, Jeth ducked out of the way of another wild swing. He straightened, hands raised—only to find the mallet hovering right in front of his nose. His eyes widened, fixed on Lily's makeshift weapon as she marched him back, step by step, until he was pressed against a wall.

"What do they mean by that? 'You stopped all the other faeries,'" she demanded.

"I became the highest power in Faerie, the High King, so I could command the fae to leave humans alone and they'd have to listen. I was born to a human mother. I've never been fully one of them."

His mind leaped to Eoghan, to what the redhead said. Now the faeries were infighting, without humans to torment. He wondered what Blackthorn Court would look like if he were to return.

Not that he could. The Moot Crown painted a target on his back. He'd stay alive longer if he weren't easy to find.

"People have been talking about that, especially here." She dropped her arm, eyes narrowed. "Queen Cailea mentioned it. The council has suggested removing faerie incident reports from their meetings, because they don't happen anymore. It's quiet."

"I did that. I ordered them to leave human settlements alone and work no harm or mischief or otherwise to them. Us. You," Jeth amended.

Could he call himself human anymore? He looked twenty, despite being eighty, and he had antlers.

"Then why are you here?" Lily asked, the mallet swinging back up to point at Jeth's nose.

He held his hands up again. "Like I said, we just want whatever you have relating to the mirrors! Information, designs, molds, whatever you have."

"Why?"

"There's one faerie I can't command. The previous faerie king, Aneirin. My...my father. He's the worst of the lot. I trapped him inside one of your mirrors, that set of five. But that means all five are doorways. He can't open them now, but he could someday. We need to break them all so he can't get out. Ever. And we need to make sure no one makes another one."

She dropped the mallet on a table with a clatter, folding her arms over her chest. She glanced back at Shae, a brow rising in silent question.

"Oh, it's true. He's sugar coating it, actually. Aneirin kidnapped me for a moon and kept me in a box. And when I wasn't crammed into the dark, he was whispering in my ear. He wanted to turn my head, turn my loyalty. A time or two, he nearly did." They frowned, gaze drifting to Jeth.

"Aneirin said he could give me things even Jeth couldn't give me once he had his power back."

Jeth's shoulders fell a fraction of an inch. *Oh.*

His heart ached for Shae, who longed to find someone they were still related to, some measure of family. Shae wanted their humanity back, to go back to a life that was long, long gone. All they wanted was a simple, normal life.

No one could give them that.

Lily studied the pair, gaze sliding back and forth. Her expression softened. "Alright, say I'm starting to believe you. I get what I want, you get what you want, the end? It's that simple?"

"Yes," Jeth said quickly. "In exchange for whatever you have concerning the mirror and the location of the other four, you can have anything."

"Almost anything," Shae corrected. "We can't bring back the dead, not really."

"Right." She rubbed her brow with one hand, the other planted on her hip as she paced. "Right, then. I want Olyver and I to be granted a title, so we can't be sent away from this place. I don't want our fortunes to change."

"I can do that."

She turned on her heel, pointing. "And Olyver gets an appointment as an archivist to go with it. He loves reading all those stuffy old papers."

Jeth nodded.

"And…and good health for our family. I'm a few moons along with our first, and I want them to have a good, long life."

"Congratulations," Jeth said with a grin.

"Thank you." Lily smiled, a hand resting on her stomach. "Olyver is so excited to raise our little one with me, but we need more security. Unless we're noble, our residence here relies on the favor of the Royal Family. So we need…"

"A title." Jeth nodded.

Shae hovered at Jeth's elbow, reaching out gently. "Is this a good idea?" they whispered.

"It's fair, isn't it?" Jeth kept his voice low, too.

"I meant that you've already cast two bargains today. Do you have enough to cast this one?"

Shae is right. This isn't good for me. I should stop…

…but this is important.

Jeth shrugged, a rueful smile on his face. He lifted his hands. Shae sighed.

The threads of the craftswoman's life were strong and bright. They were easy to follow from place to place. His pulse stabbed in his skull, but he ignored it.

What Lily wanted was already *there*. Queen Cailea leaned toward granting her friend and confidant more than just money and favor. She wanted to protect the woman who helped her see the kingdom from a new angle. All he had to do was nudge the thread, wind it a bit tighter. Cailea would grant Lily and Olyver a title—very soon, now.

The health of her family took longer, and his ears were ringing by the time he'd finished.

Thank goodness it all went off without a hitch. No tangles, nothing surprising. He was finished with the work before he felt too awful. He broke himself free of the bargain with a *snap*.

When he woke a few minutes later, his head was on Shae's lap. A damp cloth was on his forehead. His skull felt like it was splitting. Lily knelt on his other side.

"What happened?"

"You cast too many bargains in a single day, just like I thought," Shae said sourly. Their touch was gentle as they stroked his cheek, though, studying his eyes.

"Are you alright?" Lily asked.

"Yes." Jeth grit his teeth and pushed himself upright, fingers pressed to a temple. "Yes, it just takes a lot of magic to make a bargain, even for me. Whatever you have on the mirror?"

"Let me get the drawings." She vanished around the edge of a worktable, the sound of her rummaging coming from somewhere across the room.

Shae touched his brow with gentle fingers. "Does it hurt terribly?"

"Yes. I think I'm done casting bargains for today."

The changeling huffed and punched him in the arm. "Just for the day?" they asked, exasperated.

Jeth laughed softly and rubbed the ache. "Alright, a few."

Shae sobered. "You really can't, Jeth. You're out of magic reserves. You'll be lucky if you can reach out enough to pull from a source for a few days."

"Alright," Jeth said, catching Shae's hand and kissing his fingertips. "Alright. I'll rest for a week."

"That's better." Shae hesitated, then leaned in and pressed a soft kiss to Jeth's brow. "Don't make me worry about you."

"I don't think that's possible."

"Then try harder not to do anything insane."

The words hovered on Jeth's lips. *Anything for you, love.* Love. His heart ached to say it. This wasn't the time, though. This wasn't the place.

"Aha, found them!" Lily crowed.

Jeth cupped Shae's cheek, running his thumb across the skin beneath their eye. He stood a moment later, accepting their help.

Lily shoved a thick roll of parchment into his hand with a firm nod. "There you are. The sketches. All of them. Rolled them up together, clever me."

Jeth unfurled them, admiring the delicate lines, the shading, the neat notes in the margins. There was a neatly denoted list of tools she used, measurements, tips on how to get it just so. It was a piece of art.

He rolled them back up. In four strides, he was in the open air on the balcony. It took just a touch of magic to ignite them. Flames licked up the paper, hungry and eager. He dropped them, let the fire curl them into nothing more than ashen fragments on the stone. The breeze turned them into dust and carried them away.

Something else, lost to time because of him.

Who really knew how much Aneirin had to answer for?

"One mirror," he said at last, turning to Lily, "was in Ulma Dale, in Lord Perival's keep."

"Correct."

"And the rest?"

"There's one in Olmiven, in King Derik's chambers. He likes it a lot, apparently, mentions it in half his letters. And there's one in Pelusir, but that one is in the hands of a Ducal ambassador, at his country estate, I think."

"Alright." Jeth strode inside, searching for ink and a quill pen—only to find Shae already had both, and a scrap of parchment besides. They wrote as Lily spoke.

"Two more," they called.

"Right. The last two are here in Hallanor. They belong to Queen Cailea. There's one at the summer palace, which isn't really a palace. It's a hunting lodge a few days' ride to the east."

"And the last one is here, in the castle?"

Lily nodded.

"Where?"

"Where else?" She shrugged. "In Queen Cailea's chambers."

Jeth grimaced. *I should have guessed as much.*

Shae laughed softly. "Seems like that's where you ought to start."

"Me? *Just* me?"

"Someone has to be there to get you out of trouble if you get caught. Besides, it only takes one of us to break a mirror. And..." They frowned. "I don't want to see him again."

Jeth sighed. "Alright. I won't ask you to come. Lily, I need a map to the mirror, please."

"I'll give you one—if you swear on your life, you won't hurt the queen."

"On my life and on my mother's name," Jeth vowed, hand over his heart.

Lily took the scrap from Shae and drew on the back of their list. Shae came to his side, pulling the Moot Crown out of the satchel on Jeth's hip. He settled it on his brow.

"Promise me that you'll be careful?"

"Of what?"

Shae snorted. "Oh, I don't know, the terrible man in the mirror?"

Jeth clasped both of the changeling's hands in his own. "I promise. I'll be careful, Shae. I'll come back."

"Here you go. This ought to do it." Lily handed him a roughly drawn map that was little more than a series of wiggly lines with notes. 'Turn at dented armor,' 'First left x 2,' and 'Guards here' marked the way, each scribed in her careful hand.

"Thank you." Jeth pulled his satchel off and handed it to Shae. "I'll be off, then."

"Jeth?" Shae said, catching his arm. "Do me a favor and try *not* to meet the Queen?"

Jeth grinned and slipped into the hall.

ELEVEN

The castle was a tangled warren of hallways and stairs, no doubt designed that way on purpose. Any invader would be hopelessly confused, wandering for ages before finding what they were looking for and buying the defense enough time to foil the enemy.

After all, Jeth was hopelessly confused, and he had a map.

He held the parchment inches away from his face, matching each note to each turn. It was like a puzzle, with pieces becoming clear only as he came upon them.

The armor was very dented. The helmet was almost completely caved in on one side. Other sets might have some dings, but this...yes, this made sense.

The two lefts were indeed one right after the other, with no right turns available.

And, after an hour, Jeth came upon the guards.

A constant patrol of four marched up and down the broad corridor that led to the Queen's chambers. Two more stood on either side of the double doors. Jeth took a deep breath, reaching for his magic. He'd just make himself invisible, and–

–Ow. He clasped his hands to his head as a stabbing pain raced through his temples.

Without his reserves, he'd have to rely on smaller magics to get through here. No elaborate glamours, no invisibility.

Jeth watched the guards turn back and forth, back and forth, then inhaled.

If they see a strange faerie, then they'll sound the alarm.

If *they see me.*

It took just a trickle of magic, which was about all he could summon at the moment. He let it double, then triple with the help of the Moot Crown, and then released it as softly as a sigh. He was moving as soon as it left his fingertips.

The guards closed their eyes as one. They still paced or stood still, believing they were just blinking. A long, slow blink. Moving as quietly as he could, Jeth darted down the hall. The door was unlocked. Of course it was, with six people keeping watch. He slipped inside.

As it swung closed, the guards opened their eyes.

That was the hard part over, or so he hoped. He turned, taking in the comfortable sitting room all decorated in green and gold and brown. Chairs and couches were laden with blankets and cushions. It was downright cozy, more homey than he'd expected.

An open archway showed a study, with a desk and shelves. Book spines marched along them, interrupted by oddities and knick knacks. A pair of curtains hung over another archway, this one leading to his goal.

The bedchamber.

And right there, right on the wall in the corner of the room, directly ahead of him...was the mirror. His fingers curled into fists.

Make it quick. Run up, and smash it.

He moved toward it step by careful, cautious step. His own reflection stared back. Golden hair with a slight curl to the ends lay beneath the crystalline Moot Crown. Golden eyes were set in a wary frown.

"I know you're there," he said at last.

His reflection clouded, a fog filling the mirror as though someone had exhaled over every inch of it in a single breath.

Out of the fog came a soft green light, and then the shadowy, indistinct form of a man. He pressed a hand to the inside of the mirror.

The doorway didn't open.

Jeth exhaled slowly. Good. Aneirin couldn't get out. Yet.

Not that he truly expected the spell to release its prisoner so easily.

Let me out, Aneirin's voice whispered in his ear. *We can talk about this.*

"There's nothing to talk about."

There's always something to talk about. You can't keep me in here forever.

"I can try. You won't hurt anyone again, not if I can help it."

It hardly hurt them. They were just names. Who needs a name?

Jeth scowled. "Everyone needs an identity. A name is the thread that stitches together the very fabric of who we are."

You're very certain of that. Perhaps we can discuss it. We could work together, Jeth. We can change the world.

"But not for the better. Time and again, you've proven you can't be trusted. I don't trust you, Aneirin. I won't." Jeth stepped forward, lifting a hand toward the mirror's edge.

Aneirin's face swirled out of the mist within the mirror, snarling, teeth bared.

Jeth froze, heart hammering beneath his ribs. He scoffed breathlessly. "You haven't got enough power to get out. Not on your own. You don't scare me."

I should. When I get out of here, you'll suffer. I'll make sure you suffer.

Jeth grit his teeth and grasped the edge of the mirror.

"And what in the name of the heavens do you think you're doing?"

That wasn't his voice.

It wasn't Aneirin's.

It was a *woman's* voice.

Jeth turned to face her.

The woman stood with her head raised and a brow arched, her arms folded over her chest. She was a tall woman with broad shoulders. Her pale blonde hair was almost white, and it fell in loose waves over her shoulders. A jeweled necklace glittered at her throat and matched the coronet braided into her hair. Both emerald and gold pieces matched the trim on her gown, fitted beneath the bust and flaring out wide. The dress itself was a rich burgundy, dark and strong.

There was absolutely no doubt as to who she was.

"I'm about ten seconds away from calling the guard on you, faerie."

"Queen Cailea," Jeth said, lowering his hand. "Ah..."

Cailea's eyes widened. She leaned to the side. "What is *that*?" She wasn't looking at him anymore. She was looking at the mirror.

At Aneirin, glaring, his fingers hooked like claws, tips pressed against the glass. His lips were twisted in a snarl. The hatred he radiated soaked into the very air like a poison.

"Do you want the long answer, or the short one?" Jeth asked mildly.

"The short one." She planted her hands on her hips.

"That's my father."

"...alright, the long one then."

Jeth stepped between her and the mirror. "He's a faerie. He was stealing names and identities in Ulma Dale to gain power. A long time ago, he had designs on your...grandmother's throne, I think. I stopped him then, and I want to stop him now. I trapped him, but I need to destroy your mirror to keep him from getting out again."

"And he's your..."

"Yes, he's my father."

Cailea studied him, her hands folded in front of herself as she paced closer. "I had a dream about you," she said at last.

"What?" Jeth glanced over his shoulder. A dream about him, or Aneirin?

"I had a dream about you, ages ago. I was just a little girl. You...were a king of faerie, but you weren't. I remember that. I remember..." she gasped, pointing. "I know why! My mother told me about you. The faerie king of the forest, the stag with golden hair."

"What?" Jeth repeated, only growing more baffled by every word.

"One of my mother's favorite cousins disappeared in the woods years and years ago. He came back four years later, not aged a day, and said he was stolen by the faeries. He told us all about the new High King, who took the crown and freed them all. He said he followed him, the stag with golden hair and golden eyes." Her eyes drifted up to his antlers, to the crown on his brow. "That is you, isn't it?"

Jeth held his breath. There was a young man Eoghan enchanted once, a man he'd kissed right in front of him. He had the same nose, the same jawline as Queen Cailea. He remembered a parade of humans winding up dark tunnels toward the surface, toward the sun. Jeth led them all to the edge of River Tor, the town his mother had grown up in. He wished them luck. He clasped their hands.

Then he and Shae turned away to start their journey to the other faerie courts.

"I suppose it is. I freed all the humans I could from faerie control. I've protected them—you, your people—as best I can." He lifted a hand to the crown on his head.

That damn crown that he would one day lose, the crown that would undo everything he'd built and release the faeries on the unsuspecting humans living within their woods.

"Then I owe you our thanks."

"Don't thank me yet, your Majesty."

"Cailea, please. As one monarch to another. And you are?"

"Jeth. While I'm here, Cailea, I need to warn you of something. It's important."

"Something more than your faerie father in my looking glass?" She asked archly, pacing to stare through the glass, examining Aneirin like he was an animal in a menagerie.

Aneirin battered at the glass. A flash of silver power burst from his palms, but all it did was send a ripple through the mirror. Aneirin pushed with all his strength, but he couldn't get through. He snarled, lips moving in words they couldn't hear. He slammed his hands against his transparent prison door.

"Don't mind him," Jeth said softly. "He's harmless, for now. Are you aware that there is faerie blood in your veins?"

Cailea snorted softly, stepping back to shrug in Jeth's direction. "A fanciful family tale, I'm sure."

"A truth. Queen Cailea, the crown I'm wearing right now could command you to do anything I wished."

She froze, tense. Her gaze went from the crown to his eyes, her face pinched and her eyes wary. "You can't be serious."

"Yes. I won't be able to protect this crown forever. Centuries, maybe, but not forever. Someone else will take it some day, and then..."

"And then the faeries would come back. And if you can make it all the way into my rooms without raising an alarm, I imagine another faerie could do the same. Your replacement could do the same."

I hadn't thought of that. But it was true. It wasn't as difficult to get this far as Jeth expected.

"Yes, I believe they could. You, your family, and Hallanor are all in danger."
This damn crown.

What would that day look like, the day when he was no longer the High King of Faerie? What would happen? How far would the creatures he commanded into their realms and their realms alone go to exact their revenge?

Cailea walked to the window, staring out thoughtfully. "You want to destroy my mirror?"

"Yes, and the one in the summer palace."

She laughed, rubbing a brow. "Of course you do. Alright, then. Faeries make bargains, don't they?"

"We do."

"My two mirrors for your crown." She fixed him with a steady look, her blue eyes bright with determination.

"You can't use it, not unless you win it in a battle of magic." Jeth shrugged helplessly.

"I don't want to use it. I want to smash it with rocks, put it in a forge, and destroy it."

Jeth paused, brows lifting. That would...solve everything. His last commands would stand, and no one could win it back. A slow smile grew on his lips.

Don't you dare, Aneirin's voice spat in his mind. *You won't be able to command them anymore. You'll lose your power. You'll be weak, pathetic, useless!*

I was never weak, Jeth retorted, gaze sliding to meet his father's in the mirror. Even as a child, even untrained, he had more power than his father ever would. He didn't need the crown to hold his own.

No one needed this kind of power.

Jeth pulled the Moot Crown from his head and offered it to Queen Cailea. "I trust you to dispose of it, and quickly."

She took it, her fingertips brushing his. Her eyes fixed on his, blue and gold. Two kingdoms, meeting in peace for the first time in generations.

"You're not much like the stories of faeries, are you?"

"No, I'm not. I'm my own kind of faerie. If I may?" He gestured at the mirror.

Cailea swept her hand toward it, taking a few cautious steps back.

Jeth grabbed the edge, his face inches away from the glass, inches away from Aneirin's. His father screamed, spittle flecking the other side of the glass. He threw himself against the glass repeatedly, like a trapped bird.

You can't do this! What sort of monster locks their father away, imprisons them forever? What would your mother think?

Both of them paused, Aneirin's chest rising and falling rapidly as he panted, his expression softening.

Don't do this, Jeth. Give me a chance.

It was the first time he'd seen Aneirin show a glimmer of emotion beside rage or arrogance. Jeth paused, his eyes narrowing.

My mother, he thought back, as clearly as he could, *would be proud of me for knowing who you really are. Goodbye, Aneirin.*

A wordless scream filled his mind.

Jeth heaved the mirror off the wall.

With the shatter of glass at his feet, the voice in his head vanished.

Cailea grabbed his arm, towing him to the changing screen in the corner. She shoved him behind it a split second before the door to her chambers burst open.

"Your Majesty? Are you alright?"

Through the break between the screen's panels, Jeth could see the guards. Three of them crossed the room. The other three remained at the door, hands on their weapons.

Queen Cailea stood with her hands behind her back, the Moot Crown dangling from her fingers. "Hm? Oh, yes. I just bumped into my mirror and knocked it off the wall. Clumsy me. See that the frame is burned, and the glass crushed, would you? I'm going to write a note to craftworker Olyver that I'll need a new one."

She stepped daintily over the glass, picking her way across the room, keeping her back to the guards.

"If you're really alright..."

"I am. I'll just be in my study."

The guards looked after her, baffled. Jeth took the opportunity she offered. He cast the same minor spell as before. All the guards closed their eyes, and he ran, glass crunching beneath his boots while Cailea froze.

Her brows were raised, a smile on her face as she watched him go.

He slipped into the hallway and broke into a flat-out run, releasing the spell once he'd turned the corner. He pelted down the halls, around the corners, past the armor, back to Shae.

The last time he'd felt this way was before he'd taken Aneirin's throne. Before he took the Moot Crown, that cursed thing. Soon, it would be gone. Gone! Forever beyond the reach of mortals and faeries alike.

No more challenges. No more magical duels. No more High King of the Faerie.

No more hiding.

Just Jeth.

He laughed as he ran, startling a servant as he darted past, as fleet as the stag whose antlers he grew.

He'd never felt so free.

TWELVE

Last Stop stretched below Jeth. He sat perched on the newly finished stone wall encircling the city—for it was absolutely large enough now to be called such. He swung one leg idly, watching as the late afternoon light stretched out the shadows between the buildings and across the streets.

Already, the old wooden wall was coming down. Already, new shops and buildings were being erected in the new space. The air was full of the clatter of hammers and the scuff of saws and the chatter of voices.

"Here," Shae said, holding a wrapped sausage roll down to him.

Jeth grinned, taking it as he stood. "Thanks."

"You almost ready to go?"

It had been a long few weeks. They ventured the few days' ride to the summer palace, only to discover the mirror was gone. None of the servants could remember what happened to it. It was there one evening, and gone by dawn.

Rather than spend their time hunting for it, Jeth and Shae recruited Anabette Calder to keep an eye out on her travels. They asked the crafter, Lily, to keep her ears open for any hint of its whereabouts. They wrote Queen Cailea to do all in her power to locate and destroy it.

Then Jeth and Shae set out for the ones they knew they could find.

Jeth looked across Last Stop, letting his eyes wander beyond the walls. The trees of the forest marched away for miles, a gentle downslope giving him a miles' long view of Hallanor.

"I didn't think we'd be leaving again so soon," he confessed softly.

"I know." Shae slipped their hand into his. "You wanted to go back to River Tor."

"And you wanted to go home, too." Jeth sighed, taking a bite of his supper.

The changeling shrugged. They, too, studied the unending sea of trees that made up their home. "Where do you think it went? The mirror, I mean."

Jeth lowered his roll with a sigh. "Who knows?"

"Probably not a good thing we've misplaced it."

"Aneirin can't open the doors. We'll find it before anything happens. I know we will."

"You *hope*," Shae corrected.

Jeth laughed softly. "Yeah. I hope."

They were quiet for a long moment, side by side. Once more, an important task took precedence over everything else they wanted. They *had* to leave, no matter what they wanted.

Again.

At least this time, it was...different. Shae's hand, warm in his own, was comfortable. Their time apart only proved how important their time together truly was. Still...

"Shae," Jeth said quickly, "You don't have to come with me for this. You can still go home."

The changeling tensed. They gave Jeth's hand a small squeeze. "Don't tempt me," they muttered. "Of course I have to come. Who else will keep you out of trouble?"

"You don't." He grinned.

"I keep you out of *some*." Shae fought a smile of their own.

Jeth lifted their joined hands, brushing his lips over their knuckles. He turned to face Shae fully. "I'm glad you'll be with me."

"Me, too. Even if there *were* a few days there where I was very, very cross with you for leaving me with Aneirin, in a box," they said dryly.

He laughed softly, pulling Shae closer. "Never. I'd never leave you. I want you with me always."

Shae snorted, rolling their eyes again. But they smiled.

Jeth's heart raced. *No more hiding. Just say it.* His lips parted.

Shadowstep whickered impatiently below them, outside the wall.

He sighed, feeling the press of the mare's impatience. "Sounds like we ought to get on the road."

"You're not the boss of us," Shae called over the wall, sourly.

The mare answered with a snort.

No more hiding.

Jeth leaned in, kissing Shae gently. Then he kissed them again, more urgently. "Shae, you know I love you, right?"

Simple, when it actually came down to it. So simple. Why hadn't he done it sooner?

Shae turned bright pink, the color of a rose, their eyes widening. They sputtered, scoffed, huffed, and sputtered again.

For the first time, one of them said it out loud. One of them put words to the feelings they'd been carrying around for all those years on the road. It felt amazing.

Shae sucked in a deep breath—and punched Jeth in the shoulder, yanking their hand free. "Stop that! You're...you're impossible. Are we going, or not?"

Jeth laughed and turned to descend the stairs.

And though he smiled wide enough that his cheeks ached, though his chest was full to bursting with a warmth like he swallowed the sun itself, Jeth pretended he didn't hear it when Shae muttered back:

"I love you, too."

RETURN TO RIVER TOR

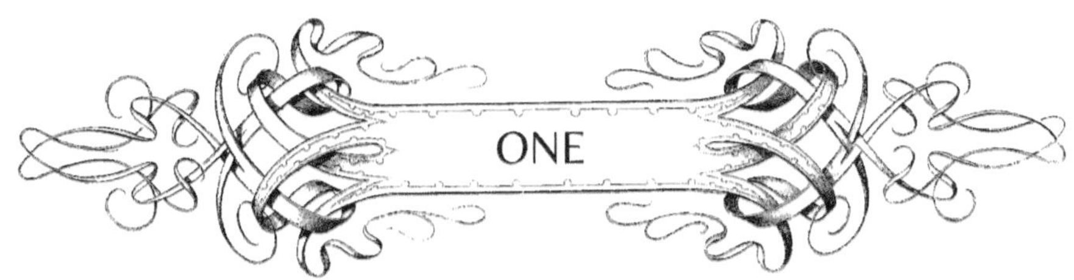

ONE

Jeth lay with his back propped against a log, head tipped back to study the sky. The stars were fading with the rising sun, though half of them appeared and disappeared behind scudding clouds that floated across the sky. He fiddled idly with the ring on his pinkie finger.

The hundredth time is the charm, right?

He and Shae, the love of his life and ten lifetimes besides, were returning to Hallanor. Again.

Back and forth, in and out, and all for what? We never get close to that mirror.

Trapping his father, the faerie king Aneirin, had seemed like a good idea at the time. The right choice, the moral one. Only the last mirror that could serve as a doorway out of Aneirin's prison had gone missing, hundreds of years ago.

Hundreds. Even thinking the word made his eyelids heavy and his shoulders sag. It tied his stomach in knots. A rush of guilt was followed by anger, and that was washed away by misery.

Rumor, hearsay, and gossip led them on a merry chase. They'd traipsed across the known lands. In and out of Hallanor, from sea to sea and back again, and more. Jeth was convinced there wasn't a single inch of the world he hadn't seen. Even so, the mirror eluded him.

Every time he and Shae got close, they'd lose the trail for a decade or longer, wandering around in the vain hope of picking up a clue once more. They'd spent their entire lives so far on the road, and nearly three hundred years of it was in pursuit of the damn mirror.

I don't feel *like I'm four hundred.* No, he didn't really feel all that different. Certainly not wiser, or braver. All he felt was...tired.

And you should, whispered a bitter voice in the corner of his mind. His own voice, irritable and dissatisfied. *Hundreds of years and nothing, literally nothing to show for it but a few pairs of boots worn through.*

Well, chasing a mirror across the world could do that to a person.

A finger pressed between his brows. Careful of the impressive rack of antlers that grew from his golden hair, Jeth tipped his head back.

Shae rubbed the crease between his brows until it smoothed, a brow arched. "You've had that thinking scowl of yours on for ages," they said. The changeling never failed to see right through him with those vividly green eyes of theirs. "What's the matter?"

Jeth sighed. "We're going back."

"Yes. And?"

"And we're still not sure we're on the right track."

"It's been five years since we've heard anything. Our best bet is to go find the Calders and ask them what they know." Shae swung their legs over the log, sitting beside his head, stroking his hair gently.

The Calders. Jeth sighed again. Hundreds and hundreds of years ago, he'd met Burne Calder, and later her granddaughter. Now, generations later, he wasn't even sure who was the head of that wealthy merchant family. Not that it mattered. Jeth, Shae, and the quest to find that damn mirror were passed down as family history. Whoever ran the family knew what they would ask.

The question was whether or not that would yield any answers. Jeth rubbed his temple, trying to push all thoughts of the mirror out of his head. "Maybe we should just get on the road."

Jeth let muscle memory guide him through the familiar motions of breaking their modest camp. Shadowstep picked her way out of the surrounding trees. She wandered as she liked, but some instinct always told her when they were ready to leave. Shae rolled up their bedrolls and affixed them to the back of Shadowstep's saddle. Jeth used damp earth from beneath a tree to put out the fire. That was it.

Shadowstep, the great black faerie steed, was well used to carrying two astride her back these days. She'd never aged, never tired, and never complained—much—since Jeth had won her loyalty in a wild ride. She turned to wuffle at his hair, the feeling of her anticipation pressing against Jeth's mind.

He snorted, gently pushing her head away. "Not you, too," he muttered, even as he swung onto her back. Once Shae was up behind him, he clicked his tongue.

Shadowstep was off, weaving between the trees of Hallanor, making her way straight toward...something. Somewhere. Jeth trusted her and whatever magical abilities she possessed to take them where they needed to go.

Shae wrapped their arms around Jeth's waist, their head resting on his shoulder. Shadowstep moved quickly, but smooth as glass, so they weren't jostled. Jeth watched the light change, the world melting from blues and purples and soft, dark greens to something brighter, like a sketch turned into a painting. The silence stretched on, broken only by the soft thud of hooves on the earth and the morning chirrups of birds.

"We need more supplies," Shae said at length.

Jeth grunted. "Shadowstep?"

She tossed her head in a nod and shifted her path ever so slightly. For once, they weren't passing through Last Stop. It made Jeth uncomfortable to see the city—for city it well and truly was, now. It was massive, with a Marquis and keep, now. The little trade stop at the border of Hallanor and Olmiven was now a coveted, wealthy title.

Ulma Dale was avoided, too, for much the same reason. The city wasn't much grown, but it was much improved. The last time they'd been, the keep was being refashioned into a proper manor estate, saving only bits and pieces of the original. The streets were all well cobbled, the houses all picture-perfect matches of their neighbors.

When Jeth learned he'd live forever, he'd never thought of what that would actually mean. He found that more and more, his worst nightmare was finding somewhere so irrevocably changed that he felt left behind. Stuck, as if he were encased in amber. More and more, the world around him changed. The endless march of years he'd never planned on was becoming a quest all its own, just to keep up.

This is why faeries go mad. This is why you will, too.

Jeth frowned at that irritable voice in his ear, looking away through the trees. A single drop of faerie blood turned one into a faerie. Shae, a changeling, was turned by years and magic and faerie food. They still looked mostly human, aside from their pointed ears.

Jeth was born of a human witch and a faerie king. Over the years, the faerie blood won out. His hair was like spun gold, his eyes like warm honey in the summer sun. His antlers grew tall from his head. His ears had the slightest bump at the tips, but had never truly turned pointed. Well, yet.

With every passing year, Jeth felt further away from the human he started as. He was a faerie, with faerie blood—and all he wanted was to be a man. Just a man. Just the man his mother had hoped he'd be.

She had no doubts what would happen to you, and she never told you, that hateful voice murmured.

Stop it. She did. She wanted more for me, different for me. She wanted me to grow up in that cottage and live a simple, happy life.

The voice snorted. *And how did that turn out?*

Jeth hadn't stopped moving since he was fourteen years old, never settling anywhere more than a few moons. What would settling down even look like?

Why bother wondering? You know you can't stop. You haven't found the mirror. You haven't saved humanity, the voice said, disdain dripping from the words like poison.

Jeth sighed heavily.

"What is it?" Shae asked.

"Just thinking."

"Again? What about?"

"Nothing, really." How could he explain to Shae that he was thinking about how fruitless the past centuries had been, running around and accomplishing nothing? Especially after he'd dragged Shae along for every mile of it.

Smoke rose above the trees in thin coils. Several trails of them, actually. Shadowstep was carrying them to a village. Jeth reached for the golden pool of magic within himself, carefully painting a glamour on over his antlers. Centuries of practice had perfected the guise. Now there wasn't even a ripple to show where the tines were.

He'd still hit them on a door frame if he weren't careful, though.

Shae solved their appearance problem by pulling on a hat, gray and shapeless, the brim flopping over their eyes until they bent it back.

Shadowstep slowed herself to a trot, then to a walk. When she stopped, the buildings of the village—a large one—were just visible through the trees. Jeth and Shae dismounted, and Shae fished a satchel from their saddlebags. Their arm disappeared further than it ought to have inside the bags.

Jeth had gotten good at that spell, too, to increase the space of a bag threefold.

The pair of them headed into the village alone. Shadowstep was sometimes...unsettling.

"Hello, hello," called a woman from her yard as she strung up her washing on a line. "Travelers?"

"That's us," Shae called, waving.

Jeth stopped by her crooked wooden fence. "Where are we?"

"Hm? Oh, Stonehill. One of the oldest little villages there is, Stonehill."

He'd never heard of it. He nodded and thanked her with a smile, then followed Shae to the modest market running outside the inn. He followed Shae around, his eyes drifting over the buildings.

There's something...familiar about this place.

It was in the trees, mostly, he thought. They tugged at a corner of his mind, familiar and yet not. And the inn, something about the worn stone building of the common room, older than the two story wooden addition behind it, something about that was familiar, too.

Jeth froze. He turned, quickly threading his way through the crowds, leaving Shae haggling with a man selling dried, salted meat. He passed around the corner of the smith's building and stopped.

It was still there. The oh-so-familiar path through the trees, with the big gnarled oaks on either side of the head of it. They were even bigger now, giant twisted things. But they were still there. Beyond, the worn path would lead to a cottage, just far enough away to be hidden but still close enough to be part of–

Stonehill.

The nameless little village Jeth had been born in, the village he'd grown up in, was now called Stonehill. Hundreds and hundreds of years ago, he left this village behind, a crystal ball in his pack, a winter storm raging.

He'd never come back until now.

Once, he'd lived here as the son of Gleda Penistone, the village witch. The cottage was full of herbs and shelves of salves. They slept in the loft above together. She taught him to read and write, and shared every piece of knowledge she had with him.

Once, they'd been walking along this very same muddy path his boots were on now, and she'd staggered, and dropped, and died.

Once, they'd lit her pyre, and Jeth had stood beside it until the last flame guttered out, until the last coal stopped glowing.

I wish I knew what she'd think of me now.

And if wishing were fishing, you'd cast a thousand lines, the voice in his head sneered.

Jeth frowned, turning away. He walked slowly to find his love, taking in the buildings around him with fresh eyes. Every small old stone house had larger, newer wood parts tacked on, extra rooms and extra space. Would his cottage look the same?

"Excuse me," he said, stopping a pair of children as they ran past. "What's up that path by the old oak trees?"

"The Harmon farm?" the little girl asked.

"A farm?" Jeth asked, brows rising. "An entire farm?"

"Yeah, biggest there is around here." The little boy rubbed his sleeve across his nose.

"Thank you," Jeth said.

The kids ran on, forgetting him entirely for the thrill of whatever game they were playing.

"Jeth, there you are," Shae called, waving. "I thought we might get breakfast at the inn before we go."

"Shae," Jeth said, pulling them into the lee of a building. Lowering his voice, he explained where they were.

Shae's eyes were wide. "This is –"

"Yes."

"And you've really never gone back?"

"No. There was never any reason to. There wasn't anything out here, and certainly not anything like this." He waved a hand at the thriving little village around them.

If he squinted, he could almost see the ghostly outline of the half dozen buildings that had been their home before this, all spread out in the little valley clearing of the forest. The houses held entire families, every generation living. Now, they'd all spread out.

The world marches on without you, the voice whispered.

A coal of fury warmed in his chest, tempered by the cold, wet reality of everything.

Shouldn't it be fine if the world moved around him? Shouldn't he be glad that humanity and the fruits of his labor were paying off, that the people of his home were thriving? Aneirin had lit their houses on fire once, searching for him. They'd more than recovered.

If you were truly happy for them, you wouldn't hate them for erasing what there was.

That wasn't the problem. Not really. It wasn't like his mother had a grave that had been disturbed. It wasn't like the villages needed witches anymore to protect them from the faeries, not since he'd sealed them all away with an edict and the Moot Crown. It was...it was...

It was that it didn't feel like home.

He'd long ago painted the little cottage in the woods as home, the happy place of his childhood. He always imagined he'd feel his mother there, see her echoed in the village itself. But she wasn't here. None of her was here.

He swallowed a few times.

Shae, watching him closely, reached out to slip their hand into his. "Where are your thoughts?"

"Everywhere. Scattered."

"What are you looking for?"

"...her."

Shae gave Jeth's hand another squeeze, hefting the laden pack on their back.

"Oi, what do you two think you're doing, skulking around in shadows like that?" A man asked. He was broad shouldered and barrel chested, and he marched over with a scowl on his face.

Jeth frowned. "We're not. We're talking."

"And talking to the children, too. My Bronwy told me you lot were asking them questions. What are you after, eh?"

"What? Nothing. Supplies, and–" Shae started.

"And you've got them. Best you're on your way, eh?" The man folded his arms over his chest.

"Samuel? What's going on over there?" A woman called.

"Just handling a few visitors that have overstayed their welcome, is all, Marjory."

She leaned out of the window of her home, eyeing them suspiciously.

Jeth fought a rising wave of nerves. The eyes of both villagers were distant and hard. They didn't care who they were, what they wanted.

They just wanted them gone.

Very rarely had Jeth been chased out of a town or village. Never did he think he'd be chased out of his own.

Well, not his own. Not anymore. That was the point. He took Shae's hand, and they hurried toward the far edge of town, heading deeper into Hallanor. The man, Samuel, followed them the entire way to the edge of Stonehill.

As Jeth led the way beneath the trees once more, he knew, he *knew* he'd never set eyes on that village again.

He stopped several lengths into the forest—Hallanor had only one forest, after all—and pressed his back against a tree. His antlers, invisible, scraped against the bark.

"That was rude," Shae muttered.

"Let's just get Shadowstep and be on our way," Jeth said softly, his eyes closed. He felt untethered, directionless, but...

The Calder line always had someone living in the same modest estate at the edge of the same small town. Hallanor wasn't a terribly large kingdom, but they'd have to cross almost all of it to reach their destination.

I hoped...

And you were wrong, weren't you? But you're getting used to that, the nasty voice interrupted. He scowled.

Shadowstep snorted as she walked sedately through the trees toward them. They packed their new provisions away in the bespelled saddlebags. Jeth helped Shae mount up, then swung into the saddle behind them and took the reins.

Jeth sighed softly.

Shae covered his hand with theirs, giving a gentle squeeze.

"I'll be alright." Jeth rested his chin on the changeling's shoulder. "It's just hard, seeing every piece of what made that place mine...gone. It's starting to sink in that I have no family, that there's no legacy of us there, that...that all this time later, there's nothing."

Shae turned their head, kissing his cheek softly, reassuringly. If anyone understood that feeling, it was them. They'd been stolen from their home long before Jeth was even born. By the time they'd returned to Shae's old home, there was nothing left. Their entire family line was gone.

"We can always find a new home," Shae offered. "Someday. After we finish saving the world."

The world will never be saved, not really, and not for long, that bitter voice pointed out.

Jeth pushed it away. "That wasn't really my mother's home, you know. She came from a place near Heartwood Hill. A little village called River Tor."

The pair of them had circled around it a time or two, but it was so close to the Blackthorn Court and Heartwood Hill that they gave it a wide berth. It wasn't often they purposefully ventured close to faerie territory.

After forbidding them to harm, kidnap, or play tricks on humans, the faeries grew to dislike their High King Jeth. He was still, technically, the High King of Faerie. And there wasn't a single court in the land that wasn't very, very angry with his rule. They wanted their freedom back, the freedom to run rampant through the forest and all the humans living in it.

Jeth spurred Shadowstep into a steady, ground eating trot. He cast one last look over his shoulder at the thin threads of smoke, wavering up into the sky over the top of the trees. He dropped his glamour, his antlers springing back into existence. He ducked beneath a tree branch as Shadowstep threaded her way through the trees.

Guilt washed over him, guilt because he was *relieved* to put Stonehill behind him. It ached, seeing the last place he'd ever really been human, seeing that it was so different. That it was gone, that something else had taken its place. The first time, he ran from his nameless village, afraid the villagers would hate him. He'd been wrong, then. This time, they'd made it clear he wasn't welcome there.

Jeth was gone, too. The fourteen-year-old boy who left the village, who went through the woods in the teeth of a snowstorm. All that was left behind was something...different. Jeth, who wasn't really a human and who wasn't really a faerie. Jeth, the powerful magician and ageless being. Jeth, the man living a life he never thought he'd lead.

"You know," Shae said, settling back against him. "We could go to River Tor."

A pang in his chest nearly drove him to say no. Jeth's lips parted, but nothing came out for a moment.

Why not? What's the worst that can happen?

This, the voice whispered. *The same thing that just did. You'll find out you don't belong here. You don't belong anywhere.*

Jeth shoved the voice back into the corner of his mind, scowling.

But what if the voice was right?

What if he didn't have a place?

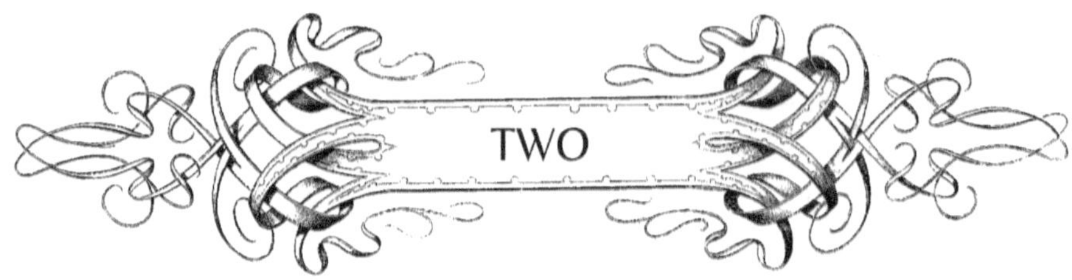

TWO

The air tasted different.

Jeth hadn't realized he'd be able to tell when they drew near the Blackthorn Court, but the magic in the air coated his tongue like nectar, sweet and heavy. The birdsong faded. In the distance, he could hear the drone of pixies.

He drew Shadowstep up short.

Which way to skirt around it? He directed the thought to the horse.

She turned her head to the left, scraping her hoof across the ground.

Shae lifted their head from where it rested on his shoulder, looking around blearily. Jeth envied their ability to sleep on horseback, so long as he was there as a support of sorts.

"Mm, where are we? How far have we come?"

"We're nearing Heartwood Hill."

Shae's nose wrinkled, and they looked around the woods in distaste. "Faerie territory."

Jeth nodded slowly. The trees grew wild here, the undergrowth thick. The edicts he'd placed with the Moot Crown didn't protect anyone who ventured into these places willingly. He didn't know how many humans found their ways to the various faerie courts. With how rare they were now, he shuddered to think what their experiences were like.

He flexed his hands, the leather of the reins pressing against the scars across both of his palms, the long-healed evidence of his wild ride on Shadowstep's back.

Every interaction with a faerie comes with a cost. How steep do they get?

"I don't want to go any closer."

Jeth paused, lips parted. He'd been about to say the same thing. The bright summer air, rippling with heat, somehow felt alive. Watchful. Malicious. He felt the prickle of eyes on them. The air crackled with anticipation.

The faeries had no love for the king who banished them all.

"I don't want to, either," he admitted, the unease knotting his shoulders. "Let's skirt around it."

The Calders' estate was located on the far side of the faerie lands and a day's ride beyond. Shadowstep turned without any urging, picking her way through the trees. Birdsong returned, hesitant though it was, the further they rode away from the hill. The sun hung high overhead in a clear blue sky, the heat of it muffled by the press of shadows beneath the thick canopy. Leaves rustled. Squirrels chittered to one another, leaping across branches overhead.

There was something about the huge, gnarled tree trunks that felt familiar. Jeth couldn't put his finger on it. Maybe it was the magic in them that tasted like his, golden and warm.

Shadowstep slowed, swinging her head to one side. *That way.*

"What?" Jeth followed her gaze. "What's that way?"

Through the trees, he could see a brighter patch of light, but–

"That's not the way we want to go, is it? We're looping around to–"

That way. The black horse turned and marched toward the light, stubborn as a mule.

Jeth frowned at the back of her head.

She shook out her mane. She knew he was looking, and clearly she didn't care.

"Where are we going now?" Shae asked, leaning around to look at Shadowstep.

She snorted.

"I don't know. She said we should go that way." Jeth swung his hand toward the growing patch of light.

Shadowstep marched out of the trees into a large, bright clearing. An escarpment filled the space, a gentle slope that rose on three sides, only to drop sharply on the fourth in a wall of stone. A few scrubby shrubs grew on the lumpy hillward side. The far side nearly met the trees of the forest, the branches reaching up the sheer stone wall and just barely falling shy of the top.

Shadowstep danced in place.

Off.

"I don't–"

Off!

Jeth sighed, helping Shae down before he swung to the ground, folding his arms over his chest and staring his horse down. "What is this? What do you think you're–?"

An excellent spot to camp, yes? Saddle, off. She presented her side to him.

Scowling, Jeth loosened the straps, quickly divesting her of the saddle and bridle. With a toss of her mane, Shadowstep trotted off beneath the trees.

Shae stood, gaze slowly sliding from the woods to Jeth and back again. "What exactly was that all about?"

Jeth shifted his burden, juggling saddle and saddlebags and bridle awkwardly. "She said we should camp here. She must have something she wants to do."

You do, too.

His gaze snapped toward the trees.

"What did she say?" Shae asked quickly.

"She says I have something to do here, too." He frowned. She'd never directed him like this before.

Jeth studied the slope, plodding slowly toward the top.

"Well, it will make a decent place to camp, at least," Shae said behind him. "Maybe for a few days, this time. We could use a rest. Hear that? Water."

The peak was a nice open space with soft grass and few rocks. The sound of water running over stones nearby played through the trees. A river, he guessed by the sound.

"How far are we from everything? Not far at all from Heartwood Hill." Jeth set the saddle down at the top, turning to admire the view over most of the trees. He could see cleared land dotted with houses and fields, not far away. The low glitter of water—of a *river*—that was–

River Tor?

The realization sparked a sudden hunger in Jeth. He'd seen it once or twice, hundreds of years ago. He hadn't gone close. Now, here it was, within his reach.

Shae followed his gaze.

For a moment, they stood in silence. The little brown lumps at the top of the treeline were rooftops, he realized. The pale ones were thatched, the darker ones capped with shingles. At this angle, it was impossible to see more, to tell more.

"You might as well go," Shae said gently, nudging him with an elbow. "I know that look. You won't be content until you do."

"But we have to–"

"I can set up camp on my own. A nice one, I think. We'll stay a few days." They turned and stuck an arm into the saddlebags up to their shoulder, fishing out the bedrolls before rooting around for more.

Jeth sucked in a deep breath. "Are you sure?"

"I am. Go on, go on!" They waved their hand dismissively. "I'll be just fine here, getting a little peace and quiet."

Jeth hurried down the hill. Before he left the clearing, he paused to weave a barrier spell around it. It was simple enough to cover the space with a dome of golden power. A little more complicated was painting the illusion over the magic, getting it just right before he let the spell settle.

To anyone who didn't know it was there, the clearing was gone. To all appearances, the woods thickened here into a tangled copse of trees and brambles that looked impassable. It was a very unwelcoming image, and one that ought to keep anyone from stumbling upon Shae in Jeth's absence.

An adventurous traveler could walk right through it, of course, but Jeth doubted there were many of those this close to faerie territory. His peace of mind protected, he left.

Jeth was no stranger to traipsing through the woods. Climbing over fallen logs, following animal trails, stepping over roots, ducking so his antlers wouldn't catch—after hundreds of years, all of it was as familiar to him as breathing.

It felt different this time, though. This time, he was on his way to do something he could actually accomplish. Going to River Tor and poking about was achievable.

Unlike the mirror, the bitter voice murmured.

Lost for hundreds of years. Jeth wasn't sure it really existed anymore, actually. A rumor nearly fifty years ago put it at the bottom of the sea—but another rumor in the same town led them off to an island, just in case. No mirror, of course.

Everywhere they went, there was no mirror.

A swell of frustration rose through his chest until it burst out of him in a huff. He slowed.

You'll never find it, the voice said.

Jeth wrenched the thought from his mind, turning instead to other questions. Different questions, and these still had no answers.

What if there are still Penistones in River Tor? What if I actually have a family, distant as they are?

Not that they would see themselves as such, since he was so...

Fae? the voice in his head asked dryly.

Different. Old, Jeth corrected.

Still, perhaps there was a trace of his family, of his mother, of his human life. Maybe that bit he'd thought he'd find at Stonehill was at River Tor instead. He pictured walking into town, pictured being drawn to one of the cottages. The door swung open, and people poured out, all of them happy to see him, to welcome him *home*, to...

You don't have a home. You don't have a family.

Jeth stopped short, scowling. He couldn't smother those bitter thoughts for long, no matter how much he wanted to. He kicked a stone, then resumed his march, mind firmly fixed on practical thoughts—like getting supplies, mending their gear, buying some fishing hooks and line. Important things. Mundane things.

He was so lost in thought he surprised himself when, as the late afternoon sun lowered toward the trees, he stepped out onto the edge of a field. A low stone fence sat a few feet away, and beyond that, the house and barn that made up the rest of the farm.

Jeth backpedaled quickly into the shadows of the trees, lifting a hand to his antlers. He was lucky no one saw him! He cast his glamours as he circled through the trees toward the coils of smoke overhead that spoke of the village proper.

The river curved into a horse-shoe shape here, with bridges spanning its length and the thick forest walling it off on the fourth side. That same river ran through the woods to their camp, Jeth realized.

When Jeth had seen River Tor last, that was all there was—a collection of houses and cottages nestled safely in the shelter of the curving banks.

It had grown.

A mill with three massive wooden wheels churned away at one edge, the water splashing and the wheels creaking. A smith's hammer clanged somewhere nearby. There was an entire stable just for the breeding, buying, and selling of horses across the water. Most impressive of all was the raw, unweathered wood of a new guards' barracks, modest though the two story building was. A few guards patrolled past in the black and tan livery of Hallanor's standing army, swords at their belts and spears in their hands.

Across the water, where once there had been roads weaving through unending forest, there were now tree-lined paths that separated four new farms—that Jeth could see. Five with the one he'd passed at the forest's edge, and thin plumes of smoke in the distance spoke to at least two more besides.

Slowly, Jeth stepped out of the woods and threaded his way between the buildings. He fought the instinct to duck and hide when someone spotted him, worried that there would be another cold welcome waiting for him here.

The roads were all packed earth, but as he rounded the corner, Jeth came nose-to-nose with a pile of stone as tall as he was, and the start of cobbles being placed outside the massive inn. There would be paved roads soon enough.

Jeth leaned around the stones, drinking in the market square before the large wooden building. Shoppers bustled back and forth, baskets over their arms and wooden crates in their hands. Coins gleamed as they changed hands. People bawled over one another, each trying harder than their neighbor to move their wares. The booths held every sort of good, from luxurious furs to little paper packets of needles.

Jeth wandered the stalls, basking in the presence of others, in the little snippets of conversation he caught as he passed.

"–get her something nice, since she's been working so hard on that quilt."

"Well, that ribbon ought to do it."

"I need four eggs more for a cake than my hens have laid, Jerim, so just you pick out four nice big ones."

"My hens only lay big eggs, Vette!"

"Can we please, please, please get some of this one, Momma? For a new dress for my doll?"

"Alright, just a little. We'll take a quarter yard, Gertie."

"Coming right up."

"Hey, la, look at this one!"

"What do you need with a sword, Urvine? You know Chrissy won't let you join the guard."

"Maybe I can convince her."

"Maybe you shouldn't have married the miller's daughter if you wanted to go off and fight."

There was laughter and shouting. Color swirled everywhere. Children ran between the legs of adults in pursuit of games their elders couldn't fathom.

Jeth stopped before a horseman's booth, admiring a fine saddle with embossed designs at the edges. He stretched out a hand to touch the smooth, polished leather.

"Oi, if you can't buy it, don't touch it," snapped the man behind the stall, smacking his hand on the wood.

Jeth paused, a brow rising. He had more gold than this man would ever see in two lifetimes—but he was still wearing his travel-stained clothes intended for hard wandering through the woods.

"What makes you think I can't afford it?"

"One look at you is all it takes. Whatever nag you have, if you have one at all, it ain't worth the feed you waste on it. That saddle is too fine for the likes of you. Just strap a blanket to the beast's back if you fancy yourself a horse rider."

"That's not a very good way to make a sale, friend," Jeth said, an edge in his voice.

"Ha! If I could make a sale off you, maybe. Go on, get out of here."

Jeth frowned and turned away.

Judgemental, aren't they? Quick to assume, quick to turn someone away, the voice murmured. *Here you are, richer than their king, and you're chased away like a street thief, a wastrel, a vagabond.*

He shook his head, trying to chase the buzzing thoughts from his mind, but it was getting harder to do so when the voice was *right*. He took a deep breath, stopping at the next stall that caught his eye.

Seeds.

He paused, eyes tracing over the little wooden signs with words and pictures both painted on, admiring the selection. Vegetables, yes, fruits, yes, but also herbs. Herbs that were familiar to him. There, foxglove for a heart that beat too weakly. There, poppy for pain. Chamomile for swollen hands and fever. Vervain to close wounds, marsh mallow for sore throats, ephedra for wheezing in the lungs. Betony, useful for everything from bleeding to hangovers! Fennel, bergamot, hyssop, and more.

His memories were as sharp as if they'd happened yesterday. He could *feel* the cottage surrounding him, smell the herbs hanging from the ceiling, hear the grind of mortar and pestle as his mother worked. Her soothing voice explained to him what each plant did, how it worked with its fellows, and more. Salves, tinctures, poultices, oils. She taught him all of them.

"You gonna buy anything or just stare? Need help to tell what's what?" The woman running the stall asked, wiping her hands off on her apron.

"What?" He looked up at her, then back down. "Oh, no. No, I won't be buying." Where would he plant seeds?

"Then do you mind? Other folks might."

Jeth pulled away at the clear dismissal, frustration warring with a pang of sadness. The woman began to cry out her wares, leaving Jeth to his own devices, his own thoughts.

Seeing those seeds felt like his mother was here, like she'd given him a small nod of acknowledgement across the centuries. A nod he couldn't—or didn't want to—ignore.

Jeth wandered the stalls aimlessly, lost in thought and staying out of the way of the strangers around him. He attracted only a few curious glances, since people passed this way often. Eventually he stopped once again, staring at the glittering metals on a young smith's table—or a smith's apprentice. A son, perhaps.

Iron implements that would burn his hand if he touched them were mixed in among polished steel. Wooden bowls held nails and rings and chain links. Flat surfaces were covered with tools large and small, everything from a plow blade to spoons.

"Anything catch your fancy, sir?" the young man asked.

"I'm just looking, really."

"Alright. Take your time." The smith turned to scan the crowd, leaving Jeth to pour over the objects on the table.

"I was just wondering, actually," Jeth said at last after a moment. "Do you have a village witch? Where do they live?"

"You need healing or some such? If you do, you'll want to go to the mender's house, over by Bear Bridge, the one over there," the smith leaned forward, pointing to one side.

"But the mender isn't a witch, are they?"

"No, course not." He snorted out a laugh that stuttered out awkwardly. "You're pulling my leg, though, aren't you, sir? Nobody needs a witch these days. What ones we have that can cast and all that, they're married with families. They only spend their time blessing fields when somebody pays them."

Jeth's brows rose. He'd seen it in other villages, where witches fell out of favor and fashion. Where their support by the villagers was deemed unnecessary now that faeries were so rare. But they still had homes, they still peddled their salves and tinctures. No witches at all was...

...and Heartwood Hill was so close. Everyone in River Tor knew Heartwood Hill was the entrance to a faerie kingdom.

Even still? The voice whispered in his ear.

"What about the faeries? Heartwood Hill?" Jeth asked the smith.

"Oh. Them."

"Yes, them," Jeth said dryly.

The smith shrugged. "Well, we give the hill a wide berth, but to be honest, sir, I don't even know if faeries are real. The old folks tell tales. Don't go too deep in the woods or the faeries will snatch you up. Don't climb on a strange horse. Could be a faerie steed and ride away with you. Don't feed strange fish, might be faeries. But plenty of us have done all of that stuff, and we come back just fine. They said Hetty got taken by faeries when she vanished two years back. I think she ran away with that trader she liked to get married."

Jeth ran his tongue over his lips, a thought rising slowly to the surface of his mind. It was still hazy, unfocused. "What's your name?"

"Coree, sir. You sure I can't get you anything? A nice spoon, maybe, for your travels? Got some with belt loops on."

"I'm sure, thank you. Coree, you know faeries are real, yes?"

"Oh, sure. If magic is real, magical creatures must be, too. I just think they left Hallanor a long time ago. Most of them."

He isn't wrong, Jeth realized. He arched a brow.

If only he knew how here and real you are, the voice murmured, urging him silently to show himself.

Jeth drew himself up straight. "You mentioned spoons?"

"Yes, sir. Got a great collection of them here, even made some of them myself." Coree pulled out a few more spoons from a wooden box beneath the stall's counter, laying them out. Most all of them were designed with a leather tie to hang them on one's belt. The smith started pointing out his favorites.

Jeth stared at the array of gleaming steel and black iron, brow furrowed. His eyes were on the young man's work, but his thoughts were a thousand miles away, following that dawning realization.

Humans didn't believe faeries were real anymore, or rather that they were real...but not a threat. Humans were lowering their guard.

And he knew exactly why. They didn't believe in them because centuries had passed in peace. No wild rides, no harassment, no tricks or traps, no lures or kidnappings. Not in hundreds of years.

Because of Jeth.

Because of his edicts.

Humans were certain their stories were just that. Fanciful tales that no longer applied to their lives. They didn't care whether or not the danger still existed, since it couldn't touch them.

And it was his fault.

THREE

"Sir?"

Someone was speaking to him.

"Excuse me? *Sir.*"

Jeth looked up at Coree, blinking owlishly. "What? Ah, sorry. I got lost in thought there for a moment. What did you say?"

Coree cleared his throat. "I said you might like this one in particular. It's got a nice polish to it." The young smith held up a nice spoon with an intricately twisted metal handle.

"Yes, that one suits me. Thank you." He pulled out his coin purse, relinquishing a handful of coppers easily enough.

"What brings you into town, then? Staying at the inn on your way somewhere else?"

"I'm considering," Jeth said truthfully, glancing up at the lowering sun. "I was hoping to run into some very, very old friends here. But I don't know if they stayed or not."

The words conjured up a thousand doubts. What if they *had* moved? What if they'd had a generation all of daughters and they'd married out of the name? How would he find them?

When they went to find Shae's family, they'd poured through the ancient records at the Lord's estate for days. It was Jeth who found the last entry. Shae's lineage had died out a single generation after Shae was taken—long before Jeth ever came to the Blackthorn Court. Before they'd ever even met.

Shae had set the papers down, face blank as a stone. Then they'd smiled and said, softly: *At least they had records at all.*

"You are? Which ones, then, sir? I've lived here all my life. I know just about everybody."

"I'm sure you do," Jeth said with a smile.

Coree gave him a stir of hope, subtle as the first sigh of a breeze. More and more, his interactions with strangers were unpleasant or downright hostile. It was nice to linger, to chat, to know that humanity as a whole wasn't rotting from the core.

"The Penistone family. I don't suppose they still live around here."

"Oh, sure. They've been here since River Tor was founded. Only three families can say that much. Mine's only been here five generations, ourselves." Coree grinned. "Friendly folks, even if they're a little odd."

"Odd?" Jeth said, dread replaced with growing hope. Horrible, tangled, painful hope. "Where are they living these days?"

"Same place they always have. At the end of that road, just there, there's a little track. Follow it through the trees and it will take you right to them. You can't miss it. It's the only house out that way." Coree leaned over his counter, pointing out the way.

"In the old witch's cottage?"

"Ha! It might have been, once. Maybe. But they aren't witches now. Like I said, we haven't got much call for witches anymore." Coree was halfway through a shrug when he suddenly straightened. He ran his fingers through his hair, squared his shoulders, and lifted his chin.

Jeth took a small step to the side as a pretty young woman stepped up to the stall beside him. She had plump cheeks the color of pink roses, and a lovely embroidered dress. She moved her little basket from one arm to the other.

"Hello, Coree."

"Hello, Jillian," Coree said as casually as he could. "Come for more needles?"

"Pins, actually. Please."

Coree ducked quickly behind the counter. A smile tugged at the corner of Jeth's lips. With a bob of his head to young Jillian, he excused himself, spoon in hand. He fitted it to his belt as he made his way down the road and around a corner.

The little track was easy to find. It reminded him of home. The sweet smell of earth and wildflowers filled the air, tinged with the scent of fresh bread from a house nearby. Long grass and thick underbrush grew on either side of the narrow path, a crooked little trail beneath arches made of tree branches. The ground was dappled with golden specks as the sun shone through the leaves. Here and there, the roots of the gnarled, ancient trees stretched across the way.

A breeze whispered overhead as Jeth stepped onto the path, rustling softly as it raced before him.

His heart swelled. He could *feel* her, here. Everything his mother taught him during his life, the way she'd chosen to live, it was because she once lived down a path like this. The plants lining the pathway, including the trees, were all useful. Edible, medicinal, or beautiful. The path was just wide enough to allow two side by side and no more, respecting the forest around it.

Jeth fought to keep his pace at a walk as his anticipation grew. He walked as quick as he could, consciously reminding himself not to hold his breath. His heart thudded, soft and determined, behind his ribs.

The light ahead grew brighter, promising a clearing. Jeth ducked into the trees, circling around the edge. He wasn't certain, after all, how he might be received. He came to a stop in the shadow of a great oak at the very edge, resting a hand on the vast trunk.

I just want to see it, that's all. I don't even really want to meet my...my family.

Liar, the voice whispered.

How would he explain who he was, though? How could he tell them where he came from?

No, this would have to be enough. Just a glimpse.

The clearing was a decent size. A small meadow stood before the house and a well with a roof over it stood in the middle. A little garden sat on one side, riotous with greenery behind a fence made of woven branches.

The cottage itself was modest, with worn stone walls and creeping ivy. The windows were closed; the shutters latched in place. A stack of furs sat in a huge wooden crate beside the door, all of them neatly laid out, one atop the other, big and small. A bow without a string leaned against the wall beside them. A few traps and coils of fine rope hung on the outside wall.

Jeth was struck by how much it felt like a *home,* imperfect and well loved. It was centuries old, he had no doubt, but it was cared for and fixed up, the thatch regularly replaced, the windows mended, the walls whitewashed and plastered over and over again.

It was a held breath, and he could feel his mother here.

Jeth straightened, eyes falling on two pairs of mud-spattered boots of different sizes. They sat beside the door, one laying on its side.

Two pairs. A couple, then? A parent and a child? Like him and his mother, once upon a time.

Jeth's entire body buzzed with the sudden need to know, the urge to investigate. He stepped into the light.

A twig snapped behind him.

Jeth froze. The hair on the back of his neck stood up. He whirled, catching just a glimpse of red, red hair as his stalker ducked behind a tree.

His fingers twitched, his lip curling. It had been a long, long time since he'd seen that bastard, the one who drove him to spend hundreds of years of his life on this wild, fruitless chase for the last mirror.

"I see you, Eoghan," he snapped.

Eoghan slid gracefully into view, abandoning his hiding place. He all but draped himself against the trunk of the tree. He was handsome, and he knew it—of course he did. He was a Gean-Cánach, a faerie of love and lust.

"I'm glad I found you, your Majesty. We sensed it when you stepped into the woods."

His voice was smooth, but his words only deepened Jeth's frown.

Damn it. They rode too close. The glittering emerald in the throne stayed lit to show the faeries that their king was alive, well, and still powerful. It must have flared when he got near enough, brightened so that they could all see.

"Don't worry, I don't plan to return to court. You can continue to pretend the throne is yours."

"But I want you to go back." Eoghan straightened, moving slowly toward Jeth, every step made with the grace of a hunting cat.

Jeth snorted a laugh before he could stop himself. "You can't be serious."

Eoghan stopped beneath the trees with a jerk, as if stopped by an invisible wall. He lifted his hand, running it through the air before him. "Can't you come here so we can talk? Your edicts are rather iron clad. I can't go any closer to that cottage than this."

Jeth frowned, taking a hesitant step closer. The space between his shoulders prickled, but he held his ground. "Why would you want me to come back?"

"I've had some time to think things over. What I did, what I said...it was rash. Uncalled for."

Jeth smothered another snort. The last time he'd seen the faerie was when Eoghan smashed the prison holding his father captive and wished every ill upon Jeth that he could.

"I know," Eoghan said, lowering his gaze contritely. He looked through his lashes at Jeth. "I'm...passionate. What can I say? But I want you to come back, your Majesty."

"Why?" Jeth asked, voice hard. He folded his arms over his chest.

Eoghan swept his hand toward the clearing. "Look at this. Look at me. This is as close as I get to humans now. I, whose magic relies on them. We're all forced to lurk in the shadows, to watch our prey and never near them. It's what you ordered, isn't it?"

Jeth glanced at the cottage. "It is."

"But now the humans, they're...expanding. They grow nearer our territory with every passing year. I've heard them speak. They hardly believe in us any longer. One day, they'll go too far, they'll cross into our lands, and then..."

He's right. You've left humanity unable to protect themselves with all your high and mighty edicts, all your grand ideas, the voice hissed in the back of his mind.

Jeth frowned. He'd thought the same thing, hadn't he?

Eoghan stepped closer, lifting a hand to touch Jeth's shoulder. "We've found what little loopholes we can, you know. It's almost enough. Almost. We watch them. We fight over what few humans *ask* us to take them. Then we wage war against one another for the right to their lives. You've made them a precious resource."

The ones who ask? He'd never thought of them. "Do they ever want to leave after you've taken them?"

"Oh, always," Eoghan said with a casual ease that sent a chill down Jeth's spine. "But they asked to come, so we get to keep them. It doesn't matter what they want, after that."

His stomach flipped, and he fought down the wave of nausea. Jeth hadn't saved all of humanity. He hadn't thought of everything.

But you did the best you could. You saved as many as possible. Who can ask for more?

His silent reassurance was interrupted by the bitter voice in his head.

You could have done better, and you know it.

Could I, though?

"Get to the point, Eoghan."

"It isn't enough," the Gean-Cánach said flatly, tossing his long, silky red hair. "Come back. Use the Moot Crown again. Limit us, if you must, but free us. Unfetter us. Let us be what we were meant to be."

Eoghan was pleading. He was begging.

Jeth's mouth went dry.

They don't know? They didn't sense when it happened? He had sensed it when the Moot Crown was destroyed, melted down in a furnace until the gold was gone and the crystals cracked. It felt like a blow to the chest. He'd fallen, struggling to breathe. Shae had knelt by his side, worried sick.

But that happened hundreds of years ago. He gave the crown to Queen Cailea four...five monarchs ago!

"I can't."

"You can. Listen, I've spent decades thinking of how to do it so you get what you want, and so do we. What we need to do is –"

"No, Eoghan. Even if I wanted to, which I don't, I can't. The Moot Crown is gone. I had it destroyed."

Eoghan went so still, he seemed like a statue. The only sign he was still alive was the faint flutter of his pulse in his neck.

"Destroyed?" he echoed after a long, long moment.

"Yes. A long time ago. Hundreds of years."

"*Destroyed?*"

A rising sense of unease swept over Jeth. Something had changed between him and Eoghan, though the faerie hadn't changed his expression or even moved, yet. Whatever truce he was trying to negotiate had failed.

Jeth stretched out his senses, tethering himself to the nearest leyline. He drew in the golden power, filling himself like a bucket, preparing for the worst.

Eoghan laughed.

He threw his head back and laughed, long and loud, the sound edged with growing madness. Abruptly, he stopped. His gaze met Jeth's, and he smiled. It was too wide. His blue eyes were too bright.

"Here I thought I'd give you a chance," the faerie said, voice shaking with fury even as he kept grinning. "But this just settles it, doesn't it? You've *ruined* us." The smile fell into a snarl, teeth bared. His hands curled into fists.

"I've changed you, that's all. You still live."

"I still live?" Eoghan spat. "And to think I once loved you."

"You never loved me, Eoghan. Just what I could offer." They both knew it.

Eoghan stepped closer, lifting a hand. Jeth stood firm, shoulders squared, braced for a blow—that never came. The Gean-Cánach caressed his cheek, glaring at him. Even in a white hot fury, he was handsome.

Jeth was very glad Shae was elsewhere. Eoghan had caused enough harm to Shae to last a lifetime, and seeing him make another move on Jeth would only make it worse.

"How do you know, Jeth?" Eoghan asked. "You never gave us a chance."

"I was never interested," Jeth said gently, not breaking his gaze. "You knew that. Go back to Heartwood Hill, Eoghan. Go back to the court and learn a new way."

"How can I? I don't have what I came for." Eoghan dropped his hand. "Lucky for us, there's always more than one solution to a problem."

Jeth caught sight of the glittering knife as it was lifted, barely. His concentration on his magic fractured, the power rushing away like a spilled bucket of water. His hold on the leyline snapped as if it were severed by the long, slender blade itself.

He threw himself back. It arced through the air in front of him, missing by mere inches.

Eoghan didn't hesitate to follow, swinging the knife with deadly grace, herding Jeth deeper into the forest. His face was fixed in a mad mask of mingled glee and anger.

"It's so simple, your Majesty! All we need is your death, your blood, and our spells!"

Blood magic!

Long forbidden by human and faerie alike, blood magic was powerful but unpredictable. Many of the spellcasters died as often as their sacrifices.

Jeth ducked around a tree trunk, cursing as Eoghan lunged for him. He reached for the leyline, darting to one side–

–only to swing around a tree and come nose to nose with the Gean-Cánach.

Instinctively, his hands shot up as Eoghan thrust the knife toward his chest. He caught the faerie's wrist and braced himself. It took every ounce of his strength to hold him at bay, and still the knife inched toward his neck, a hair's breadth at a time.

Jeth grit his teeth. "Just stop it, Eoghan! I don't want to hurt you!"

"Liar! You've hurt me and every other faerie for *centuries*. All for your precious humans, all for your loyalty to some mortal whore," Eoghan raged, spittle flying from his lips.

Sweat ran down Jeth's brow as they wrestled. He scowled. "Don't speak about my mother that way," he spat.

One last time, he reached for the leyline, stretching his concentration and his strength to both limits.

Golden power flooded him. He pushed it into his muscles, into his arms and legs. Then, he coated his skin with it, turning it into a shield around every inch of himself, an invisible armor stronger than any steel.

Then Jeth let go.

He stepped back.

Eoghan didn't expect it. The knife flew forward, glancing off the magic barrier on Jeth's chest and sliding down. The way it had slipped twisted it. Momentum carried it backwards from there. Eoghan stumbled.

The knife met flesh.

Eoghan grunted, eyes widening. He was still. They both were. His fingers uncurled from the hilt of the blade one by one, his eyes fixed on where it rested in his chest, angled up between his ribs.

His breath rasped. With a cough, blood flecked his lips. He'd hit his lung.

"No. No, Eoghan!" Jeth caught him as his knees gave out, lowering him to the ground. "Hold on, I can heal this. Just don't move."

I didn't want this; I didn't.

He felt the voice in his mind, the bitter, angry voice, watching his movements, judging him.

Eoghan caught Jeth's wrist in a vice-like grip as he reached for the knife. "Don't," he managed, crimson blood staining his lips. "Don't. This is...better than what you...you left us with." He choked. He coughed.

"You just have to adapt, Eoghan. We all change, you can change." Jeth felt Eoghan's grip on his wrist weakening. "Let me help you."

"No," the Gean-Cánach murmured, voice fading. "You have done enough for me. You destroyed me and everything I love. And you...you don't even care."

The faerie's hand fell by his side. Jeth moved quickly, grasping the knife and sending his magic down the blade, into the flesh around it, racing to find the worst damage. "I can mend it."

Eoghan grabbed his wrist again and wrenched it up before Jeth could stop him. The knife was still in his hand. He felt it as the blade slipped free, felt flesh give beneath his hand, saw blood flow freely, heard the sickening squelch.

Jeth shouted wordlessly, throwing the knife aside and pressing both hands over the wound. There was so much blood. He reached for his magic, but it slipped beneath his grasp. He couldn't concentrate.

"*You did this,*" Eoghan whispered. "You killed me."

The light faded from his eyes, the sapphire blue dulling to gray. His body went limp. His handsome face went slack, a single drop of blood running down his jaw.

Jeth froze, stunned. His breath came too fast, as if by breathing for both of them he could bring Eoghan back. His chest felt too tight, like something was trying to break free and never could.

This isn't what I wanted.

Isn't it? You let go, the voice murmured.

No!

He wasn't a killer.

This isn't what he wanted.

Slowly, he lifted his hands from Eoghan's body, staring at them. They were painted red with blood.

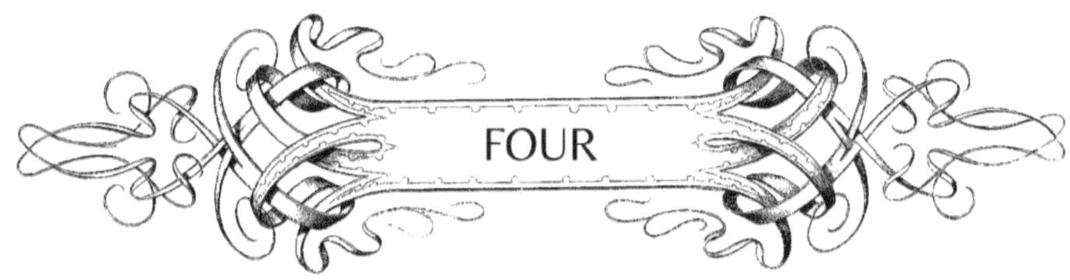

FOUR

The sun was sinking. No one was at the cottage, but they would return before nightfall, most likely. Eoghan lay, staring sightlessly at the sky. Jeth fought the urge to scream, to run, and to empty his stomach.

I can't leave him here. Not like this.

Numb inside and out, Jeth gathered his power and parted the earth at the base of the grand oak tree at the edge of the clearing. He lay the dagger on Eoghan's breast, wrapping the Gean-Cánach's hand around the hilt, and closing his eyes. His fine robe, a rich dark green with brown embroidery, was stained red down one side. Jeth couldn't do anything about that.

With as much dignity as he could, he lay Eoghan to rest. The earth flowed over the faerie's face, more like water than dirt.

Jeth stood.

It was as if something broke in him, then. He staggered into the woods, steps quickening from a walk to a jog to an all-out run.

Branches snapped and crackled around him as he ran headlong through the trees. His hands were stained with rust and red smears. They almost looked like earth, but Jeth knew better.

He knew.

His pulse roared in his ears. His stomach churned and flipped inside him. Chilled through as he was, he hardly felt the scrapes of branches, the sting of leaves as he charged through them.

You killed him, the voice murmured.

It wasn't my fault!

You killed.

For the first time in his life, he'd taken one. Eoghan, of all people! Eoghan, who was a thorn in his side, but never so overtly malicious—until today—as to deserve an end like that. Jeth stumbled to a stop, bracing himself against a tree. He retched up a mouthful of bile.

I killed.

Murdered, the nasty voice all but purred.

Worse, if what Eoghan said was true, the faerie courts were in turmoil. They laid the blame for their unrest squarely at Jeth's feet.

And humans were entirely unaware of the danger of faeries, unaware of how close their lands actually were to the borders of the courts. They were in danger of forgetting them entirely, already believing them to be nothing more than stories.

And you still don't know where the mirror is, do you?

Jeth shook his head, but the voice was growing stronger. It was *right,* damn it. It was right.

He didn't know how long he stood there panting, the bark digging into his forearm. His racing pulse slowed. He stared unseeing at the ground. Hesitantly, the faint sound of evening birds filled the air.

There was another sound beneath the birdsong. A rumble. A rush. It took him several moments to piece together what he was hearing.

Water.

Jeth lurched forward, the sudden need to be clean overtaking him. His knees threatened to buckle with every step as he pushed through the trees and underbrush.

The river cut through the forest, through the earth at his feet, the shore lined with stones rounded by time. Here, the water moved quick but calm. A little way ahead, it rushed around a series of rocks, frothing white. It was that part that made the sound.

Jeth waded in, the teeth-chattering cold of it hitting him like a slap in the face. He gasped, and sucking in that lungful of air was enough to remind him to breathe again. He thrust his hands into the water, scrubbing at his skin with his sleeves.

Dark swirls flowed away from him like coils of smoke, vanishing into the water as the river ran on.

I didn't know that would happen. I didn't.

Was that enough of an excuse to justify how he was chipping away at his fading humanity? He'd killed, and it had been so easy. He'd killed, even if it were an accident. In the moment, he hadn't cared what would happen if he stepped back. He just *did.* Only afterward did the feelings of guilt rise until they threatened to choke him. He was like a drunk, acting without thought of the hangover that would follow his mead.

Jeth's teeth chattered. His hands were clean, but he still scrubbed, and scrubbed, and scrubbed.

The endless march of time robbed him of memories. It stole his friends and loved ones from him one by one. Now, it chipped away at his soul. He had an unending number of years to look forward to, unless he was killed.

Like Eoghan.

What will you be like in another 200 years, I wonder? The voice mused. *What will you do when the world changes on you again and again? How do you even fit into the world as it is?*

There was no place for faeries in Hallanor. Not any longer. Jeth saw to that himself. But he couldn't ignore what he was any more than he could ignore the antlers growing from his head.

He couldn't pretend he was human, either. No matter how much he longed for it, it was something he could never get back.

For a moment, he understood the fluttering madness he'd inflicted upon the faeries, the sudden panic at discovering he had nowhere to go, that he was nothing, no one. The shift in his heart that said he no longer fit into the world the way he had an hour ago.

But I didn't hurt Eoghan for pleasure. I didn't hurt him for my own gain. Jeth never wanted to hurt anyone at all.

Bit too late for that, isn't it? The voice asked.

He sank to his knees, the water enveloping him up to the chest. The cold cinched around his lungs like a vice, leaving him gasping. He closed his eyes, wondering what would happen if he just lay down and let the water take him. If he survived the rapids, would he come out cleansed?

"Jeth?"

Water sloshed and streamed off him as he pushed to his feet and turned, locking eyes with Shae. Beautiful, patient Shae, whose wide eyes were fixed on the cuffs of Jeth's sleeve. Even with the river, the fabric was stained red.

Shadowstep stood behind the changeling. Her concern pressed at the edge of his mind before she slowly backed into the shadows beneath the trees. Jeth felt her leave.

She knew who Jeth needed in this moment. Shadowstep brought Jeth the one person who might be able to help him.

"Shae," he breathed, wading toward the shore. "Shae, I..."

He trailed off. What words would say enough here?

"Alright," Shae said after a long moment, holding out their hands. "Come out of the water."

Jeth's numb, icy fingers wrapped around Shae's, the heat of the other faerie warming him like a fire. He left the river.

Shae wrapped their arm around his shoulder, guiding him to a boulder and urging him to sit. The changeling sat beside him, taking his hands in theirs and rubbing life back into them as gently as they could. "What happened?"

Their voice was soft and comforting. They weren't asking in judgment, but concern.

"Eoghan came at me with a knife. Shae, I...I killed him with it."

Before he could stop himself, every detail of what happened was falling from his lips. Shae listened, asking gentle questions here and there. They never once let go, never once pulled away.

As the last of the story left him, his thoughts and feelings followed. He was empty, out of words at last. He stuttered to a stop, numbness swallowing him whole.

Shae pulled Jeth to his feet. They held his hand, towing him through the trees. The branches gave way to the clearing and the hill the pair of them had claimed for their camp. Shae had been busy. A fire crackled merrily in a low circle of stones. The rarely used tent sat behind it, the inside padded with their bedding and packs. A battered tin kettle was warming on a flat stone at the edge of the flames.

The changeling sat Jeth on a cut log. They disappeared inside the tent, pulling out a set of dry clothes and a sachet of herbs. Jeth changed. Shae steeped a pot of tea. They swathed themselves in blankets as the night grew cold around them. Neither said anything until they sat side by side, nursing small tin cups that smelled of bergamot and cloves. The warmth seeped through Jeth's palms and up his arms, bringing life back to his numb body.

"Do you want me to tell you that it's alright, or that the pain of it will fade in time?" Shae asked softly, their head tipped back to study the stars.

"I want you to tell me the truth."

"The pain will fade in time. Who knows how long it will take, but it will. You didn't do anything on purpose. You didn't kill him. You didn't draw the knife. But the pain you feel is still real. The wound is still there."

Jeth studied the tea in his cup, saying nothing. His brow furrowed.

"In a fight, you can't control what happens. Instinct takes over. Fear sits at the edge of everything. Survival becomes the only thing that matters. That's what you did, isn't it? Survived?"

"I could have held him at bay with my magic," Jeth said harshly. "If I could have just concentrated for a *moment–*"

"Yes, because concentrating as a knife comes at you again and again is so very easy," Shae drawled.

Jeth scoffed, but the knot inside his chest eased. "He said killing me could undo the edicts and free the faeries."

"That isn't even how it works. I read all the books in the castle's library. It takes the Moot Crown to do it, or nothing. He'd have a right to wear the crown if he killed you, but the crown is gone."

"What about blood magic?"

"No, blood magic demands too much. To do a work that size, they'd need to bleed half the keep *and* you."

Jeth turned the cup in his hands, watching the tea slope up the sides, threatening to spill over the edge.

Shae put a hand on his cheek, drawing his attention to their eyes. "Don't worry. The people are safe from our kind."

Our kind.

The words echoed in his mind. Jeth sighed. Even Shae, who only needed to wear a hat to pass for a human, knew the truth. They were faeries. It didn't matter what else they *wanted* to be.

And there's no going back.

"Shae, I..."

Jeth grit his teeth, the words dying on the tip of his tongue. Quickly, he swallowed half his cup of tea. It was hot, nearly scalding his tongue, but the ball of fire that slid down his throat and into his stomach was a balm. A little more of the numbness faded away.

Shae said nothing, turning to add another log to the fire. They were waiting, Jeth realized. He'd never met anyone as patient as Shae. Once the changeling decided someone was worth being there for, they would wait for as long as it took.

"I can't even begin to sort all this out," Jeth said at last.

He could, though. He wanted to open his mouth, to let all the words tumbling through his mind into the open air. He wanted to tell Shae, to ask them what to do.

I'm tired, and nothing is working. Nothing seems worth it anymore. Something has to give, and I don't want it to be me. It's been so long, Shae. Haven't I done enough? Can't I...stop?

What if he told Shae, and the changeling hated him for it? They'd spent hundreds of years on this quest, together. They'd traveled across the continent more times than Jeth could count, together. It was Shae's quest as much as his own, wasn't it?

What if Shae wasn't done yet?

"Things will be clearer in the morning, maybe." Shae slipped their hand into Jeth's, giving it a gentle squeeze.

They both lapsed into silence, staring at the leaping flames. Jeth finished his tea. The silence itself was as soothing a salve as the contents of his now empty cup. He passed it to Shae. The changeling wiped it out with a handful of clean grass and set it aside for a proper wash in the morning.

They put the fire out with a breath of magic and crawled into the tent. Shae had lain the bedrolls out right beside one another, making a single large bed. Jeth sprawled on his back, staring blankly at the canvas overhead.

Shae pressed against his side in the dark, warm body molding to his own. Jeth wrapped his arm around their shoulders. In the silence, in the calm, it would be so easy to just relax.

Jeth couldn't get the knot in his shoulders to ease. He couldn't keep his mind from racing. He fought the urge to toss and turn. The deep, even breath of Shae beside him meant the changeling was asleep, and he didn't want to wake them.

Exhausted and frustrated, Jeth resigned himself to staying awake all night if that was what his mind wanted.

...and the next thing he knew, he woke to find it was morning.

The tent flap was pinned open. Shae was outside in the foggy morning air, fussing over the fire and starting breakfast.

Jeth felt...fine. A night of sleep put a wall between him and his guilt. It was still there, but distant. Detached. It only drew closer if he examined it too closely. So he didn't.

You're not bothered? The voice asked.

Shae is right. It wasn't my fault. I didn't draw the knife.

Then why did the blood on your hands scare you so much?

Jeth frowned, sitting up. He had to do something, to hold those thoughts at bay. He slipped out into the open air, wrapping his arms around Shae's waist from behind. He brushed his lips against their cheek.

"Morning, Shae."

"Morning. Feeling any different?"

Not better. Jeth was glad Shae hadn't asked if he felt *better* about murder, as if a new day could erase what happened.

"Different?" Jeth mused. "Yes. Determined, I think."

Shae turned in his arms, a brow raised. "Oh? Determined to do what?"

Jeth brushed a blond curl out of the changeling's face. "I need to warn the humans about faeries. I need to give them a chance, at least. If I can convince even *one* village witch to remain vigilant, it would be enough."

The changeling studied Jeth for a long, silent moment. Their thoughts ran across their face in brief flickers of the brow, little quirks of the lips. "You want to protect them?" they asked at last. "Even still? Even knowing they'll be alright?"

It was true. The people of Hallanor were alright. Faerie magic was unsettling. It was unlikely they'd build into faerie courts, and certainly not in the next few hundred years.

Then why do you still want to protect them? The voice asked with a sneer.

Jeth's lips parted, then closed. *I...*

Just last night, all you wanted to do was stop, but now you've changed your mind? Why?

I can't just stop. This is what I do. This is who I am.

Is it?

"One more try," Jeth said slowly. "Just one. That's all."

"And the mirror?"

Shae's green eyes fixed on Jeth's, and he knew that they *knew.* They knew he was tired.

Jeth pulled away. "We can talk about that later. Soon."

The changeling nodded, pressing a warm piece of flatbread into his hands. "Well, go on. I'll have dinner waiting for you when you get back."

Jeth smiled. *I like the sound of that. A place to go back to.*

He reached out to the corner of his mind where his bond with Shadowstep lay. The mare came out of the trees, tossing her mane and whickering softly. The morning sun was already burning the fog away as he mounted her bareback. A simple nudge with his mind, and they were in among the trees.

The way Shadowstep moved through the woods was like wind or water, flowing along the easiest path as quick as thought. Her deep black coat and her too-intelligent eyes were enough to unsettle most people, but Jeth had grown fond of his wild faerie steed.

Still, he drew her up short a mile away from River Tor. He appreciated her, but he wasn't certain if the villagers would. He slipped off the massive horse's back and gave her neck a good scratch in thanks. She arched her head, leaning into his hand for a solid minute. Then she straightened, tossed her mane, and went trotting off through the trees.

She disappeared in moments, leaving Jeth alone.

For a moment, he wondered what she got up to out there when she was alone.

I'm wandering. Don't you ever just wander, just look at things? She asked.

Jeth's brows rose. *No, I don't think I have.*

You should try it sometime.

The mare closed the connection between them abruptly. Jeth shook his head, a tiny smile on his lips, though it faded quickly. He turned back toward River Tor.

You really think convincing one village witch will be enough to protect the entire kingdom? The voice was back, more disdainful than ever. *You're throwing buckets of sand into the sea and hoping it will hold back the tide.*

One witch can spread the word to another.

Across the entire kingdom and back again? You're one faerie, one of the last faeries. You can't change the minds of a kingdom overnight.

I can try. All it will take is—

"So you say," a female voice said, laughing. It was faint, somewhere through the trees.

"Yes, so I say. There's nothing wrong with a good rabbit stew, Effie, but now and then, a body wants mutton." That one was male.

Jeth slowed.

"We don't catch sheep in our snares," the woman, Effie, teased. "Here, lend me your knife. The line is stuck."

Jeth turned, threading his way through the trees, drawn by the voices, by the casual way they taunted one another, comfortable and familiar. His exhaustion made the laughter sound warmer, brighter.

"Careful, Effie."

"I'm being careful! Oh, whoops."

"Are you alright?" The man asked, alarmed.

Effie laughed.

The man made a disgusted sound. "I swear to the heavens, Effie Penistone, you scare me like that again and..."

Jeth froze in his tracks. The voices were loud and clear now. He heard every word. He heard *Penistone.*

Penistone.

His breath caught.

The people in the woods ahead of him were his family.

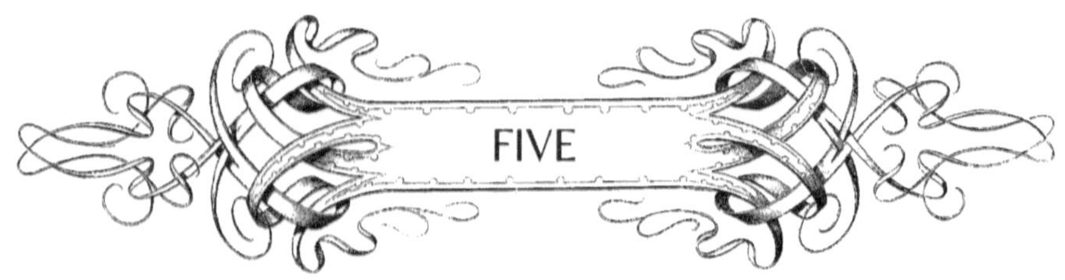

FIVE

The undergrowth was thick, both a blessing and a curse. The wild grass was tall, the shrubs thick.. Jeth used a touch of power to cast a faerie spell of silence on himself, hiding his passage as he moved closer. He dropped to a crouch, easing into place behind a shrub a head and a half taller than his antlers. He peered through the branches.

And there they were. His family.

His family!

The woman, Effie, knelt in the loam. She was smiling, a wide smile that crinkled her cheeks and the corners of her eyes. Her hands were busy resetting her snare. Her hair was black, wavy, and wild. She'd plaited it down her back, but tendrils escaped along its entire length. Her eyes were large and gray.

The man tied a rabbit to the brace already hanging over one of his shoulders. He was built slimmer than his wife, gangly to her solid, tall to her average. He was whippet strong, though, every inch of him muscled. Friendly green eyes glittered beneath his shaggy brown hair. He was smiling, too, and he shook his head.

"Have you got it?" the man asked.

Effie nodded. "Think so. Ought to hold for at least a few more rabbits before the whole thing needs replacing." She held her hand up toward him.

The man pulled her up fast, faster than she was expecting. She all but flew to her feet and into his arms. He grinned, and after a startled moment, Effie laughed at him, smacking his chest lightly.

"What are you thinking a thing like that for, Olfric? In the woods, of all places," she scolded fondly.

"I can't help it. We've been married a whole year soon, and it's got me remembering…" Olfric captured her hands in his, pulling back—only to start a village jig, humming under his breath.

Effie couldn't have smiled any wider if she'd wanted to. She danced along. "It was more fun with a skirt on."

"It was more fun with real musicians!" Olfric laughed.

His laugh was infectiously cheery and loud. It filled the air beneath the trees. Jeth found himself smiling until his cheeks hurt, watching them spin and hop and clap their way through the dance.

They slowed, pausing face to face. Effie leaned in, kissing him gently.

"I love you, Olfric."

"I love you, too, Effie. Thanks for giving me a chance."

Effie snorted. "What does that mean?"

"You knew Abrem was going to inherit the farm, and you decided to take a chance on a second son, anyway. I know it's been a long year, teaching me the trade. I'm getting a little better though, aren't I?"

"A little," Effie teased. "You might catch a rabbit of your own some day."

Olfric laughed. "Or a pheasant."

"Don't get too far ahead of yourself." She looked down at the snare. "I think we should take another look at the game trail, see if there are any new branchings."

The pair ambled beneath the verdant canopy of branches, and Jeth moved slowly after them, enthralled by the simple way they bumped one another with their shoulders, how their fingers brushed, how they glanced at each other when the other wasn't looking.

Jeth drank in their appearance. *They aren't in rags. Those are nice leathers, actually. And the cottage was in good repair.*

His family, his *mother's* family, was doing well for themselves. That was why he was captivated, he realized. Here was proof that his mother wasn't gone, not entirely. Effie moved like she did. She had the same gray eyes.

"Effie," Olfric said, tipping his head back to study the canopy of leaves overhead.

"Olfric."

"What do you think about us starting a family soon?"

Effie stopped in her tracks, face blank with surprise. Jeth ducked behind a tree, peering around the trunk. His antlers blended in with the branches just enough that they wouldn't notice him if they turned, he hoped.

Olfric held his hands up, shrugging. "I'm not saying I'm in any rush. I'm just starting to think about it. And I was wondering if you are, too."

Effie put her hand in his, lacing their fingers together. "I am. I just...have some concerns."

"Tell me about them?" Olfric drew her over to a fallen log. He sat facing her, their knees touching. "I'm listening, Effie."

"Well, let's start with you."

Olfric looked stricken.

Effie raised her hands quickly. "No, not like that! I meant that with you still learning the trade, we might have a lean season. I'll get too big around to do much, near the end. At least, I won't be able to fit between the trees." She laughed.

"Which means I'd be in charge of the run on my own," Olfric said with a heavy sigh.

"Exactly. And it would be nice to time it out so the child arrives in the spring, when we aren't the primary source of meat for the village."

Olfric grimaced. "Yeah, the hunting. I was awful at that last year."

Effie patted his arm, laughing softly. "You've been practicing. But I'll want to wait a bit, to make sure of that. And there are a few other things."

"Besides me?" Olfric teased.

"Besides you," she taunted. "What about the future? We're living pretty tight at the moment, since we need to pay the thatcher for a new roof, and there's two pots we need mended, and all that will cost coin. But once the baby arrives, they'll cost coin, too. I haven't got any clothes for them. We'll have to pay or trade for those."

Olfric's brows rose steadily toward his hair. "Right. Roof, pots, clothes, then baby."

"Well, not quite."

"Not quite?" Olfric asked, voice rising in pitch. "What else is there?"

"After the babe arrives, I won't be on the trails for a while. They have to feed, and so do I, so we'll need some extra food. And that–"

"–will require trading or coin," he finished with a sigh.

"Exactly. We'll need good hunting luck all winter, and then you'll need to do very well this spring, which means going further, and looking harder. And then as soon as we're both ready to go on the trail, someone from the village will need to watch—"

"No, no, we can bring them with us!" Olfric said quickly. "What's more Penistone than learning to hunt and trap before you can toddle, hm? I'll carry them like I do the rabbits."

"Slung over your shoulder?" Effie asked with a laugh.

"No, on my back." Olfric was grinning. "Then they'll be with us if they get hungry."

"They might cry and warn the animals off," Effie warned.

"We'll adjust."

Effie dropped her gaze to their laced fingers, smiling softly. "I can't say I'm not still nervous, but...I'd like to try."

Jeth inhaled slowly, eyes widening. The next Penistone. They were discussing the next in his family's long line.

But they're worried, the voice in his head murmured. *They could starve after the babe arrives.*

He frowned. *I won't let that happen.*

Oh? And how are you going to stop nature itself from taking its course?

Jeth cleared his throat.

Both Effie and Olfric turned toward the sound. Olfric was on his feet at once, drawing a dagger from his belt. "Who's there?"

"A friend," he said slowly. "I didn't mean to frighten you."

Effie stood, her eyes sweeping the bushes. "What do you want?"

"To help you, if you'll let me. With your needs. Your family. Your luck."

If I have anything to say about it, they won't starve. The Penistone line will carry on long after even I am gone.

"Our family? Our *luck*?" Effie repeated. She scoffed. "No one can promise that. Who do you think you are, a faerie?"

Olfric's eyes narrowed. "Show yourself."

"I don't want to frighten you again. If I show myself, will you let me explain?"

"Just show yourself," Olfric said through clenched teeth, grip tightening on the hilt of his dagger.

"Remember, I just want to explain," Jeth said carefully.

Then he took a deep breath,

and stood.

Jeth's antlers rose over the shrubbery first. His golden hair and golden eyes followed. He stepped into the open, dressed in a simple traveling jacket—for him. Faerie garb was designed to last an age, but also decorative. Always. The green jacket had gold embroidery along the back and sides, down the front closures, and on the cuffs of his sleeves. He looked like what he was.

That is to say, he did not look human.

He held his hands up as he stepped into the light. "I don't want to frighten you. I mean you no harm."

Effie's eyes were wide, a hand clutched to her chest. "It's...it's..."

Olfric staggered back, his arm dropping. After all, what use was a knife against a creature of magic? "It's a faerie," he breathed.

"Please, stay calm. Let me explain."

"No! Effie, don't listen to him," Olfric snapped, stepping between Jeth and his wife. "Everyone knows faeries only spout honeyed words to trick you into bad bargains!"

"Not all faeries," Jeth pointed out. "Aren't there other stories?"

"Shut up!"

"Olfric," Effie gasped.

"Let's go. Run, Effie, Run!" Olfric grabbed her hand. The rabbits swung as he turned, nearly falling off his shoulder.

He and Effie tore off into the trees.

"Wait!" Jeth cried.

For a stunned moment, he just watched them run, flashes of brown and white clothing between the tree trunks growing smaller and smaller.

I just wanted to help my family.

Clearly, they don't want you, that nasty, bitter voice said.

You're wrong. They just don't know.

Faeries can't live with humans. You can't be their family. Not anymore.

Stop it.

You're alone, in the woods, between two worlds—and you always will be. Just you and Shae, forever. No one else, ever again.

Stop it!

Hands clenched at his sides, Jeth started off through the trees after them. Once he explained, once they understood, surely...

It was his family.

He had to try.

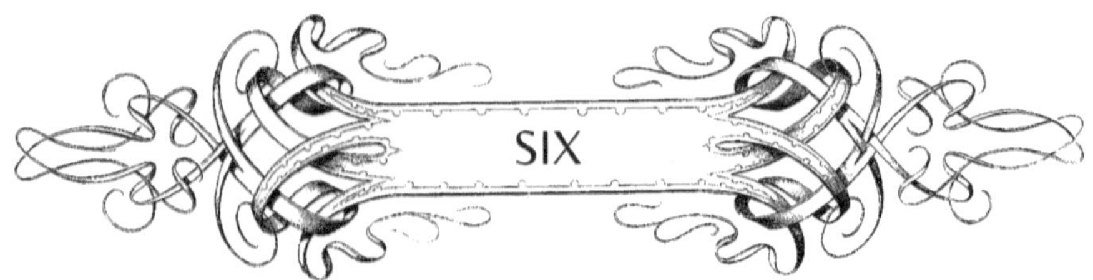

SIX

Jeth moved slower through the woods than Effie and Olfric Penistone. His plan to speak to the head of the village and any witch he could find was forgotten entirely as he moved after them. He reached the edge of River Tor just as the noonday sun reached its peak. He stood in the safe embrace of the shadows beneath the trees as he pulled on his glamours, feeling them settle on his skin like an itchy wool sweater. This time, he made sure to disguise his clothes and put a spell of inattention on his face. No one would notice him, not unless he wanted them to.

Only then did he step out of the trees.

The streets were busy, but not crowded—at least, not until one reached the market square. A handful of men were digging away, laying the first of the cobblestones at the foot of the inn's door. A group of children were laughing at a puppet show. Several women were at a booth with embroidery thread, chattering with one another. The inn's common room was busy, too. It did a bustling trade in lunch options, it seemed, with a whole throng of people at the tables and benches outside the door.

Jeth scanned the crowd. It would be simple. He'd find them and pull them aside. He'd explain everything. He would tell them all about his mother and his own history, and then they'd at least listen to him explain his bargain. Right?

One step at a time.

There!

Effie held Olfric by the sleeve, dragging him into the shadow of a market stall. Their heads were close together. Both of them were frowning, both talking in low voices, both moving their hands in sharp, jerky movements as they argued. Olfric turned away again. Effie held his arm fast.

Jeth started through the crowd toward the pair of them. He nodded to those he passed when they noticed him for all of a second before his spells took hold, their gazes flitting away as quickly as they fixed on him.

"Olfric," Effie said in a loud whisper, just missing his sleeve as he started away from her again. "Olfric!"

Olfric didn't hear her, or if he did, it didn't stop him. He marched to the tables in front of the inn and climbed on top of one. Two men cursed and pulled their food away from the hunter's booted feet. The brace of dead rabbits still hung from his shoulder, and they swung back and forth as Olfric steeled himself.

What is he...no. Oh no.

"Everyone, listen to me! Listen. Effie and I just saw something awful in the woods," he shouted, waving his arms.

Effie stood in the lee of the market stall, her shoulders hunched and her frown directed at the ground. Around her and Olfric, the conversation faded. Others turned at the sudden hush, and it grew and spread like snowfall across the market square.

Olfric held his hands up. "Listen to me, please. You need to know. Effie and I were in the woods, and we saw...we saw..." He trailed off, struggling to find the words to describe Jeth.

Jeth flushed slowly. *I'm not that strange. Am I?*

"A bear?" one man called.

"Someone get him a drink."

A few people moved toward the door of the inn.

"Was it a boar, lad?"

"No, none of that," Olfric said, waving his arms for silence. "We saw a faerie, an actual faerie. He looked like a man but spun of gold. It was in his skin and his hair. His eyes were made of it. He had antlers like a great stag, and he was dressed in leaves."

Jeth looked down at his green jacket, frowning. It was made of perfectly normal cloth! The gold, however, he couldn't deny. The faintest glimmer of it in his skin, the change in his hair and eyes. That was the work of the crystal ball his mother had given him long ago. When it shattered, he absorbed it—and its magic.

For a moment, the market was quiet, utterly quiet. Jeth felt a prickle of unease run up his spine.

And then someone laughed.

Soon the entire square was laughing, and someone pressed a mug into Olfric's hand.

"Good one, lad."

"Had us going there for a minute."

"A faerie! Ha!"

"But I'm telling the truth," Olfric shouted, frowning. "He tried to trick us into one of their deals. He said he wanted to help us."

"Help you what?" A woman shouted. The group around her tittered.

"Help us...well, we didn't listen, now, did we? We ran away. Effie will tell you. We saw it."

Effie looked pained, a few fingers pressed to her temple. She sighed and stepped forward. "We did see a faerie. A forest faerie."

Jeth grimaced as more laughter raced through the crowd.

"Come off it, now," one woman called.

"He tried to spell us so we wouldn't run away," Olfric cried.

Saying 'don't be afraid' is a spell now? Jeth scowled.

"Olfric," Effie whispered, the word hard and irritated. She tugged at the hem of his jacket. "Get off the damn table."

"You know, I saw a faerie just a few days ago, myself," an old man said solemnly.

The crowd hushed.

"A faerie princess, and she wanted to marry me and make me king under the hill," the old man finished. He howled with laughter that was echoed by everyone around him. He was not a handsome old man, by any stretch.

"Hort, if you ever married, the sun would rise in the west," a portly woman bawled over the noise, which only made the laughter double.

"Only because you keep turning me down, Krissi, and a damn shame, that." Hort smacked his lips in her direction.

She waved him off, though she was smiling.

Olfric's hands balled into fists, frowning down at everyone around him. "But we aren't joking. We all know there are strange things in the woods. We've all heard the tales."

"That's all they are," another man called. "Tales! Told 'round the fire to keep the little ones from straying off."

The children by the puppet show were watching the entire exchange with wide eyes. The puppets hung limp as even the puppeteer listened in on all the excitement.

"If you saw a faerie and came back here to tell about it, they'd have to be right close to River Tor, eh?"

If only you knew, Jeth thought, a brow raising.

"They were. Less than a mile off," Olfric waved his arm toward the woods.

"There you have it, then. Impossible." Krissi smacked her hands together.

"But I swear," Olfric started.

The people gathered muttered. A few boo'd. Effie tugged at his jacket again, and this time, Olfric climbed down.

"A fine story, lad. Next time, don't take the jest so far," Hort said as he passed, clapping Olfric on the back.

Olfric scowled. "They don't believe us," he muttered.

"Would you? If it were anyone else saying this, would you believe it? Come on, I told you this was a bad idea." She looped her arm through his. Together, they walked toward the little trail that led to their cottage.

Scattered laughter followed them.

Jeth slipped onto a seat at the end of a bench, watching the crowd with a frown. *Effie and Olfric think I'm a monster or something. The way they talked about spells and my bargains, I am the monster.*

Aren't you? the voice whispered in his ear. *Aren't you more faerie than man? Aren't you losing who you are? Do you even remember what it is to be human?*

Krissi set a clay mug of beer down in front of Jeth with a *clunk* and a rattle of wooden dishes down the way. She didn't even look at him again as she hurried to Hort's table.

"Refill?"

"After that tale? I'll need three."

A few men around Hort laughed.

"Can you imagine? Faeries," Krissi scoffed. "Going to have the children a mess for weeks with a tale like that."

"Or sneaking off to the woods to try to find one. Fat lot of good it will do them," another man chimed in.

"What would you know, Edmund?" Krissi arched a brow. "You haven't got any kids."

"Dani does. Don't you, man? And grandchildren, to boot!"

Dani sighed mournfully. "I'm going to have to watch them close for a few weeks, aye."

"Those Penistones," Hort said, the words dripping with disdain. "Always the odd ones. They might be one of the oldest families here, but that just makes them all the stranger. They say one of them married a faerie, once."

Jeth's brows rose. *Not quite, but it seems more of my mother's story survived than I thought.*

"You stop spreading tales, too, Hort. You'll put me off my drink," Krissi whined, plopping onto the bench across from the men.

"It's folks like them that give this place a bad name," Edmund said, mulling over the contents of his mug.

"What are you talking about, a bad name?" Dani asked.

"Well, we look at River Tor, and we see a lovely place. Good for families, friendly community. But you put a rotten apple in a barrel..."

"And the whole thing goes rotten," Dani finished with a frown.

"Exactly. And the Penistones may have been around a while, but they've always been half out of their minds."

"Only half?" Hort asked.

Everyone laughed.

Jeth felt his frown harden, and his hands clenched around the mug before him. He watched the foam on the top fizzle and fade. Every popping bubble felt like a chip at his patience—which was already wearing thin.

"Ought to find something to do with those sorts of people." Dani banged his mug on the table.

"Oi, you're gonna break it," Krissi scolded, yanking it out of his hands.

"Fill it up for me, will you, Krissi?"

Krissi stood and sauntered back inside.

"You're not wrong, though, Dani," Edmund said, looking up from the depths of his mostly empty mug. "Folk like that don't improve over time, they just get stranger. And then they get dangerous."

Dangerous! Jeth scowled. He might not know the Penistones very well, but he doubted they were dangerous—especially not for telling the truth.

It's your fault they don't believe, the voice murmured. *And your fault again for showing yourself to your family. You set them up.*

Jeth fought down the pang of guilt. *I did not.*

The voice said nothing, but he felt it, smug and self-satisfied, in a corner of his mind.

"I swear, the day isn't far off when the best of us are going to have to run the worst of them right out of town," Hort said, waving his arm expansively. "Keep everything nice and safe. Orderly. All that."

"Run them out?" Dani's brows rose. "The Penistones? But there's always been a Penistone at River Tor. My grandfather told me the town was founded by them once."

"Well, they don't run it any longer, do they? It's our town, now, and we have a duty to it."

Edmund nodded along to Hort's speech, clapping him on the back. "Now there's a notion, Hort. Chase them right out of town. And if they won't go..."

Hort grinned. "Oh, we know what to do with rubbish. Burn it."

The last bubble foam on Jeth's beer popped with a little spark, even as Jeth's grasp tightened until his fingertips went white. *They'll what? To my family?*

He stood, instinctively reaching out for the nearest leyline. He wasn't even certain what he planned to do. Blast Hort and his henchmen to pieces and leave them scattered across the market grounds? Curse them, wrapping them in such dark magic they and their families would never escape? Maybe he would just curse the entire village, curse everyone here in the market who heard Olfric's story and didn't believe him.

If being told you don't exist didn't convince them, this will, the voice whispered, elated. At last, it had what it wanted.

Jeth was on the knife's edge. One little push was all it would take to break.

"Best do it before they start to breed," Dani said airily, watching the door for his drink. "Folks get mad when you hurt babies."

Jeth and the bitter voice in his head were in agreement for once, clicking together with an almost palpable snap. Effie and Olfric were discussing starting a family within the year, and here were people who would hurt them the moment they found out about the impending baby.

No one, no one, *will hurt that family.*

Jeth touched the leyline, letting it flood him with power.

He turned toward the three men, drawing himself up, his eyes glowing with the magic that crackled through his veins.

He lifted his hand.

SEVEN

A small, slim body inserted itself between Jeth and the men, grabbing his hand and yanking it down. Jeth growled, the magic dancing around their joined hands for a moment—until he realized who it was.

Jeth's head snapped to the side, gold eyes falling on an all too familiar face. "Shae?"

Shae had their head ducked down, their hat firmly over their ears. Despite the tingle of magic running over their arm, they kept hold of Jeth's hand, their gaze never wavering. Bright green eyes bored into him.

Jeth tensed, a wave of guilt pushing the magic right back out of him and into the leyline where it belonged. A few people were looking at them. At Shae, rather, as Jeth's glamour of inattention was still intact.

"Come on. Please." Shae jerked their head toward the edge of the woods.

"You don't understand," Jeth started, heat rising in the words.

"You're right, I don't," Shae whispered, glaring at Jeth. If a gaze could melt stone, Shae's would have.

Jeth's protests died on his lips. He cast one last glance at the trio of men, now accompanied by Krissi and a pitcher of beer. Shae drew him away, towing him along by the hand.

His thoughts raced, the voice inside him raging like a thunderstorm at being thwarted. He warred with it, hardly noticing when the shadow of the forest fell over him. The chatter of the village faded. The only sounds were birdsong, the chatter of chipmunks, and their passage.

They needed to be stopped.

They needed to believe.

We could have given them both, the voice whispered, over and over.

Jeth's brow furrowed. *But we were about to...*

Yes, the voice exalted. *We were.*

I don't want to be like that.

It laughed in the corner of his mind. *And what did you want to be? Nothing? Extinct? Forgotten?*

"What were you doing?" Shae asked, breaking into Jeth's thoughts.

"I..."

"It's half rhetorical. I'm not as powerful as you are, but even I can sense a curse."

A curse was a powerful bit of magic, and complex. There had to be a way to break it. A smart curse was placed with some impossible loophole that would take years or generations to break. To weave one required hundreds of threads of magic, artfully woven together.

Jeth planned to curse the entire village.

Jeth was powerful enough to do so. Few enough were. Three. Four, perhaps.

The curse Jeth planned to weave was complicated enough that it would have taken generations to pick apart.

It might have wiped out the entire village before it was broken.

What was I doing?

His stomach twisted itself into a knot and the taste of bile coated the back of his throat. There were children at the market. He hadn't planned to spare them.

They're just humans, the voice in his mind said idly.

Jeth's disgust doubled. How could he have listened to that dark corner of his soul, the spreading black stain that didn't care about the people Jeth was trying to save?

People who don't even appreciate it.

Stop, stop it! Jeth forced the voice as far out of his mind as he could.

Shae cleared their throat. "Jeth, what happened?"

"I found my family," Jeth said heavily. "I tried to speak to them, but they ran away. When I followed..."

"What?" Shae asked when Jeth didn't continue.

"They told the whole market that they saw a faerie."

"So the village knows? I'd have thought they'd react more."

"They heard, but they didn't believe. They laughed at them, Shae."

"And you thought a curse would help?"

Heat crept up the back of Jeth's neck. "I didn't *start* with a curse. I overheard them talking about driving my family away. If they wouldn't go...Shae, they threatened to kill them."

"What?" Shae's steps slowed, their brows raised.

As the two threaded their way beneath the trees, Jeth relayed the entire story from start to finish. It was late afternoon by the time they reached the hill that housed their camp. They stepped out of the trees to find everything painted gold.

Shae let out a sigh. "It's complicated, isn't it? Even standing here, looking at that comfortable little camp, it's complicated. The village is complicated. Having a family hundreds of years removed from you is complicated. I can see why you snapped, but...Jeth."

Jeth picked his way up the hill, swinging Shae's hand lightly. "I know."

"Everything we've done, everywhere we've gone, it was all to protect people. All of them. We never asked if they were good or bad before. We never asked if someone deserved help. And here you are, ready to throw it away in a tantrum? We don't do that, Jeth. We're not like *them*. We haven't spent all this time changing the world, so *you* could be the one to ruin lives."

Shae sat on a stump, stirring the embers of the fire to life and adding a few logs.

"I know," Jeth said heavily, sitting across from them. "But once they threatened their lives, once I knew they were in real danger..."

"They haven't been attacked yet," Shae pointed out.

"If you'd heard those men... They were serious, Shae."

The changeling looked at Jeth as flames licked over the sides of the logs. "But you chose a curse instead of a protective spell."

A flush crept over Jeth's cheeks. "That's...that's true."

For a time, both of them were quiet. The wood popped and crackled as the fire grew strong. Jeth peeled his glamours away layer by layer. The first stars appeared in the pink and purple sky overhead.

Somewhere, someone was singing. Someone else would be holding the hand of the love of their life. Children were laughing or crying. Parents were lecturing. A farmer was seeing to their herd, and a shepherd to their flock. All over Hallanor, people were living their lives.

Jeth was part of why.

They are what I wanted to protect. Their way of life, the way my mother taught me.

And how long has it been since you've lived that life? The voice sneered. *What sort of person are you, this far removed from it?*

He stared at his hands, flexing his fingers. It was true. Centuries passed while Jeth drifted from place to place, untethered, unmoored, like a ghost ship at sea. The feel of earth beneath his hands, the tasks of mixing herbs and brewing tinctures, the simple act of going to market—he hadn't done any of that in a long, long time.

Is that why my humanity is finally fading?

He ran his tongue over his lips.

"You're angry," Shae said suddenly.

Jeth jerked, gaze lifting to meet the changeling's. "What?"

"You're angry. You're furious, and trying so hard to bottle it up. What are you mad about, Jeth?"

"I'm not angry."

"You're not?"

That bitter corner of his mind laughed again, and suddenly Jeth wasn't sure.

Shae shifted around the fire until they could lean against Jeth. He wrapped his arm around the changeling's shoulders.

"I think you have some questions you need to ask yourself. And I think you should try to speak to your family again."

"Really?"

"They're there, and you said yourself that you didn't get to introduce yourself. One last try before we're...on our way again." Shae sighed softly. "Just...you need to sort this out. Before you hurt someone. Before you hurt them."

"Them," Jeth echoed.

"The humans. The village. Your family. Them."

Jeth nodded slowly.

Shae pulled away and went to the packs, pulling out supplies for their supper. They left Jeth to his thoughts.

What are you mad about? he asked himself.

The sun set. A darkness that matched Jeth's black mood swallowed the world.

EIGHT

The sweet sound of birdsong filled the morning air. Light slanted down into the clearing as the sun rose. Jeth stood with his face tipped back, letting the rays play across his skin, savoring the warmth. The seasons would turn soon, as they always did. The leaves would start to change and fall. But for now, the warmth of a late summer sun rose around him.

The day would be clear and beautiful, a sharp contrast to his still muddled thoughts. He was no closer to answers, no closer to knowing himself any better. Still, as the morning dew glittered like jewels at his feet, it was hard to feel anything bad.

His questions for himself could wait.

Movement behind the window of the cottage in front of him drew his attention. Just a flicker of it behind the shutters, but still. It meant the Penistones were awake. He stayed still, standing in the sun before their home, waiting.

Jeth could almost picture them arguing, as they had in the market square. Their heads close together, their voices low, their hands moving through the air. They both gestured when they spoke. Jeth liked that they matched that way.

With a creak of the hinges, the wooden door swung open. Olfric stepped through the door. He didn't close it behind him. His hands were empty.

"Good morning," Jeth said, hands tucked behind his back.

"What do you want?" Olfric asked.

"To introduce myself. Please. I want you to understand."

"Understand what?"

"Who I am to you."

Olfric snorted. "You're nothing to me."

Jeth smiled, though it was weak. "And you might decide that's still true after I tell you who I am. I hope not, though." He cleared his throat. "May I?"

"Fine. If it will make you leave." Olfric folded his arms over his chest, puffing himself up protectively.

"My name is Jeth Penistone."

"What?" Effie blurted from inside, her voice high and shrill. She appeared in the door, shoving her head into the open. "Liar!"

"No, I'm not. You see, a long time ago, right here in River Tor...a woman named Gleda Penistone caught the attention of a faerie."

"I know that story," Olfric said slowly. "Effie, you told me that story." He glanced back at her, brow furrowed.

Effie's expression went from stunned to angry, then eased to something faintly confused. "It was just a story, Olfric. Just some silly family legend."

"The woman ran off with the faerie to be his queen in their kingdom," Olfric said.

Jeth grimaced. "Not...quite true. She found herself with child and made a bargain with the faerie to protect the baby. Once she had the faerie distracted and unable to stop her, she ran."

"How do you know?" Effie asked, scowling. She pushed her way into the open air, standing beside Olfric and mirroring his posture. Both of them frowned at Jeth over their folded arms.

"Because the child she had was me."

Effie snorted.

"That would make you...really old," Olfric said slowly.

"A few hundred years," Jeth admitted with a slow nod.

"And a faerie. He could be lying, you know," Effie said, looking him up and down.

"Faeries can't lie."

Olfric glanced at his wife. "He's right. All the stories say so."

Effie sighed heavily. "Fine, you're not lying. But how did a human's son become a faerie?"

"Even a drop of faerie blood turns you into one, eventually. The more I cast magic, the more I changed."

"Is that why your hair is all...gold?" Olfric asked, gesturing at his own hair. "I mean, Penistones all have black hair and dark eyes. Always."

Jeth smiled. "Yes, magic did this." Not over time, but it would be difficult at best to explain how he'd blown up a crystal ball. "When I was young, I had hair black as ink, I promise you that."

Effie glared at him for a moment, then let out an explosive sigh. "You'd better come in for breakfast, then. I guess we have a lot to talk about."

Olfric's brows shot up, and he followed his wife back inside. "Wait, you can't be serious! Faeries curse people for being poor hosts."

"Family doesn't curse family, or I'll skin him," Effie muttered.

Jeth stepped up to the door, peering inside. It was a modest little space. A sleeping loft, a bed in one corner, a table, a large hearth and a few chairs. The air smelled of nothing more than soap and leather. He stepped inside.

Effie was setting breakfast on the table. A handful of hard-boiled eggs, bread and butter, tea and cream. Olfric opened the shutters, letting daylight pour into the room.

Jeth took a seat, careful of his antlers in the small space.

"This is about the strangest thing I've ever done," Olfric muttered as he sat across from Jeth, his eyes drifting over him from head to toe.

"It's not normal for me, either. This is the first time I've reached out to family."

"For a bargain, right?" Effie asked, setting a wooden plate and mug in front of Jeth, and another set in front of her husband. She sat down with her own dishes and served herself.

"Yes, originally. But now I want to do something different than that."

"Different how?" Olfric asked sharply.

Jeth slowly, cautiously explained what he'd heard in the village after the pair left, even including the part about the baby. Effie's eyes were wide and full of a deep ache. Olfric was furious, his hand clenched so tight around a butter knife that his knuckles were white.

"They want to chase us out? But even *my* family has been here for an age," Olfric exploded at last.

"There's always been a Penistone in River Tor," Effie said slowly. "It's our home."

"And I want that to remain true for as long as possible." Jeth set down his half-empty mug of tea. "My mother loved it here. I know it was one of the hardest things she ever did to leave. I want to protect that. I want...I want to protect you."

"You're proposing a protection instead of a bargain?"

"Well, yes, and no," Jeth said slowly as the seed of an idea began to grow. "I want parchment, a quill, and ink. In exchange, I'll put a protection spell over this house, this corner of the forest, and the Penistone family. I'll protect your home so you can start your family knowing that you're safe. I'll protect your entire line. Our...*Our* entire line."

Effie passed a hand over her eyes, shaking her head. "This is insane. How can we trust you?"

"Ah. That's another story."

As briefly as he could, Jeth told them the events of the last few hundred years. When he finished, breakfast was gone, the plates cleared and the mugs empty. Lunch had been set and eaten, too.

He spread his hands on the table. "As you can see, I'm not quite a faerie. I'm not human anymore, either, but I've always remembered how I started. In a cottage sort of like this one, only with a bigger garden." His gaze drifted over the familiar plaster and wood walls.

"All that time, and you never had a home?" Effie asked softly.

"Home is where you make it, isn't it?"

Olfric snorted. "Sure, but you have to *make* it."

Jeth shrugged, clasping his hands. "Let's get back to the bargain."

"It seems really uneven," Olfric said slowly.

"It's as much of a gift as I can give within the boundaries of the spell. There has to be some kind of trade. I could ask for a few rabbits instead, if you'd like?"

"No, we have parchment and ink." Effie stood to dig through a drawer in a cabinet. "And you'll be able to keep us here, and safe?"

"Yes. I can't change what the villagers feel about you. But I can make it so that whenever they come out here with the intent to cause harm, they'll forget. Add a good luck charm to the area, and one to our family line, and..." He shrugged.

"If you really are my great uncle, if we really can trust you, then I want to do it," Effie said, smacking a small stack of parchment down on the table. The dishes rattled.

Olfric stood, gathering them and taking them to the sink. He hauled on the pump and water sprayed out. "I can't say it sounds like a bad deal. I'm worried about the way Hort and his lot were talking, to say the least. They're well known for being bitter old men, but it doesn't make my mind rest any easier. They'll do whatever they like and get away with it."

Effie wrinkled her nose. "They've gotten away with quite a lot of scandal, actually."

Jeth wasn't surprised to hear that the righteous, self-important villagers of River Tor were actually some of the worst. He'd found it true everywhere he went. On all his travels, there was always someone who thought they were right, they deserved more than they had, and who fought to take it no matter the harm to others.

"Then we have a bargain?" Jeth held out his hand.

Effie clasped it, giving a firm shake.

"Welcome to the family, Uncle Jeth. Now let's do something about saving it, hm?"

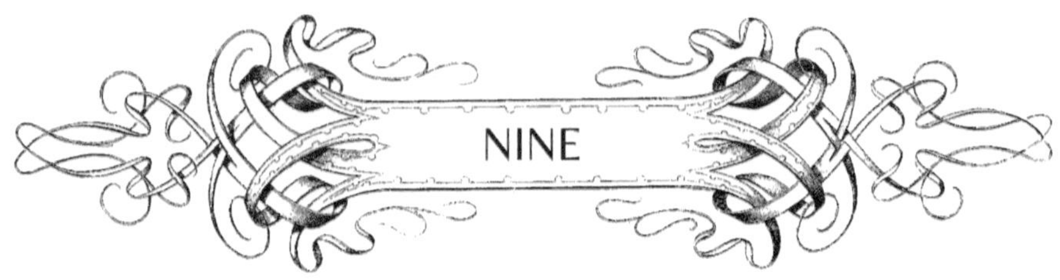

NINE

By the time all the spells he wanted to weave were cast, the sun had set and night was setting in. Crickets sang in hidden corners. Glowbugs flew through the air, winking in and out of sight as they did. Jeth held a small satchel of parchment, quill, and ink slung over his shoulder.

He shook Olfric's hand, then Effie's. "Thank you for letting me help you."

"All that paper, it's so you'll write, yes?" Effie asked lightly.

"What?" Jeth's eyes widened. *That wasn't what I had in mind.*

"Are you really my uncle?"

"With a few dozen greats in front of it, yes," Jeth said slowly.

"Then you'll stay in touch. It's what's family does."

"You want me to write? I may not even be here in a few days."

"An excuse," Effie insisted, poking him in the shoulder.

"It is not."

"Then you'll write, even if you're on the road?"

Jeth's mouth hung open. He shot Olfric a bewildered look.

The man laughed and held his hands up. "Look, I'm just glad it's your turn to be badgered into something entirely reasonable. It's better to just agree when she gets like this. She's right, and we all know it."

Effie looked smug.

Jeth exhaled, smiling. "Well, what can I do, then? I'll write."

"Good." Effie stepped forward, wrapping Jeth in a hug. "Travel safe, Uncle Jeth."

Jeth's breath caught. Slowly, he returned her embrace, then stepped back.

This is what I was missing. This is what I wanted.

Something real. More than just him and Shae alone on the road day in and day out. Something that bound them to the world they moved through.

Family did that.

Jeth never considered Aneirin a part of his family. The faerie was his father, but there was no tie there, no bond. As new as his relationship with Effie and Olfric was, it felt right.

"I'll be going, then." Jeth turned toward the woods.

As he stepped beneath the boughs of the great spreading oak, he stopped. He put his hand on the wood, feeling the pulse of magic in it, now. It absorbed power from Eoghan's body, a body Jeth hadn't told his family about. Around the base of the tree, late blooming wildflowers grew rampant—when they hadn't before. The tree, and Eoghan, served as an anchor for many of the spells, and it would for generations to come.

"Uncle Jeth," Effie called as he dropped his hand.

He turned.

"Introduce us to Shae before you two go off again, alright? Your family is our family." She smiled.

Jeth smiled back, then vanished into the trees. Olfric and Effie waved until they vanished from view.

How strange. What Shae wanted all along was here. What I wanted all along was here.

And now you have to leave it, the bitter voice murmured. *After all, you and you alone have to save the world.*

Jeth scowled as he picked his way through the underbrush. That damnable voice and its poisonous words. He hadn't heard it all day, and now –

He stopped walking.

I didn't hear it all day. I didn't hear it when I was... What, with his family? Happy, for however brief a time? If that was all it took to silence it, Jeth knew what came next.

It was time to listen to that voice in his mind, to confront it once and for all. Sometimes, one had to step into the shadows to really see them. As he ducked beneath a branch, Jeth opened his mind. All the thoughts, fleeting, furious, or miserable as they were, came flooding out.

What are you really mad at, Jeth? Shae's voice asked.

His mind flitted through a thousand different images.

Aneirin, smugly studying himself in a mirror and choosing his clothes. He knew Jeth didn't have what it took to end him. He knew he was safe.

Stonehill, the village that had once been his home, and the hulking man, arms folded, who told them to leave.

Hort, Edmund, and Dani, sneering at anyone different over the rims of their mugs.

The countless little interactions he'd had throughout the years where people slung sharp words, where they made certain he felt unwelcome. Humans, one and all.

Then his mind turned to the faeries. They had been monsters, but honest about it. They were still as destructive to humanity as wildfires were to the forest. Jeth didn't regret separating the races, even if it seemed it would take faerie-kind far longer to adjust to the new way of things.

Jeth was mad at them all.

He was angry at Eoghan above all others. He saw the flashing knife and felt another surge of guilt. In defending himself, he'd taken a life. Eoghan made sure it was Jeth's fault the knife was pulled free. He made sure it was Jeth's burden to bear. It was one step too much, too far. This journey –

This journey was taking bites out of him with every new turn, and soon there would be nothing left. Jeth felt drawn taut as a lute string, and just as likely to snap at any moment. Death, destruction, cruelty, the things he couldn't fix – all of them littered his past.

One step at a time, his mother's voice whispered.

Shae's followed on her heels. *What are you really angry at, Jeth?*

"I'm angry at myself," he murmured.

Why?

Jeth stopped walking, closing his eyes and listening to the night hum of insects.

Why? Shae repeated.

"Because I can't save the world. Because I'm not strong enough."

I could have told you that. Jeth recognized Aneirin's voice, though he hadn't heard it in his head for centuries.

Jeth scowled, eyes flying open. That voice wasn't welcome here.

Aneirin laughed in his ear. *And why not?*

"Because I'm mad at you, too," Jeth shouted, rounding on – nothing. He was still alone. "If it weren't for you, I wouldn't have to leave."

Why do you have to leave? His mother, Gleda, asked. Her voice was soft and curious, brimming with patience.

"Because we have to find the mirror. We have to make sure Aneirin can't get out of his prison and hurt anyone. We have to protect humanity."

Just us, and us alone? Shae asked.

Just the two of them had traveled the faerie courts. Just the two of them had found and broken four mirrors out of five. They traveled the continent dozens of times, side by side. Just them, and them alone.

But did it have to be that way?

They'd met others, fleeting as they'd always been. There was always a Calder running a merchant route, raised with stories of Jeth and Shae. There was always a lord or lady in Ulma Dale who knew the tale of the stolen names. The King or Queen of Hallanor knew of the faerie with a stag's head who fought for them in the shadows. As fleeting as their lives seemed to Jeth and Shae, who didn't age or change, they were still people that helped and hoped and searched.

So was he really alone?

Others can help us. Others have helped, Shae said.

Other people wanted to save their world as much as he did.

"But that doesn't mean they can do it. I can. I can do it."

Do what? Aneirin sneered. *What have you even accomplished in the last hundred years? Two hundred?*

A flush crept over Jeth's cheeks. The past few centuries had been uneventful. Jeth led the way from rumor to hearsay, chasing a mirror that was never there when he arrived. Shae followed after him. They both loved one another very dearly, very deeply, but Jeth was the one who insisted on all the travel.

Shae never complained.

"But that doesn't mean he likes it," Jeth murmured.

Why do you have *to leave?* Gleda repeated.

A surge of anger sparked through him like lightning.

"Because someone has to find the mirror," Jeth said loudly, voice cracking. He pressed the heels of his palms to his eyes.

Gleda hummed softly in agreement.

Do you want to? Shae asked.

"What?"

Do you want *to leave?*

The anger faded, bleeding away like water into the earth. His head bowed, his shoulders hunched, Jeth considered the question for the first time.

He pushed the answer away before he could finish thinking it.

"It doesn't matter what I want. Someone has to do all this. Someone has to go."

But why you? Gleda asked softly.

Jeth's breath caught.

Why does *it have to be me? No one ever told me I had to save the world. When did I start to think that everything, everywhere, was my responsibility?*

He lowered his hands. "Why does it have to be me?"

Jeth started walking, then running. He had to get to Shae, to speak to the changeling, to see if this was real or if he was losing his mind. He moved fast and sure as a stag through the trees and undergrowth, his heart hammering beneath his ribs. In time with his steps, with his pulse, two words echoed again and again.

Why me?

Why me?

Why me?

There was no answer. There was no answer because it didn't have to be him. He could stop, if he wanted. He could *stay,* if he wanted. If he didn't like his life as it was, he could choose a different one.

Couldn't he?

Jeth spent his entire life, a life that spanned *hundreds* of years, torn between two worlds and belonging to neither. In all the time he spent in faerie courts or wandering human settlements, he never found somewhere he felt like he belonged. He spent his time on the outskirts, as lost and haunted as a ghost.

Until here, until River Tor. This tiny settlement, so close to the forest and the Blackthorn Court, was the first place that felt like home. It was the first time he felt like his mother's son in a long, long time. It was the first time he wasn't painfully aware of his antlers. He *looked* like a faerie. And if one walks like a duck and talks like a duck...

No. No, whatever he was, it wasn't a faerie. It wasn't human. It was...*He* was...

Jeth. Just Jeth.

Aneirin once stole names, taking entire identities with them. A name was the glue that held a person together. When they were stolen, a person's identity became the thing they were over all others. The minds of their neighbors and family plucked a single string to define them. When a person was reduced to a single hobby, a single task, a single description, how did they reconcile everything else around it?

If Jeth had his name taken today, now, what would be left? What had he accomplished? When all was said and done, what was he? What words would the world decide to call him by?

Hero?

King?

Stranger?

Or would they say nothing, nothing at all?

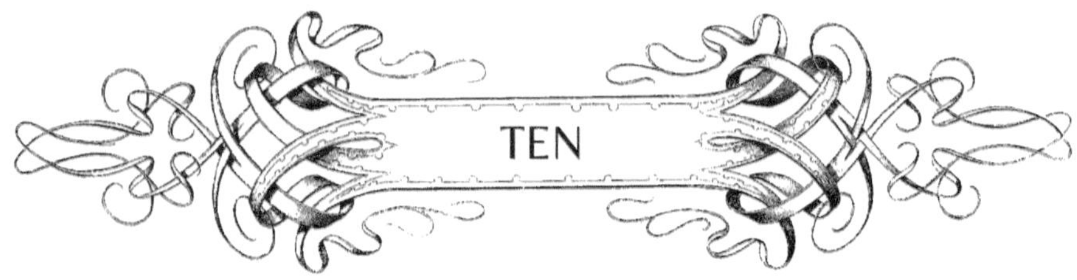

TEN

"Shae?"

Jeth burst out of the trees at the foot of the hill.

Shae stood by the fire, arms full of sticks. Their head was tipped back to look at the moon, hanging low and full in the sky. At Jeth's call, they turned, and a smile broke out on their face. "Jeth. You're back."

Jeth climbed the hill, bursting to tell Shae everything. He kept it all in check, barely, and slowed as he stopped beside the changeling.

Shae turned back to their study of the moon. Their presence, their calm, was a balm to his racing heart. Jeth turned to the sky as well.

"You were gone all day. Did it go alright?"

"Talking to Effie and Olfric? It went better than alright. They want to meet you."

"Me?" Shae asked with a start, sticks rattling in their arms. Their smile returned, twice as bright as before and warmer than the fire. "I'd love that. They really don't mind us being...you know. Not human?"

"At first, I think," Jeth said slowly.

Shae bent to set the sticks down in their sizeable wood pile beside the tent.

Jeth turned slowly, studying all the work Shae had done in his absence. The campsite was more elaborate than their usual sort. The tent, yes, but there was more than that. Shae had washed laundry, stringing lines of twine between long sticks they'd shoved in the ground. Cloth stirred in the breeze where it hung. A mending kit was out by one of the stumps, and a few socks and shirts were piled beside it. The log and stumps that they used as seating around the fire were rearranged, the earth beneath them dug out enough that they wouldn't teeter or rock underneath someone.

Shadowstep had a small pile of cut sweetgrass from the meadow waiting for her, though she was nowhere to be seen at the moment. She had a cleared area to lie in.

The hillside was showing the start of a path. Grass lay flattened, and some stones and low scrub bushes had been dug out to make it easier to climb.

Shae spent their time settling in while Jeth was away.

Roots.

A person needed roots, an anchor, a tether, a tie. Somewhere to return to or somewhere to go.

"Did you eat dinner? I've got a little stew going." Shae turned to the fire.

Even if Jeth had eaten, he would have said he hadn't. He smiled. "Stew sounds perfect."

Only after both of them were seated on the log with bowls of steaming stew in their hands did Jeth break the comfortable silence. His shoulder brushed Shae's.

"I've been thinking."

"Should I be worried?" Shae glanced at him sidelong, a hint of mock suspicion on their lips.

"About me? Always. But I've been thinking about what you asked."

Shae nodded. "When I asked what you're really mad at?"

"Yes."

"And?"

"I think I'm tired, Shae," Jeth said slowly. "I think we've traveled forever, and I never asked you twice if this is what you wanted to do, and we've spent a few hundred years failing to find a mirror. If it hasn't opened by now, will it ever?"

"Probably when it reaches a thousand years. Isn't that how all the stories go?" Shae asked, blowing on a bite of stew. "Or never. For all we know, it's already broken."

Jeth nodded. Every time he'd scried for it, he saw nothing but darkness. That meant it was either in the dark, or it no longer existed. Either way, if the mirror was out of the way...

"We don't actually have to keep going," Shae said, echoing Jeth's thoughts. "I mean, I will if you want to. I always will. But if you *don't* want to..."

I don't want to.

Jeth nodded. "We've done our time, haven't we? We spent enough time trying to help everyone."

Shae nodded. "It's good to let people help themselves once in a while, too. They seem to be doing alright for the most part, don't they? On their own?"

"I don't know. They seem like a mess. But it also seems like we can't fix that. We're not...one of them."

"Does that mean you want to go back to faerie?" Shae asked, the spoon hovering halfway to their mouth.

Jeth heard the unease in the simple question, despite how light Shae kept their words.

"No. We're not faeries either, not really. We're somewhere in between, and we always will be."

"Then where will we go?" Shae's brow furrowed.

"Nowhere." Jeth set his bowl down, spreading his hands. "Here. We can stay right here, between Blackthorn Court and River Tor."

Shae smiled, ducking their head to hide it. "Here? We can stay right here?"

Jeth nodded, grinning.

"Good. I like it here. And what will we do out here, on our own?"

Jeth's heart began to swell. Shae was just as tired as he was. No, tired didn't even explain it. What they felt was a bone deep weariness formed year after year. All that time was layered atop itself like bricks in a wall, threatening to crush them beneath its weight. This was a thousand thousand days, and nothing ahead of them but the promise of thousands more.

No, they were *done.* And that meant they could do anything.

"We can make salves and tinctures like my mother taught me. We can have a garden and grow our food. A little flock of sheep, maybe. Three, four? At the bottom of the hill, there. Chickens. A dairy cow. We can just live, spending our days doing nothing and everything we want. On seventh days, we can take things to the market and sell them or trade them. You'll wear your hat, and I'll wear a glamour. We can give bargains to people who wander into our little corner of the land and become a story all our own."

Jeth turned, grasping one of Shae's hands in his own. "We can settle, Shae, and live. We can write to my family, the Calders, and the King. You can mend and spin. You can draw. I'll grow all the herbs and sweep the floor with a broom made of straw. We could grow straw!"

Shae's eyes grew wider and wider with every word, but at that last enthusiastic idea, they burst into laughter. It was sweet as honeysuckle, filling Jeth's ears and heart at the same time. "If we're going to have sheep and a cow, we probably ought to have straw, yes."

"We'll build a cottage."

"A cottage?"

"Yes, with a kitchen and an enormous table, a bedroom and a loft. Shae, if we settle, we can have guests. We could have a–" Jeth stopped abruptly.

Shae's smile bloomed slowly. "A family?" they finished.

Heat raced across Jeth's cheeks. They'd never talked about children or a future. He paused, realizing he was right. They'd never talked about a future, about what they wanted when their journey was over.

We never thought it would *be over, did we?*

He frowned.

Shae's fingers pressed at the crease in his brow. "I have always wanted a home," they whispered. "What you're telling me? That sounds like a home to me."

Jeth's eyes stung, and he cupped Shae's cheeks, kissing them deeply. "Then can we do it, Shae? Can we be done?"

Shae snorted, their face still cradled in Jeth's hands. "Honestly, I was ready to be done a hundred years ago."

Jeth laughed, letting them go. His head spun. Pressing his fingers to his temple, Jeth shook his head. "Just like that?"

"Just like that."

It was so easy. All this time, and it was so easy.

"Get the lantern, please," Jeth said, opening the satchel that still hung on his hip. "I have some letters to write."

Shae stood, abandoning their half-eaten stew. "Letters?" they echoed.

"The Calders will know what supplies we need. I want to write them first. We need tools, after all, and I don't even know where you go to buy a sheep."

Shae laughed. "I can ask around at River Tor, maybe. I can go to the market and get a few things to get us started." The light grew stronger as Shae lit the lantern and held it aloft.

Jeth spread the paper on his lap and balanced the inkwell on the log beside him. He paused, looking up at Shae. "Are you ready?"

"To start a new life with you?"

Jeth nodded.

Shae leaned in, kissing Jeth gently on the cheek. "I'll think about it. Are you going to write that letter or not?"

Jeth grinned, dipping the quill into the ink. *Dear Percy Calder*, he wrote.

A deep sense of relief faded to a peace as comfortable as a quilt wrapped around his shoulders. The quill scritched and scratched across the parchment as he wrote his letter, with suggestions from Shae here and there. The fire crackled. The crickets hummed. In the distance, the faintest twinkle of light from River Tor broke through the trees.

Jeth savored every piece of it, even as he and the love of his life planned what came next. That was because, no matter *what* came next...

He was home.

ELEVEN

One end was always the start of a different story.

Rich earth, dark and brown, crumbled easily in Jeth's fingers. *It feels like silk, almost,* he thought, smiling. Good, healthy earth was its own treasure. It smelled like growing things and looked like the richest of chocolate.

The late spring sun warmed his shoulders as he dug between the sprouts of the garden, hunting for weeds. There weren't many, not with magic and inter-planting—but it was always good to check.

A basket beside him held the first harvest of his herbs. He spent the winter preparing the house for his new craft. Well, his old craft. He'd hammered nails into the rafters, built shelves on the wall for his jars and bottles, and built himself a fine, sturdy worktable.

A few small carrots, some beets, and a handful of arugula sat in the basket as well. He and Shae would have a nice stew tonight, with the first of their home-grown vegetables.

Home. He loved that word.

The rooster cackled from the chicken run, peering through the wood and rope fence Shae wove. It fixed its beady black eye on Jeth and cackled again.

"Alright, alright," Jeth said with a soft laugh. "You act like I've never fed you before."

He picked up his basket of spoils and started up the hill.

Fences of wood and thick rope surrounded the two terraces they'd built on their little hill. It was crowned with a small palace of a cottage. It was two floors tall, as space was limited, but it had a nice chimney and a tall peaked roof, big windows of bubbled glass, and a fresh coat of whitewash. It looked magical, like something Jeth knew once in a time long past.

I think they call it old-fashioned these days.

Still, he loved the curl of smoke out of the rough stone chimney, and the brightly colored wooden shutters over the lead-lattice windows. He loved the way the door, carved with flowers around the edge, looked when it was propped open with a spare brick.

Shae and Jeth put the finishing touches on the whole thing just before the snows had set in. They spent a winter sitting before their new hearth on tree stumps, eating with their camping supplies and sleeping on the floor in their bedrolls—but they knew they'd be cutting it close with the turn of the seasons.

Once the weather had warmed, they started making improvements again. Shae found they had an aptitude for building furniture, and even better, a passion for it. Their talents grew quickly, and with Jeth's help they soon had a dining set, a bench inside and a bench outside the front door, a few chairs further down the hill, and soon, a bed. Shae was inside, even now, tightening the ropes that would hold their mattress up.

Jeth would add sweet-smelling herbs to the wool they would shear from the sheep in a few weeks. They had three, milling contentedly about in their little paddock at the bottom of the hill. They had a little lean-to that they shared with the cow, and all four were quite content.

After that, Shae would stitch the wool between some cloth, and they'd have a proper mattress, warm and cozy.

He couldn't wait. *When was the last time I slept in a proper bed?* Years, at least. It would be better than sleeping on a cloud.

Jeth paused beside the chicken run near the house, tossing a handful of feed out for the rooster and the hens.

There was a letter from his family that he had to read. Shae brought it back the night before, after a trip to River Tor. Things were going well between Jeth, Effie, and Olfric. The Penistones loved Shae, too. And his family was growing! Effie was expecting. In fact, Jeth expected the letter to announce her successful delivery. The baby's gift was already prepared. Jeth fashioned a rattle out of seeds and a large acorn, with the help of a bit of magic.

Jeth paused as he headed for the door, glancing down the hill. "Hey, Shadowstep. See you tonight?" He called.

The mare stepped out of her modest barn—on the opposite side of the hill of the livestock, of course—and shook out her mane. She danced in place, then trotted off amongst the trees. She came and went as she pleased these days, but had decided to stick around. She seemed just as relieved to have somewhere to come back to.

Jeth felt at peace more and more with every sunrise. Finally, all the muscles within him were uncoiling, relaxing. All his fears and doubts were smaller, manageable and mundane. Life was simpler. Safer.

This is how I wanted it.

He ducked inside, mindful of his antlers on the doorjamb. It already bore a few scratches from his tines. The kitchen inside was modest, but it had a pump sink he'd built himself. Except for the well, that is. That, Jeth dug out with magic. There was a second pump outside for when they needed it.

He dumped the vegetables into a large clay bowl. The hinge of the pump squeaked as he filled it with a few swings of his arm. He cleaned everything thoroughly and set them aside, laid out and waiting for their journey to the stew pot.

Then he started on the herbs. He brought each bundle to his nose, inhaling deeply before he rinsed them clean, wrapped a bit of twine around them, and then set them aside. The sharp scents filled his nose, each one unique. Thyme, rosemary, sage, mint. A half dozen others, too. Once they were clean, he strung them from the nails he'd put in the rafters. He smiled as he stepped back to admire them.

It looks just like my mother's. The neat little bundles would soon festoon the rafters, waiting to be put in jars and stored until they were needed. Salves, tinctures, poultices. He remembered how to mix them all. Just like his mother taught him.

Shae's arms slipped around Jeth's waist from behind as the changeling snuggled up to his back. "How is everything outside?"

"Decent. I think we'll have a good harvest of squash by fall. They're growing well."

"I'll have to ask for some recipes in town," Shae said, stepping back. They went to their chair beside the fire and the pile of fine clothes there. "I'm thinking I might cut these up to make a quilt. The cloth is fine, but we won't have much cause to wear it all."

"A quilt?" Jeth grinned.

"It would be nice, don't you think?"

"I do." Jeth stepped around Shae. "This isn't all of them, is it?"

"No, I saved a few. Just in case."

Just in case they had to leave again and impress someone, no doubt. He hoped 'just in case' would never come. No, he'd rather every single piece be cut up by the love of his life and stitched together into a fine quilt. It would warm them and remind them of all their adventures, a soft nod to a different time. Made of faerie fabrics, it would stay as beautiful as the day it was made for all the hours, days, weeks, months, and years of their lives together.

And they would spend it with one rooster, a few hens, three sheep, and a dairy cow. They'd spend it in the cottage on the hill with the stone chimney and little wood shutters. They'd spend it gardening and mixing salves, sewing, mending, tending, planting, harvesting, making. They'd eat here, and sleep here, and they'd do it next month, and next year.

The knowledge that this was his life, simple and beautiful, filled Jeth's heart.

"Can you take a few of these carrots and beets down to the root cellar?" Shae asked. Their cellar had been dug into the hillside's steep drop, and required walking down and around the hill—but it was naturally cool and dry, and therefore ideal for storing these things for next winter.

Jeth took a handful of each, kissing Shae on the side of the head. "I'll be right back."

"You better be. I need help moving the bed frame."

Jeth laughed.

As he stepped outside, the sun was lowering toward the trees. The canopy was a rich spread of greens both light and dark. The warmth played over his skin, sinking in until he was warmed all the way through. His cheeks ached from smiling as he tipped his head back and closed his eyes, savoring every moment.

There were no other voices in his head anymore. Not his mother's, not his own. No one whispered about what he should do or where he should go. No one tried to tell him what he wanted.

Because this is what I want. In a way, it always was.

If his mother never died, he would have grown up to live this way in the village that would one day become Stonehill. He would have fallen in love and tended a garden. It took him a long, hard path to get back to where he wanted to be.

And now here he was.

And I don't need anything more than this.

He embraced that thought as he picked his way down the clear, half-cobbled path he was laying up the hillside. Here he was, living between two worlds. The Blackthorn Court and Heartwood Hill on one side, and River Tor on the other. Just like his home, he was something in between.

Just like his home, the only world he would ever truly belong in was his own.

He stopped again, gaze drifting over the trees to the distant, flat-topped peak of Heartwood Hill. Underneath the ground there was a throne of thorns, and he would never sit on it again. He would never be a faerie, much less a faerie king, again.

His gaze swept toward the distant curls of smoke from River Tor. He'd never be a human, either.

Neither thought made him sad or confused, as they once had. Neither thought sent a pang through his chest.

Because the only thing I know for sure, Jeth thought as he paused by the paddock to give the sheep a good rub between their ears, *is that this is the life I want.*

This was the life he'd never had. This was the life he'd been raised to. This was the life his mother had always, always wanted for him. The life *he'd* always wanted, too.

Jeth looked up at the cottage. Shae crossed in front of a window, their arms full of cloth. He smiled. After he put the roots up, he'd go help with the stew while Shae worked. They'd move the bed frame. They'd watch the sunset together.

In the morning, Jeth would harvest and dry herbs for their mattress, using just a touch of magic. He and Shae would prepare their salves and tinctures for a trip to River Tor's marketplace. They'd smile and hold hands and talk about the cow over breakfast.

Yes, this was the life for him. Simple and fulfilling. Full of love. Full of peace. This was the life he once thought lost made real.

This was real.

This was his.

This was the life of a witch's son.

The story will continue in
The Book With No Names

Acknowledgements

Where to even start? I guess with the making of. My thanks to Rachel Brune, who edited Glimmers in the Night when it was written — a full year before the next three. To Vicky Gavin, who edited the other three in a very short time frame. To Joze, who did my covers for the individual stories as well as this full volume. To Amphi Studios, who does all my typography and does it beautifully.

To Mystel, the whole reason behind why I wrote three more stories to go with Glimmers in the first place, and to Stella, my first fan-artist. Your drawing was inspiring, and I loved it. This piece wouldn't exist without you two. Two thirds of this book is your fault (in a good way)!

To Dills for putting up with me while I struggled through all this. You listened to me go off about the covers and titles and outlines a thousand times. To Emily, who sat with me every few weeks while I got all caught up on every step of the process. To Megan, Marshall, Emily, and Natalia for getting excited about the covers when I shared them, and helping me get amped up to get through this project — my first indie project — start to finish.

To Vincent, who unwittingly began this series with a joke in TWT's Facebook group. To Venessa for talking me through a bunch of the story, and who runs TWT, because that writer's support group is half of what keeps me going.

To the people trapped in between. When nowhere works for you, make your own space. You've got this.

Last, but not at all least, to you, dear reader. Because you read my story, I can keep doing what I love.

About the Author

October K Santerelli is a fantasy author presumably from Denver, Colorado and not from a faerie realm in any way, shape, or form. He lives there with his two dogs and thousands of books. He spends much of his time crafting stories for various mediums, including novels, short stories, comics, and more. A disabled and LGBTQ+ author, October crafts stories with queer elements in the theme whether or not there are queer characters in the tale — though this one clearly has both.

To find out more about October K Santerelli and sign up for his newsletter, please visit octoberksanterelli.com.

Also By October K Santerelli

NIGHTFALL:
City of Day
City of Night
City of Death (Coming Soon)

OTHERS:
Storm's Eye (An Out of Time novel with David Brin)
Mi Jaculpo (Hold Your Fire anthology)

www.ingramcontent.com/pod-product-compliance
Lightning Source LLC
Chambersburg PA
CBHW022018310726
48972CB00006B/1714